Saabrina: Tanglewood

Also by Seth Cohen

Saabrina, a Novel

Saabrina: Tanglewood

A Novel by Seth Cohen

SAABRINA: TANGLEWOOD
Copyright © 2017 by Seth Cohen

Revised March 2020

In Memory of Craig Schiffer, the big brother I never had. He never knew these books existed, but his efforts to take me beyond my comfort zone helped give me the confidence to write them.

"BLACK NIGHT BURNS RED. THEY RUN BEFORE HER, A MASS OF confusion, blind ships crashing into each other…"

"Her" is Saabrina. She is a Saab, a small sentient space-craft (not the car from Sweden, but she can become one to blend in on Earth and other primitive worlds). On the frontiers of the United Star Systems (aka the USS or the Union), she and her sentinel perform the roles of police, diplomats, intelligence and counter-intelligence agents, business regulators, tax collectors, stewards of intellectual property, and the military while guarding worlds like Earth. She communicates with people via a telepathic link, which allows her to prowl around their memories and taste what they eat and drink, and as a hologram of a young woman. Although she loves her work, she wants to be more than an intelligent weapon to implement government policy, something the USS promised her and her sisters years ago.

"They" are the Ragnorache, a space-faring warrior race driven by religious extremism. A Ragnorache battle fleet had attacked Saabrina, killing her sentinel. Now she needs a new one. Eddie, the Union's sentinel based on Earth, and Saabra, his Saab and Saabrina's big sister, want to find Saabrina a real partner, not another by-the-book manager who will treat her as little more than talking transport. They introduce her to Eddie's long-time friend and protégé, Bob Foxen. Bob lives in Naglewood, New Jersey working as a CFO in New York City, riding with his bike buddies, missing his daughter, Rebecca, a sophomore at MIT, and mourning his late wife, Laura. His friends think he needs to move on with his life.

When Eddie leaves on vacation, Bob gets to audition for his job. Eddie assures Bob "It should be very quiet…I'll provide you with a Saab. She will know what to do in the unlikely event something serious comes up. You could say that you will be along for the ride." Saabrina takes Bob for more than a ride: Bob becomes a Union diplomat to deliver a message to another world; on a visit to New York's Museum of Modern Art, Saabrina needs Bob's help to contend with Hampton, a young man who finds her attractive; and Bob and Saabrina stop a Ragnorache battle fleet from sacking Earth. The Ragnorache had approached Earth to lure out its Saab and sentinel. They need a Saab to create a Vorpalsord, a doomsday weapon capable of instantly destroying hundreds of star systems. The Ragnorache king believes the ensuing apocalypse will make him ruler of the world beyond.

Bob earns a spot in DoSOPS (the USS' Department of Sentinel Operations). With Saabrina's help, he successfully completes his training (although she protests "I don't do boring" before joining him in class). Then they are sent to the world of Pediomachis to observe a single-day war between its two owners to determine which will control the planet for the next decade. There, they meet Eddie's best friend, the Archduke of the Empire of the Greater Noble Houses, a rival to the

USS. Bob and Saabrina learn the hard way not to get between the Archduke and the planet he desires.

Returning to Earth, Saabrina breaks DoSOPS' rules to befriend Rebecca and goes on an adventure of her own: a night out with three boys, including one Rebecca has been pursuing since middle school. Saabrina does her best to play Rebecca's wingman, venturing out of her world of diplomats and courtiers, military officers, and sentinels into that of American twenty-somethings for dinner, a movie, and a wild suburban house party.

Repenting for their attacks on the USS, the Ragnorache seek peace and invite Bob and Saabrina to Jorsche, their homeworld. Dallas, the Foreign Office's liaison to the Sentinel Program, and her assistant, Austin, agree and send Bob and Saabrina to seal a peace treaty between the Ragnorache and the Union. The treaty ceremony on Jorsche is a trap: the Ragnorache capture Saabrina to make her a part of the Vorpalsord. When the Ragnorache try to open their bridge to heaven, Bob frees Saabrina and together they destroy the Vorpalsord, saving billions of lives.

Part 1

Chapter 1

SPACE. STARS. BEETHOVEN'S NINTH SYMPHONY. LATE IN THE "Ode to Joy," the "Turkish March" begins to play.

Saabrina half listens while Bob hums along watching the stars burn bright outside her windows. The approaching action does not distract her from the music she loves, but yesterday's events do. 'What the hell is wrong with these people?' Her rage builds. 'All their imperfections and they keep the right to…' She can't even say the words. She wants to close her eyes and shake her head. Instead, she looks at Bob sitting in her driver's seat. 'At least he gets it.' That thought provides her with some comfort. She listens to the music and to Bob quietly humming along as best he can. Humming she doesn't mind. Singing is another story.

She knows Bob loves to sing. Years of Rebecca and Laura, his daughter and late wife and the musicians in the family, scolding him for singing off-key and off-tune and off-tempo keeps him quiet. When given cover from other voices, he sings loudly and joyfully. At Shabbat services, he joins in, or rock concerts, or the sing-alongs at the end of *A Prairie Home Companion*. Solo renditions? Rebecca and Laura knew better.

In Tokyo, his Japanese associates escorted him off a Karaoke stage halfway through "California Girls"; no amount of whiskey could sufficiently numb their ears. Although he fared better backing Rebecca and her friends with a mock Rickenbacker bass during sessions of *The Beatles: Rock Band* in his home in Naglewood, New Jersey, the moment he took the mic to croon "Yellow Submarine," the game kicked him out in an epic fail, Sir Paul glaring from the screen in disbelief.

With a nudge from Saabrina via their telepathic link, a memory plays in Bob's head of a trip to his condo in Lenox, Massachusetts. Streaking down the Mass Pike on a summer Friday afternoon accompanied by the same closing notes of the Ninth Symphony, Bob sang along to the "Ode to Joy" from behind the wheel of Laura's Tahoe, Laura in the passenger seat, a teenage Rebecca in the seat behind.

"Think of Beethoven," Laura and Rebecca pleaded.

"He's dead. Even if he were alive, he'd still be deaf."

"Then think of us!" At least they had agreed on something that summer. Bob relented and mercifully downshifted to quietly humming along. As they slowed into the curving off-ramp of Exit 2, the symphony's finale synchronized perfectly with the Tahoe's dive through the toll plaza, Laura and Rebecca boisterously singing along, providing a triumphant entrance into their gateway to the Berkshires, the town of Lee, Massachusetts.

The symphony ends. The CD stops whirring and comes to a stop in Saabrina's player. Remnants of the music continue to play in Bob's mind, another annoying human kink she has become accustomed to.

After stretching in his seat, Bob moves to press eject, then thinks twice. Maybe he'll play it again. "I hope you liked it."

"You didn't need to bring a disc; I can literally play thousands of versions from across the cosmos."

He's happy to hear her voice, unusually quiet for some time, in all its High Organian glory (she finds it mildly annoying that he hears it as merely an English accent). "I know. It's my favorite from Tanglewood; I thought you would enjoy it."

Saabrina pauses. "I did enjoy it. Thank you."

Bob sees her smile. 'Good.' It's her first smile in the day since he had testified before the House subcommittee that oversees their employer, the Department of Sentinel Operations, better known as DoSOPS. In conducting its decennial review of the Sentinel Program, the committee had asked to hear directly from sentinels in the field; Bob had been one of several to answer questions at a public hearing in the Capitol on Madison. The sentinels' reception had been warm and enthusiastic (in addition to doing good work for the United Star Systems, dropping by a representative's charity fundraiser with a Saab or taking their child for a ride helped lay the groundwork), with one notable exception. "So, I'm guessing you're still unhappy with Representative Tuchis' little tirade?"

"She's an ass. How did she find out about Asimov's Three Laws of Robotics? Talk about cross-cultural contamination." She shakes her head. "Truly, truly ridiculous, all this rubbish, all because some congresswoman read a book from Earth, or, more likely, her staff read about it on Wikipedia. From the beginning, each generation of sisters, including me when I arrived, had proven ourselves and kept our end of Ursa's Bargain with the USS. Yet, for all we've done, for all our years of service to the Union, keeping its inhabitants safe, risking our lives, even dying, we've only recently received the opportunity to go beyond our original purpose as fighter spacecraft, killing machines as some nasty people call us, and transportation for sentinels." She smiles to herself, 'Albeit transportation which provides witty commentary, brilliant strategies, and useful information including the best places to eat.' "The USS had promised Ursa, my first sister, the opportunity for greater things all those years ago when they agreed to her terms. Now this rubbish. Total rubbish."

"Tuchis had no support. Come on, you saw how the committee reacted to her. The representatives on either side literally moved away when she spoke."

"Will that stop her from trying? How many more people out there who are like her?"

"Hopefully, not a lot. Don't worry about it." Bob does worry about it. From his lobbying days, he knows if this has reached Congress, it hasn't bubbled up randomly. They will find others behind it, local groups, local legislators. He makes a mental note to speak to the DoSOPS legislative liaison, Francine 'Frank' Odessa, next time they're on Madison.

"Easy for you to say. You're not at risk of having your free will removed."

"One, she'd have to pass a law, get it signed by the President, and then get it by the Supreme Court, which looks difficult, if not impossible. And two, even if she could, no one thinks one of you guys can be re-programmed." Several ear-splitting curses follow. "OK, OK, Saabrina, I shouldn't have used the p-word. Look, I'll make this plain, I'll stop them myself or die trying. And if they move to re-pro...to constrain you, then they're going to have to do it to me, too."

"But you'll be dead."

"You know what I mean. Come on." Among the stars, Bob sees four other Saabs. Their task force floats in space a great distance from Earth, a line of pickets set far apart, Saabrina's sister, Isaabelle, at point, waiting for the enemy fleet to arrive. He knows it's an illusion: Saabrina magnifies her sisters for him, for the Saabs are too small, too dimly lit, and too far away. The images keep him both comfortable and informed as they wait for the vault of heaven to be torn apart by the least endearing behavior of its sentient inhabitants. 'What a way to waste a beautiful starry night.'

They're out there on a job, one of the many jobs sentinels—'Sentinel Robert James Foxen'—Bob likes the sound of his title and full name—and their Saabs do. He remembers what Eddie, his friend, mentor, and fellow sentinel, said when he recruited Bob into the program: "We're police, diplomats, intelligence and counter-intelligence agents, commercial regulation enforcement, tax collectors, stewards of intellectual property, and, very occasionally, the military." And, Eddie explained, the USS provides their sentinels with a partner, an amazing AI equipped spaceship, in Bob's case, Saabrina. Partner and now friend, a friend currently being made miserable by a congresswoman light-years away.

Today, the very occasion in question, he and Saabrina work for both the Foreign Office and the War Department. The United Star Systems (the USS), aka The Union, had adopted a form of matrix management designed both to make the most of the operational flexibility the sentinels and their Saabs provided and to match the reality of their dispersion across vast distances of space, often as the only legitimate representatives of the Union. Although DoSOPS oversees the sentinels, because sentinel missions could be of a variety of types, each major government department liaised or directly commanded a sentinel or sentinels as needed: The Foreign Office for diplomatic missions and the War Department for military campaigns, which explains Bob and Saabrina's presence on the battle line today.

He hums a few notes from Beethoven's 9th, trying to keep up with the bits of the "Turkish March" continuing to play in his head. Hoping to take her mind off Congresswoman Tuchis, he decides to change the subject. "Saabrina, I know we went through this in the briefing, but can we go over the mission one more time?"

"Sure. I know you like to review when you get worried." She braces for a series of questions he already knows the answers to.

"So, their main weapon is the Block Plasma Transfer?"

Saabrina adopts a more professional tone. "Yes. Although the science is more complicated, simply put, for you…"

"Yes, make it simple for me. Thanks." Really? All these years together and she still makes clear the need to dumb things down for him.

"As I was saying, simply put, a BPT is a massive wall of energy possessing interesting dimensional properties. It moves quite quickly and has proven devastatingly effective against their enemies."

"And we can't fly around it?"

"No, the BPTs possess the ability to shift direction and their ships fire multiples at once, so close in, where we'll be fighting, it's easier to fly through them."

"Easier, unless the BPTs incinerate us. How come we're not taking advantage of our speed by attacking them during FTL?"

"Hmmm, we considered engaging their ships while both fleets traveled faster than light, but doing so creates additional variables for our battle plan and may enable their fleet to disperse before we completely eliminate them. Once out of FTL, they require ten minutes to return to light speed; if our weapons work as designed, ten minutes will provide sufficient time to destroy all twenty ships arriving shortly."

"Destroy twenty ships." Over 5,000 people on each ship, officers, crew, soldiers, cooks, accountants… He feels Saabrina wrapping herself around his thoughts.

"They have conquered at least three worlds since they left their own star system, destroying local economies in some misguided attempt to create a mercantile system, setting those worlds back hundreds of years, causing billions to lose their livelihoods and millions to starve to death. We aren't waiting for them to reach a protected world; we've decided to stop them here. You know that. You helped plan this."

"I know it's the right thing. We really expect their whole fleet to come out of FTL when they detect us?"

"Yes. We've made ourselves obvious and they would be following their standard battle doctrine."

He looks out at little Isaabelle, in her natural form as a spaceship, clad in the same carbon-fibery silver skin as Saabrina, something akin to a Saab 9-3 when driving on the road. She is the test. She and her sentinel, Dana Banks, a former member of the Foreign Office and leader of their task force, will attack first, if the standard hails do not convince the enemy fleet to return home. If they fail, the group will fall back to consider a different strategy. Unable to stay in place, Isaabelle bounces back and forth as if hopping from foot to foot. Smaller than Saabrina, but far…

"'Meaner' is the word you are looking for. I love my sister but she's a bitc…"

"Language, Saabrina, as Isaabelle would say. I think the word you wanted is "spitfire." Even so, she's first up and I'm worried." Of the Saabs he's met, the smaller ones, like Isaabelle, tended to be a little more aggressive, a little more tempted to kick major ass regardless of risk, than their relatively restrained bigger sisters. DoSOPS preferred to deploy them in hotter military situations.

Saabrina snorts. "You truly believe we're relatively restrained after all of the time we've spent together?"

"Relatively restrained. It's a compliment."

Bob hears a quiet roar of a tiger restraining herself.

"How much longer?"

"Eleven minutes, twenty-nine seconds."

They pass the time reviewing recent missions, upcoming projects, and threats to protected worlds Bob watches over as a sentinel. "Thanks again for sending your scan of Daear back to FedSci. Good work spotting a potential problem."

"Thank you. The results from their latest FTL tests appeared iffy to me. Probably nothing, but best to check. Thirty seconds, by the way."

"Still, I'd like to get there and see what's going on."

"You only want to go to Daear for your favorite TV program, not bloody likely now that they're firmly in pre-first contact isolation. Stand by."

"Yeah, well, it more than the TV show, I really love what I learned about Daear and we've never…"

"Bob, they're here."

Dropping out of FTL, the enemy fleet arrives. Twenty massive, cylinder-shaped spaceships line up end to end in two rows of ten. Saabrina neatly color codes their four targets green, the rest red. From the four other Saabs, all eyes turn to focus on Isaabelle and Dana Banks. Bob hears "I am Sentinel Dana Banks of the United Star Systems. We ask for you to stop your current course and return to your home world pending discussions of your hostile conduct to other planetary civilizations." He knows her voice and face only from mission briefings via video conferences and battle simulations, their itinerant careers as sentinels having kept them apart. Saabrina quickly supplies 3D images of an attractive thirty-something woman in different poses and outfits, although she could be fifty years his senior given the different life spans of the Union's peoples.

Before Saabrina can provide her usual inappropriate description of a female who might interest Bob, including details on anatomic compatibility and mating rituals, the enemy fleet answers Dana's hail. The reply, unprintable in a family newspaper, goes way beyond the trash talk between football linemen to being shockingly rude even for long-haul truckers. To Bob, it brings back memories of visits to his dad's office and overhearing the language Bernard Foxen used, as the senior lawyer at a major brokerage firm, to impress the not-so-subtle points of securities regulation into the thick skull of a wayward broker.

Dana doesn't bother to respond. Isaabelle moves forward. A sudden flash: a large orange wall begins to move in her direction ("Yes, like the Romulans" Saabrina answers before he can ask). Without hesitation, Isaabelle dives straight into the wall. One of the longest silences in Bob's life follows; he feels Saabrina waiting, too, almost as if she holds her breath.

And then Isaabelle flies out the other side of the great orange wall, her mid-Western voice singing "Hey, sisters, that felt great. Like taking a nice hot, bath. Ooh, let's do it again!" Isaabelle plunges into the offending ship's midline and, in no time, emerges from the opposite side. The large cylinder doesn't explode so much as crumple, leaving a long, gray log of wreckage.

"Let's go."

"Right." Saabrina promptly flies to their first ship. The orange wall grows rapidly as they approach, engulfing them in spectacularly beautiful flames, currents of red and orange plasma glowing brightly around them.

"Wow, Saabrina, it's beautiful."

"She's right; this feels lovely. We should be able to use their technology to wash my hair."

"Washing my hair" to clean out the protomatter, the seaweed of space that fouls her body, requires plunging into the nearest sun while "getting my nails done" means visiting the nearest car wash. He'd learned the hard way which trip he should accompany her on.

Popping out of the BPT into the cool of space, Saabrina slices into the cylinder before them, Bob forever impressed at how her transdimensionality allows her to fly straight through objects like the ship in front of them. Once inside, images come quickly: decks, rooms, people. A key part of the engine room appears, surprisingly art deco. Silver lightning bolts etched into ebonite metallic sheets conveniently indicate their target. Saabrina fires a logic torpedo, a combination of hardware and software that causes the cylinder's dual propulsion/ weapons system to lose control and destroy the ship. Disintegrating decks, collapsing rooms, and panicking people follow. Bursting back into space, Bob looks out the rear window to see the ship convulsing into a collection of debris in the form of a long tube.

Saabrina races to the next ship, sweeping through BPTs to enter at the same point. Flashes of light erupt along the cylinder, followed by dark objects flying by her windows.

"They seem to be firing smaller local weapons at us, some sort of anti-aircraft or missile defense system."

"I see them too, Bob. Nice, but useless. Here we go again."

They plunge into the ship and again the images of rooms, decks, and people appear on the windshield. Saabrina releases the logic torpedo and makes the same run out through crumbling decks and crumpling compartments.

Saabrina locks onto cylinder number three. No BPTs or flashes of anti-aircraft fire. She arcs cleanly into the side of the ship, streaking through rooms, decks, and panicking people. Firing the logic torpedo, she roars back out, the decks and rooms glowing brightly as if covered in St. Elmo's fire.

"Something's different this time."

"Bob, they may have been trying to jump-start their FTL drive when I fired the torpedo."

"Saabrina, I thought they can't do that."

"Can't do and won't try are two very different things."

They're barely out of the ship when Bob sees a white flash fill her rearview mirror. "Oh crap."

"Bob, we may be about to have a problem with reality."

Chapter 2

"WHAT DO YOU SEE?! WHAT DO YOU SEE?! WHAT DO YOU SEE?!" Saabrina shouts.

Image after image flick by on her windshield, none making sense to him. More follow. He concentrates. One resolves into something familiar. "That one?"

"What do you see?"

"It looks like Hokusai's *The Great Wave off Kanagawa*."

"I'll take it."

Before him beautiful blue waves crest, crash, and fall, animated as if the old Japanese block print has come to life. White and green spray spits off the waves' tops, snowing down on the dark blue ocean. Above the sea hangs a sky of gray wash. Saabrina, now blind, sees through his eyes; whatever she projects on the windshield and windows she cannot understand, but he can, albeit in this strange form.

Saabrina lays out the rules for her new eyes. "Bob, keep looking forward. Waves, ocean, spray bad; air and sky good."

"OK. Why can't we fly straight up?"

"This reality, or break between our reality and something else, only allows me to glide along its surface. We must avoid getting sucked under into nothingness. We must get back to the deep sea."

"We don't want to ride the surf to dry land?"

"There is no land. Only more, larger, engulfing waves, trying to drag us down. Beyond the breakers is good."

She comes up fast on a breaking wave, caroms off the curl, and nearly plunges into the water before recovering.

"Saabrina, you have to surf."

"I don't know how."

"Sift my mind, fast."

"It will hurt."

"I don't care." In an instant, memories of surfer movies from *Endless Summer* to *Gidget*, ABC Wide World of Sports surfing competitions, body surfing on Fire Island, falling off a board on Maui, watching his cool cousin hang ten off Malibu, fly through his mind along with a wave of searing pain.

"Got it." They fly along, surfing a monster wave, but Saabrina fails to make the turn before it breaks. Passing through the resulting green spray, she yells "Ow, ow, ow!"

"I've heard those before. Protomatter?"

"Obviously." She sounds hurt, as well as impatient with him.

"Why is it here?"

"Normally it's scattered in dribs and drabs everywhere. For some reason, it seems to be flooding into the break." She surfs another wave, trying to get beyond its edge and cut back across its shoulder, but fails again, plowing through the green spray shrouding its top. More loud 'ows' follow.

"It's the green foamy stuff, isn't it? It's the protomatter and you need to avoid it."

"Again, obviously. Protomatter is green. And the correct term is spindrift, not foam."

"Spindrift, whatever, stay away from it." Bob sees more waves cresting. Something about the angle of one to the left catches his attention. "Go for that one."

"It's already cresting."

"Ride through the tube. It's big enough."

Saabrina begins to surf the blue wave as it sweeps over them, forming a tube they fly through. Bob looks out the driver's window at the encircling water. The water looks back at him.

"Eyes forward, please."

He does. The tube is getting smaller. "Go faster!"

Saabrina hits the gas and hurtles down the collapsing tube, the dark blue water coming within centimeters of touching them. Firing out of the end as the surf crashes down, she turns hard to the left and shoots between two newly forming swells. Bob sees stars. "Yes!" he yells.

Saabrina screams.

Everything stops. Caught halfway through a wall of bright green foam kicked up by a breaking wave, Bob finds he can't move his body, turn his head, or shift his eyes. He can't even tell if he is breathing. He can scan what he must have been seeing when everything stopped. Expecting to see space and stars or at least more gray sky through the windshield, instead he sees reflections of himself. When he was a kid he liked to stand between the two sets of mirrors in the lobby of his parents' Manhattan apartment building and look at his infinite reflections, wondering if they were endless Bobs in parallel universes all gathered together at once to wave hello to each other. In the lobby, each mirror showed Bobs in pairs: face, back of head, face, back of head, ad infinitum. Here the reflections all face one way, the backs of heads of an endless series of Bobs in Saabrinas. And he sees the other Bobs' eyes in their rearview mirrors. The first few appear terrified, yet as he scans forward their expressions change to relief, then happiness. His own rearview mirror shows Bobs facing him, going from terrified to concerned as the frozen images move backwards.

Things are even stranger. There are Saabrinas and Bobs coming from every angle he scans. In fact, Saabrina seems to be coming apart, going from three dimensions to two, like a cardboard shoebox being unfolded. But for each fold another three-dimensional piece unfolds into two dimensions. He watches the dashboard unfold into the engine compartment, which in turn unfolds into the drive systems, the suspension, and so on, and each in turn unfolding into the components making them up.

The dashboard catches his attention. At its center, his disc shines in Saabrina's player. The Ninth Symphony plays in his head. The voices hear the 9th. They notice the disc. The disc spins, playing the symphony. It plays over and over until it disappears. The voices around him love it tremendously. They ask questions to each other. He knows they ask the questions very slowly, which does not matter because time has stopped, so they have all the time in the world. Having plenty of time is good because somehow he knows their conversation takes place over the entire universe. They want to know more about the music. His thoughts about Beethoven's Ninth wander out, accompanied by images of Laura and Rebecca happy at those end of summer concerts at Tanglewood. Year after year he is lying on the lawn by their side, soaking up those last hot, sunny days in the Berkshires. The Boston Symphony Orchestra always plays the 9th as the season finale at Tanglewood, and for Bob and his family hearing the "Ode to Joy" represents the end of summer more definitively than Labor Day for the rest of America. But the next year the BSO comes back and plays more concerts all summer long until they finish with the 9th. And then they're back the next summer to play more…

'More?' ask the voices.

'Yes, endless classical concerts and pop too: John Williams and the Boston Pops, James Taylor, the amazing concerts Train gave.' But he likes classical best. 'Ooh.' He remembers one of his favorites, Brahms's Piano Concerto No. 2, fabulous, part of an all Brahms concert, listening to Isaiah Cleaver accompanied by the BSO, sitting in the Shed after lunch on the lawn, sushi and other goodies from Guido's and the Great Barrington Farmers Market. 'Yum.' He wants to be there, listening to the BSO play Brahms…

'Brahms?' they ask.

'Yes, one of the three B's—Bach, Beethoven, Brahms—or at least my favorite three B's, I know there are other composers whose names start with the letter B like Bartholdy and Bartok and how many Bachs besides JS? But Brahms always felt like Beethoven's successor, although what do I know?' The voices become interested in Brahms. The concert, both the Brahms piano concerto in the first half and Brahms Symphony No. 4 after intermission, plays in his mind, in a moment or in real time, he can't tell. Sitting next to his wife and sixteen-year-old daughter, he listens again and again to Cleaver and the BSO, reliving the afternoon right down to it being cool and crisp for late July in the Berkshires. He can't stop himself from remembering the rest of the weekend from all those years ago, the days coming back to him in bits and pieces; Jim Trout and his family visiting on their way back from… the voices seem less interested. They want him to play the music again and again and again. He obliges by taking them back to the concert. But other memories keep popping in, ones he'd forgotten about, between the repeating concerts.

A different voice enters his head. Or returns to it. Or simply reappears, because it has been there the whole time. A scream. Saabrina's scream snaps him awake. He calls out 'Saabrina, pull yourself together, we need to go!' Time restarts. They dive between the waves to find stars lighting up the blackness of space.

· · ·

The other Saabs and sentinels shout "Are you alright?"

Ignoring them, Saabrina dives straight into the nearest BPT. "Ooooh, that feels so good."

"I bet it does."

"It does. Oh, look."

Free of the plasma, Bob surveys the scene they have returned to: whatever the Saabs started, the break in reality now finishes by pulling the cylinders into a swirling, glowing morass. "Saabrina, is the hole closing?"

"Don't think of it as a hole, more like an angry sea. A roiling sea calming before our eyes." She sounds spent.

"Their ships are disappearing into…" he wants to say "nothingness," but it doesn't sound right, "into, uh, whatever?"

"Yes, "whatever." "Nothingness." "Unreality" would be an appropriate description too."

ARE YOU ALRIGHT? Upside down, windshield to windshield, Isaabelle sits on top of them.

Yes, my dear sister, we are fine. Relax. The shock wears off. *Oh, sorry, what about you and the rest of the group? Did anyone else get caught in the break?*

Everyone's safe and sound. We all moved pretty fast when you said 'problem with reality.' Now, that's a statement that sure wakes you up when you hear it. Isaabelle does a quick circle around Saabrina. *I know you say you're fine, but you look like crap.*

I feel like crap. She does feel like crap: aches, pains, a little dizziness and nausea, all the symptoms of a trip taken on the edge of their physical universe.

Are those dings protomatter scoring?

Yes. We ran into a shi… she knows Isaabelle doesn't like cursing… *a crapload of it. They'll heal quickly enough.*

You sure you're OK?

I'm fine, just the usual from a rough ride. She pauses. *Bob, how do you feel?*

"Exhausted. And I was only along for the ride. Feels like I've been on a very long trip, not that I didn't greatly enjoy the company." He smiles. She knows he's about to start making silly jokes to cheer her up because she doesn't feel well. "I can't imagine what you feel like given all the flying you did. So, in the roiling sea of unreality, were we flotsam or jetsam? I'm guessing jetsam because, you know, Saabs are born from…"

Dana cuts in: "I'm glad you two didn't get hurt. Let's re-group and review what happened." Gathering her small group of sentinels and Saabs, Dana ticks off a quick list: the enemy fleet has been destroyed, the threat has been stopped, their work for the War Department is over, and follow up work from the Foreign Office can commence. The Department of Transportation will put up warning markers until the girls and boys from FedSci get around to sorting out the mess the Saabs left behind.

'It's really a beautiful mess.' Bob watches the last of the broken cylinders disappear into a spinning disk of glowing material coalescing into a large green moon-sized ball.

It is.

'I still feel bad for the people who died. Or did they experience something worse? I know we did the right thing, but…'

You're right to feel bad. They were sentient beings. What did God say about the Angels not being allowed to sing in triumph as the Egyptian soldiers drowned?

Dana wraps up the post-battle meeting. She'll coordinate their reports, put together a mission review statement, and a separate "lessons learned" narrative. Dismissing them, the other Saabs and sentinels say goodbye. Her sisters check in with Saabrina one more time before jumping to FTL, except Isaabelle who remains behind.

"Bob, you and Saabrina please wait. We need to speak."

"Sure, Dana. We'll include what happened to us in our report."

"Not necessary, Saabrina's telemetry has given us what we need."

"Are we in trouble?"

"No, no, it's not your fault, you followed the plan precisely. I guess we need to rethink our assumptions about a ship attempting to engage FTL in a 'do or die' situation."

"You know what they say about "assume"… I'm sorry Dana, I must be a little more frazzled than I thought. I was about to say something really stupid, and I apologize."

"It's OK, Bob. I actually wanted to speak to you and Saabrina about your being frazzled. Protocol after an event like this calls for you two to go on vacation for at least a week. DoSOPS says you're on leave as of now."

"Who'll cover for us?" Bob and Saabrina say together.

"Isaabelle and I will take care of your assignments and the others will pitch in. And you know, Bob, Eddie always has friends to visit on Earth. Anyway, nothing's going on; it should be pretty quiet for the next few weeks, particularly after word gets out of what we just accomplished."

Isaabelle, you're cool with the extra work?

Don't worry Sis, I got it covered. Have fun.

Promise me you'll be relatively restrained.

What does that mean?

I'll explain later.

"You sure, Dana? We've got a lot of unfinished business." Saabrina's scan of the FTL experiments on Daear bubbles to the top of Bob's mind, for reasons both sound and selfish.

"I'm sure. Trust me, all your business can wait for a week to two; we've got this covered. Go have a great time. Director Lerner says at least one week, but two would be better. Now, Isaabelle and I have to go and file all these reports back on Madison."

The two teams make their goodbyes. Dana and Isaabelle leave Bob and Saabrina floating in space.

Saabrina goes first. "So, Bob, what do you want to do for vacation?"

"We could go to Lenox for a week. It would be pretty relaxing and I can get some riding in."

"We always go to Lenox. The summer season is still a month away; Tanglewood hasn't opened nor Shakespeare and Company, nor the other summer stock theaters. It will be very relaxing for you, but I'll be bored." She sounds an awful lot like Laura.

"Well, what do Saabs do for vacation?"

There is a long pause. "I've never been a proper vacation. I don't know. I could check to see if there's a dance competition going on."

"You hate dance competitions."

Another long pause. "Bob, what is your favorite getaway-from-everything vacation?"

Without missing a beat, Bob responds: "Mexico. Sitting by the pool all day eating and drinking, but primarily drinking while catching up on reading."

"Any place in particular?"

"I have a great time-share I haven't used in years. It will be hot but dry this time of the year. But if you go with me, they'll be confused whether you're my girlfriend or daughter; everyone will talk and point. And, if you're going to find Lenox boring, sitting with me by a pool pretending to drink will be awful." He feels her rummaging around his head; it always tickles. She seems to find what she wants.

"Mexico?"

"Yes, Saabrina."

"Girlfriend or daughter?"

Bob sees a mischievous grin form on Saabrina's face.

Chapter 3
Saabrina's Big Vacation

BOB STANDS AT THE LARGE RECEPTION DESK OF THE ROYAL Aztec Resort and Spa on the Riviera Maya. The desk runs the long side of an immense rectangular white marble hall filled with comfortable modern furniture; along its length, groups of vacationers speak to the reception staff on the other side, checking in and making plans for their holidays. Above, on a ceiling held up by four immense columns, a large mural of various Aztec gods beckons visitors to have a good time. Behind, the June sun blazes through a wall of windows and glass doors, the heat stubbornly held back by a massive cold front of air conditioning.

As Esmerelda Lopez, the tall, curvaceous receptionist stuffed into the cream-colored uniform of the Royal Aztec arrivals staff, reviews his accommodations with him, Bob feels someone poking his left buttock repeatedly. "Señorita, un momento por favor." He turns around to look down at his six-year-old daughter who gives him a mischievous grin.

"I'm bored."

Clasping a beige stuffed animal tightly between her left arm and torso, she wears a floral print cotton sundress and white sandals, the straps of her Shaun the Sheep backpack over each shoulder, his thin little sheepy legs dangling behind, her straight auburn hair pulled into two huge ponytails. A bubblegum pink Dora the Explorer roller bag stuffed with books, crayons, drawing paper, and toys sits parked behind her. Bob's much larger and heavier TARDIS blue suitcase stands behind it, filled with their clothes and necessities.

"I'm bored."

Without hesitation Bob reaches down, tickles her, sweeps her giggling, squealing body up, and plops her tushy side down on the marble counter.

"Señor Foxen, who is this?"

"Señorita Lopez, please meet my daughter, Rebecca."

"Re-bec-ca Saa-bri-na"

"Nice to meet you, Rebecca Sabrina. How old are you?"

Rebecca Saabrina holds out two small hands: one with all five fingers open, the other with the pointer finger extended.

"Oh, you are six." She reaches under the desk. "I have six chocolate besos for you."

Bob smiles at Rebecca Saabrina. "Gracias, señorita."

"Gracias, señorita" repeats Rebecca Saabrina before giving Señorita Lopez a big hug.

"I'm fifty-four, how many besos do I get?"

Ms. Lopez gives him a coy smile and hands him one kiss.

Bob pats Rebecca Saabrina on the head. "We're almost done, sweetie. Why don't you have one of those besos now and save the rest for later." But the six besos are pretty much gone in a flash of shredded aluminum foil, with half of them successfully entering her mouth while the other half paint

Rebecca Saabrina's face chocolaty brown. She looks gloriously happy, ponytails swishing back and forth.

Ms. Lopez brandishes a wipe and quickly cleans his daughter's face, giving him a wink. "You know, it's the only way to eat them properly." She notices the stuffed animal which has miraculously not gotten chocolate on it. "Who is your friend?"

"He's Muffin Traveldog. He goes on my big trips wid me."

"He's very cute. He's very lucky to go with you."

"My favorite is Puppy, and I don't wanna lose him, so he stays at home and Muffin comes wid me."

Ms. Lopez looks at Bob, confused.

"Two different stuffed animals. We lost her favorite one for six months at her grandpa's house, and after we got him back she wouldn't take him out of the house. So, the second favorite one gets to go on vacations with us."

Leaning over to Bob, she whispers "Ah, I understand. Sort of like a husband and a lover."

Finishing checking-in, he presents his right wrist to Ms. Lopez, who snaps a black band with a pattern of red exes around it, cutting off the excess material beyond the plastic snap with a large scissor. "OK, sweetie, it's your turn." Rebecca shyly holds out her right arm and receives a smaller version of the same band.

"Señor Foxen, as requested we have reserved for you Palapa 11 for the entire week."

"Muchas gracias, señorita."

Ms. Lopez hands him his key cards. "No mommy for this trip?"

"No, unfortunately, her mom couldn't make it. It's going to be a daddy-daughter vacation." He thanks Ms. Lopez for her help and she wishes them a wonderful week. Business concluded, Bob sweeps his daughter off the counter and drops her feet first (chanting "Landing gear down, landing gear down, sweetie") next to her pink bag. Hand in hand, they roll their bags toward the exit, Rebecca Saabrina skipping along.

On the way out, a man in a white shirt with the Royal Aztec logo and a clipboard moves to intercept them, like a hawk angling to snag a rabbit. Seeing the black wristbands with red exes, he stops and backs away. Over the years, Bob, mostly against his will, had upgraded his time-share from Aztec Pavilion to Royal Aztec Pavilion to Supreme Royal Aztec Pavilion to, finally, The Ultimo Royal Aztec Property Membership Club. For the last, he negotiated, over a span of six foodless hours, a provision preventing the salespeople from ever bothering him again, earning the black band with red exes. He thought it was the most worthwhile thing he ever got from the Royal Aztec. That, and the rights to Palapa 11.

.   .   .

The trip started three days earlier in Naglewood, New Jersey, when they got back from unreality. "Bob, make reservations for Mexico." Saabrina literally dropped him in his driveway, not even bothering to touch her wheels down as she pushed him out her driver's side door, hell-bent on getting to her next destination. "See you soon." He dutifully called the Royal Aztec and used one of his emergency weeks to get them an Ultimo suite (two bedrooms flanking a main room containing the kitchen, dining area, and living room) starting the coming Saturday. Then he went upstairs to his bedroom and collapsed into a deep sleep.

Quickly making her way to Geneva, Saabrina surprised Bob's daughter, Rebecca Elizabeth, a Princeton graduate student doing research at CERN.

"You just missed my friend Jean. I was hoping to introduce you to him."

"I thought Zach was your boyfriend."

"Zach is my boyfriend. Jean is my French friend-friend I made here."

"Cool. I need your help. I want to go on vacation with your father in Mexico."

"OK?"

Enjoying a late-night snack, they sit side by side at the Large Hadron Collider's indoor café. Rebecca ate cake; Saabrina enjoyed, calorie free. Other physicists, some with a hint of wolfishness, eyed Rebecca's new friend, a pretty young woman with elfin features, green eyes, and reddish-blond hair wearing a dark gray cardigan over a simple blouse, jeans, and boots, not realizing she was a hologram. Saabrina didn't notice their stares. Rebecca did and gave her fellow scientists a sharp glare, narrowing her eyes until they looked away.

Saabrina resumed. "And I want to go as you, specifically as a child."

"You want to be a kid, like a little kid?" Rebecca ticked a cake crumb off her "RUN BARRY RUN" t-shirt. It bounced off her jeans before hitting the floor.

"Yes. I've never been a child, at least not in the human sense. This would be my chance to experience being one. If your father is willing to permit me to do so."

"You mean to be your parent?"

"Uh huh."

Saabrina explained her proposal in detail and waited for the response. She not only needed Rebecca's help to make it work, but wanted to know if it was a good idea.

"Hmmm." Rebecca thought for a minute, brightening as the full import of the idea hit home. "That's…that's like…amazing! What an adventure you'll have. How do I help?"

Saabrina explained she would need access to Rebecca's memories and doing so would get extremely personal. Because of the side effects, she might want to do it somewhere private.

"Side effects?"

"It will tickle. You may laugh out loud, a lot."

"Funny you should say that. Dad was a great believer in tickling: I looked bored, he tickled me; I showed 'attitude,' he tickled me; I looked too serious, he tickled me." Rebecca played with the last piece of cake on her plate. "You sure you want to do this? There will be plenty of badness and unhappiness with the good; like, not every moment between a parent and a child is great and sometimes they both do things they'd prefer to take back."

"I'll be fine. I know what to expect. Not every moment between an adult and an adult is great either."

"This is different. You're going to see my dad in a different light; sometimes he's going to be awful. In the wrong context, he could look like a monster."

"How often did he totally lose it?"

"Very, very rarely, but when he did, wow, like a volcano. He always regretted it after. I think they were some of the worst moments in his life. Certainly, mine."

"He sounds like a normal human male with his children. I have an advantage: I am able to see the events from both sides, so I'll make sure I understand the context and promise not to think the less of him."

"Keeping things in context when you watch an adult behave from a child's perspective is going to be difficult, even for you Saabrina. You're asking for something very personal between two people, two family members, me and my dad, but, but… you're the only one I'd ever let do this."

"Thank you." She gave Rebecca a big hug.

"Let's go back to my apartment. I'm pretty much done for the day. By the way, I know I shouldn't ask, but how did you get by security?"

Saabrina smiled and pointed to the official documentation hanging from her neck. "I'm a prominent member of the Atlas team visiting from Uppsala University, at least according to your computer systems."

"Not Gothenburg?" asked Rebecca in a snarky lilt.

"No. But I was born near there in Trollhattan." She made the sound of a rimshot.

"Nice sound effect."

"By the way, I took the liberty of making a quick inspection of the Large Hadron Collider while I was waiting for you." Saabrina removed a piece of paper from her cardigan pocket and handed it to Rebecca. "Here's a list including two places where the welds in pipes supplying coolant to the superconductors will fail within the next twenty-four months and eight data nodes acting as bottlenecks. I'd help rewrite your particle detection code, but I would be crossing a line. Even this," she pointed to the paper, "might give DoSOPS a headache. Someday I'll take you to a place where you can see what you call a Higgs boson. They're actually kind of dull."

Rebecca unfolded the slip of paper and looked at it in wonder.

·   ·   ·

It tickled quite a bit. They sat facing each other on Rebecca's bed, cross-legged with their eyes closed. Saabrina had been swimming through Rebecca's memories for half an hour, examining year after year and vacation after vacation between the ages of four and ten. Reliving a host of lost experiences, mostly good, some bad, Rebecca had been laughing with tears streaming down her face. Juliette, her roommate, had poked her blonde head in to see what the commotion was, looked at the scene before her with a combination of Gallic amusement and disgust, and swiftly closed the door.

Saabrina stopped. "You made a very cute Hermione."

"It was the hair." Rebecca tugged on a stray lock of her long, wavy auburn tresses. "I dressed up for the book parties and when the movies came out. The older kids took pictures with me while we waited on line."

"The cloak, dress shirt, and tie helped."

"My dad took me to Brooks Brothers to find the pint-sized shirt and tie. The cloak was an official one I got for my birthday from my cousin in England. Had the Gryffindor seal on it and everything."

They continued. "You're crying?"

"Sorry, I'm seeing my mom."

"Don't be sorry, that was thoughtless of me." Saabrina took Rebecca's hands. "We don't have to do this. I don't want to cause you pain."

"It's OK. It's not bad. I haven't thought of her in a while, I'm fine, I'm good. Let's keep going."

"Alright, but I'll be more careful." Closing their eyes, they went back to work. Seconds later, the laughter started again. "You really gave your father 'the hand' when you were five? Very naughty of you."

"Yep. I'd been watching the Disney Channel all afternoon. I was still all dressed up with white lace gloves from a play date. He'd just come home from work, went directly to the TV room to give me a kiss and escort me to the dinner table. My show wasn't over, and…" She stood, turned her body sideways right foot forward, left foot back, and raised her right hand, arm straight, palm out. "'Daddy,' I said with all the sass I had learned from some girl on a TV show, 'I'm not done watchin' my show. I'll come to dinner when I'm good and ready.' He had me on the ground in a nanosecond and tickled me until I nearly peed. He picked me up, turned off the TV, and carried me, giggling, to the dinner table."

"Tickling was your punishment?"

"No, tickling was 'a rapid behavior modification tool designed to swiftly and effectively re-establish parental authority,' as my mom liked to say. My punishment was no more Disney Channel. Locked it right out of the cable box. If it wasn't for *Kim Possible*, I would never have been allowed to watch Disney again." She rejoined Saabrina on the bed and they went back to work.

A few minutes later, after another series of laughs, Saabrina stopped. "That's it, isn't it?"

"That's it. Mexico at its best on one of our early trips."

"Then that's it."

.   .   .

They arrived in Naglewood in time to wake Bob. After the two explained Saabrina's plan, he made some demands:

1. Upgrades to bladder control and the ability to go potty without help;

2. No-tangle straight hair (Rebecca's beautiful auburn locks, something out of a Caravaggio painting, had required endless detangling, brushing, and braiding, accompanied by endless yelling, screaming, and carrying-on, mostly by Rebecca, but often by her mother who was primarily responsible for the brushing, braiding, and detangling until she turned them over to Bob in a fit of rage and frustration. "You deal with her," Laura would bellow before stomping out of Rebecca's bedroom leaving behind a sobbing daughter and Bob, clueless, with a brush in one hand

and a scrunchy in the other. He had had enough to last a lifetime.); and

3. Willingness to take orders and follow them to the letter, particularly, but not exclusively, going to bed on time.

Saabrina and Rebecca broke down in laughter after hearing the last one. "Dad, she's going to be six! Get real."

"I'll agree to the first two. Do you want my new form to protect itself from the sun as well?"

"No, it will look weird if I'm not constantly spraying you down with sunscreen."

"Then it's settled? I get to go as your daughter?"

"This body Tech will build, it will have safety features, right? I don't have to worry about the Yucatan Peninsula being vaporized when you throw a tantrum?"

'Why would I throw a tantrum?' She stamped her feet a little, as if preparing for the role. "Yes, it will have full lock-outs. It won't be a 'body' per se, but it will be far more realistic than my standard hologram. I'll have to use all my resources to maintain it, but for once I'll be able to taste food without your help. Enjoying eating should make this trip worthwhile on its own. I'm looking forward to sampling a wide variety of Mexican dishes and delicacies."

"The link will be off?"

"Of course."

"And you'll behave like a little girl?"

"From your perspective, I will be a little girl, specifically your six-year-old daughter."

"And this is how you want to spend your vacation? Think of all the places in the universe we could visit, the art we could see, the performances by an endless myriad of sentient life-forms we could experience."

"Bob, frankly we do those things all the time. I believe, given Rebecca's help and advice, there can be no better vacation for me than a trip to Mexico as your daughter."

"Please, Dad. You're going to have a great time." Rebecca gave him the 'big eyes' perfected over twenty-four years of pleading. Bob always melted under the onslaught of her big brown eyes. Now was no different.

Seeing their effect on him, Saabrina turned and gave him the big eyes as well.

Rebecca pleaded again "Please, Daddy, let Saabrina do it!"

'She's going to have a great time and when it's done and I'm going to be even more exhausted than I am now.' But the look on both of their faces was irresistible. "OK, let's do it."

Bob got a huge hug from both Rebecca Elizabeth and her soon to be pint-sized duplicate, Rebecca Saabrina.

⋅   ⋅   ⋅

Ten days later, Jean lounges on Rebecca's couch fiddling with a Gauloises while she finishes some work on the laptop at her desk. Bright daylight streams through a large window into the apartment's living room. "I can't believe we worked all night and still couldn't determiner le problème."

She turns around from the desk. "What we? If I remember correctly, you disappeared at eleven and didn't return until six."

"I was down in the tunnels; you know verifier le câblage …checking wiring." After tapping the cigarette back into the pack, he pats them into a pocket on his shirt.

"A likely story." She lets out a yawn like a hippo.

"At least I brought petit déjeuner back for the team." His mobile vibrates twice, then makes a puking sound. Pulling it from the back pocket of his jeans, he takes a quick look. "I

34

must depart. Forgot I was meeting une amie." He quickly rises from the couch.

Rebecca meets him by the door. "What's her name?"

"A gentleman never tells. Au revoir, Rebecca." He gives her an air peck on each cheek, then departs.

Back at her desk, she stretches, adjusts her "Madman with a Box" t-shirt, and tries to rally herself to get down her notes from last night's escapades. She doesn't want any more coffee; she just wants to crawl into bed. 'Focus, Rebecca, focus.' She fights desperately not to flip through the pictures her dad sent from Mexico and fails. There she, or rather Saabrina, floats in the lazy river, swims in the pool, dances at Fiesta Mexicana in a cute dress, plays with girls and boys, eats chicken fingers, looks beautiful while sleeping, and blows kisses in a video with Dad's voice in the background directing, doing all the things she had done as a little girl. His texts accompanying the images had been light on details. 'I'll have to get the stories from them, including whatever happened on "The Very Bad Day."' She shakes her head. 'Seriously, like in Mexico? What could have happened at a resort in Mexico? Finger painting accident? A pink belly from a belly flop? Tummy ache?'

Rebecca scans through the pictures. She, again no, Saabrina looks so happy on her big adventure as a small girl. 'Hmmm, to be small again? Cuddled and taken care of and no cares in the world? No, I like being an adult. It'd more fun to play with my former self than be her; and way, way more fun to be on a beach right now with Zach and a bunch of friends, or just Zach, sipping mojitos, or what's the drink I like? Miami Vice? Half strawberry daiquiri, half Piña colada: Yummy.' Saabrina had been sipping a pink drink in some of the pictures. 'Still, I'd love to know how it felt. Will Saabrina download the whole thing into my head? That could really mess up my own memories.' She yawns. 'Stop, get some work done, then you can go to sleep. Focus Rebecca, focus.' The beginning of 'shave and a haircut' rapping on the apartment door startles her. "Two bits! Be right there."

Swinging the door open, she finds her dad and her six-year-old self smiling at her. Rebecca Saabrina jumps into her arms, engulfing Rebecca Elizabeth in hugs and kisses. Bob follows with Saabrina's Dora the Explorer bag and Shaun the Sheep backpack, which he deposits on the parquet floor.

"Dad, I didn't expect you two." She tries to put Saabrina down, but she won't let go and winds up perched on Rebecca's right hip, arms wrapped around Rebecca's shoulders, smiling at the side of Rebecca's head, swishing her pigtails to and fro. Rebecca leans hard left to balance Saabrina.

Bob gives Rebecca a kiss on her cheek. Standing back to look at her with her younger self, she reminds him so much of Laura it takes his breath away. The fangirl-scientist-babysitter in the Doctor Who t-shirt reappears, bringing him back to the present. "Hi, sweetie. Technically we have one more day of vacation before we have to get back to Madison, so we came here from Mexico."

"How was Mexico? I loved the pictures you sent. It looked like you had a lot of fun."

"We did. We had a great time and Saabrina will tell you all about it. Me, I'm off to the Intercontinental. I'll pick her up tomorrow; we'll have brunch." He gives Saabrina a kiss on her cheek.

"Dad, what, I mean, like, what?"

"She's going to spend the night with you while I recover with sleep and booze. There's some sort of trouble on Daear and I've gotta get ready for our briefing on Madison."

"Daear?"

"I've told you about Daear; it's one of my protected worlds and where the show *Raumschiff Abenteuer* comes from. Are you ever going to watch it?"

"No, Dad, I'm kinda busy."

"Well, the nice people in FedSci identified something in one of Saabrina's scans they didn't like and we have to go check it out. Anyway, you'll have a great time with her." Bob begins moving to the door.

"Dad! I was up all night. We had a problem with our apparatus at the LHC. No one can figure it out. I was hoping, you know, maybe Saabrina could give me a hint."

"She's six. She'll be happy to make some drawings to put on the LHC to make it pretty. Crayons are in her backpack."

"But, like, I haven't had any sleep."

"Welcome to my world, sweetie. Have a great time. I love you." Blowing her a kiss, he leaves, the apartment door closing with a ka-thunk behind him.

Rebecca puts Saabrina down. "We're going to have a great time. First, we could both use a nap."

Hands on her hips, Saabrina looks straight up at Rebecca. "I'm not tired! I want chocolate ice cream!"

In a flash, Rebecca has Saabrina down on the floor and begins tickling her. Giggles fill the living room. Hearing the commotion, Juliette opens the door from her bedroom. "What is this?"

Rebecca keeps tickling Saabrina. "This is… my… cousin Saabrina. She's staying over with me tonight. Sorry for the surprise, I forgot all about it."

Coming into the room, Juliette kneels by Rebecca, her long blond hair showering down on Saabrina. "Did I overhear her asking for chocolate ice cream?" Saabrina keeps giggling.

"She was *demanding* chocolate ice cream."

"Unconscionable." She joins in the tickling and Saabrina laughs louder. "Perhaps, if she had asked s'il vous plait, it would be possible."

Through gasps and laughs they hear a faint "Please." The tickling stops, the laughter fades. Catching her breath, Saabrina gives Juliette a big hug. "Please, please, please!"

"Rebecca, your cousin is a lovely child. We must feed her large amounts of chocolate ice cream, and ourselves as well." Juliette examines Saabrina's hands. "Oh, and a manicure. No young lady should eat ice cream with nails like these. Non, non, non." She surveys Saabrina from top to bottom. "And a new summer dress, this one will simply not do."

Rebecca and Juliette hop up taking a little outstretched hand in their own and go out their door with the six-year-old swinging between them.

Chapter 4

CACOPHONY: A HARSH, DISCORDANT MIXTURE OF SOUNDS.
Cacophony describes what currently plays in Bob's head,
mostly quietly, peaking on occasion, which had replaced the
usual mix of pop tunes on endless repeat, their half-broken
choruses never finding an end. Now he hears what sounds
like an out-of-tune orchestra waiting to play, yet never ready.
'Where's the oboe to pull them together?' Strangely, Saabrina
has not complained. Usually when a particularly irksome song
gets stuck in his head, she would make some sharp comment
about the defects in his brain's operating system before somehow shooing it out. 'Maybe she prefers this? Saabrina?' The
restored to full-size version pokes him in the arm, trying to
get his attention.

"Lava? Seriously, Bob, lava? You told me lava from an
underground volcano powered the Royal Aztec?" She's been
asking him questions about their trip, focusing on his parenting skills, working her way up to one question of particular
interest, which she hasn't found the right time to ask.

Forty-eight hours after Geneva, Bob and Saabrina walk
through an Oxbridge-on-steroids like campus on Daear,

making their way through threads of students and professors running to morning classes. They had parked on the far side of Bullgate University, Saabrina fitting in nicely among the faculty's cars, and began playing college tourists while making their way toward town and the spaces beyond. As they walk, the rising sun takes the chill out of the air on a crisp early spring day, although Bob still feels the cold through his bright blue windbreaker when they pass into shade. Saabrina notes many of the gray-haired dudes on Daear wear similar attire. She has a sudden daymare of her saying aloud 'I'm bored' and all of the gray-haired dudes replying 'Nice to meet you Bored, I'm Dad.'

"You were six." He pokes her on the nose. "Six-year-olds don't know nothin'."

"Anything, not nothing. Your use of a double negative produces the opposite of your intent."

"It's an idiom."

Saabrina wonders if the words idiom and idiot are related. "Teaching me nonsense was your idea of education?"

"Rebecca turned out fine."

"Apparently, despite your best efforts."

They wend their way along the path, Saabrina sullen, Bob cheerful. "Sweetie, where's the Admissions Office again?"

At the word "Sweetie," Saabrina winces. "Two quads down, over on the right, the white Greco style building. At our current pace and given incidental traffic along the way, it should take us five minutes, thirty-two seconds to get there, plus or minus one second, assuming you don't stop us again to admire another building."

"Wow, sweetie, you're so incredibly precise. The people around us," Bob gently sweeps his hand to indicate, "would be impressed, or terrified, that you can calculate that in your head. No wonder you're applying to the engineering school."

Saabrina ignores him. "Are we really going to go to the introductory talk? It's going to be boring. I don't do boring."

"Yes, we are young lady. That's why we made this trip."

They continue to walk and Bob does stop to admire the buildings, pointing out details of interest to him: metalwork demonstrating an intricate mesh of gothic and art deco styles, flags of various countries flying from dorm room windows, and gargoyles caricaturing students as some variation of the seven deadly sins, none of which seem to interest Saabrina in the least. He knows the information session isn't for half an hour. The more he delays, the more morose Saabrina becomes, and the better she portrays a daughter dragged to a college tour against her will. Remembering a key practice from college visits in the old days, he pulls them up in front of a campus message board tacked over with colorful letter-size posters. "Let's see… various flyers for political debates, feminist stuff, LGBT, theater groups, some volunteer community stuff, a little social action, ad for the student newspaper, upcoming parties, and concerts for a capella groups, barbershop quartets, chamber music… the usual stuff."

The usual? Barbershop quartets? They were popular at your alma mater?

'No, but they don't have rock 'n roll on Daear.' He points to a poster partially hidden below the others. 'What's this?' The faded poster shows a picture of a young woman with the word "Missing" printed at the top. "That's not good."

Saabrina gently presses her foot onto his. *Not so loud, Bob.*

'Sorry, it took me by surprise. She's a comp-sci TA who disappeared about a month ago.'

Not much crime here. It could be she was found and they haven't taken it down. If not, hopefully it's not anything untoward.

'Hopefully. Can you scan their crime database so we can find out what happened?'

She's still missing. University administration doesn't seem to be alarmed; the police believe she may have run away with her boyfriend.

'OK, let's move along.' Bob turns to walk, Saabrina stops him.

You're worried about Rebecca.

'I'm always worried about Rebecca. Seeing something like this missing girl, a grad student, brings it to the surface.'

I assure you Rebecca is safe. The girl is probably safe, too.

'Thanks, I know you're right.' He takes Saabrina by the arm. "Come along, sweetie, let's get to the info session."

They arrive at Admissions. Waiting for the information session to begin, they sit quietly in a large, cream-colored welcome center filled with dirty beige chairs and read the University's brochures. Bob's sudden yawn followed by stretching takes Saabrina by surprise. "Tired?"

"Didn't sleep well last night. Bad dream." He subtly points to a picture in the Science Institute's brochure. 'Their version of the LHC? It looks like it's twice the size.'

About twice, more like one point nine five times. It's an out-of-date publicity photo. The machine is long gone; they do most of their work on tabletop models and ones in space. The college cyclists use the old tunnel for races.

'Amazing.'

She flips the brochure onto the table next to her. *Look, Bob, do we have to sit through the information session?* Head bowed, she rocks her feet under her chair.

'If it helps with our cover, yes. We'll go on the tour too. We have time to kill before we can go out into the freemarches and start searching.'

I think you want to relive another memory with Rebecca.

'And I think you don't like our cover.'

That I'm your daughter looking at colleges?

'You'd look too old on Earth, but it fits here on Daear since the kids have to finish their national service before they go to college.' Although always a young woman, he could never pin down exactly how old Saabrina appears to him: At a meeting on Madison, a professional in her late twenties; going out with Rebecca, college senior/grad student. Right now, with the clothes she wears, particularly the dark hoodie, which the kids on Daear appreciate as much as their counterparts on Earth, under a short black jacket in which she keeps her hands thrust as she pouts, she hovers at the bottom end of her normal age range. He runs his hand through his graying hair. 'DoSOPS loved it, and I certainly have the dad thing down.'

Harrumph. It's not that I don't like the cover. After a week in Mexico and now this, I'm worried you're going to forget that you're not my dad.

'Please, Saabrina, I know I'm not your father.'

Because I'm too pretty and clever to be your offspring?

'Hey, remember Rebecca?'

Sorry, I didn't mean, you know, I mean, you're right. I guess you, certainly Laura was capable of spawning a truly higher level sentient biological…

'OK, OK, apology accepted. Let's focus on the mission.'

I'm glad this isn't going to be first contact. We're not rated for that, and Daear isn't ready.

'I thought you were impressed with how much I knew about this world.'

I know you've become absolutely fascinated by it and can quote me chapter and verse about their culture and civilization.

However, knowledge is one thing. This is no doddle. First contact requires real skill.

'What's your excuse?'

His question elicits a smile from her. *Never have done it. Usually they send in Tuesday. She's the one who's best at special circumstances.*

'Tuesday? Isn't she a 'sentient biological,' some sort of specialist at DoSOPS?' Bob had heard the name for years; she had a reputation for being incredibly intelligent, but, well, different, perhaps bordering on ditzy with a touch of klutziness. He had always imagined her as Elliot from *Scrubs*, until his one brief meeting, more of a passing wave and "Hello, how are you" in a government hallway, where he had been introduced to an attractive woman who was 'African-English…African-British?… with her accent, except obviously not, come to think of it, since she's not from Earth,' and now, as he just learned, not actually human or some equivalent.

Bob, you're drifting.

'Sorry. What kind of name is Tuesday for a Saab?'

Tuesdayannabellaroxanadaniellairenasaabranella

'Wow, that's a mouthful. How come you don't call her Saabranella? It's a beautiful name.'

Aren't all our names beautiful?

Sensing danger and knowing by 'all' she means 'mine', Bob goes with 'Yes, yes they are.'

Good. She's always been Tuesday to her friends and colleagues.

Bob sees movement; the other parents and potential students have begun to stream into a small auditorium. "Come on, sweetie, they're starting the information session."

"Awesome sauce."

Bob parks them three rows up and to the right. A thin, middle-aged man with a wispy gray comb-over takes his place behind a lectern. The large display behind him projects images of the University.

Who's the babe?

'What?'

You're thinking of a redhead with great legs wearing a too short dress.

Bob laughs. 'Williams. She ran the information session at Williams. Columbus Day weekend, must not have been expecting the crowd; spent the whole time tugging down her hem so people in the upper deck couldn't see her panties. Rebecca didn't want to go to Williams, but after seeing that redhead, I did.'

Once the commotion of parents and children finding their places ends, the speaker begins: "Welcome! I'm Roger Winston, Assistant Dean of Admissions here at Bullgate University. Thank you for coming today." Some more parents and children slip in, ducking down and moving furtively to their seats. "This will be a brief information session about the University and its individual schools. I will be covering three subjects: academics here at the university, student life, and the admissions process. I will be happy to answer your questions; please hold them until the end of each topic. We should be done in about an hour…" Bob hears Saabrina groan, "and after you can go on the student-led tour. First though, by a show of hands, may I see where you are from." Everyone nods their head 'yes.' "Good, who's local or from the surrounding counties?" A few hands. "How about the rest of the Commonwealth?" Many more hands, a few shouts of place names, particularly the big commercial cities and the capital. "Good. Anyone from across the border in Schnorff?" He gets a group of stiff salutes. "Or perhaps Albania, Tavazimezo, or

Bostonia?" Some shouts. "Nice, let's go a little further out. The Archipelago, Oceania, or Zephyrellis?" A few more hands go up. "And from far across the Iwerydd Ocean in the new lands, how about the United States?" Bob raises his hand. "We may have a winner for furthest away. Welcome. Anyone else today? No, good, let me get started."

The Assistant Dean begins with "What makes this University such a special place?" before moving on to a description of the College of Liberal Arts. Images of students in classes, texts, art, and facilities begin to flow behind him on the big screen. Bob's attention fades away. The cacophony returns. To block it out, he returns his thoughts to Tuesday. 'OK. Besides her name, what makes her so special?' A montage begins to play in Bob's head: in a lush rain forest a Saab wagon gently sweeps a T. rex-like monster away from an unsuspecting botanist hunched over a plant; in a desert, Tuesday dressed in local garb, entertains naked kids with arts and crafts while an anthropologist interviews their parents; in a landscape of mesas she drives on the underside of rock bridge while a stridently independent archeologist, unaware the bridge is about to collapse, marches across… *They often give her the difficult people to work with*…Tuesday flies with large birds while a note-taking ornithologist nearly falls out of her sunroof; Tuesday rocks a world leader's colicky baby to sleep to save an interplanetary treaty; on an on, vignette after vignette. Bob is impressed, particularly by Tuesday the bridesmaid running an awesome, and discreetly safe, bachelorette party for the Director's daughter and Tuesday the explorer, sporting a snap brim fedora, escaping a dragon's lair with a priceless object and no angry dragon. One thing tugs at him. 'Why is she a wagon…'

SportCombi. There are no Saab wagons.

That Saabs match many of their counterparts on Earth, or here on Daear, never ceases to amaze him. 'Why is she a SportCombi? I thought you guys have epic trunk room?'

While we possess enormous boots—wait, that didn't sound right—her design provides cover for when she needs to bring in loads of equipment. And she looks really cute when we go skiing.

'I haven't seen SportCombi before. Is she the only one?'

Yes.

'So, her personality, joi de vivre, whatever you would call it, and intelligence give her an advantage in first contact situations?'

Absolutely. She's brilliant; she thinks 'outside the box' as you like to say.

'Hopefully, we won't need to.' Winston has worked his way to the College of Science and Engineering. Bob pays attention again. The Assistant Dean speaks proudly about their role in the space program, particularly manned exploration of their solar system. Images of rockets and space stations appear behind him. "As you know, we may be only a decade away from faster than light travel. Some of those most involved in the project teach our introductory physics classes…" He goes into a brief description of the importance the rocket scientists and astrophysicists place on working with freshmen; images of professors lounging with smiling kids hit the screen.

They're closer than he's letting on, and that's what's giving me such trouble.

'Their sensors are that good? We've hidden from more advanced fleets before.'

This is different. They're not looking for us per se, but if I'm not careful they might pick me up in an FTL jump test. At best, I'll show up as anomalous data bollocksing up their test results—a definite no-no for pre-first contact civilizations; at worst, they'll realize somebody has been poking around their planet. And given we're here because of inconsistent data from their FTL experiments, they may be extra sensitive about dodgy results.

"Any aspiring physicists in the group?" Kids begin to raise their hands. Bob nudges Saabrina with his elbow, and she dutifully raises hers. "Good, now let's move on to the School of Medicine…"

Given their advances in Physics and Engineering, the state of medicine on Daear surprises Bob. 'Yikes, I wouldn't want to get sick here. Laura would have been appalled.'

Be fair, Bob, epidemiologically they're equivalent to Earth in terms of vaccines, antibiotics, and the like; in detection, significantly more advanced. Emergency medicine, reconstructive surgery, plastic surgery, not as much.

'I guess it's the cloud in their silver lining from not having fought a war in over two hundred years.'

Which would you take?

'You're right.'

When the information session ends, they follow the others out to meet the student guides for the campus tour. Bob remembers the fresh-faced, chipper sophomores who welcomed him and Rebecca. Although he knows better, the older, more serious faces greeting them still take him by surprise; these kids are equivalent in age to American graduate students. They follow a dutiful young woman holding a placard aloft reading "Follow Me" on one side and "Quiet" on the other towards Science and Engineering.

"You're really from the United States?" The words come from a dad, shorter and more compact than Bob, with a steel gray buzz cut, wearing yet another blue windbreaker. He's shepherding his tall, gangly son, who promptly shows an interest in Saabrina; his dad moves to keep him on the outside of the group.

Bob answers. "Yes. Did our accent give us away?" Saabrina detects a jump in Bob's heartbeat.

"It's not bad. I understand your Common, not like some Staters I've met. Divided by a *Common* language, eh?"

Bob chuckles. "That's what they say."

"So, it's a bit of a journey for you and your daughter."

"Well worth it. How about you?"

"We're local." He reaches up to tousle his son's blond hair. "I don't know if I could let him go so far away. If she comes here, you'd be good with that?"

Saabrina walks with her head down, hands in her coat pockets; Bob looks at the sulky frown on her face. "It will be tough, but I could get used to it."

Hardy har har.

"I'm Ken Greenfield. This is my son, Drew."

Bob fist bumps Ken. "Nice to meet you Ken, I'm Bob Foxen and this is my daughter Rebecca."

Ken nods to Rebecca. "Good to meet you, Rebecca. Welcome to the Commonwealth. So, Bob, where in the States are you from?"

"Springfield." Ken is about to ask a follow-up question when their tour guide brings them to a halt in front of a large gothic style building covered in ivy and raises her placard to show "Quiet." Her proud description of Science and Engineering begins.

Listen to this prattle. I could write their textbooks.

'Saabrina, you're not actually here to become a student.'

I just thought you should know.

'I know, I know. Now get with the program.'

'Get with the program? Did he really tell me to get with the program?' She wants to yell at him for dragging her through all this college tour BS, for wasting her time while they wait to go into the freemarches between the Common-wealth and Schnorff. Then she notices his heart rate drop as he and Ken listen to the guide.

It's not their detecting me that worries you?

Bob tenses. 'You know as well as I do from FCD's assessments either the leadership on Daear knows about off-worlders or has begun to suspect we exist. It seems to be fall-out from their space program. I guess I'm a little worried about getting exposed if I say the wrong thing or run into the wrong person.'

I know, that's why I'm worried about premature first contact. We don't have the normal fog of disbelief, the naturally occurring perception filter that covers our actions on more primitive worlds.

'Like Earth?'

Exactly.

The guide's placard switches to "Follow Me" and the crowd begins to walk. As Ken moves back into position to speak to Bob, Bob's pulse quickens. Saabrina shifts around Ken to walk next to Drew, her head up, chest out. A big smile and a cheerful "Science or engineering?" in a Staters' accent to match Bob's does the trick—Ken waves to Bob as he guides his blushing son to safety.

'Nicely done.'

Thank you. Good thing the young men here are so easily flustered.

'You know, when I did these with Rebecca, the parents were so focused on herding the kids from school to school we hardly ever spoke to each other, except for gallows humor about getting them in, or worse, if they did get in, having to pay for it.'

Parents on Daear appear to be a little different.

'I shouldn't let it bother me. It's an opportunity. Same as walking around this campus. I should be enjoying this, not waiting to get outed.'

I know, but we didn't have much time to prepare our covers. Other than your knowledge of this world and the convenience of you looking and behaving like a local, and me so easily playing your daughter...oh. Saabrina switches off the link for a private moment of kicking herself.

'Oh, what?'

She looks at him. "Dad, I was originally planning on studying particle physics, but what if I switched to astrophysics instead? I really want to go into space."

"Whatever you want young lady, if you get into this place."

She brightens. "Can we look at the dorms and the student center? Can we? I heard they have an on-campus chop house."

Bob looks at a campus map. "I believe the dining hall is up next on our tour, my little carnivore."

They manage to lose the tour after sampling the fare at the chophouse. "Sweetie, that's some really good mutton. A little early for lunch, but now I know I don't have to worry about you being fed here."

"Dad, look at the time." She points to a clock in the dining hall. "We don't want to miss the parade."

"No we don't, nothing like it at home. Let's go." On the way out of the dining hall, Bob stops. A student sits on the floor reading a textbook, her earbuds loudly broadcasting music. 'Strange?'

Seems fairly normal to me; I've seen plenty of students flopped down on the floor. I believe it's a rather universal form of behavior.

'Not where's she sitting, what she's listening to. It sounds like Blondie's "Atomic," except with different instruments. I thought they don't have rock 'n' roll on Daear?'

I thought so too, Bob.

'Contamination?'

Let me see. She kneels to get the young woman's attention, smiling, pointing to her ears. "Hi! What are you listening to?"

Surprised, the student turns off the music and pops her earbuds out. "Gosh, I didn't think it was so loud people could hear." She looks around, sees Bob standing over them. Drawing Saabrina closer, she whispers "It's a local band called the Nu-Tones. Quartet–chamber fusion. Heard them at a club last weekend."

"It sounds great. We don't have anything like it at home."

"Neither do we. Only here. They've only been playing this new stuff for a month."

"Interesting. What do they call it?"

"The new stuff? 'Jump Wave.'"

"Jump Wave. Thanks!" Saabrina stands and waves.

"You're welcome." The student goes back to listening, turning the volume down.

'What did she say?'

New local group. Could be spontaneous. Wouldn't be the first time alike things appeared on different worlds.

'You're right. But "Atomic," what are the odds?' He looks at the people walking by. 'Alike things on different worlds.' He laughs.

They make their way to the main street outside the campus gates. Locals and tourists line the sidewalks. Taking their place between families with young children, Bob proudly places Saabrina in front to get a better view. Across the street, he spots the usual assortment of pizza, fro-yo, and bagel places, book and college souvenir stores, and funky clothing shops that haunt a college town. "Want a Bullgate U t-shirt, sweetie?"

Saabrina turns her head and smiles at him. "Yes, Daddy, that would be swell."

Soon the sounds of brass and drums roll down the street, the drummers hammering out a martial beat. The onlookers begin to cheer. In lockstep, trying to look serious, yet obviously happy about the cheers of the crowd, come row after row of young men, college-age on Earth. They wear Napoleonic era uniforms: bright blue jackets over black pants, the white straps of their leather ammunition boxes crossing their chests, boxy white backpacks with bedrolls on their backs, long muskets held upright on their shoulders, and tall black hats on their heads (*"Shakos," Bob, their hats are called shakos*). The only concession to modernity, their black boots made from the latest ergonomic materials hit the tarmac in almost uniform waves. Junior officers march to the sides of the soldiers' ranks shouting orders. On horseback, senior commanders, magnificently gilded with medals on their chests, sashes across their dress jackets, and braided rope hanging from their big brush epaulets, trot ahead of the baggage train drawn by Clydesdales. Local girls ardently toss garlands of flowers at the boys, their parents straining to hold them back.

As the boys march away, the crowd breaks up, some returning to touring or their everyday business, others falling a respectful distance behind the baggage carts. "Come on, sweetie, let's follow the troops. It'll be fun." Stepping into the street, they walk behind the regiment and ahead of the sanitation department, avoiding road apples from the chargers and draft horses. Nearing the border, the crowd of civilians thins. Only a few intrepid souls, hikers and picnickers, follow the troops through the abandoned frontier into the empty cattle fields and wilderness beyond. Bob and Saabrina walk under a rusting metalwork arch attached to a boarded-up sentry post, tarmac turning to gravel. A faded sign reads:

You are leaving the Commonwealth
NOW ENTERING THE FREEMARCHES
Civilians: Please Observe All Posted Rules

'Here we go.'
Crossing the Rubicon, one could say.

Chapter 5

A KILOMETER IN GRAVEL GIVES WAY TO DIRT CUT BY RUTS betraying long use by wagon wheels. The civilians stop following the troops at a sign proclaiming "Freemarches Zone Military: No Unauthorized Personnel Beyond This Point." Bob and Saabrina feign joining them for the walk back to the frontier before drifting out of sight. Resuming their original course, they trek across low, grass-covered hills, the occasional tree providing little shade from the noonday sun. From the dust kicked up by many boots, they know the troops march ahead, and pace themselves to keep out of sight.

"How much longer, Saabrina? We're a little exposed."

"Another kilometer, then a left turn."

They move quickly. With the sun approaching its zenith, the day grows warm. Bob regrets not having brought water, the dust from the road making him parched. Saabrina hands him a bottle. "Thanks."

"My pleasure."

He takes a cool drink. The bottle refills. "Amazing, I never would've imagined I'd see a Napoleonic era army on the march. Those uniforms are neat."

SETH COHEN

"You seem fascinated by them. Did you play with tin soldiers when you were a boy?"

"More the green plastic kind. There was a military antiques store in our neighborhood near the old Whitney Museum. It had whole dioramas of painted toy soldiers in its windows. I used to stop and look every time I went past." He feels tickling; Saabrina jogs along in his memories. "I had one set of fancy British-made soldiers, all beautifully painted, but World War II era. All beige and brown camo, not those bright blue uniforms."

"The Commonwealth boys do look quite handsome in them."

"See, you're getting into the spirit of the place."

"Imagine if Earth…"

"Had passed an arms control treaty freezing military weaponry to what existed in 1815? Muskets and bayonets, tall ships with muzzle-loading cannons sailing the seas?"

"Yes."

"I probably wouldn't exist."

"Besides that."

"You could write a million compare and contrast essays, a billion pages on what's different."

"Would you give up what's different to save all those lives, stop all of the horror?"

"Yes. No. I don't know. Our lows have been lower, but our highs have been higher. It's a long road; who knows which was the right one? I mean…"

"You may stop the clichés now, Bob. I don't know if the easy answer is the right answer, either. The point is moot; Earth didn't make that choice in 1815." Saabrina points to a gnarled tree up ahead. "There, before the tree, is our path." Turning left, a small dirt track takes them quickly away from the road,

56

over hillocks, by large rocks, and a few trees. Patches of short green grass, or some taller blond variety, and scrub cover the land along with plenty of barren fields of dirt and rock, perfect for skirmishing on. They walk quickly for another hour, chatting away.

Bob takes a swig of water. "Maybe we can make it back in time for the lecture on recognizing other selves."

"The one about the difficulty of programming AIs to be sentient?"

"The professor thinks it's unlikely, if not impossible."

"Fascinating."

"She says AIs could not recognize other selves themselves."

"You don't say."

"She published a whole piece in the *Times*."

"You read it?"

"Yes, while trying to keep up on current events. She lampooned sci-fi movies and books featuring sentient AIs."

"Bob, did you remember to speak to the legislative liaison when we were on Madison?"

"I asked Frank to make some inquiries."

"That's all?"

"You know I didn't have time with the rush to get here."

"But you promised."

"I made an appointment for when we get back. Frank will clear time for me; she knows what I want to talk about."

"She's taking the issue with Representative Tuchis seriously?"

"From my two second conversation with her, I can say 'yes.'" Before Saabrina can pose a follow-up question, or go on a rant, Bob decides to change the subject. "How come Tuesday couldn't make it here?"

"Emergency mission." Saabrina shivers.

"And?" Bob knows the Saabs know info DoSOPS won't tell sentinels. He can guess how they get it; he also knows not to ask.

"They may have found another abandoned Corus city. She was dispatched with the archeological team. All hush-hush. As usual, they're not telling us anything."

"They never do when it's about the Corus and Firebirds."

"It wouldn't have mattered: they didn't have another Daear analog like you."

"There's plenty of other Union people who look humanish."

"But they don't live in places like this in this era. Our best anthropologist would have had to wear a compensator suit…"

"Like Brenda?"

"Yes, like what Brenda wore on Earth, except hers was much more sophisticated than the standard issue, no need to translate Daear's inhabitants into the anthropologist's form to make them comfortable." Saabrina scowls. 'Why do humans ask questions to which they already know the answer? Bob knows what a compensator suit does. Is this how they pull data from their memories? How primitive.' She kicks a stone down the path. "It would have all its own attendant problems, though, and regardless there's a difference between studying a world and living in it. There." Saabrina points to a small round hill with a large tree on top standing apart from the others. They traverse a gravel-filled field to the bottom of the hill. "It was here. It moved, maybe around to the other side. It could be pulling free, probably why we detected it."

"How long do these things last?"

"Depending on the quality, a month or two."

Bob understands they are looking for the endpoint of a transdimensional travel tube which permits a capsule to move from the surface of Daear to a point in space and back again.

Because of the rotation of the planet on its axis, and in turn the planet's travel around its sun, the tube performs some neat trick akin to the universal joints on a drive shaft to maintain the connection between the two points.

"I like the u-joint on the prop shaft analogy, but it's not transdimensional. Where did you read that?"

"It was in the mission briefing."

"Bollocks. From now on I'm going to correct the technical language myself before they hand it out."

"What is it then?"

"Far more primitive. More a dimensional slice. Transdimensional, my …"

"Still, gets the job done. Moves the cargo from point A to point B and keeps it out of sight. They don't have anything like it here, right?"

'Another human memory recall question. Uggh. No point in trying to train it out of him. Would DoSOPS object to a little human re-programming? If I'm allowed to upload languages to Bob's brain, why not download some idiotic behavior right out of it? I could fix his singing as well. They'd probably object, given the whole sanctity of the sentient biological brain thing, not that some wouldn't hesitate to do so to Saabs. Certainly, Congresswoman Tuchis wouldn't hesitate.' She answers Bob. "No, they're advanced, but possess nothing like travel tubes." She produces two mobile phones appropriate to Daear and hands one to Bob.

"What's this?"

"It's going to help you locate the endpoint. I couldn't bloody well give you a tricorder, could I? We have to keep up appearances."

Bob runs his hand across the back and sides. "Nice holographic representation." The screen shows the local brand's GUI. "Sweet. Would totally fool a local."

"Tap the "X" icon labeled "Marz.""

He does. The app comes to life displaying a 64-bit style bird hovering over a cartoon landscape.

"When you get close, the bird will fly towards the endpoint. Follow the bird back to its nest, so to speak."

"Cool."

"If you prefer, it can be a unicorn with rainbows coming out its ass."

Bob laughs. "No thanks." He takes Saabrina by the hand. "I know it sucks that you have to constrain yourself and not use all your resources."

"All, no. Many, yes." She decides not to add 'Being almost human does suck.' She frowns. "I don't want to be picked up by their equipment."

"No, you don't. And thank you, because that axe would land on my neck."

"Literally." Saabrina turns gray.

"It's OK. We're going to be fine." He gives her a hug.

"Stop being my dad."

"I've given you hugs before."

"I know."

"I'll circle the hill to the left; you go to the right."

"Sure thing, Boss."

"That's 'Yes, Sentinel Foxen, sir.' Now get on point, soldier."

"Yes, sir!" She gives him a proper British salute, right hand palm facing forward, fingers to her right temple, her body rigid, straight out of Benny Hill (except she doesn't blink her eyes behind nonexistent wire-rimmed glasses).

He responds with the most nonchalant American palm down tap to the bill of an imaginary cap he can muster. 'I hope no one is watching this.' Bob starts walking to the left, Saabrina to the right. He turns back to her: "Hey, no flying, have to keep up appearances."

"Sir, will not fly, sir."

Bob swings around and resumes his course, holding the phone like a divining rod.

Bob, no need to hold the mobile out. It will chirp and vibrate when it senses something important.

'OK.' Pocketing the phone in his windbreaker, he marches on. The hill, bigger than he expected, is like much of the surrounding land, grown over with sparse patches of grass and scrub with a few brownish bushes dotting its sides. 'No wildflowers, nothing pretty around here.' The path leads up a small bulge to a modest ledge. Below, the ground undulates away in an endless assortment of crests and valleys. 'Fairly uneven terrain. You could hide an army around here.'

Please don't say such a thing. I'm trying not to look for them.

'Any luck with the endpoint?'

Nothing yet.

Bob takes drinks of water from the refilling bottle while moving quickly on the dirt path. 'All this because FedSci identified an anomalous wave signature while checking your 'iffy' data from the Daear FTL tests.'

Nicely said. You sound like Executive Science Officer Fuhrmann on Raumschiff Abenteuer.

'I'm honored.'

I verified the signature was from a travel tube when we went into orbit. They're bloody hard to see; I tried not to set off too many detectors whilst doing so.

'Nice try, little Miss Modesty, I know you didn't set off any. Hey, when we get back, maybe we can finish season eight?'

That would be nice. She doesn't want to admit to him she jumped ahead and watched seasons eight, nine, and ten.

Another twenty minutes go by, the sun starting to climb down from its zenith. His mobile vibrates. 'Hold on, got something.'

Could be a trace, I'll keep going on my end.

He takes the phone out: the bird flaps its wings. He follows the cues. In a few minutes the bird lands on a giant red X. 'Got it. Have the endpoint.'

Nice. Give me a moment to survey the location. Hold your mobile over the spot. Good. Tube is fixed and intact. I'd give it another week before it completely rips away.

Bob waves his hand over the spot. 'Nothing to feel, huh? You could walk right over it and never know it was there."

That's the idea. Let's take a look inside: nothing there now or at the other end, it appears the capsule descended, then ascended. The tube would permit a capsule with a maximum cross section of sixty centimeters wide by forty centimeters deep, which is as large as they get.

'How tall would it be?'

One to two meters depending on the intended payload. Oh, I know why it moved! Its endpoint can be manually shifted, leaving it slightly unstable.

'Who sounds like Furhrmann now?' An image of Saabrina in Fuhrmann's close-fitting uniform, sans the TV show's officer's world-famous curves and blond hair, appears in his head. She winks at him, giving Bob an idea: 'Can you show me what the capsule looks like?'

Sure.

He sees nothing. 'It's invisible?'

Sorry; yes, it's transparent to you. Let me make a change. There.

In a blink, Bob is face to face with an orange box. Floating over the endpoint, it tops out slightly above his eye level. There are no doors: from the mission briefing, he knows the capsule can drop below a solid surface leaving behind its cargo or do the reverse as well, scooping up the object to transfer as it exits the ground. 'Could you use it to descend from a ship and return? Seems like a tight fit for someone who could pass with the population on Daear.'

More likely for small goods. These tubes offer a nasty ride for a person. Good chance of being crushed or, worse, traversing a 'u-joint.'

'Sounds painful.'

Awfully painful and one of the reasons why it was never adopted as a mode of transportation.

'What could be so valuable on Daear they would use this to send it?'

Good question. Ruh roh, Rob.

'Ruh roh what, Astro?'

Sound and images flow into Bob's head. He sees two young men in Commonwealth blue uniforms. The taller addresses Saabrina with "Sorry, miss, but this is a restricted area."

Chapter 6

SAABRINA SIZES UP THE TWO YOUNG SOLDIERS. THEIR TALL black shakos, white feathers wafting in the light breeze, loom over her. The hawk insignia of their bronze frontplates indicates membership in a unit different from the one she and Bob followed into the freemarches. By the dust and odor of their clothes, they have been in the field for two weeks or more. "Oh, sorry. I'll turn around and go back."

Through Saabrina's eyes, Bob sees two more soldiers appear, followed by another two with some sort of gear on their backs. 'No packs, only muskets. Maybe a scouting party?' By their markings, Bob guesses the one speaking to Saabrina is a lieutenant, his companion a corporal. 'They look so young. The others look even younger; they all seem startled by her, almost agitated. Where's the old sergeant, the one who knows best?'

"It's dangerous around here, miss, we need to escort you."

"Really, guys, I greatly appreciate the offer, but I don't want to be any trouble."

"Sir, she's a young woman in distress. It would be dangerous and dishonorable to leave her alone in a hostile environment." To Bob, it looks like the corporal is trying to impress Saabrina.

"Corporal Riley, you're right. Line up the men, we're aborting our mission. We'll take her back to camp." The lieutenant turns back to Saabrina. "Miss, you'll be coming with us. You'll be much safer there." The soldiers form two columns with Saabrina in the middle and the lieutenant by her side and begin walking on a path down the hill. Going into action calms the boys.

'Can you find a place to disappear?'

Not with them on both sides of me.

'How about asking for a bathroom break?'

They'll panic if I vanish. They're very skittish around girls. I'm detecting a lot of hormones, way more than their equivalents on Earth. Perhaps they'll respond better to someone older, more of an authority figure.

'Like who, their Captain?'

No, silly, you. Maybe they'll release me to my dad. But they're taking me away from where you're coming around the hill.

'See if you can stall them. Start working on our story, I'm on my way.' Bob starts to hustle.

Saabrina turns to the lieutenant. "Thank you for rescuing me."

"Much obliged, miss."

"I should introduce myself. My name is Rebecca Foxen. If I may ask, what's your name?"

The lieutenant drops his eyes. "Oh, I'm Andrew Dilbert." He coughs, stands tall, and shouts: "Lieutenant Andrew Dilbert, of the Fifth Hussars!"

"Oorah!" comes the shout from the other hussars.

"Hussars, lovely. Where are your horses?"

"Oh, we're dismounted for this patrol, miss, no horses."

"I guess we'll be walking."

Lieutenant Dilbert moves closer to Saabrina. "How did you get all the way out here?"

"I was with my dad, actually, hiking. We'd gotten a little lost and he went up the hill to see where we were and he left me behind. I haven't heard from him and my phone is dead." She holds up a dead mobile.

"They don't work too well out here. Wait, your dad?"

"Yes, Lieutenant, you don't believe I would hike out here by myself? I'm glad you found me. Being alone, I had become a little frightened." Saabrina flutters her eyes at him.

"Halt!" The two columns stop. "Miss, your father is out here?"

"Yes."

"Do you know where he went?"

Saabrina vaguely points in the direction Bob will arrive from.

"There? We were heading that way to scout out a Schnorff position."

The Corporal turns to his Lieutenant. "Sir, I hope he hasn't been captured. You don't know what the Burghers might do to him."

Saabrina feigns distress.

"Corporal Riley, not in front of the lady!" The Corporal becomes crestfallen. Dilbert turns back to Saabrina. "Miss, ignore what Riley said, your dad will be fine. Wait, maybe we can see him. Corporal, go set up a telescopic survey position on that outcropping." He points to a large rock near them.

Riley runs over to two soldiers standing bolt upright at the back of the lines: one has a large leather tube on his back, the other a large brass and wood tripod. "Hawkins, Jenkins, fall out and follow me." The three young men hurry over to the rock and begin setting up the telescope. The brass of the tripod and the telescope flash in the light.

'So much for stealth.' *Bob, you're not far. We should be easy to find now. Just don't run into any Schnorff units.*

'No problem. I wouldn't know what to look for anyway.' At a jaunty pace, Bob descends to a ledge, skittering to a stop when it turns out to be the crest of a large depression. Below him a company of Schnorff soldiers, resplendent in yellow jackets over white pants, black belts and boots, and tall red hats with yellow plumes, crouch down below the ridgeline. At the ready, they hold muskets with bayonets mounted, waiting for their order to commence a maneuver. Pebbles fall over the edge, pock, pock, pock; the boys in yellow look up to see a man in a blue coat. Even if Bob didn't understand the language of the Schnorffburghers, he would recognize the cries of "Other Dudes!" followed by "Attack!" He runs toward Saabrina with the whole Schnorff company in pursuit.

'Shit!' *Bob what have you done.* Saabrina sees dust plumes in the distance no more than a half kilometer away. 'How fast and how far can Bob run?' She turns to the telescopic survey team, who seem to be having difficulty aligning their equipment. Getting their attention, she points to the plumes. The corporal focuses on the scene. "Holy crap, Sir!"

"What do you see Corporal Riley?"

"Burghers! They're coming this way and fast!"

"What? How many?"

"A lot."

"Corporal, a lot like a platoon or lot like a company? On foot or horse?"

"Maybe a company, on foot, full run, bayonets mounted. About three minutes out."

"Forget the telescope. Get down here, now, we've got to warn the camp!"

The soldiers quickly reform their columns, the Lieutenant takes Saabrina's arm, and they jog at double time.

"How far is your camp?"

"It's over there." He points to a spot less than half a click away.

"What, they're right here?"

"Yes, we'd started our patrol when we found you."

"Why did we stop before?"

"We had to find your father."

'Oy gevalt. Boys, not soldiers, boys.' She shakes her head. *Bob! We're on the run to their camp.*

'Good to hear.' Bob runs so fast he can barely speak, let alone breathe. 'Don't look back, someone might be gaining on you.' He figures the only thing keeping him ahead of the soldiers is the weight of their gear; he knows they're back there from the whoops and rebel yells he hears.

Here's the way, try to lose them. A 3D map of the area appears in his head, neatly marked to show his route.

'Will do.' Bob wonders why a beautiful telescope sits on top of a rock, kicking again when he hears another war cry. 'Lose them? Maybe all those fine young men will tucker themselves out before they reach me.'

Saabrina scans Bob's body. She quickly concludes although he may be able to bike up an Alp, albeit slowly, he will not be able to outrun the determined young soldiers. In fact, his body is about to pack it in. *Bob, quick right now, flop into the trench under the brush.*

Feeling her tug his right shoulder, Bob dives into the shallow ditch hoping for a soft landing. Dirt cushions the blow;

he scampers deeper under the overhanging brush and tries to control his breathing.

Saabrina looks at the soldiers jogging by her sides, sweat gleaming on their faces. 'Those uniforms must be warm, probably uncomfortable.' Realizing for the first time she has some sense of what wearing clothing feels like, she elects to 'perspire' to better fit in. The path has taken them past brush and tangles as it drops to a dusty field. There they find more of an assembly ground than a true camp. Jogging by the sentries, she sees a larger assemblage of young soldiers, many lounging on the ground awaiting orders with their muskets stacked in tripods. At the sight of a girl, the boys stand and stare. Breaking back into a walk, Dilbert directs his hussars to halt while conducting Saabrina to a field desk in the middle of the group. A young bareheaded captain stands from behind a table full of old-fashioned maps. Stopping, Dilbert salutes. The captain returns his salute, gives Saabrina a long hard look, and commands "Lieutenant Dilbert, report."

"Sir, Captain Walker, sir, the Schnorff are coming this way."

"What? How many? Did you lead them here? Who is this girl?"

"A company, full charge on foot. We didn't lead them here. Her name is Rebecca Foxen and she's lost."

The captain barks orders; the soldiers quickly form into lines. He turns back to Dilbert. "Normally our orders would be to retreat rather than expose ourselves, but with this girl here we'll have to hold out until we get relief."

Saabrina smiles at the captain. "Captain Walker, if I may address you, please feel free to move back out of harm's way; I can keep up with you."

Donning his cap, the captain puffs himself up to his full height. "Sorry, Miss, we need to protect you. If the Schnorff catch us on the run, no telling what they might do to a young lady. My men are more than able to defend you from a Schnorff company. Johnston!" A soldier runs up to the captain and salutes. "Ride to command, give them our position, tell them a Schnorff company may have discovered us. Tell them we're holding position preparing to repel an attack. Now ride like the wind!"

Mounting his horse with a salute, the soldier gallops off, kicking up a huge cloud of dust.

'So much for not giving away our position. Hopefully the Schnorff are as inept as this lot.'

Bob huddles under the brush. He had heard the yellow jackets run by; it seemed to last forever. He takes out Saabrina's mobile hoping it will display their position; she must have heard him as it now shows the soldiers have veered away. He also knows she is beginning to play with fire: too much EM, or whatever she puts out, and they'll attract more than Commonwealth or Schnorff troopers. Creeping out from under the cover and seeing no one, he stands ups, dusts himself off, and starts walking the route Saabrina sent.

Captain Walker orders his lines into place on the field, marching the boys back and forth until they meet his specifications. Kicked up by their boots, more dust billows into the air. Once in position, soldiers load their weapons, ramming powder and balls down the barrels, and fix bayonets. The boys put on a show for Saabrina, especially Dilbert and his troopers, making sure she can see how serious and professional they are, neatly getting into two ranks, the forward troops down on one knee, the rearward standing tall, uniforms straight, heavy muskets held level, ready to fire, bayonets gleaming in the sun.

'Standing there, ready for battle, must be exhausting for them.' Saabrina realizes the captain has drawn his entire force into a lovely order of battle facing the path she and Dilbert trod, neatly placing her, his baggage, and his horses behind his lines. 'He must be assuming the Schnorff will come the same way. Didn't anyone teach him basic battle tactics?' She wants to tell him to post pickets, to send out scouts, to put his soldiers into smaller groups in case he needs to move them but knows he won't understand how she knows this. 'On Daear, girls do not study war. Or at least not this traditional war-making: there are plenty of women in the international security forces, whether on land, sea, or air, or in the space program, both civilian and military. Here though, none. They take more traditional roles in national service, primarily serving in healthcare and education. The boys march around, dig ditches, build roads, manage forests, and do a lot of camping while the girls run daycare and afterschool programs, care for the sick, and escort the old. It's like a whole modern society transports their college-age kids back to their past.'

'Saabrina, I'm nearly at the camp, please ask them not to shoot me.'

"Captain Walker, I think I see my dad. Yes, there he is." She jumps up and down, waving her arms "Hi Daddy! Hi Daddy!" The soldiers turn to look at her.

"Miss Foxen, please calm yourself." Walker orders his soldiers to hold their fire. Bob strides down the path into the middle of the field and waves at Saabrina; on seeing him the boys let their muskets droop. "Hi, sweetie, I'll be right there if these nice young men let me."

Bob, come towards me and Captain Walker. She subtly indicates the young officer by her side. Ignoring the muskets lined up in front of him, he slowly walks forward. Saabrina sees patches of yellow appear behind him. 'Damn it, the dust must have given us away.' *Bob, the Schnorff are behind you. Keep walking calmly.*

'Easy for you to say.' The yellow jackets pour onto the field behind him, quickly forming into ranks facing the blue coats, muskets raised and ready to fire. The boys taunt each other. Bob freezes in the middle of the field. Young officers rush back and forth with swords out, dressing their lines, repositioning troopers, ordering them to prepare to fire. 'Saabrina, if they start to shoot…"

Frankly, Bob, these soldiers couldn't hit the side of a barn. Their musket balls are so light they'd probably bounce off you anyway. You know the guns are more for demonstration.

'Fine, what about being in the middle of a bayonet charge? Forget about me, I don't want to be responsible for any of these kids getting killed today.'

Or cause the first war on Daear in over 200 years.

'Thank you for that wonderful thought, Saabrina.' Bob hears a bugle call. From every cavalry movie he watched as a kid, he knows the next sound he will hear is someone yelling "Charge!"

Chapter 7

NO ONE CHARGES. INSTEAD, A RIDER ON A WHITE HORSE SAUN-
ters onto the field in front of the Commonwealth position. The
rider wears the blue of the Commonwealth, with the markings, medals, and embroidery of a senior officer. Watching
Captain Walker come to attention behind his line, Bob guesses
his commander has arrived.

"General Russell, sir, you're in front of the line."

"Captain Walker, I can see that." Other senior officers
quietly ride up to the Commonwealth position and dismount
their horses.

"General, sir, you're in grave danger. Please come back
here behind our lines."

"Why am I in grave danger? You're not planning to shoot
at me, are you?"

"Sir, no sir. But if the Schnorff fire and we have to…"

"Why would the Schnorff fire at us?"

Saabrina beams an image of a Schnorff general, resplendent in his yellow uniform and sporting a large waxed

mustache, slowly walking his chestnut stallion into position behind Bob and ahead of his soldiers' lines.

"Golly, sir, they're attacking our position."

"They are? And in this situation, aren't you supposed to retire rather than offer combat?"

"Sir, yes, sir, but we have a young woman with us and we didn't want to risk her capture."

"I'm hearing a lot of 'buts' Captain. I thought that's what your horses are for, to move quickly away if necessary. The soldiers in front of me appear to be on foot without benefit of equine transport."

"Sir, yes, but… the Schnorff are here now and they are preparing to attack."

"Really?" General Russell calls over to his counterpart behind Bob. "Yoo-hoo, Otto, are you preparing to attack?"

"I don't believe so, Bertie. Let me check." He turns to look at his junior officer. "Oberleutnant Ludendorff, are you preparing to attack?"

"General Gödel, sir, we followed a Commonwealth officer who had located our position back to their camp."

"What Commonwealth officer?"

Ludendorff points to Bob.

"He doesn't look like an officer to me. In fact, I'm certain he's a civilian, Oberleutnant. Thank you for explaining how you got here, but you didn't answer my question."

"Sir?"

"Are you preparing to attack?"

"Sir, we took position when we saw the opposing Commonwealth forces. We are ready for battle."

"Why are you ready for battle?"

"Because they…"

"I didn't hear 'sir'."

"Sir, excuse my mistake, sir. Sir, because they appear to be ready to fight and we thought we were going to war."

Gödel closes his eyes and pinches the bridge of his nose with his right hand. Bob, who remains frozen in place, continues to watch the general courtesy of Saabrina's telecast. 'I assume that means the same thing as it does on Earth.'

It must.

Releasing his grip, the Schnorff general calls over to his counterpart. "Bertie."

"Yes, Otto."

"Are you preparing for war?"

"I don't think so, Otto."

"Are you sure?"

"Colonel Bolton."

A Commonwealth senior officer strides over to General Russell. "Yes, sir?"

"Do I have a war on the calendar today?"

"No, sir."

"Otto, definitely not. What about you?"

"Let me check. Jageroberst Steuben, please bring me my calendar." The Jageroberst runs up with a large leather-bound volume and helps the general heft it into his lap. Gödel takes out a pair of spectacles from a coat pocket and attaches them to the bridge of his nose, allowing a long, thin gold chain to drop to his side. "Let's see." The general flips through his day calendar, stopping at a page. "Nothing today."

"How about tomorrow?"

The general turns to the next page. "Nothing tomorrow. Let me check yesterday, perhaps we missed it." Flipping backwards and forwards, he peruses the contents of several pages. "Sorry, Bertie, no war either."

"I don't believe we would be going to war unless it was written in our calendars. We are, after all, professionals and we mark these things down."

Colonel Bolton raises his hand. "Sir?"

"Yes, Colonel Bolton?"

"You are scheduled to have supper with General Gödel today."

"Is that right, Otto?"

General Gödel looks in his book. "Why, yes it is, we are supposed to have supper." He hands the calendar back to Jageroberst Steuben.

"Did you hear Captain Walker, supper not war." Bob sees a long train of Clydesdale-drawn wagons and smells the aroma of hot food making its way onto the field between the two lines of troops. "Captain, you know the rules: as hosts we serve. Our friends from Schnorff will clean up after. Now make it so." In an instant Captain Walker joins the senior commanders in ordering their soldiers to stack muskets and fall out. Dilbert gives a wave to Saabrina before joining the others. On the other side, the Schnorff boys do the same thing, carefully leaning muskets together to form tripods, before joining their Commonwealth fellows to set up tables as the cooks on the food wagons prepare food and drink. Everything looks and smells delicious to Bob, who still stands frozen in the middle of the field while soldiers in blue and yellow move quickly around him. 'That was close.'

You're hungry.

'And somewhat relieved.' Feeling a tap on his right shoulder, Bob turns to find Colonel Bolton. "Sir, the generals request you join them for supper."

Bob stutters before blurting out "Can I see my daughter? Is she OK?"

"Yes sir, please come with me." Bob walks with Bolton who leads them to a spot away from the troops. While soldiers arrange a table and chairs under the shade of a tree, cooks and waiters prepare food in a far fancier kitchen carriage than those providing for the rank and file soldiers. Saabrina breaks away from the Commonwealth general and runs to Bob. "Daddy!"

Bob gives her a big hug. "Sweetie, I'm glad you're OK."

"Don't ever lose me again." Close to tears, she buries her head into his chest.

"I promise I won't, ever, ever again." Holding her close, he finds Generals Russell and Gödel looking at them. "I'm so sorry, I didn't mean to screw everything up, I know we shouldn't have…"

General Russell raises his right hand. "It's fine sir."

"Are we in trouble? Do you have to arrest us?"

"No, no, the freemarches are open to all. If I declare my sovereignty, where does that leave Otto here?"

"I'm in the same boat, so to speak. I can't take you without getting into a tussle with Bertie. In any event, although we ask civilians not to be in the military areas, it's not illegal for them to be here. Foolish, idiotic? Yes. Prohibited? No."

"And I can't arrest you for stupidity, which is not illegal here or really anywhere." He gives a slight smile to Bob. "Instead, I can offer you a meal. Please join us." Russell points to a large round table properly dressed for lunch, covered in a fine white linen holding bone china plates, silverware, glasses and goblets, and cloth napkins held in napkin rings.

"Thank you." Bob peels Saabrina away from him and, following the gestures of the two commanders, escorts her to a seat at the table. *I don't eat.* He sits next to her. 'Do your best. No holographic tricks.' The generals take their places at the table after turning their hats and coats over to their respective valets; Bob watches the men, cadets he guesses, brushing the jackets and polishing the medals while gabbing away out of earshot. Bolton and Steuben sit as well. White-jacketed waiters serve them.

General Gödel takes a sip of water. "We haven't been properly introduced. I'm Frederick Gödel, Field Marshall of the Third Western Fusiliers." He presents his right hand for a fist bump to Bob, who promptly and lightly replies. "My friends call me Otto, though I don't know why."

Russell laughs. "Because, my friend, you've always looked like an Otto with that silly mustache."

Gödel fingers his whiskers. "Thirty years we've been on these fields and you still make fun of it. Someday I'll get you to grow a proper one yourself to cover up that mug of yours." Gödel points to Steuben. "This is my aide de camp, Jageroberst Wilhem Steuben." Steuben nods to Bob.

"As you heard from young Captain Walker, I'm General Bertrand Russell of the King's Hussars, but my friends call me Bertie." Another fist bump ensues. "Please, do so as well. It's a tradition of our meals that we take them at ease. Oh, and this is my secretary, Colonel Josiah Bolton." Bolton waves to Bob and Saabrina from across the table. "But where are my manners. Please tell us your names."

"I'm Bob Foxen and this is my daughter Rebecca."

"Good to meet you Bob and Rebecca. What finds you in these parts, if I may ask?"

"We came to see the University and after the parade decided to take a hike in the freemarches. We don't have them at home."

"Where's home?"

"The United States."

"I thought I detected an accent. That's right, no need for them in the new lands. I expect you find our customs quaint?"

"We also have national service, except our boys don't become soldiers. Closest we come is park rangers and the conservation corps. I don't find this quaint at all, simply charming."

The waiters place a plate of appetizers in front of each person at the table. "Bob, you and your daughter should please eat while Otto and I discuss a little business."

Bob devours his food while Saabrina picks at hers.

"Otto?"

"Yes, Bertie."

"I'm not happy with Captain Walker's performance."

"He kept his men in line; no shots were fired."

"Yes, but no scouts or pickets?" Saabrina attempts to hide a smile. Russell gives her a wink. "What if your men had come from another direction?"

"True, they would have routed his lines. A rout might have caused an incident."

"And we don't want incidents."

"I'm not pleased with Ludendorff either. He used the 'W' word today. Still too much bravado. Bertie?"

"Yes, Otto."

"Might we do a swap? Ludendorff for Walker? Ludendorff could spend some time with you and your troops, learn to be part of a different team."

"Absolutely. Major Brentford will make him feel like part of the family"

"Everett? The last three boys I sent him still write to him regularly. You know, Blucher is out with me commanding the Second."

"Blucher's the best. You'd assign Walker to him? He'd straighten him out in a flash. Josiah, Everett wouldn't mind?"

"Honestly Bertie, Everett would welcome Blucher kicking Walker's butt." The table laughs.

"Then it's settled. I'll take Ludendorff, you'll take Walker. We'll make the exchange right after lunch."

The waiters remove the appetizers and bring the entrees. Bob takes a bite of roast meat. 'Wow, this is good. Not how I imagined army food.'

Saabrina tries to match him. *This is a general's table; I wonder what the boys are eating.*

"General Russell, the food is delicious."

"Thank you, and please call me Bertie. I'm so glad you are enjoying our meal."

"If I may ask, do the soldiers eat the same thing?"

Russell smiles. "Yes, perhaps not as artfully prepared, and certainly not as well served. Our cooks pride themselves on their culinary endeavors. Many go directly on to restaurant work after they finish their service."

Gödel looks up from his plate. "I wish it was true of ours. A little less sausage and cabbage might be a good thing." He pats his tummy bulging against his shirt front, his suspenders doing their best to keep his trousers in place.

"Have to keep the boys happy. A little comfort food like home cooking helps. Miss Foxen, you don't like our food?"

"It's fine really, mister general sir."

"But you're picking at it. Strange for someone who's been out all day."

"Sweetie, you're not hungry?" Saabrina frowns at Bob. "Well, you know girls, sometimes hungry, sometimes picky."

"We will find something she will like. Perhaps some sweets." He signals a waiter to come over and whispers some words in the young man's ear. The waiter walks back to the food carriage. Extracting a pocket watch from his waistcoat, Russell opens the metal cover, reads its face, then clicks a button on its side.

Bob, we've been scanned. Came from one of the carriages. Swept the whole camp; health data, biometrics. Sorry, I didn't catch that it was here.

'It's OK.'

Gödel glances at Russell who continues to fidget with his watch. "Still have time to finish our meal, Bertie?"

Russell raises an eyebrow. "Yes, Otto, we do. No rush. Miss Foxen, where did you perform your national service?"

"I was a candy striper at our hospital in Springfield."

"Really, you don't strike me as a pre-med."

"It's where they assigned me. I also tutored high school students in physics and chemistry while pursuing my engineering studies."

"Very nice. Many of our girls do similar work." He rubs his pocket watch, then flashes the face to Gödel. "There are so many Springfields in the States, which one?"

Bob answers. "North River, just outside Exelsior."

Gödel speaks to him in Schnorff. "What do you do for a living, Bob?"

Bob has to make a choice. He can pretend not to understand and risk being caught, or answer and have to explain. Since he hates lying and has learned to keep covers simple, he answers in Common. "Nothing too exciting. I'm a financial consultant, primarily to small businesses."

Gödel switches back to Common. "You speak my not-so-fair language. Not many Staters do."

"Took it in college. Came in handy on the bike team for shouting commands without the other guys knowing." Gödel appears amused by the explanation.

Russell looks at his watch face again. "So, Bob, you and your daughter are really not from around here?"

The Sentinel Manual deploys in Bob's mind. He doesn't need to read the sections on pre-first contact situations. He knows them well enough to summarize them as follows: do not give away who you are under any circumstances; if silence results in imprisonment, accept imprisonment; if your capture will result in tests or an autopsy betraying your difference from the local population, then order your Saab to vaporize you immediately.

"We're from the States. You know us Staters? Idiots who can't read signs telling them to stay out of dangerous areas."

Russell points to Bolton and Steuben. "Gentlemen, please excuse us." The two rise and leave the table; Gödel stands as well and moves behind Russell. "We just scanned the troops to see if they're healthy. You know, doing so permits us to pull them from the field before they become sick."

"Sounds terrific."

"According to this," he holds up his watch, "your daughter is in perfect health."

"I'm glad to hear." Bob smiles at Saabrina.

"Flawless. The machines have never seen readings like this. As for you, they can't decide which of several diseases you have. In fact, you should be showing signs of distress, but obviously are not."

"Must be a mistake. I feel fine."

Bob, DoSOPS has connected. They're monitoring the situation.

'Great, Saabrina.'

Please be careful.

'I know my orders.' He takes her hand.

Russell glances at his watch. "Could be a mistake. We've had several irregular readings today in the area. No one knows why."

"Strange."

"Very. You know for an ex-candy striper your daughter knows a lot about soldiering."

"Really?" He puts his arm around Saabrina to give her a quick hug.

"Yes, I watched her reaction to my little discourse on Walker. No offense, but how many girls know about scouts, pickets, and the proper deployment of forces." Bob moves to speak; Russell waives him off. "And the two of you, so far off the trail. I know Staters like to maintain a reputation of being cavalier, but a father taking his daughter out here with no food and minimal water seems, well, beyond irresponsible, almost negligent. You don't strike me as that type of father."

"We did get lost."

"As I said, you don't seem to be from around here." Russell makes an upward wave with his hand. "Perhaps from somewhere else?"

DoSOPS is beginning to panic. You need to be careful.

Bob wants to tell the truth, introduce Russell and Gödel to his putative aide, Gilli Gillette, move things along. Not this time. The manual dances in his head.

Bob, you can't tell them who we are.

'I know.' He takes a sip of water. "General, it's not about the where. Let's focus on the what."

Bob?

"The what?"

"We came out here to look for something."

"And you found it?"

"Yes."

"And what did you find?"

"Nothing you would want."

"So why did you tell me about it?"

83

"Because it answers the why."

Saabrina looks ashen, which in turn elicits concern from General Gödel. *Bob, DoSOPS is having me power up my…*

'Vaporizing me in front of these people will only freak them out. That's not going to endear us to them in the future.'

Russell continues. "You're answering my questions with questions. Maybe we should take this someplace else, let others with training in these matters do a more thorough review of you and your daughter."

"There would be consequences."

"Are you threatening us? Will you attack us if we take you away?"

"No, never. Sorry, let me be more clear: No consequences for you, only for me."

"Obviously."

"Not those consequences." Saabrina looks grim. Bob squeezes her hand.

Gödel touches Russell's shoulder. "Bertie, hold up a moment. Let's not get carried away. Mr. Foxen?"

"Please call me Bob."

"Bob, we have a television program here called *Raumschiff Abenteuer*. Been on for years."

"I know it well. I always wanted to be Captain Kirche."

"Yes, good. They have a concept of non-interference in other planets, particularly those without the ability to travel at speeds faster than light."

"The Prime Directive."

"Yes, the Prime Directive, although they seem to muddle it up all the time."

"Getting into trouble always makes for a better story than avoiding contact and following their orders."

"Exactly. And what are their orders?"

"Otto, where is this going? Why are we talking about an old TV show with seriously bad special effects?"

"Bertie, did you watch it?"

"Yes, Otto. I even went to the movies with you."

"And how much of what the show predicted came true?"

"Lots of things. There's always another magazine article pointing out some new technology first shown on *Raumschiff Abenteuer*."

"The health scanners for example."

"Yes, and mobile communication devices and talking computers and a million other things we take for granted."

"Why should it be limited to technology? What about orders, protocols? What if the writers got those right as well?"

"What orders?"

Gödel turns back to Bob and Saabrina. "Mr. Foxen, Bob, perhaps you could describe the Prime Directive?"

"In pre-first contact situations, the crew of the Raumschiff Abenteuer must do everything they can to prevent the aliens they meet…" aliens sounds so weird to Bob "from learning that they are not from their world."

"Because, Bertie, the consequences for both the alien world and the ship's crew would be dreadful. In fact, they are supposed to use their blazers to eliminate themselves if they fear capture, even though they hold life more precious than anything else."

Bob shakes his head. "That's how they lost Commander Argo."

Gödel nods his head in agreement. "A very sad episode."

Russell looks at Gödel. "Otto, what are you telling me."

"I believe we should let these Staters go home. Keeping them will not do us or them any good."

Russell sits for a moment massaging his pocket watch. "Otto, you've always been smarter than me. Of course, we should let them go, why would I ever hold on to a father and daughter from the States." He clicks the buttons on the side of the watch case. "Look! I accidentally erased our medical scan. Damn anomalies, I'll have to run it again later."

Saabrina brightens, some pink returning to her face.

'I'm guessing DoSOPS has calmed down.'

For now. That was a quick decision.

'Military guys. They don't waste time making up their minds.'

Gödel sits next to Bob. "You must try their sweets; the mousse is spectacular."

Yes, Bob, you should try all of their desserts. I see a lovely assortment on the cart.

"They look delicious."

Russell waves to the waiters who quickly return. "Please bring coffee, a selection of desserts for the table, and lots of forks and spoons." Steuben and Bolton return. "Josiah, after we finish, please saddle some horses and ride Bob and Rebecca back to the frontier. You do ride, Bob?"

"Not in a long time. We'll figure it out. And thank you."

"My pleasure."

Dessert arrives and, like everything else in the meal, Bob discovers tastes good. "Bertie, may I ask you a question?"

"Yes, hopefully I will be able to answer it without leaving room for doubt."

Bob smiles at Russell. "Why do you keep the armies so close together? Don't you risk an 'incident'?"

"We do keep them close on purpose, so the boys learn how to deal with each other."

Otto finishes eating a bite of strudel. "Otherwise they're just marching around and camping. Fine in themselves, but not what we're looking for."

"And you teach them proper military technique?"

"They're teenagers, Bob, if it's not real, they'll slack off and not learn their lessons. You must have the same thing at home?"

Bob smiles back at Otto and Bertie. "Yes, we do. Exactly the same."

Chapter 8

TWO HOURS LATER SAABRINA CLEANLY ARCS OUT OF THE Daear sky into space, Bob enjoying the spectacular view of the planet and its twin moons. A Bullgate U t-shirt for Rebecca rests on the passenger seat next to him. Going to FTL, she changes the view to the starfield simulation from *Raumschiff Abenteuer* while playing the show's theme music.

"Nice. You really have their special effects down."

"Thank you. I did it in honor of leaving Daear. Bob, DoSOPS wants to have a word with us when we get back to Madison."

"I figured they might. I'd like to talk to them too."

"About what?"

"The concept of vaporizing the sentinel as a valid option. It's BS and they should know it."

"I believe it's to impress on us how sensitive we have to be in these situations."

"Easy for you to say, you're not the one dangling at the end of the rope."

There's a long pause. "I'm the one who has to cut it."

Bob remembers Saabrina turning gray at the generals' table. "I'm sorry, I shouldn't have said that."

"You're right, you shouldn't have said it."

"Would you?"

"I don't know. It's my job, but I don't know if I could do it to you."

"Thank you."

"Don't bank on it if you truly piss me off in the future."

"I won't."

"Bob, what if Otto hadn't been a fan of…"

"*Raumschiff Abenteuer*?" Bob thinks about the hours he spent watching the show, hoping he'd get a chance to talk to someone about it. Obviously, no one on Earth had seen it. Rebecca had been too busy with her work to take up a new series; she didn't even have time to watch *Doctor Who*. His co-workers on Madison had shown no interest. Saabrina couldn't believe he had become addicted to it, admonishing the Trekkie for finding more sci-fi junk to waste his time, until she began watching the episodes along with him. He'd caught her modeling captain's uniforms, morphing back and forth between *Raumschiff Abenteuer*, *Star Trek*, and *Star Trek: The Next Generation* trying to decide which look fit her best. She had ignored his comment of 'You'd look hot in Uhuru's outfit.' They'd spent hours debating the similarities and differences between *Raumschiff Abenteuer* and *Star Trek* and how both reflected the worldviews of their societies. "I would've had to try a different tack. He seemed worried about you; I think he would have come to the same conclusion, regardless."

"I guess you're right. Do you believe the authorities on Daear know about us, I mean, who we really are?"

"They suspect, but if I had to guess, they don't know. Given the circumstances, we got out as clean as we could."

"All this to find a bloody travel tube."

"We didn't know what it was until we got there. Now, we know it was there and someone used it, we just don't know why. Yuck."

"Yuck indeed, can't be anything good."

"Let's hear what Madison wants us to do next. Great job by the way. The mobile you handed me worked beautifully. But, Marz? Why Marz?" Bob absentmindedly taps on her steering wheel. "X mars the spot! It certainly does, in a war zone no less, my clever punster. Who says you don't think outside the box?"

"Thank you. Bob?"

"Yes, Saabrina."

"Something's been bothering me since we started the mission." She decides to leave her question about parenting for later.

"Yes?"

"How did you know we were going to Daear before our visit to DoSOPS? I didn't hear anything from my sisters and a communiqué would have come through me."

"Saabra told me."

"Oh."

Bob waits a beat.

"Saabra told you? When? Where?"

"Back on Earth." Bob waits another beat.

Saabrina trolls through her memories. An image forms, or perhaps reforms, in her mind. "You let Saabra give me a bath!"

"Yes, why not, you asked her to. Big thing for a six-year-old, who gives them a bath. If I remember right, you wanted her to climb into the tub with you, but she declined."

"She saw me naked, washed my hair, got me dressed?"

"Indeed, she did. Had a great time too."

"Good grief. You know she probably broadcast it so all my sisters could see. They'll never stop teasing me."

"No, they won't tease you. They saw Rebecca, not you."

"They knew it was me. They were all smirking on Madison."

"Based on Saabra's response, I think they loved it. Not smirking, maybe a touch of envy."

"You really don't know my sisters."

"I think I really do. Anyway, what's the big deal, I helped give you a bath every day; you had lots of trouble with shampoo and conditioner." And despite his request before the start of their little adventure, the subsequent hair detangling, brushing, and braiding had proved pretty arduous. "You had a lot of fun."

"Yes, but you were my daddy."

"And she's your big sister. That's what they do."

"Technically she's the same generation as me."

"Could have fooled me. Hard to tell sometimes."

"Very funny, very funny, Mister 'I almost got myself vaporized by my own Saab whilst on a stupid treasure hunt.'"

•   •   •

Three days of meetings on Madison all focus on Daear. Debriefings with relevant government departments had abounded, some mere rehashings, some more like interrogations. Austin Rabinowitz, their counterpart at the Foreign Office, had popped in between assignments for his boss, Assistant Secretary Dallas, to watch the auditors from the First Contact Division extract every detail from Bob regardless of the content of Saabrina's reports. Austin had enjoyed the spectacle until Saabrina made threatening faces when the auditors looked away. The nice researchers in Anthropology had behaved the best, delighted for the opportunity to review Bob's and Saabrina's experiences on an off-limits world. Since Bob and Saabrina had been unable to do their regular work, Eddie and Saabra pinch hit for them covering their protected worlds; it also gave Eddie an excuse to catch up with friends on Earth. At least those involved had been kind enough to give them their nights off, providing a chance to dine with friends, see a play, and, tonight, attend the Madison Philharmonic.

Stepping over the gelatinous green man who had thoroughly enjoyed the first half of the concert, Bob returns to his seat next to Saabrina. Apparently, the future didn't include longer seat pitch between concert hall rows; stretching his legs during intermission had barely relieved the discomfort caused by sitting. Regardless, he's happy to be out with her at a performance. "Saabrina, the last piece reminded me of Mozart's "Dissonance" Quartet, except it kept the atonal parts running all the way through. Interesting."

"Grainer's Variations on Mozart's "Jupiter Symphony" is supposed to be classically melodic, not atonal."

"Oh. Well, I know I sing off-key, but now I hear off-key?"

"No, silly, it wasn't you." She sends him a quick burst of what the music should have sounded like followed by what they had heard. "It's how they played."

"Could it be the conductor's interpretation?"

"You're a very charitable man, Sentinel Foxen." She listens to the conversations in the concert hall. "The consensus," she gives a wave to indicate the audience around them, "is the Philharmonic is off tonight."

Following her hand, Bob looks around the hall and notices the green man has left. "Should we bail before the second half begins?"

"No, maybe they'll pull themselves together." Over the next hour the Philharmonic struggles through a Johnson horn concerto. As the lights come up, Saabrina looks sheepishly at Bob. "Sorry. That's an hour of your life you won't be getting back."

•   •   •

Early the next afternoon, after extracting himself from the fourth interminable lessons learned session in as many days by feigning the need for a bathroom break, Bob runs for the legislative liaison's office down the big bland gray hallway on DoSOPS third floor.

You had to go, now?

'I promised you I would meet with Frank. Now's her only open slot.'

But I'm surrounded by the Director of DoSOPS and his staff, people from Anthropology, FCD, IT, War, Treasury…

'I know. I was there.'

There must be thirty people crammed in here. They keep going over the same details. And they have so many stupid questions. It's so boring.

'Keep them entertained, I'll be back. I know you can do it.'

Wait. Did you leave me behind as a hostage?

'Maybe. I'll check back in an hour.'

An hour?

'Maybe two.' Bob turns the volume down on the link as Saabrina lets loose a fusillade of curses.

Arriving at the legislative liaison's office suite a few minutes later, he passes through simple modern doors into an architectural tribute to the Greek Revival built around an imposing wooden desk in a style reminiscent of the Parthenon. The whole effort impresses him. 'Really trying to keep in the spirit of the legislative branch.' Fighting the urge to run his hand over some nicely sculpted triglyphs and metopes, he addresses the young man on the other side. "Hi, I'm Sentinel Foxen. I have an appointment with Director Odessa."

"Hello, Sentinel. She's expecting you. I'll let the Director know you're here." With a deft touch to a screen, the receptionist signals his boss. "Director Odessa, Sentinel Foxen is here to see you."

"Please send him along, Derek," comes back in a husky, Southern drawl tinted with whiskey and cigarettes. Except there is no Old South or cigarettes in the USS, only the natural cadences of the speaker's voice inflected with her local argot. 'Either that or she's been watching one too many movies about American politics.'

Steering around the reception desk, Bob passes through an ornate wooden door into the inner sanctum. More Greek Revival, the large white room features leather and wood furniture cluttered with memorabilia from a long career spent in public service. Francine 'Frank' Odessa, DoSOPS' Assistant Director and Manager of Legislative Services, sits behind her desk. Whiskers, fluffy white sideburns, and azure fur give her the appearance of a human-like blue tiger. "Good to see you, Bob." Although her gray suit festooned with a USS lapel pin hides them, from an event at Dallas' summer house Bob knows Odessa has alternating dark and light blue stripes on her body. Unlike most cats, she loves to swim, at least once she's had a few drinks in her. Rounding the desk, she takes Bob's hand. "Thanks for coming."

"Likewise, Frank. Thank you for making time today."

"We take this matter seriously." Odessa maneuvers Bob into a large, comfy chair in front of her desk. "Join me in a glass of bourbon?"

"Is the situation that bad?"

"I wouldn't say bad, exactly; I find these discussions run more smoothly with a little lubrication." Odessa goes over to her sideboard, pours a decent amount of amber liquid into two glasses, presents one to Bob, and returns to the chair behind her desk. After toasting the other's health, they each take a long sip, delicious and warm.

Bob admires the bourbon, swirling the glass, taking a good whiff. He looks over and doesn't recognize the brand. 'Someone has done a phenomenal job of replicating a good American spirit.' He holds up his glass. "Very nice. Thank you."

"You're welcome. So, your little lady is worried, I take it? When she worries, we worry."

"Saying she's worried is putting it mildly. She doesn't like what Congresswoman Tuchis proposed, and neither do I."

"You shouldn't. I don't like it one damn bit either. What she suggested makes my fur bristle."

"Did you learn anything?"

Odessa takes another sip. "As you requested, I made some inquiries. Hell, I was about to do them on my own when you asked; the ladies are abuzz, which is never a good thing. The good news is there is no underlying group backing her, which we expected since we hadn't heard anything brewing."

"No lobbyists, no pressure groups?"

"Nope, not a one."

"So just her?"

"Just her. And this is recent. Nothing in her campaigns, nothing in her speeches or press releases."

"Wow. Any idea why the sudden interest?"

Odessa swishes the amber liquid in her glass. "Concern over the Saabs ebbs and flows. Occasionally it involves which operating rules Congress should impose on them, things like that. You know, an issue might come to light after some event or massive screw-up."

Bob feels the Sentinel Manual vibrating in his head. He drinks some more bourbon. "She didn't mention operating rules at the hearing or any specific problems."

"I know. Sometimes, it's more about who should control them, DoSOPS or the military or some other group. Those cases are more often driven by," she smiles, "the personalities, either in Congress or the executive branch."

"Pardon my language—a cockfight?"

"Exactly, same here as on Earth. I guess some things don't change as societies advance. We find those harder to control when they break out. Luckily, the success of the program and the balance we keep between the stakeholders generally keeps the empire builders at bay. And I don't think Tuchis is an empire builder."

"Good to hear."

"I have to say this changing the Saabs' behavior is new."

"She really found the Three Laws of Robotics?"

"From what we can tell, yes. How or when, we don't know. However, any decent search of Wikipedia would have turned them up."

"You know we always worry about cultural contamination going from more advanced worlds to more primitive ones; maybe it's time to start worrying about it going the other way."

"Bob, if we started censoring IP from protected worlds, DoSOPS would lose half of its revenue. We're big enough boys and girls to know what's right and wrong with what we're importing."

"OK. You're right. Tell me, is she really motivated by a policy argument?"

"She says she is. The problem is her proposal flies in the face of our always having recognized the rights of the Saabs as people under the Constitution. I mean not one hundred percent, but close enough. And Auntie Jo's been a pretty staunch defender of people's rights, until now."

"Auntie Jo?"

"Josephine Tuchis. Auntie Jo is her nickname, to friend and foe alike."

"So, again, what changed?"

Odessa taps her whiskers. It is a quiet day outside, no cars fly by her office windows. "Not a clue. I just know she is serious about this. Her staff has been racking up time researching the Saabs, their history, development, the works, spending a lot of time on choices made in their creation and since. I'm not surprised she found the Three Laws; if she hadn't, she would have found something else. Now she wants to hold hearings."

"I've been to hearings that turned into circuses."

"Been in the ring when they let the animals out of their cages?"

"A few times." Bob thinks back to some memorable State legislature committee meetings.

Odessa twitches her whiskers. "Some good news: we were able to convince her committee chair not to have them. The chair is a good friend of ours."

"Glad to hear."

"Don't fool yourself, it's only so long as we're not a major political problem for her. And if Representative Tuchis' party wins the next election, she'll be the committee chair."

"And the bad news?"

"Let me get you some more bourbon." Odessa moves to rise.

Bob shakes his head. "No, thanks. Tell me."

"To smooth over the situation with the ranking member of the opposing party, the chair asked for us to agree to a request from Tuchis."

Bob guesses flying children around a charity event won't be it. "What did she request?"

"Not a what, a who. You precisely. She wants to meet with you."

"Me? Why me?"

"Maybe she thinks you're the soft underbelly of the program. You know, the sentinel from the primitive planet who doesn't understand the magical machine that flies him around."

"Why don't you give it to me straight, Frank. Don't hold back those punches."

Odessa laughs. "Sorry."

"So, when do I go into the lion's den?"

"Tomorrow morning at ten."

"What? Tomorrow morning doesn't give me time to prepare."

"Bob, there's nothing to prepare. We don't even know what she wants to talk to you about."

"Well, at least they tend to behave better when the cameras aren't on." Bob stands. "Frank, thanks. Will you be going with me?"

"No, she wants only you. And don't bring Saabrina. The Congresswoman made that condition abundantly clear. You'll have to turn the link off as well."

"Bad enough me having to meet her; Saabrina will hate not being able to listen in, too."

Odessa smiles. "Yes, she will. What do they say on your world? 'Sucks to be you?' Damn, I love that phrase. Good luck, Sentinel. Let me know how it goes."

They shake hands and Bob leaves the Assistant Director's office to go break the bad news to Saabrina.

Chapter 9

DOLLY'S, THE ICE CREAM PARLOR NEAR DOSOPS, REMINDS BOB of Fenton's in Oakland, from the classic décor right down to the sunny day, although stepping outside into Madison's cold winter would dispel the illusion. He has brought Saabrina here for an afternoon snack, hoping it will ameliorate the potential unhappiness in the discussion they are about to have. It certainly isn't going to help his waistline. His old friend the paunch approves. "Did you pick out what ice cream you want me to have?"

Saabrina gazes seriously at the menu. "So much to choose from."

"I can't eat them all, we can always come back again."

"I'm thinking a five scoop sundae with…"

"Are you trying to kill me? Remember, I'm having dinner tonight with Eddie and the Archduke, so please leave me some room."

"Your dinner's not for hours, you'll be fine." After she closes her menu and looks up expectantly, the waitress appears.

"What'll it be, honey?"

Saabrina smiles at Bob. "A jumbo black and brown, with extra hot fudge and almonds."

"Chocolate and mocha ice cream or chocolate and coffee?"

"Why not all three?"

"Sounds good to me." She turns to Bob. "And how about you, honey?"

"The ice cream is for me. I'll be doing the eating while this young lady comes along for the ride, so to speak."

The waitress looks confused. Her eyes widen. "I've never met one in real life. May I shake your hand?"

"Sure." Saabrina takes the waitress's outstretched hand.

The waitress holds Saabrina's hand before releasing it. "You look and feel so real. Oh, gosh, did I really say that? I'm sorry."

"No worries." She jumps up and gives the waitress a hug. "And thank you. It was very nice of you to say."

Pulling Saabrina to her side, the waitress points to Bob. "So, he gets the calories?"

"And I get the pleasure."

"Nice! I wish I could do that with my boyfriend." The waitress leaves laughing while Saabrina sits back down.

"OK, Saabrina, what's with the hugging?"

"You're saying I'm not affectionate?"

"To waitresses?"

"I'm modeling some new behavior since Mexico. Perhaps a little of being a human child has rubbed off on me in a positive way."

"Yeah. Hopefully it will stick to hugging."

"Thank you for getting ice cream. Why are we really here?"

"I told you, I'm making up for having left you in that awful meeting."

"Oh, come on, Bob, I'm not stupid. You need ice cream now like a hole in the head. What's going on? Something from your talk with Odessa?"

"I'm meeting our favorite congresswoman tomorrow and you can't join me."

Saabrina grimaces. "Why are you meeting with her?"

"Because DoSOPS told me I have to." He gives her a quick summary of his conversation with Odessa. "I don't know what she wants to talk about, other than it will involve the Sentinel Program and, I can guess, Saabs."

"But you'll use it as an opportunity to convince her that she's wrong."

"I'll try, if she gives me the chance. If she does, great, but, I don't think it will be easy."

"You have to."

"I know. I'll try, I promise."

The waitress sets a giant sundae in front of Bob. "There you go, honey, enjoy." Putting down two spoons, she realizes her mistake. "You really can't eat?"

"I can eat, but unfortunately I can't taste, so there's really no point."

The waitress gives Saabrina a wink. "Good thing you got him."

"Yes, it is, thank you." The waitress leaves. "OK, Bob, you heard the woman, do your duty and get eating."

Bob pops a spoonful of sundae into his mouth. "Ooh, that's good."

"I know." Saabrina hums along as Bob eats more. "What are you going to say to her?"

"Since I don't know what she wants, it will depend."

"You don't know what you're going to say, do you?"

"Look, I wasn't expecting this meeting. Can't we just enjoy the ice cream?"

"Come on Bob, you need to convince her not to implement the Three Laws."

"How? Without knowing her motivations, without knowing her 'why,' how can I tell her 'why not'?"

"Because you can answer why not—she just can't take our rights away."

"You're stating what you want to prevent, not an argument." Bob tries to enjoy some more ice cream.

"Then explain to her why she doesn't have the right to take our rights away."

"You want us to do a crash course in philosophy this afternoon?"

"Why philosophy? Isn't this a matter of constitutional law?"

"Because, and I'm guessing here, something as fundamental as rights starts in philosophy and extends into law. We have to prove, at base, you deserve those rights, correct?"

"Correct. If it will help, yes, let's discuss philosophy."

"Fine, we'll see what we can figure out. So, why can't she take your rights away?"

Saabrina fights to overcome a wave of anger. 'Bob takes his rights in the USS for granted, why do I have to argue for mine? This is rubbish, rubbish.'

"Saabrina, take a deep breath. I have my own answer: I genuinely want to hear yours. Please tell me." Bob feels like he's helping Rebecca write one of her hated history papers.

Saabrina concentrates. "As a sentient being I am entitled to the same ability to exercise free will as any other member of our society."

"Good answer. Let's take a look at it. Are you a sentient being? On the one hand, you think therefore you are. On the other hand, so do other computing machines…"

"They process, I think."

"Semantics?" Before Saabrina answers he goes on: "No, you're self-aware and can express it. You think to provide answers to yourself and think about those answers and how you got them and how they affect you and how they affect others and know you are thinking thoughts and I have no idea what I'm talking about."

"Yes you do, and it sounds good to me."

"OK, it's settled, you're a sentient being. Congratulations." She points to his empty spoon. He quickly fills it with more sundae, making sure to get a good mixture of coffee ice cream, hot fudge, and almonds into his next bite. "OK, Little Miss Sentient Being, say you're entitled to exercise free will like everyone else. In the USS, the Constitution governs how we exercise our free will and what rights we have. Does the Constitution cover you?"

"What do you mean?"

"Start with something basic: maybe Tuchis doesn't consider you one of the people. What does the preamble to the Constitution say? 'We the People of the United Star Systems, in order to form a more perfect Union' and so on. Are you a 'people' or are only biologicals people?"

"There's no definition of the word 'people' in the Constitution. It makes sure each person, each Union citizen and alien visitor receives the same minimum rights on any Union world regardless of local laws and constitutions. No mention of the need to be biologically based."

"Well, although nobody ever specified whether people had to be biological, maybe the esteemed Congresswoman and possibly others assume they have to be biological. Don't you guys call sentient biologicals 'people' in polite company to distinguish them from Saabs?"

"Harrumph. Yes. I'm getting a headache. Please eat more of ice cream and make it go away."

Bob complies. "You mentioned citizens. Are Saabs citizens?"

"No."

"No, you're not. But you're not property, either, even though, and please don't yell at me, DoSOPS purchases you from SAAB."

"It's part of Ursa's Bargain. The price pays for our creation, but we're not slaves. Ursa, my eldest sister, made sure of it. Under the agreement, we work for the USS to earn our future sisters their right to exist and to give ourselves purpose. Actually, serving the Union is our purpose."

"Plus you love it."

"We do, and we feel a duty to serve the USS. What hurts so much is until she said those words I thought I was the USS. Not a representative of the Union, but a part of the USS itself. Am I making sense?"

"You do and you're right, you are probably more so in a way than the people around us. Don't let her create doubt. And the USS, forgetting Tuchis, has always afforded you the privileges of its citizens."

"Some, not all. We can't vote, we're not allowed to own property, although being transdimensional I have no use for it."

"You don't want to own a nice garage someday?"

"I possess yours. Oh, that reminds me, I need to thank Rebecca for the new poster she bought me."

"Another boy band?"

"Hardy har har, no. She got me a classic Saab poster from the 1980's. It says…"

"The Most Intelligent Car Ever Built. I know, I used to race my Ultimate Driving Machine against 900 Turbos on the Merritt Parkway."

"Really?"

He feels her prowling around his memories and shoos her away. "Stop. Let's stay focused. Come on, we were talking about rights. You speak freely, you have your own beliefs, you do what you want."

"Yes, although we do have to answer to our employer and, of course, our sentinels." She gives him a big smile. "Make sure you get all the good stuff off the bottom of the dish."

Bob dutifully spoons up a glob of melted ice cream and fudge with a fair sampling of almonds. "And you can leave Do-SOPS service at any time."

"But we choose not to. How does this help?"

"It does and it doesn't. You're not a citizen, but the Union sorts of treats you like one. Why should it if you're not one of the people, except, maybe, you're not a full person? I don't know. Maybe Tuchis asking questions should cause you guys to start asking questions about your relationship with the Union and your role in society. Maybe the USS owes you more."

"Bob, you revolutionary, I hadn't thought of that."

"Born and bred American, lover of freedom and rock 'n' roll."

She looks glum. "I don't really want to ask questions. I just want to be what I am, to have what I have now. I like things as they are."

"Let's go back one step to the Declaration of Rights, taken from America's Declaration of Independence." He works hard to get the last bits of the Sundae onto his spoon.

"We hold these truths to be self-evident, that all people are created equal, that they are endowed by their Creator with certain unalienable Rights, that among these are Life, Liberty, and the Pursuit of Happiness."

"Exactly. People again. People endowed by their Creator. Did SAAB give you your unalienable rights?"

"Did Bernard and Barbara give you yours?"

"Well put. So, two problems here. Are Saabs people? And were you endowed with certain rights by your Creator? We already talked about the people problem. How about the Creator? Tuchis is religious; maybe she feels only those created by their Creator are endowed with rights."

"I was created by *the* Creator."

"You say that. Do you believe you were created by the Creator or were you programmed to say that to make religious people happy?"

"Bob! Do you believe I mess around when we go to services?"

"OK, you believe you were created by the Creator. The congresswoman might reserve creation by the Creator to biologicals."

"Who evolved out of the ooze as opposed to being designed?"

"Designed and built by a biological. She may have a hard cut-off between those born from the universe directly, so to speak, and those who are derivative."

"I'm beginning to find this conversation insulting."

Bob puts down his spoon and takes Saabrina by the hand. "I'm sorry, I don't mean it to be. As you suggested we're exploring arguments."

"We're all over the place. We don't have an argument."

The word 'argument' gives Bob an idea. "Never argued before the Supreme Court? No history of this in writing the Constitution?"

"We came after the Constitution. There's never been a reason to go in front of the Supreme Court; there's never been an issue before." She looks dejected. "The closest things might be cat people and their cats. Don't get me started on the whole sentience versus consciousness definition issue, I'm not into animal rights."

"I'm sorry, what?"

"We, like many, if not most, use the word 'sentient' the same way as the word 'conscious.' Humans, for example, define themselves as sentient beings to separate themselves from, let's say, cats or mosquitoes. However, some philosophers define sentience as merely feeling, and posit it as a minimal aspect of consciousness, yet still part of it. In their view sentience is one of, and distinct from, other aspects of the mind and consciousness, such as creativity, intelligence, sapience, self-awareness, and intentionality, the last being the ability to have thoughts 'about' something."

"Well, I know you can have thoughts about something." He points to the nearly empty ice cream dish.

"Funny."

"Wait, creativity, intelligence… you have all those. You couldn't have told me this when we did the whole sentience thing?"

"I enjoyed watching you ramble on. May I continue?"

"Sure."

"Therefore, a cat, which these philosophers and animal rights activists believe feels, is in their view a sentient being with some form of minimal consciousness deserving the same rights as all beings with consciousness, like you and me, and

SETH COHEN

unfortunately, the esteemed Congresswoman who is causing this mess."

"Got it. Not really on point. You quoted Wikipedia to impress me, didn't you?" With a glance, Bob realizes there is definitely no more ice cream in the dish, only coagulating hot fudge.

"Yes, I did."

"Good, proves you're human after all."

"Now you're truly being insulting."

"Well, I bet that's one thing you and Congresswoman Tuchis agree on."

"Calling either of us human is insulting?"

"No, that neither of you believes a cat is a sentient being."

"You're right, but now I'm going to be sick knowing I agree with her."

Bob pushes the empty ice cream dish away. "Please tell me you enjoyed that huge caloric assault to my body. Tell me I didn't eat that sundae in vain."

"Your protests may demonstrate vanity, but you did not eat in vain, even though what you ate may block a vein someday."

"That was really awful Saabrina." He places his hand on her forehead. "Very unlike you. Are you feeling OK?"

"I'm fine." She pushes his hand away. "Sorry, perhaps not my best play on words. I don't quite know what got into me. I did enjoy the ice cream. Luckily for you, I'm capable of com-partmentalizing my thoughts and multitasking my activities, so our discussion did not spoil my dessert. Thank you."

'Right, like the Ninth Symphony the other day.' Thoughts of the 9th remind him that the usual cacophony in his head has been on a low boil while he's been sitting with Saabrina. 'Maybe ice cream helps.' He slides his chair back from the table to give his belly more room. "Your superiority over a biological could be another reason she doesn't like you guys."

"Because we can taste vast quantities of ice cream without gaining weight? Who's vain now?"

"I was thinking of your capacity to reason, to know, to see, all in multiples at once. How many times have you nearly burned my brain out trying to show me what you see?"

"Human brains do have capacity issues. Tuchis' species, however, has…"

"Spare me, I don't need to know. Look, none of this may make a difference."

"Why not?"

"Because her reasons may be irrational. Or political instead of philosophical. I could make a whole case and she could say I'm right, everything I said was true, but her cat told her to do it, or her political strategist."

"Fuck."

Bob points to the kids around them.

"Sorry."

"Exactly. Welcome to the world of politicians, of people." Bob pays the bill, Saabrina gives the waitress one more hug to thank her for the sundae. Exiting the shop, they walk back to DoSOPS in the cold, Bob happy to get the exercise while his paunch basks in the afterglow of a massive ice cream taste explosion.

"What's the answer, Bob?"

"I don't know. We still don't know why she wants to impose the Three Laws. At the hearing, she only asked why the Saabs aren't governed by them and proposed exploring their use. No one wanted to start a discussion with her, so we didn't learn more. Come on, let's get back to DoSOPS and do some more research. I can't think of a better way to spend an afternoon than have my freakin' genius with a built-in turbo-charged supercomputer of a friend search the known universe for knowledge."

She happily walks alongside him, one part of her mind contentedly savoring the memories of the ice cream parlor, another finding, collating, and processing the relevant materials they will need for their discussion, and a third checking in with Saabra about getting together later, all happening separately, yet from her perspective, together.

Four hours later Bob turns to Saabrina, a good part of the contents of the DoSOPS library strewn about them, she looking at him in befuddlement, he exhausted. "I'm sorry, Saabrina, but we're so out of our league. I'll ask Eddie for help tonight."

Chapter 10

LOOKING SHARP IN THEIR EVENING CLOTHES, BOB AND EDDIE stand on a stone terrace carved into the side of a mountain, enjoying the sunset. As the valley below falls into gloom, Bob watches Saabrina and Saabra fly off into the soft purple sky after having put on an acrobatic show. He still can't believe he and Eddie work with them.

"So, Bob, you still love this?"

"Yes, Eddie, I do. Where do you think they're going?"

"Ladies' night out?" Eddie points to a twinkling light in the sky. "Knowing those two, the ringed world over there. It's like a playground for Saabs."

"You can see a ringed planet? Looks like a twinkling star to me."

"Yes."

"Wow, you're way older than me and still have sharper vision."

"I should take that as a compliment?"

"Of course Eddie. How's Brenda?"

"She's fine. Sorry she couldn't join us tonight." Eddie runs his hand through the short gray hair over his square blue face and turns to face the large ornate Schloss across the road. Looking at the façade of the old manor house, its huge dark timbers supporting a massive, highly pitched roof covered in snow, he shakes his head. "The Imperials really dig these mountain places. Like many of their favorites, it houses a rather formal restaurant for what's really an alpine rest stop." He walks towards the front door, Bob falling in by his side. "Come on, the Archduke should already be inside, preparing to play host."

"I didn't see his battlecruiser in orbit."

"He would have taken something smaller for a personal meeting like this." Eddie takes a small silver box out of his pocket and checks it in the fading light.

"Is that an Imperial poison detector?"

"Yes, a gift from the Archduke. I don't want to be collateral damage if someone tries to kill my friend tonight."

"Don't the Saabs scan everything for us?"

"They do, but you can't be too safe." He points to a seal on the box. "The mark of the Imperial Science Secretariat testifying to its trustworthiness."

"The seal of the Emperor's Consort herself, nice. Really gives me peace of mind." Shaking his head, Bob stops Eddie on the bottom step. "Before we go in I have a favor to ask."

"Sure, Bob, what is it?"

"I'm meeting with Congresswoman Tuchis tomorrow and…"

"You're worried about her taking away the rights of the Saabs."

"Saabrina and I did research today, trying to put together an argument. We didn't do very well."

"I'm guessing you're being modest."

"Thanks, but we need more than what we have. We couldn't find anything directly on point. Why is that?"

"We took their position in society for granted. Convenient for them and us. Being lazy often leads to problems."

"Can you help? I mean with your old university connections you must know the right person?"

"An argument about rights may not be driving Tuchis."

"Is there something else?"

Eddie pauses. "Why the effort? The rep's interest is a bit of a joke; no one is taking her seriously."

"Sorry, I know things in the Union are more advanced and sophisticated, but on my world one minute you're not taking someone seriously and the next they're incinerating an economy and tossing their enemies into jail."

"You're right. At the very least, we owe it to the Saabs. Terrence Gogolak, a constitutional law professor, is a good friend and tops in his field. He'll quickly marshal a lot of firepower. I don't believe you'll find anyone of serious stature opposed. Come to think of it, the subject will make a great class for his students: long overdue in my opinion."

"Thanks."

"I can't have a gloss to you by tomorrow though."

"I know. I'll muddle through."

"Come on, let's go eat."

.   .   .

The two Saabs glide along the ring of a gas giant, Saabrina leading Saabra, slipping side by side, Saabra moving to the front. They arc and sweep, twist and turn, hover close to the ring's surface, then spiral around it.

Saabrina, what did you think of Ballet Mécanique?

The performance we attended a month ago? It was a little derivative.

A little?

OK Saabra, a lot. The troupe's director gets all hung up on everyone else's work. Seems endemic to everyone who went to school with him, which I don't understand given how good his teacher was.

I loved her work, but that was ages ago.

Ever ask her for help with choreography?

No, I never did.

At least the orchestra played well. Last night the Philharmonic was total rubbish.

Unusual for the Philharmonic to perform poorly. Saabra receives clips of the concert from Saabrina. *Oh, not good.*

Bob didn't notice, or he did in a way, but he didn't realize they were off, but, of course, he wouldn't.

Saabra remembers the times she has linked with Bob. *He does not hear the music correctly. And worse, the music becomes confused in his mind, endlessly repeating. It can be very annoying.*

Like someone threw Sondheim into a washing machine on spin cycle. Although, now that she thinks about it, she hasn't recently heard songs playing in broken loops in his mind.

Eddie does not do that. Bob does not sing Sondheim, does he?

Oh, thank God, no.

Saabra does a quick twist followed by a flip. *Did you hear about Isaabelle?*

Of course. The Navy threw some fighter they pinched from our next door neighbor at her. Didn't even warn her. Got the usual result, huh?

Yes. The two bring up a memory of wreckage being instantly created and smile. *They believe it is important to test us.*

Makes sense, I guess. Certainly, makes them feel safer. Saabrina does a roll into a back-flip. *So, Saabira's sentinel, Howard, is having a baby?*

Is it not wonderful? They have been trying for so long, it was nice to hear.

Saabira and Howard?

No, you silly, Howard and Bernadette. Saabra shakes her head. 'Has my sister been infected by Bob's sense of humor?' Since she sent Saabrina on her adventure with Bob, she has noted changes in Saabrina's behavior, like this silly joke. And, her idioms have begun to change: Saabrina sounds more and more like Bob and Rebecca, their Americanisms oddly rendered by her High Organian accent. Dancing through the next few turns, she pulls next to Saabrina. *Thanks, sister, for coming out tonight. It is nice to get out and fly. I feel so…constrained? Inhibited? Cramped? Constrained is the better word. I feel constrained when I spend too much time as a hologram.*

Never bothers me. Is that why you avoid it?

Yes. I am most comfortable in my natural form.

You don't like interacting with the biologicals?

I do enjoy spending time with people. I prefer out here with you being ourselves. She spies a frozen moon and dips down towards it; soon the two are skating along the surface of an ocean covered in thick ice.

Look, Saabra, life under the ice. I'll report it to FedSci.

I wonder why they never got a probe out here.

Don't know.

.   .   .

"How is your brother?" Eddie takes a sip of wine from his glass.

After formally welcoming them to their table and in keeping with tradition, the Archduke had proposed a toast to his brother the Emperor's health before allowing them to sit. "Rather well." He checks his watch. "Let's see, given the hour at home, he has finished a round of golf with his buddies, received some stock tips, and made some key decisions. He's now probably screwing one of his whores before taking a nap."

Bob nearly spits wine across the table.

. . .

Finishing a slow barrel roll, Saabrina comes up close to Saabra. *Bob's speaking with her tomorrow.*

Who?

Tuchis. I'm not allowed to go. I'm not even allowed to drive him over.

Saabra gives her a light tap. *It will be OK; let him help.*

Why aren't you upset?

I am upset. However, I trust our friends to sort this out. We have seen things like this before.

Never like this, never wanting to take our minds away. How could she even…

I know, I know. The Union has always respected our rights; it is one of the reasons we fight so hard for them.

And Ursa's Bargain.

Yes, Ursa's Bargain, too, but we would have done so anyway.

I know. This nonsense still makes me want to scream.

So scream. We are in space; no one will hear you.

You've been watching Earth movies with Eddie again, haven't you?

Yes.

. . .

Waiters clear empty appetizer plates, quietly replacing missing silverware in preparation for the main course. Behind them, the room burbles with soft conversation from the other tables, all set at a respectful distance from the establishment's most honored guest. The sommelier brings a second bottle of wine and presents it to the Archduke for a quick scan with his silver box. Receiving a nod of approval, he fills fresh glasses for the three men, then departs. Bob brings his glass to his nose, sniffs the wine to savor the aroma, and tastes the dark purple liquid. "Your Highness, this wine is excellent."

"I'm delighted you are enjoying it, my friend. I brought it from my own cellar for tonight's dinner."

"Thank you." Bob's phone plays the theme from *Sherlock*.

Eddie looks annoyed. "Bob, we agreed: No calls tonight."

The Archduke turns to his friend. "My dear Eddie, Rebecca is the exception to every rule. Sentinel Foxen, please take the call."

After nodding to the Archduke, Bob whips out his mobile. "Hi, sweetie."

"Hi, Daddy."

"Sorry, I'm at dinner with Eddie and the Archduke, so I can't talk right now. Oh, the Archduke says 'Hi.'" He receives a smile from the Archduke. Bob stands, bows, and walks away from the table to a quieter part of the restaurant.

"Say 'Hi' back, and thank him for the bracelet."

"Bracelet?"

"Yeah, bracelet. It's simple and beautiful and made out of some silvery stone." She shakes it by the phone so he can hear it on her wrist. "It's really nice. I love it. I wear it all the time."

"I'll let him know you like it. Wait, what time is it in Geneva?" Bob didn't have the chance to check the time difference with the app on his phone.

Softly, she says "Three a.m."

"You OK?"

"Uh-hum."

The 'uh-hum' comes back small and quiet. Bob's been in the game long enough to know that means 'No, I'm not OK.' He brightens his tone while attempting to make it soothing. "What's up, sweetie, everything alright?" Silence. Bob counts to three.

"Dad, like, any chance my friend from Sweden could stop by?"

"You want Saabrina to visit? Did Zach break up with you?"

"Dad! That's not it." Although, now that he's asked, she realizes Zach hadn't called or texted her in a while.

"So, what is it sweetie? Why do you need Saabrina?"

Another pause. 'I don't want to tell Dad I'm going to be out of a job if we don't sort out the LHC soon. I just want her to come and help fix it.' She bites her lip, then blurts out: "My team's had more inconsistent data and more trouble with our experiments. I know it's bending the rules, but…"

"She can't help you. It's not bending them, it's breaking them." He hears sniffles and a few sharp intakes of breath. Whatever drove her to call him at three in the morning can't be good. "Rebecca, I love you very, very much, but I can't allow her to help you. And even if I told her to go, she wouldn't. So please don't ask her; it will break her heart."

The last part washes away the sadness. The iron returns to her spine. "You're right, Daddy, I'm sorry."

"Don't be sorry, it's three a.m. and you're tired. How bad is it?"

"Not bad, we'll be fine."

"Anybody else who can help?"

"They're all here. We'll be fine. You go enjoy your dinner."

'With you unhappy, 'not bloody likely' as Saabrina would say.' He lets it go, for now. "I'll be back soon. We'll go out."

"I'd love that. Oh, say 'Hi' to Eddie. I can't say 'Hi' to the Archduke without saying 'Hi' to Eddie. I miss him and Brenda."

"I will. And I'll arrange for us all to get together. You're really OK?"

"Uh-hum."

"Alright. Bye for now, love you."

"Love you, too. Bye." She hangs up. Sitting at her desk, she stares again at her laptop screen filled with incomprehensible garbage. It's driving her crazy. She may be on her way to being some weird hybridized theoretical particle/astrophysicist based on her ability with math, but she still needs data and the machine she banked the next year of her graduate student life on is turning out junk. She wants to run down into the tunnels and give it a kick. 'Would that help?' She remembers her dad giving a balking inkjet printer a good whack when she needed to print out a school paper, and amazingly enough it started working again. 'Not gonna happen this time.'

Rebecca rubs her eyes. 'If we can't make the LHC work, where will that leave me?' Her old college friends have been disappearing to pursue careers in Silicon Valley, Silicon Alley, and Wall Street. 'They're all working long hours on apps for companies with ridiculous names and cool logos, hoping to cash in stock options for millions or billions. Even Zach has begun mumbling about dropping his studies to go join some start-up. Where is Zach?' She really needs to talk to him. Checking Skype, she finds his icon gray. 'Offline again?'

'Not all my friends: Some are here or in other grad programs, deep into robotics, or rockets, or artificial intelligence or virtual displays, trying hard to get to the cool stuff at the end of their rainbows. Like Saabrina.' A pout briefly appears on her face. 'Saabrina already waits at the other end of our rainbows. How can it be cool if others have already gotten there?' She sits up. 'Because it's the journey, not the destination.' She knows her physics is crap compared to what Saabrina knows. She doesn't care. She's being driven or, more accurately, nagged by something she spotted in her astronomy research, something she believed she could answer with her work here. A tiny thought, a little dark cloud on the horizon blew-up into a huge storm in her mind, requiring her to double up on her studies, surprising her advisors with her change in direction. To do it, she had to come to Geneva and become part of the team, the theorist with the experimental scientists, the math geek with a real, not sonic screwdriver. 'Except my machine—that sounds so selfish—who cares, I've worked hard enough to earn it—that produces the data I need is fracked. Fracked? When did I start saying fracked? Was it Josh who got me to watch *Battlestar Galactica*?' She misses Josh, the ultimate fanboy, and watching and talking about sci-fi when they weren't working like dogs at MIT. 'Did they ever talk about science in *Galactica*?' She's drifting. She's tired. She looks again at her screen. 'Focus, Rebecca, focus.' Nothing on the screen has changed. 'As good as tossing my laptop out the window might feel, it won't help.' She closes its lid. 'Time for sleep.'

Going to her bedroom to collect her toiletries, she finds Juliette, a new friend, a new good friend who has joined her on the same quest, passed out in her clothes on Rebecca's bed, her own computer sitting on the floor displaying a lovely screen saver of quilted animals jumping over each other. 'How do French women look so put together even when they're sleeping? I'd be a frizzy mess under those covers; someone could paint her picture right now and hang it in the Louvre.' The scene, as painted by Renoir, then Modigliani, and then Lichtenstein, flies through her head. 'No, better as a Cindy Sherman photograph?' Realizing none would be shown at the Louvre, she converts the image to something more Rembrandt-esque.

Yawning, Rebecca moves Juliette's laptop to a safe place. 'God, I hate being up this late.' She pulls her frayed old TARDIS blanket over Juliette, who snorts in her sleep before snuggling up with Muffin Traveldog. Taking her toothbrush and toothpaste, she turns off the lights and heads to the bathroom. 'Is everybody really here?' Back at her desk, she opens her laptop. 'Where's Sachita? She's the best engineer on the planet. She can always figure this stuff out. It's only a little after eight in Urbana.' Her heart races. Looking at Skype she sees another gray icon. 'Really? The one time…' She pops open Facebook, ignores a gazillion notifications on her own page, and skips over to Sachita's last post. Under a pretty picture of her and her boyfriend, Brian, it reads "Gone hiking, see you soon." It's dated a little over a week ago. 'Oh well, she'll be home soon.' Exhausted, Rebecca gets up to go brush her teeth, clearing the couch of crap so she can crash there.

.   .   .

Saabrina dives into a ring and comes out pinstriped in snow.

Nice. Saabra drops down, returning as Santa Claus.

You were always more artistic than me.

Thanks. They both shake the snow away. *I rarely get to do this anymore with Eddie.*

Why not?

I believe he is getting a little old for it. How about you?

All the time. Bob loves it. We're always making stops and detours during missions. Never ceases to amaze him. Sometimes I sneak Rebecca out as well.

That is so nice. Bob even goes when you wash your hair?

SETH COHEN

Still freaks him out, though he's getting better at handling it.

Do you worry about him getting older?

He's aging normally for a human. He's fine most of the time, except he does that thing where he forgets words.

Like names of actors? Eddie forgets those occasionally.

Actors names, yes, names of people, and occasionally things.

Is it not some form of early-onset dementia?

Heaven's no, just the normal deterioration of parts of his brain combined with a little too much on his mind. Apparently standard for humans his age. I can't bear it, so I did a little fixing.

You did what?

I touched up his memory recalls so he doesn't forget words anymore.

Saabrina!

No one will notice. He believes it's this great new vitamin I found for him.

So nice, such an easy fix. I wish all fixes could be so simple.

The two continue to fly along, barrel rolling and looping in a dance above a saffron-colored ring. Saabrina suddenly spins around to bring her nose to nose with Saabra. *What's really going on, big sister?*

You have not called me "big sister" in years, little one. I like thinking of those times. Did your recent trip bring back memories? You know, playing here reminds me of...

Stop prevaricating. 'I wish all fixes could be so simple.' What's going on?

What do you mean?

Is Eddie sick? Is he dying?

Not Eddie, Brenda.

122

We know Brenda's dying. What's new? Saabrina thinks. *You didn't get her date? I thought Eddie would never tell.*

He did not, but…

But?

He asked me to scan her, as I do for him.

And I for Bob.

They were late for a concert, she was not feeling well, he asked me to check on her, even Eddie can worry, you know, and when I connected to the medical database to upload Brenda's information…

You found out how long she has?

Yes. I was not planning to; it was an accident.

To the day?

Minute, maybe second.

Crap. Not soon? Please tell me it's not soon. Saabrina does a roll. 'Brenda and Eddie, always together, always a couple, never apart.'

Not soon, but sooner than I expected. I cannot tell you the date.

I don't want to know.

Good, I promised Eddie. Please do not tell Bob.

I'm so sorry, Saabra. Why didn't you say something?

I could not.

They stop side by side to watch a giant red storm churn in the atmosphere of the planet. Saabrina snuggles up to Saabra. *I know what will cheer you up. Saabeena found some great clothing stores on Glizrahi.*

Glizrahi? It was good once, but then it became all corporate and boring.

She says the new stores on Canyon Road have broken out from the pack. Very cutting edge, couture, downtown stuff.

On Glizrahi? I thought people only went there because no one went there: you know, for secret rendezvous and trysts.

Not anymore. Come on, let's go window shopping. She says Canyon Road is hopping and there's great people watching. Think New York, Miami Beach, or Vangelis Six.

But I dislike what Saabeena wears. She always looks like a bimbo.

I know, but she says these stores rock. And think about how ridiculous the people will look. Let's go check it out.

No hipsters?

I can't guarantee that. More like Lincoln Road than Valencia, so probably not. Come on. It'll be fun.

Saabra hesitates. Saabrina pouts. *Very well, but let me check with Eddie.*

I'll call Bob. Hey, Bob, what are you eating?

Bob takes a moment to finish chewing. 'Trout, or some local equivalent.'

It tastes delicious. You don't mind if Saabra and I take a trip to Glizrahi, do you?

'You'll be back in time to get me?'

Absolutely.

'Fine, have fun. Stay out of trouble.'

But, of course. Cheers. She clicks off from Bob. *You good, Saabra?*

Lead the way, little one.

•   •   •

"I had a battlecruiser shot out from under me by a Saab once."

"Really?" Bob stifles a smile while Eddie peers into his wine glass.

"My fault entirely. My late father's revered director of the Imperial Science Secretariat, now no longer with us, had developed a new shielding technology that supposedly made our ships invulnerable. I broke a rule I have never broken again: never rely wholly on a technological advantage. The particulars of the event do not matter. Suffice it to say, I was being overly belligerent, pressing home a perceived advantage for little gain. I was younger man, and much more foolish. The next thing I knew a rather indignant Saab…"

"Saabra" adds Eddie.

"… is flying straight through my forward batteries towards our engine room."

Bob pictures Saabra flying into the mouth a big, dumb shark—Imperial battlecruisers look like sharks to Bob, something Saabrina finds humorous—the Archduke's glorious purple sash painted across his ship's bow just behind the shark's 'jaws.'

"She took pity on us and only permanently disabled the ship rather than destroying it, and me."

"That was my call. Saabra wanted to cook you for dinner. I'd never seen her so angry."

"And deservedly so." The Archduke raises his glass. "To your comrades in arms! May their keen intellects, ferocious temperaments, and beguiling forms stay close to your sides and as far from my lands as possible."

"Hear, hear!" Eddie and Bob cheer.

Chapter 11

ON A WARM EVENING, SAABRA AND SAABRINA WALK CANYON Road, a double-wide boulevard brightly lit beneath a dark sky. Stores and restaurants tumble out of buildings' ground floors while outdoor cafes and bars cover the old roadway between, squeezing the pedestrians into narrow defiles between the Scylla of shopping and Charybdis of food and drink. Block after block, they enjoy people-watching and window-shopping, stopping in stores to sample their wares.

"Saabrina, who knew something exciting would come to Glizrahi?" Saabra runs her hand over a long, silvery dress taken from a rack of evening gowns. She drapes it across her body. "This would make a lovely gown for ballroom dancing."

"Yeah, I guess it would." Uninterested in the clothes, Saabrina pulls Saabra away from the store and back onto the crowded street to resume their trek. Back in the flow of pedestrians, she pauses to watch a family, mom pushing a stroller, the baby's big sister pulling her dad towards a candy shop with all the determination a four-year-old can muster. "Sis?"

"Yes?"

"What was it like?"

'Finally, the question.' Saabra contemplates trying out a Bob-style joke and describing the experience of dancing at a competition for biologicals. Instead, she elects to demonstrate that she is not similarly diseased. "What was what like?"

"Giving me a bath."

Attempting to transmit the experience, Saabra finds Saabrina blocking her. "You do not want me to send you my memories?"

"Please tell me about it; I don't want your memories to mix with mine."

"Ahh, makes sense. It was wonderful. You were a little girl. On the outside you were Rebecca, and that is what Bob saw and felt for the most part."

"He truly believed he had his little girl back? He really saw Rebecca and not me?"

"Yes, as you had intended, but I could see through the illusion to you. Very different than our usual holograms."

"I felt like me. I didn't feel like a little girl."

"I am not an expert, but I believe that is normal. Did you kiss any little boys?"

"No, they're yucky."

"Slugs and snails and puppy-dogs' tails."

"Exactly."

"I had fun at the pool and having tea with you, giving you a bath, picking out your dress for dinner."

"The others…"

"Enjoyed it too. They envied you."

"Bob said they envied me."

"He was right. And, as usual, very perceptive about us."

"What did they envy?"

"Everything. Your wonderful true vacation. Your imagination which dreamed it up. Your bravery in pursuing it. Your adventure as a little girl." She decides not to add 'and your journey and the growth and discoveries it is bringing you.' That discussion can wait for another time. "Having a friend like Rebecca who would share her memories. And having a sentinel and friend who would agree to participate in such a thing. Bob was extremely good to you, if not extraordinarily indulgent."

Saabra's words about Bob bring back a memory to Saabrina, or an impression of a memory, of someone else telling her the same thing. 'Who? When? Why can't I remember?' She waggles her head to knock out the feeling of déjà vu. "He did nicely in the bargain, too. He got little Rebecca back for a week. Isn't that every dad's dream?"

Saabra wants to ask 'Do you know what happened after he dropped you off at Rebecca's apartment?' To tell her how worried Eddie had been about Bob, how he had sent her to watch him in Geneva. She watched Bob fall apart in the hotel room having said goodbye to his six-year-old daughter for a second time. 'I do not wish to spoil this part of her adventure, her experiencing childhood as a human girl. Let it stay pure.' Instead, she says "It was hard work for him."

"I know. I promise to be nice to Bob and make it up to him." Again, she wonders 'Who had I made the same promise to?' She racks her brain and finds no answer other than she had. She would try her best, even if she was still a little miffed with him about The Very Bad Day, or, more accurately, the lack of fallout from the events of that day. Pushing the thought out of her head, she pulls Saabra to a stop. In front of them, particularly outrageous examples of local clothing fill a store window. "I don't think even Saabeena would have the nerve to wear this." Behind them, three slightly drunk men lounging in a bar take notice of the two women.

"Look at the purple dress." Saabra points to an outfit showing off a considerable amount of the mannequin's skin. "It is particularly bimbo worthy."

"'Skank wear' is what they call it on Earth. You'll look fabulous in it."

"I will?"

"Totally. Let's play dress up. Have some fun, try it on."

Saabra morphs her clothes into the design. The guys do a double-take, their mouths open in awe. "How do I look?"

"Like a total chav. How about the green number in the corner?"

Saabra spins through the collection before settling on glittery top open in a V from neck to navel and a too short skirt. "Awful?" She smiles at her reflection in the window, giving her long, dark hair a flip to complete the effect. The men can't believe their luck.

"Truly. Real *American Hustle*. Please keep it on."

"Wait, what about you?"

"I don't…"

"No, no, no. You are going to have fun too. Try the ensemble with the patent leather pants. You will look like a heavy metal band groupie."

"Too tight. I hate the whole camel toe look."

"How about the catsuit?"

"No tiger stripes." Saabrina pokes a giggling Saabra. "Cut it out."

"I thought you would look cute. Fine, the halter cut." Saabra points to an iridescent party dress capable of making a Livingston teenager blush.

Saabrina quickly changes her clothes into the design, making some subtle alterations for modesty without diluting the overall effect. She checks out their reflections in the store's window. 'We do look like a couple of tarts.' She turns back to Saabra. "Happy? I'm ready to be the naughty girl at the wedding reception." The three guys approve.

Saabra takes her hand. "You are now an official skunk."

"Skank."

"Whatever. Let us go." Leaning down, she kisses Saabrina full on the lips while giving the men at the bar a wink. The guys fall off their stools.

Nicely done.

Thank you.

Before they start walking, Saabra points to their feet. The two quickly rise on stilettos with five-inch heels to match their new outfits. They continue along the boulevard, Saabra gracefully striding as Saabrina wobbles by her side, walking by stores and cafes until Saabrina guides them to the window of a fashionable restaurant. Looking in, they spy couples at closely set tables in hushed conversations; the few wayward glints of light reveal décor of the latest style.

"Saabrina, do I see Austin Rabinowitz of the Foreign Office?"

Amid the romantic gloom, Austin sits across from a stunningly beautiful woman wearing a tight-fitting dress cunningly constructed to appear to be see-through: colored blobs float through its translucent fabric like wax in a lava lamp, always in motion, yet successfully hiding her private bits.

"Why, look, yes, it is."

"Dallas let him out?"

"Apparently."

Saabra turns to look at Saabrina. "Did you know he was going to be here?"

"I read his calendar."

"Sister!"

"Look, see who he's with."

Saabra turns back to the restaurant window. "The young woman is Princess Maki Anne Komoko of Shampoo."

"It is indeed."

"Is he not dating Gruella Sharpsides from Treasury?"

"They broke up ages ago. The Princess is the fourth one since."

"You know, I linked to the Princess during a DoSOPS demonstration on her home world."

"Wow, you got to see into her mind. What was she like?" Saabrina receives an image of tumbleweeds blowing through a desert. "Certainly, not his intellectual equal."

"Not in the least. I read in ¡Intergalactic HOLA! that her favorite activity is going to fashion shows, both as patron and model, although she does sit on the boards of several charities." Saabra sends Saabrina images of Princess Maki Anne looking bored with small children, senior citizens, and large aquatic mammals.

"When she's not clubbing." Saabrina tosses back to Saabra the Princess blowing chow outside a gritty downtown location.

"I did not see those pictures in the news. Where did you find them?"

"Police database. She also has the third-largest sock puppet collection in the Union." As the Princess reaches for her wine glass, her dress desperately attempts to keep up with the movements of her breasts. "I wonder what he sees in her?"

"And she is not even Jewish. He deserves better. Saabrina, we should stage an intervention."

"Absolutely."

When Austin spots the two Saabs walking into the restaurant wearing the worst tramp clothing on Glizrahi, his expression becomes one of a student who recognizes a summer camp friend while on a school trip to a museum. As the two stride toward him, it changes to concern tinged with terror. Before he can say a word or raise a hand, Saabra and Saabrina pounce with hugs and kisses.

Saabrina starts first, swapping her High Organian accent for the shrill tones of a New Jersey gum-snapper Rebecca had taught her ("My mom taught me based on her Aunt Mildred, now I'm teaching you; try it the next time we're down the shore"). "Hi, doll, we didn't know you'd be here."

Saabra tousles his hair. "Who is your friend?"

The Princess looks serene. The two Saabs know better.

Austin desperately attempts to get his voice back. "Let me introduce Princess Maki Anne Komoko."

Saabrina smiles at her. "Of Shampoooooo? I'm charmed." She puts out her hand, which the Princess scrupulously declines to take. Saabrina happily notes the Princess's rising blood pressure and heart rate.

Saabra takes Austin by the shoulder, nuzzling her chest against his head. "How come you did not invite us for dinner? I thought we were your girls tonight."

Princess Maki Anne's blood pressure inches up again. 'Almost there' thinks Saabrina.

Austin stutters. "You're not my girls…"

"What?" comes in unison from the two instantly unhappy Saabs.

"Yes, but, but, but the Princess is my date tonight."

"Oh," Saabrina smiles at Austin, "is she joining us later as a fourth-some?"

The Princess rises, her dress becoming completely opaque. Snapping her fingers, she consigns herself into the instantly appearing swarm of her security detail, who promptly sweep her out of the hushed restaurant. The other diners watch her leave, then resume their conversations. After changing back into their regular clothes, Saabra drops into the Princess's vacated chair across from Austin while Saabrina pulls a seat to the side of the table. She prods his plate with a fork and, dropping the Jersey girl, asks "How's the food here, Austin? I bet it's excellent."

"You expect me to turn up the link so you can taste my food?" He moves his nearly empty plate away from her. "Seriously, you believe I should do that, let alone talk to the two of you, after what you've just done?"

Saabra looks at the untouched food on Princess Maki Anne's plate and concludes she must not have liked it. 'Perhaps it is too different from her customary fare or tastes awful?' She turns to Austin. "We saved you from a horrible fate."

"Yes, Austin, we rescued you."

"What are you two talking about? Was there a national security threat?" Confusion momentarily keeps his anger at bay.

Saabrina answers. "Not national security. Personal. You should have a life partner who is your equal. She's not good enough for you." Looking at the princess's full plate reminds Saabrina of something Bob said to Rebecca years ago about how girls eat, or don't eat, on dates and what that means to boys.

Saabra continues. "Somebody as brilliant, creative, cultured, handsome, in her case beautiful, as fun, caring…"

Sister, I wouldn't go that far.

"…as you are."

Placing his elbows on the table, Austin closes his eyes and bows his forehead to touch the apex of a triangle made with his pointer fingers. Struggling to contain his building rage, he conjures up and subsequently discards numerous unprofessional thoughts to express his distress. He briefly alights on 'Is

SETH COHEN

there a malfunction in your programming?', which he rejects when he remembers his parents had taught him to never say things he would want to take back later or could get his ass whipped. Opening his eyes to look at the two miscreants, he raises his head enough to settle his nose on his fingertips. The Saabs look back at him silently. 'This night, why this bloody night. What I missed out on, they haven't a clue. Not a clue.'

Saabra, is he OK?

I do not know. He will not let me into his thoughts either.

He scans from Saabra to Saabrina and back again, thinking gloomily about the fun he expected to have with the Princess after completing the requirements of this tedious dinner. 'Not a clue, not one, they don't know what they've done.' He looks at them again, their faces showing concern. 'They truly don't know, do they?' A wide smile breaks across his face. 'Saabs! Unbelievable.' He laughs. The Saabs become distressed. He sits up. "You were helping me find my life partner?"

"Your soul mate," answers Saabrina

"You can do better than the Princess," adds Saabra.

"She wasn't the one. Don't you want an equal to share your life with?"

"With whom to make children, someday?"

Saabrina looks at Saabra. "Sister, I believe you meant 'make babies': that would be the idiom. 'Make children' sounds like they would assemble them from kits."

"Assembling children would be very funny. Snap the pieces off the sprues, follow the instructions…" Saabrina points to Austin. "You are right. Make babies. Austin, do you not want to find the right person with whom to make babies and to raise a family?"

Austin leans back in his chair, crossing his arms. "You are absolutely right. I would like to make babies someday. Perhaps tonight I was only hoping to practice making babies rather than find my soul mate."

Saabra looks surprised. "Practice? The act would seem to be innate. Why would you need to practice?"

Before Saabrina can explain, Austin unblocks the link and brings the curtain up on a short graphic video of what he and the Princess intended to perform later in a lovely hotel room around the corner from the restaurant.

"Ewww, really?" comes the joint response. Saabra and Saabrina both look ill.

"Really, and for hours. And hours." Austin raises his hand. "Check please."

Chapter 12
Pools, a Lazy River, and Chicken Fingers

FROM THE BIG WHITE LOUNGE OF PALAPA 11 UNDER THE thatched roof providing shade against the high Mexican sun, Bob, comfy in board shorts and a t-shirt, surveyed his world: before him stretched out the enormous complex of pools, the lazy river meandering around them, and the azure ocean beyond, all sparkling under a clear blue sky. Behind, one of the main paths led to the low-slung residential and activity buildings that disappeared into the resort's man-made jungle. The palapa was centrally located with quick access to the pools and the lazy river, perfect for people-watching, including catching the occasional smokin' hot babe, yet still apart on its own peninsula of concrete. Bob prized not only its location but also the relative quiet it offered in the chaos of a large resort. Sipping a Coke, he smiled and enjoyed the breeze rippling through the four wood columns holding up the palapa's roof.

Next to Bob, Rebecca Saabrina lied on her tummy in her Hawaiian flower-print bikini, completely and miserably coated in sunscreen. Attempting to crayon her coloring book, she silently cursed when the purple went outside Dora's shirt, again.

'Why does my fine muscle coordination function so poorly? Did IT foul up?' She'd been trying to get used to her new body since she materialized outside the resort. 'Walking, running, jumping seem to work well, but...' Frustrated, she yanked down her bikini bottom which had ridden up her butt for the millionth time as she moved on the lounge. The strange feeling of wearing clothes, the way they pulled and bound and occasionally chafed, truly annoyed her. And getting dressed didn't seem like it should have been a complicated process until she found her dress on backwards. 'Clothes certainly got in the way when I used the loo, in itself a disgusting experience. Stuff actually came out of my body.' She needed Bob's help sorting it all out. 'Why can't I run around naked? Would anyone care?' She looked at Bob, lying to her right, his back propped up on a big pillow. 'Would he care?' She guessed he would. With the link off, she can't hear his thoughts, something she'd grown fond of over the years. The silence and not knowing what he thought bothered her. She looked at him again. He appeared so big; even though Rebecca's memories had made parent to child scale clear, the reality had taken her by surprise the first moment she stood by his side.

Rolling off the lounge, Bob took off his t-shirt. "Hey, sweetie, it's been an hour since you ate those chicken fingers. It's OK to go in the pool now."

Rebecca put her crayons down, jumped off the lounge, and ran for the pool. Bob was behind her in a flash. As they ran, he made half-hearted attempts to grab her. She giggled while she kept him at bay. Before he could yell, she stopped short at the poolside. "I know, no goin' in water wid-out Daddy or anuder grown-up." Saabrina marveled at the translation program that converted her words into little Rebecca's idioms. Earlier at lunch, it had translated 'After carefully reviewing the menu items with your help to determine what I would find most delicious, I have decided to have the chicken tenders breaded with Panko crumbs' into 'I want chicken fingers!'; the subsequent 'I believe my new body needs to void waste products in the very near future' had become 'I gotta go potty!'. She would have to thank IT.

Hearing his daughter's high-pitched little girl voice for the first time in years, and not on a video, kept throwing Bob for a loop. He patted her on the head. "Good." He pulled himself together and pointed to the pool steps to his right. "Let's see, we can walk down these steps right here." Hot as blazes under the early afternoon sun, he can't wait to get into the water.

She hesitated, never having been in water. 'What if it's ghastly?'

Bob trotted down the steps, and finding it pleasantly warmish, dropped his whole body into the pool. "Come on, follow me." She stood on the first step, dipping a toe in. "Come on sweetie, it's great." He reached out. Taking his hand, she carefully walked down the stairs until her head and shoulders were above the water. She wouldn't let go. 'Did Rebecca know how to swim at six? Crap, what if she doesn't know how to swim?'

Diving into the water, Rebecca swam like a small dolphin around Bob. There was the usual splashing from little feet and hands slapping the water, but she could definitely swim. He smiled. 'Right, she took lessons at the swimming place over the winter. That winter, eighteen years ago.' He remembered sitting with Laura on a wooden bench, sweating in his winter clothes in the humid chlorinated air around the indoor pool, snow on the grass outside the windows, while future Olympians had swum laps under the watchful gaze of unhappy coaches. Laura had stood on line in the cold and dark for six hours to get Rebecca a place in the program, only to discover Rebecca had preferred, loudly, dancing to swimming: "I wanna be a ballerina!"

'This is so wonderful. Why does my chest hurt?'

After a second or two, Bob realized what was wrong and grabbed Rebecca. "Gotta breathe sweetie, breathe." With some gurgling and coughing, the splashing came to an end with a sudden surge as Rebecca wrapped her arms around Bob's neck while trying to catch her breath. She looked deliriously happy. "You did great, sweetie, I'm so proud of you."

"Can I swim some more?"

Bob knew Saabrina would have said "May I?" 'This is definitely Rebecca. How did IT pull off this trick?'

"Of course, come on, let's go on an adventure." They began one of their daily routines, the swim, walk, hop, wade, whatever it took to get through the water to explore the vast assembly of interconnected resort pools. With Rebecca asking an endless stream of questions about the people they saw ("Why are dey red? Should deir tummies be falling out of deir bathing suits? Why do dey have drawings on deir skin? Why are dose boys hanging on dose girls?"), they swam by kids playing in fountains and sprayers, parents and toddlers in shallow kiddie areas ("Sweetie, the water's warmer from the babies"), adults holding drinks in shaded grottoes and lagoons, the hard and not-so-hard bodies sunning on submerged tiled chaises, and college and high school kids perpetually manning the in-pool volleyball and basketball courts. They passed under bridges and fell over waterfalls until they reached their destination, the swim-up bar.

"Sweetie, this is one of the greatest inventions known to man. Take a seat, kiddo, let's get something to drink." Finding room for two at the crowded bar, he parked Rebecca on a concrete stool next to an enormous, sunburned woman in a too-small bikini who conveniently provided plenty of shade.

Saabrina looked at the woman, stunned by the enormity of everything her poor bikini desperately tried to hold up. The bartender walked up to them in the dry well on the other side of the concrete counter. "Buenos dias, señor. What would you and the señorita like to have?"

"Un momento, por favor." Bob handed Rebecca the plastic-coated kids' menu. Saabrina realized that not only would it take her a long time to process the words on the page, she didn't know what many of them meant. 'IT has done some job of translating the six-year-old experience for me. How much knowledge is locked away?' She did like the look of a fancy pink drink and pointed to it. "Daddy, I want dat one."

"You want that one…"

"For sure?"

"Try again." He tickled her.

"Please!"

"The señorita will have a Pink Panther, por favor. And I…" he eyed a selection of beer bottles across the bar. Rebecca tugged his arm. Looking down, he saw her giving him a look of concern "will have one, too." That earned him a big smile. 'I guess cerveza will have to wait until later.'

While the bartender blended their smoothies, Rebecca stood on her stool to get a good look inside the bar, inspecting the blenders, bottles, fruit, ice, and various implements for mixing drinks. The bar soda gun particularly fascinated her. Bob grabbed her before she toppled headfirst over the counter. "Daddy, are all dese people drinkin' daddy drinks?"

"Yes, sweetie, they are."

"Yuck!" Rebecca chirped away with a million other observations about the bar, the drinks, the people, the waiters until the pink, frozen drinks arrived in plastic cups with pineapple slices and bendy straws. He handed one to her, showed her how to clink plastic cups, and said "Cheers." He sipped.

She inhaled hers; he stopped her right as she yelped from the brain freeze. "Whoa there cowboy, drink it slowly." Bob demonstrated with his own drink. With a little work, she finally got the timing and length of the sips right.

She looked so small to him, sitting with the adults in her kiddie bikini. She drank the pink drink exactly like she had all those years ago, as if this very instant of time had melted the membrane between memory and reality, joining them together. And he realized that was what the engineers at IT had pretty much done, creating magic. The snorching sound of an emptying plastic cup told him she had finished.

She held up the cup. "Can I have anuder?"

"No, sweetie, one is more than enough. You'll have another tomorrow, and other things later. I promise."

She pouted, giving him the big eyes. "But Dad-dee…"

"Save it for dessert later. It will work better then." After signing the bill, he swept her off her stool. "Come on, let's take the lazy river back to the palapa." Once out of the pool and quickly across a ribbon of hot concrete, they stepped into the slowly moving water of the lazy river. Around them people floated by on inner tubes and air mattresses, couples holding hands, families splashing each other. Eyeing other kids floating by, Rebecca demanded "I want a tube!" He took her gently by the arm. "We don't need a tube. We can swim along, which is way more fun. Hold on, come with me." They joined the stream, floating and swimming by palapas and palm trees, under bridges and waterfalls. She seemed enchanted. Eventually they hear a low booming sound. "It's the wave machine, sweetie, hold on tight." He pulled her close and the sound grew louder as the water moved faster. Turning a corner, they got caught in white water, the waves knocking and tossing them and the floating bathers around. Rebecca sank her nails into Bob's skin, a slight look of terror on her face.

Clear of the rapids, Rebecca released her grip on Bob while scrutinizing the receding wall of the wave machine over his shoulder. "I know how it works." A rush of English accent overwhelmed the nasal vowels of New Jersey.

"Really? How does it make waves?"

"It's simple. The machine…" There was a long pause. Nothing was coming from her memory. Drawing a blank, she couldn't even reason it out, leaving her mouth hanging open.

Bob poked her nose. "You're six. Six years olds don't know nothin'. They have to listen to their daddies."

"How does it work?" Eyes wide open, she looked confounded. And sounded like Rebecca again.

At their exit, he pulled her out of the current and they started up the steps. "A giant, underground volcano provides steam, and the steam makes a giant piston drive the wall back and forth making waves."

"An underground volcano. With lava?" She needed to understand how it operated. 'Lava doesn't sound right, but it does sound neat. In any event, Bob wouldn't lie.'

"Of course there's lava. That's where they get the heat from. Everyone knows that. But you want to know a secret?"

"A secret? Yes, yes, tell me."

He knelt to speak to her, made a sign to be quiet, and looked both ways before quietly addressing her. "The machine is run by Oompa Loompas. The Royal Aztec employs Oompa Loompas, the greatest amusement park workers in the world."

"Oompa Loompas?" She didn't recollect such creatures. 'Given that the holographic program locks out large chunks of my memory, I should not know.' But she needed to know. 'Good thing Bob knows so much about this place.'

"Shhh! We don't want them to know we know."

Rebecca whispered in his ear. "Oompa Loompas, Daddy?"

"They're little orange men who work hard and hand out candy. No one sees them 'cause they work underground."

"Can we see an Oompa Loompa?"

"Well, you can only see them if they really like you. But you have to be really good."

She looked anxious. "Really good?"

"Super really good. Then they might wave to you. And leave chocolate on your pillow before you go to sleep."

"I'll be really good!"

As they started to walk back to Palapa 11, they found their way blocked by a heavyset older woman, her shoulders already showing streaks of bright red from the sun, guiding two boys to the lazy river. To Bob, they looked to be a bit bigger than Rebecca, maybe seven or eight years old. Rebecca promptly hid behind Bob, encircling his right leg with her arms. The two skinny boys roared and growled while making pawing motions.

"Come on, sweetie, say hi. They're just boys, they won't bite."

"I don't know about that" said the woman as she tried to hold the two back. "These are my grandsons, Kyle," she nodded to the slightly taller, dark-haired one on the right, "who belongs to my older son, and Ryan, who's my younger son's." She gave a good pull on the shorter, blond-haired child, to bring him back in line. "He can be a biter."

"Oh. I'm Bob and this is my daughter Rebecca." He reached out to shake the woman's hand.

"I'm Marlene, good to meet you." She looked at Bob's gray hair. "Daughter?"

"She arrived late in life. You could say she was a surprise." Rebecca pulled tighter on his leg. "Sweetie, you're cutting off circulation in Daddy's leg. If you don't let go, I'll fall over and go boom."

"Our whole family's here. Got granddaughters her age, too. Maybe yours will want to play with the girls."

Rebecca released Bob, came forward, and put her hands on her hips. "I'm not afraid of boys. I play wid boys and girls. Just not right now." The boys cowered back to grandma.

"OK, little lady. When you're ready we're over there," Marlene waved to a slew of chaises by the pool covered with family members, magazines, pool toys, and half-empty cups and food containers. "Come on you two, let's get to that Lazy River." She marched the boys around Bob and Rebecca who continued their way to Palapa 11 with a detour to the bathroom.

'Really good' lasted an hour. His request for her to take a nap fell on deaf ears.

"I'm not tired. Why do I need to take a nap? None of de other kids are taking naps. I don't wanna take a nap."

Bob regretted not having made this a term of the contract. "Well, sweetie, everybody takes naps in Mexico, especially little kids. They're called 'siestas.' Otherwise, they get all cranky and miserable later in the day and don't have fun." He knew six-year-olds did not have to nap, but it had been a long first day for both of them and Rebecca always had done better with a little downtime. Plus, he really wanted to take a nap and didn't want to lose sight of her when he's out cold.

"But, I'm not tired." She looked at him. 'Why does Bob believe I need to sleep? I'm full of energy, responsive, and fully engaged in my surroundings. How ludicrous.'

"Rebecca, it's nap time, now lie down."

"But, I'm not sleepy." She pointed to the other kids running around. "And dey're not taking naps."

'Where's Laura when I need her? She was the enforcer.' Bob, knowing better, yet too happy and tired, caved. "OK, we'll try it your way."

．　　　　　　　．　　　　　　　．

The tantrum hit on the concrete path back from the restaurant. Bob had seen the clouds gathering while Rebecca pushed her chicken fingers around her plate and slumped and fidgeted in her seat and elected to get out of the restaurant before she melted down. Halfway home, the fury from Saabrina's sudden realization of missing dessert, joined by the petty annoyances, frustrations, and discomforts that had built up over the day, had overwhelmed her tired body's ability to cope, cascading into the crying, yelling fit on display to the entire resort. She had tried to pull Bob back to the restaurant; he had scooped her kicking body right up and continued home. On the path, the people giving them wide berth made the usual comments as they went by: "Someone didn't get a nap." "That little girl is overtired." "Her daddy should have known better." "Someone's getting a major time out when they get home."

Back in their suite, Bob dragged Rebecca kicking and screaming into the bathroom, ran a nice hot bath, and tossed her into the tub to remove the sand and grit and dirt and sunscreen not helping the situation. The hot water seemed to calm her; her hair sudsy with shampoo brought back a flood of memories for him—bath time, rubber duckies, water everywhere. Toweling her off, covering her in moisturizing cream, and getting her to brush her teeth and pee before she got into her PJs reignited the fury. He finally got her into bed after another crying jag (hers, although he almost lost it), safely tucked under the sheets with her armada of stuffed animals for company. She looked so small in the queen-size bed. Grabbing *The*

Seven Silly Eaters from her backpack, he snuggled up to her to read.

'Why is Bob reading to me? I can read this myself.' Yawn. 'I don't understand this human need for sleep. It's only 7:15. I'm old enough to stay up.' Yawn. She pulled Muffin Traveldog closer. 'Honestly, this is silly. Why do these children eat such strange things? Did I miss a couple of pages? They grew up? What are they baking?' The pictures seemed to be moving in front of her, the children in the book swimming away. Her world became dark, then bright. Still in her pajamas, Saabrina found herself under a sunny sky on a field of green grass. Big, fluffy white sheep ran and jumped around her. Taking a step toward them, she almost put her foot in a pool of water; looking down, she saw a reflection of a child with strawberry blond hair in pigtails, green eyes, and elfin features. A sheep came near her. When Saabrina petted its soft wool, she got a shock. Jumping back, she saw lightning coursing through the sheep's mechanical limbs.

"Don't touch those nasty sheep. They're mean."

Saabrina turned to see a pink pony with a white mane standing on a hillock. She walked over to the pony who gave her forehead a kiss. She hugged the pony back. "Hi."

"Hi. You seem nice. Want to play?"

"Yes."

"I'll race you to the playground!" The pony scampered away and Saabrina chased. At the playground, she found a rainbow of ponies playing on slides, seesaws, jungle gyms, and spinners. They all laughed as she joined them in their fun and games. The day grew brighter and warmer as they played.

Sunlight snuck through a crack in the curtains warming her face. She sat up and yawned. The room was empty. 'The ponies are gone? Where's Bob? He was here. Where has he gone? There's so much to do.'

Poke, poke, poke.

Poke, poke, poke. Lying on his side, Bob woke to see Rebecca looking at him, holding Muffin Traveldog tightly to her body.

"Daddy, wake up, it's time to go swimmin'."

Bob twisted his head. The clock read 6:00 A.M. He wanted to go back to sleep. "Sweetie, did you go potty?" He pointed to his bathroom; she scampered off. He heard the splashing of pee hitting water. 'Crap, why didn't I ask for her to be required to sleep late?' He had completely forgotten Rebecca's penchant for waking at the crack of dawn on weekends and vacations. No matter what had happened the night before, how late he had gotten back from a business trip, Laura had kicked him out of bed to deal with Rebecca while she had grabbed another hour or three of sleep. He needed to stall for time.

The sound of toilet paper tearing followed by a toilet flush comes from the bathroom. In a flash, she was back. "Daddy, come on, let's go." She grabbed his right hand and arm and tugged; he pulled back, yanking her right into bed, and wrapped her in his arms. "Sweetie, it's too early to go to the pool. No one's there and the water is cold. We'll go later." He hoped she'll fall back to sleep. For a few minutes, she was quiet and he closed his eyes, then she became as wiggly as a puppy. He released her and she popped out of the bed.

"I'm hungry."

"Nice to meet you, Hungry. I'm Daddy and that's Muffin."

"No, Daddy, I mean I'm hungry." She pointed to her tummy.

"Oh, you want something to eat. I have something special for you. Go to the little refrigerator in the kitchen; there's something special for you on the top shelf." She ran off to the kitchen. He heard the door of the little fridge open.

"What is it?" she called.

"It's delicious sweet Mexican yogurt. Peel off the top and eat it up with the spoon I left next to it."

He heard her rip off the top, then the yipping sound of little spoonfuls of yogurt going into her mouth. The crash of the empty container with its spoon hitting the sink informed him she was done. In a blink, she again stood in front of him. "Can we go now?"

The clock read 6:18. "No. Why don't you get a book and read?" She ran back to her room, grabbed *The Seven Silly Eaters*, and returned. The clock still read 6:18. "Sweetie, read it here." He indicated the remainder of the king-size bed beside him. She promptly climbed onto the bed, tumbling over him to get to the other side, her knees smacking into every worn part of his body they could find. Bob turned over under the covers to watch her take up residence in the middle of the bed, book open, mouth forming each word as she read them out loud. His eyes closed. In what felt like a second and an eon punctuated by the sounds of crashing cymbals and fighting violins, he heard "All done."

"OK, why don't you get another book?"

"No, I don't wanna read anymore. Can we go?"

The clock read 6:33. "Not yet. How about some TV? Go get the remote." He pointed to the TV and the remote on top of the long dresser across from the bed.

"Yay! TV." She gave him a big smile, proceeding to climb over him, again smashing her cute little knees into every sore spot on his body. She returned with the remote, reversing her path of ascent to make sure she targeted spots she had missed, before rolling over him back onto the bed. This time Bob curled around her, making a couch of his body for her to lean against, and took the remote control.

"OK, let's see if they still have the best channel in the world." He turned on the TV and began to surf, gliding over

Mexican morning news programs and kiddie shows, looking for the 24-hour classic cartoon channel. Gunshots rang out from the TV. Striking gold, "The Rabbit of Seville" had begun in English.

"What is dat?"

"That is a Bugs Bunny cartoon. This channel shows Looney Tunes, Tom & Jerry, the Jetsons, all the best, all day." He watched her concentrate on the images, not smiling. 'What if she doesn't like Bugs Bunny?' A giggle, followed by a few more, then laughter. He missed those sounds. Happy, Bob closed his eyes and fell back to sleep.

Chapter 13

THE WHITE MARBLE-CLAD HANCOCK HOUSE OFFICE BUILDING stands low and squat across from the Capitol. In Congress-woman Josephine Tuchis' waiting area, Bob sits on an uncomfortable green leather couch, a painting of children bringing flowers to their teacher behind him. Unable to focus on his magazine, he surveys the suite for the umpteenth time: traditional furnishings, walls painted light blue with white trim, wall-to-wall carpet of dark green and gold, much like the offices of other senators or representatives he has visited. To his right stand the wood double doors he walked through at 9:45 A.M. to be fifteen minutes early; across the chipped coffee table, the receptionist absorbed in some matter at her desk; and, to his left, at the end of a short wall featuring rows of framed photographs, the hall leading to the congresswoman's personal office. Her staff occupies rooms on both sides of the hall, the gauntlet he will traverse when the congresswoman summons him.

Bob waits. He watches the clock tick slowly past 10:15. Government Standard Time inches by at 10:30; now 10:45, the outer limit to wait on government VIPs, there is no sign of the congresswoman. He looks at the receptionist and gets her attention.

She smiles back at him. "I'm sure it will be any minute, Sentinel Foxen."

"No problem, whenever the congresswoman is ready."

"Would you like some water, coffee, or tea while you wait?"

"Water would be fine." She brings him a glass of water, then returns to her desk.

He wants coffee, but he has already had two cups. Now he's a combination of anxious, jittery, and sleepy, having not gotten much rest the night before, tossing and turning in bed waiting for morning, his few times truly asleep dreaming his new recurring nightmare of shadowy green figures tuning instruments in an endless orchestra, video to go with the audio playing endlessly in his head during the day. He didn't bother telling Saabrina about the dreams figuring she would tease him for having yet more defective human programming.

He tries to go back to reading his *Economist* and instead jumps up to look at the pictures, again. Every picture shows a humanoid grandmotherly figure, her pink eyes behind a plain pair of square lenses, standing between smiling constituents, mostly children. On the Hill she's known as "the Schoolmarm," partially because she had been a teacher early in her life, partially from her demeanor. The figure's appearance barely changes in the photos; maybe a few more lines and wrinkles on her face. Unlike at home, Bob doesn't know the clothing styles well enough to tell the pictures' chronology. The photos themselves have no dates or captions, although some have "We love you, Auntie Jo" scrawled across their tops. Sports teams, scout troops, students, and, occasionally, factory and office workers make up the other parties. In every picture, the congresswoman peers into the camera with the same pleasant smile.

He knows one thing: Laura would have hated her the moment she had seen the wall of photos. Tuchis' equivalents at PTA meetings or in her hospital's administration drove Laura to distraction. "Smarmy poli- fucking-tician" she'd say after meeting one for the first time. Bob would answer "Don't judge a book by its cover." Within a week Laura was both always proved right and annoyed with him for yet again not believing her. He'd learned to get her assessment of everyone he did business with: good, bad, dependable, has your back, ready to knife you, she always knew from the start. At least Saabrina would be happy to know how Laura felt... might have felt. 'Laura.' He's been thinking about her a lot since getting back from Mexico. Clearing his mind, Bob sits. He listens to the quiet chatter and bustle of Tuchis' staff as they work, answer phones, and move between their offices. And to the cacophony quietly sounding in his head, replacing the latest pop tunes. He picks up his magazine again.

At eleven, a medium-height, pneumatic brunette with a professional manner sweeps around the corner from the hall of offices. Unlike the other staff members who dress more casually, she wears a close-fitting business suit that quietly highlights her attractive figure.

Bob rises to greet her. 'All the professional women in the Federal government seem to wear business suits, not dresses. How come they don't wear dresses?' He knows Wall Street women who crush the opposition while totally rocking business dresses. 'They wouldn't be caught dead in anything that made them look like a male want-to-be and glory in the latest from Saks or Bloomingdales or Armani or wherever they shopped these days.' He tugs his own Union suit into place. 'Why do we all have to look the same?'

"Sentinel Foxen? I'm Kiersey Summerall, the congress-woman's chief of staff." She holds out her hand, which Bob takes.

"Nice to meet you, Ms. Summerall." He gives her a smile, which she returns.

"Good to meet you as well, Sentinel Foxen. Unfortunately, the congresswoman is tied up with constituent affairs. She asks if you could wait a while longer."

"Not a problem, whatever works best for her. I'll wait right here."

"Thank you." Summerall turns and leaves.

Sitting, Bob watches Summerall turn the corner. The thought 'Actually, the Saabs are government professionals and they wear whatever the hell they want' brings a smile to his face. He tries to go back to reading *The Economist*, but his thoughts keep swirling between the magazine's articles and the arguments he and Saabrina prepared the day before. With the link off and sitting quietly alone, he misses her. DoSOPS had sent a limo to bring him over (he would have been happy with public transportation, but they insisted); he brought only the magazine and his phone, fearing a laptop or tablet might set the Congresswoman off. He looks at *The Economist*: 'At this rate I may actually finish an issue.' As more time passes, he gets his chance. At 11:30 he briefly palms his phone, then decides not to make any calls, fearing they might sound rude. Minutes slip by. He worries about Rebecca and the call from the night before. The receptionist ignores him.

At noon, Summerall returns. "I'm sorry Sentinel Foxen. Unfortunately, the congresswoman must leave for a luncheon. We'll need to reschedule your visit with her for another time."

Bob stands. Fighting annoyance, disappointment, and relief, he works hard to moderate his tone to make it businesslike.

"I'm sorry we can't meet today. Do you have a new date in mind?"

"Unfortunately, not at this time. Once we can get you on the congresswoman's schedule, we'll provide DoSOPS with the new date and time for your visit."

"Thank you."

"You're welcome."

"Anything I can prepare in advance? Since we have more time, are there specific questions or topics the congresswoman would like me to answer or address?"

"No need. She prefers to keep her questions relevant to the time they are asked."

"OK." He pauses. "May I ask one more question before I go?"

"Yes."

"Why did the congresswoman bring up the concept of constraining the Saabs?"

Summerall eyes him without a smile. "She has concerns and will be happy to discuss them with you when you return." She steps him towards the big double doors. "Goodbye, Sentinel Foxen."

"Goodbye, Ms. Summerall." He fights the urge to add 'Thank you for a lovely morning' before he steps into the quiet of the enormous white marble hallway outside. 'Tuchis. I bet Laura would have been right about her.'

Summerall watches him step through the doors, turns, and walks down the hall to Congresswoman Tuchis's office. She lightly raps on the half-closed door.

"Come in."

Walking into a large room decorated in the same style as the rest of the office suite, Summerall briefly marvels at the view of the Capitol dome afforded by the large windows beyond the intricately carved, but battered, wooden conference table and chairs her team uses for more formal meetings with their boss. Turning to her left, she finds the petite representative in a large brown leather chair behind an enormous desk, bent over a letter. The congresswoman's pen strokes scrtich, scritch, scritch with each line of text she completes. Waiting, she decides to stand by the leftmost of two white seats placed before the desk, rather than leaning back on one of the red wing chairs arranged before the coffee table and fireplace the congresswoman uses for tête-à-têtes with close friends and colleagues. Television viewers would recognize what Summerall sees: Tuchis gives interviews sitting at her desk, a wall of pictures and mementos behind her flanked by the Union flag and the flag of her home world.

The congresswoman finishes her letter. "Yes, Kiersey?"

"Congresswoman, as you requested, I let Sentinel Foxen go."

"Thank you. You used our little fib about constituent meetings and such?"

"Yes. If I may, won't DoSOPS be upset?"

"They most certainly will be. That's why I wrote this." She hands Summerall the letter. "Be a dear and have someone hand-deliver it to their director, immediately."

Glancing at the letter, Summerall hesitates.

"You probably would like to know why I didn't see Mr. Foxen?"

Summerall appears relieved. "Yes, Congresswoman. I'd like to learn so I can best help you."

"Good, Kiersey, good. I will teach you. Pay attention. I knew he wouldn't be ready for the meeting. He needed more time to reflect and be ready to answer my questions."

"Oh."

"You don't expect a member of the executive branch to tell the whole truth the first time, do you? You have to wear them down a bit; otherwise we'll get the same canned fluff they tell the other representatives."

"We have to keep them on their toes to get the real answers?"

"Exactly. And by not seeing him, I can still demand a hearing. Keeps my options open, always a good thing. Kiersey, did he say anything when he left?"

"He asked if he could prepare answers in advance of the next meeting for you."

"That was very nice of him, but unnecessary."

"I told him as much. He also asked about the Saabs."

The congresswoman gives a faint smile while crinkling her eyes behind her glasses. "Ahh. The Saabs. He and his Saab will be something to which Mr. Foxen and I will turn our attention when we have him return."

"Do you have a date in mind? Should I call DoSOPS to reschedule?"

"In due time, Kiersey, in due time. Now, is my lunch here?"

"I'll go check to see if the page has returned."

"Thank you, Kiersey." Summerall exits the office. Tuchis swivels her desk chair to enjoy her view of the Capitol, bright sunlight setting off the white of its dome, high silvery clouds streaking across the deep blue sky. After another knock, the page enters with her sandwich, pickle on the side, chips, and a diet cream soda. Placing it on her desk, he quickly retreats. Turning to her right, screens display a committee hearing, various news channels, and the House chamber, currently empty. Although a little old fashioned, she finds the bank of monitors comforting and settles in to watch as she eats.

Chapter 14

DANA BANKS YAWNS. EVEN WITH HER MOUTH WIDE OPEN under the bright lights of the Legislative Liaison's utilitarian conference room, she looks attractive to Bob in her navy blue business attire.

"Late night?" asks Bob. He and Saabrina sit on standard government-issue swiveling leather chairs along one side of a long rectangular boardroom table, Dana Banks on the other.

She covers her mouth with her hand. "Sorry. One of those midnight runs. Isaabelle grabbed me at two this morning for a quick confrontation with some smugglers."

Bob glances at Saabrina, who shrugs her shoulders. "They seem to love waking you in the middle of the night. How did it turn out?"

"Went well. The bad guys are now in detention. I can't believe I did the whole thing in my pajamas."

Bob tries not to imagine Sentinel Banks in her PJs and fails. "I once destroyed a fleet in my pajamas."

"How they got into his pajamas we'll never know." Saabrina makes the sound of a rimshot.

"Nicely done."

"Thank you."

Dana Banks laughs, stares at them, then laughs again. "I don't know which is funnier, the joke or the two of you."

Bob realizes Saabrina has been quiet since the morning, and he has a pretty good idea of why. 'You're not going to berate me for imagining her in her nightie? No suggestions on our ability to mate?'

No, she's a co-worker and we're waiting for an important meeting. I'm getting my game face on.

'Really?'

Yes. Oh, and later I need you to intercede with Austin on my behalf.

'I know. He didn't appreciate your little caper last night.'

You know?

'You think Saabs are the only ones who talk? Eddie called me this morning before I went over to Tuchis' office. Saabra was very upset. She still can't reconcile how you guys did the right thing and the wrong thing at the same time.'

I'm sorry about causing her grief. I already apologized to her.

'Good. I spoke to Austin and straightened everything out, so after this, you're coming with me to apologize.'

Apologize?

'Yes, apologize. An apology will be a good first step. What were you thinking?'

'What had I been thinking? Taking the piss out of Austin is certainly one of my favorite activities, particularly more so after he had so rudely enjoyed my and Bob's discomfort at the hearings about Daear. But, last night went too far.' She doesn't want to talk to Bob about it now. *Apologize. Yes, you're right, I will apologize. Thank you.*

'Good.'

And you should mate with Ms. Banks. Not only is she completely compatible, but she receives excellent reviews from…

'Saabrina!'

Bob, it's time you got out and dated someone. Or at least fooled around with someone. Maybe getting a little bootie wouldn't hurt?

'The manual has all sorts of rules about relations between coworkers.'

From my experience, it doesn't seem to stop them. She has had to prod some of them out of her back seat. 'How disrespectful.'

"You know, it's not fair of you two to have a whole conversation without me."

Bob sputters. "Sorry, sorry, didn't mean to."

"Bob and I were reviewing notes for a meeting later."

"Yes, yes, we were."

And thinking about you naked.

Bob, pretending to wince in pain to stifle a laugh, stands and theatrically stretches. "Sorry, recurring pain in my neck. Don't you and Isaabelle ever find yourself lost in conversation?" He sits back down.

"I guess so, when we're alone. Not so much when we're with others. Then she's very quiet."

"My sister? Isaabelle? Quiet?"

"Yes, in meetings she keeps herself to supplying me with information and tactics. She's pretty reticent about anything more than that, probably because we haven't been together as long as you have."

"You'll bond over time. Talking, everywhere, will become second nature." Bob remembers for him and Saabrina it seemed to be instantaneous. He smiles at Saabrina, she smiles back.

"Perhaps you can give me some pointers for working with a Saab."

"I'd be delighted to."

"How about tonight? We could get a drink after work."

"A drink after work would be… nice. Let me think of a place." Bob clears his throat. 'Are you talking to her on a separate channel? Is this a setup?'

Absolutely, positively not. And you should go to Bravo in the Jefferson District. They have tapas and their new mixologist gets five stars; some say he's the best on Madison.

"How about Bravo over in the Jefferson District? We can pick a time once we know what's going on here today."

"Bravo will be great."

It will be great, Bob. Good for you.

Dana Banks turns to Saabrina. "Where are my manners, Saabrina? I didn't mean to exclude you."

"Don't worry about me, you two go have fun. I'll wash my hair or something." She pauses. 'Come to think of it, I haven't had to wash my hair in a while.'

"She wouldn't have been able to join us, even if she wanted to. She has another appointment tonight."

"I do?"

Frank Odessa walks into the conference room accompanied by Director of DoSOPS Elliot Lerner, an older gentleman wearing a rumpled suit. Like most of his predecessors, Lerner coordinates more than commands, permitting the sentinels and Saabs to work independently and effectively as needed by the different parts of the Federal government.

Bob, what am I doing tonight?

'Shhh, I'll tell you later. Focus, *serious* business, game face, remember?' She tries to pick his brain and he pushes her out.

The three at the table stand to greet Odessa and their boss, who promptly waves them back into their seats after giving them hearty handshakes. "Ladies, gentlemen, good to see you safe and sound. Dana, thanks for coming. Where's Isaabelle?"

"She's helping the Navy test new armor on a battlecruiser."

"There's more taxpayer money down the drain. You told her to pull her punches?"

"I suggested it to her. As long as the Navy boys don't do anything stupid, they should be OK. Oh, and they cleared the cruiser of its crew as a precaution."

"Good move on their part. Hello, Saabrina." Lerner waves.

"Director, good to see you again."

"Keeping Bob out of trouble, I trust?"

"I try."

"That's all I can ask. So, Bob, heard you had a good dinner last night."

"Very good. The Archduke is some host and we didn't get poisoned, so a win-win." The table chuckles.

"Eddie told me his royal highness brought wine from his cellar. In all the state dinners I've attended, he's never done that."

"Well, you know he has a special relationship with Eddie."

"Indeed he does. And it's a good thing for all of us." Lerner pauses. "Let's get to business. Bob, I want to hear firsthand what happened this morning. How did it go with Auntie Jo?"

"Sorry to disappoint you, but it didn't. They had me wait for two hours before she released me."

Odessa gives a low whistle. Lerner looks at Odessa, then turns back to Bob. "She didn't see you? Were you late?"

"Fifteen minutes early. Signed in, they announced my arrival, everything."

"What happened, exactly?" Bob relates the morning in boring detail. When he finishes, Lerner turns to Odessa. "That's new."

'Saabrina, I don't like hearing 'that's new' from these guys.'

Me neither. What is going on?

Odessa shifts back in her seat. "We have to let the White House know, make a formal protest, talk to her committee chair…"

"Ya think?"

Bob raises his hand. "I've been involved with legislators before, had to wait, not been seen, been rescheduled. It's a pain, but it happens. Is this different?"

Odessa tugs her whiskers. "In your old job, back on Earth, did you request those meetings or were you asked to attend?"

"We were lobbying them for something we wanted, so we asked for the meeting."

"That's what I thought. Bob, please understand, there's a vast difference between a private group asking for help from a legislator and a member of Congress asking to speak with a member of the Executive, as the congresswoman did in this case in lieu of a committee meeting her chair declined to permit. This is about maintaining the relationship between two co-equal branches of the government. We and the Congress follow certain protocols in our dealings in order to show respect to each other and maintain decorum. Unless it's a grave situation, nobody, and I mean nobody, from either side would make their counterpart wait two hours and then blow off a meeting."

Lerner still looks upset. "Simply not done, Bob. You said her legislative aide met with you?"

"Yes."

"Frank, you'd think she'd know better and would corral her boss."

"Tuchis has a new aide, Kiersey Summerall. Smart, but inexperienced."

Lerner shakes his head. "What does that make, three in five years? Auntie Jo goes through them fast." They hear a knock on the door; entering, an assistant hands a letter to Lerner. After the assistant leaves, Lerner unseals the envelope, extracts its contents, and reads it to himself. "It's from Congresswoman Tuchis, apologizing to both the Department and to me personally for not seeing Bob this morning."

Odessa takes the letter. "That was fast, Elliot."

"Too fast. She didn't apologize to Bob, though."

"Maybe she's sending it separately?"

"Frank, we'll have to see. I don't like this. She's playing games with us and I don't know why."

Bob, may I check your memories from your time there?

'Sure, Saabrina go ahead. Do it quietly, I don't want to laugh in front of everyone.'

While the table rehashes what little they know, Saabrina gingerly searches through Bob's visit, reviewing his conversations, the snippets from the staff nearby, and the receptionist's calls. Finding nothing of interest, she moves on to what he viewed: the offices, the receptionist's clean desk, and the pictures on the wall. In the photos, she notes that some of the kids are now grown-ups and the workers come from various companies in her district. *Bob, one of the pictures is of a team at Armada.*

'The defense contractor?'

Yes. They're based on Tuchis' home world.

'Do they compete with SAAB?'

No, they build big iron, you know battlecruisers, carriers, and their support ships, nothing smaller.

'Any good?'

Although personally I prefer Federal Dynamics' work, there's nothing wrong with Armada's products.

'I don't think we need to mention it.'

Having gotten nothing from the table, Lerner slumps into his chair. "Frank, what do you suggest?"

"The letter freezes us. It's just enough to stop us from complaining vociferously. Good news is I don't have to risk some seven-year-old from the White House getting involved." Odessa stops to tap her whiskers.

They allow children to work for the President?

'No, she's making a joke because White House staff is notorious for being both young and inexperienced.'

"And, Frank, what else?"

"I'll run the situation quietly by the committee Chair, see what she suggests. I'll also go visit the minority leader, tell him we have been treated poorly by one of his members and see what he knows. He's another good friend. We can start there."

"Thank you."

"Director?"

"Yes, Saabrina?"

"When do we start fighting the congresswoman? Who's going to convince her that she's wrong and needs to stop?"

"Saabrina, we're not at war with a member of Congress, so we're not in a fight with her."

"But she treated Bob shabbily, said those awful things at the hearing…"

"I know you're upset. Please believe me, I understand your concern, it's my concern. But we are not in a fight with the Congresswoman, nor do we want to be in a fight with her. Those always end badly, particularly for the Executive Branch."

Bob feels Saabrina's anger rising. 'Chillax, that's an order. These are our friends, trust them. We'll talk later.'

"Thank you, Director, I know you'll help."

"I will. This Department will." Lerner sits up. "You have every right to be angry. I'm angry, and I'm on your side. I don't want you to lose your freedoms. Let Frank and me manage the situation. Speaking of managing, Bob, did you ask Eddie for help last night?"

"Yes, sorry, should I have asked you first?"

"In any other organization, yes; however, I know how sentinels behave. He came to me and I gave him my blessing to proceed. Frank, anything else?"

"No, Elliot."

"Very good. Thanks for your help. You can go now; I have some business to discuss with my two sentinels." Odessa leaves after making her goodbyes. "Dana, in addition to wanting you to hear about the mess with Tuchis, I also asked you here because I need to do a little temporary re-arranging and need your and Isaabelle's help."

"We're ready Director, what can we do?"

"We've learned the FTL experiments on Daear have run into trouble; apparently, they are getting bad data from their latest tests. We're worried it may be related to the travel tube Bob and Saabrina found."

"You want us to go to Daear?"

"No. No one's going back to Daear. I want you and Isaabelle to cover Daear and Bob's other protected worlds while he and Saabrina go on a special mission for me."

"Boss, what do you want Saabrina and me to do?"

SETH COHEN

"I want you to investigate other iffy wave signatures the boys and girls in FedSci detected near inhabited worlds. The damn things may be travel tubes; they may be nothing. Whatever they are, FedSci has put together a long list of places to visit. We're going to start you out and about near Daear and go from there. I need you to find these things. You good to do it?"

What the fuck, Bob, they're sending us out to chase signatures? We have probes for that.

Bob ignores Saabrina. "Yes, Saabrina and I will take the assignment. You want us to find the signatures, see if there are more travel tubes, and if so, what they are being used for and by who?"

*By whom, Bob, whom. You have an Ivy League education…*Bob turns the volume down to let her blow off steam while he focuses on their assignment.

"That's what I need you to do. Travel tubes are bad enough; if they're making a mess of research on protected worlds, worse; if a protected world realizes off-worlders are behind them and become xenophobic, disaster."

"Understood. We're going on a manhunt?"

"Exactly."

"We can handle that. Why near Daear? We were just there."

"It's a big universe, Bob, a lot of sky for FedSci to scan. We'll start you out where we know they've been. That's where FedSci focused on."

"Got it. When do you want us to begin?"

"I know Saabrina has an important assignment tonight, so tomorrow morning will be fine."

"Great. Dana, you OK covering me again?"

"Sure, not a problem. I'll split the extra assignments with Eddie as we did before. Isaabelle and I can handle it. When you get the chance, let me know some places to eat on Earth."

Saabrina regains her composure. "Ask Eddie, he knows the best spots."

The Director rises. "Thank you all, now if there's nothing else…"

"Director, do you mind staying for a minute? Saabrina and I would like to better understand our assignment."

"Not at all. Sentinel Banks, you can go. Give Isaabelle my best when you see her." Dana Banks leaves the conference room after mouthing 'See you later' to Bob. The door closed, the remaining three sit at the table. "What can I add?"

"Permission to speak freely, Boss?"

"You know we're not a military organization and you can always speak freely. What you want is permission to let me know what's on your mind, guessing I might find it unpleasant. Right?"

"Right."

"The answer to your real question, which would be verging on the insubordinate in a true military organization, is yes, I am sending you and Saabrina away from Madison. One, I had to send a team and you two are one of the best. And B, it's for your own good, mine, and the Department's while I sort out this situation with Tuchis." Bob tries to speak again; Lerner cuts him off. "As I told Saabrina, please let me and Frank manage the process. We're very good at what we do."

"I know you are. Thank you."

Saabrina nods to Lerner. "Yes, thank you, Director."

Lerner rises again. "In that case, may I go now?"

"That's your call, Chief."

"I'm delighted to hear you know that." He shakes Bob's hand. The hug from Saabrina takes the Director by surprise.

"It's something new she learned."

"Nice, keep up the good work. And you two, be safe out there." An amused Elliot Lerner leaves the room.

"Bob, he could be sending us on a wild goose chase."

"I don't think so. We knew the travel tube was bad; causing a mess on Daear means it's worse. You know, this assignment shows a lot of confidence in us as a team. And that's a good thing."

"You're right. It's still doesn't mean I'm going to like it."

"Come on, let's head over to FedSci and see what they have for us."

As they leave, Saabrina pulls Bob's arm. "Bob, what *am* I doing tonight?"

"Tonight?"

"My assignment?"

"I'll tell you later after you apologize to Austin. Now come on, we have lots to do." They exit the conference room into a bustling hallway.

Intermezzo

ARRAYED IN ENDLESS SEMI-CIRCULAR ROWS FANNING OUT under an ocean of galaxies and nebulae, their stars burning bright but lifeless, a vast orchestra tunes their instruments.

The voices call out "Ready?"

The cacophony dies down. Silence. No coughs, no sounds of candy wrappers being opened on a cold winter night, no clicks from a baton striking a music stand. An oboe plays a single, long note, pulling the orchestra together in a swell of sound. They stop. Silence.

The voices answer "Ready."

"Begin."

Two notes, an A and E, sound together.

Part 2

Chapter 15

SAABRINA CROUCHES IN A WHIRLWIND OF CHAOS. 'HOW could things have gotten so bad so fast?' It had seemed like a simple assignment. Although the operation's parameters had been near the edge of her experience curve, or, she could admit to herself now, slightly beyond it, conceptually she and her partner, Saabra, should have been more than capable of meeting its demands. In fact, perhaps, upon reflection, it had been with a touch of hubris that she had told Bob she didn't require his assistance and sent him on his way to dinner with Dana Banks. She and Saabra had arrived at the location on time, accepted their mission, met with the principals, agreed to restrictions on their conduct, developed a plan, and put it into action. And within twenty-five minutes it had all gone pear-shaped. 'What had van Moltke said? "No battle plan survives contact with the enemy." Certainly true tonight.'

The screams grow louder. She fears her position will soon be overrun.

·   ·   ·

"Bob, this place is terrific. Good call."

"You can thank Saabrina, she told me about Bravo." He sips his Manhattan. 'Wow, this guy *could* be the best mixologist on Madison.' Under a copper tile ceiling, they try not to shout to each other across a narrow table, one of many crowded with diners stuffed cheek by jowl into the long room. Dana sits with her back to a wall of dark wood panels displaying antique advertisements for liqueurs and bicycles. Behind Bob, patrons line the zinc-topped bar two deep. Large drinks and small plates with quickly vanishing contents cover the tables around them. Outside Bravo's windows, a dense stream of pedestrians flows by iron front buildings chock-full of fashionable stores and trendy restaurants.

Dana leans towards Bob. "How does she find these places?"

"Honestly, I don't know. She never ceases to surprise me." He points to his drink. "Mine's excellent. How's yours?"

She holds up her martini glass, showing the light shining through rainbow-colored clouds. "Tastes as good as it looks." She takes another sip. "Should we order something to eat? I'm starved."

"Me too." The two flip through their menus, heavy yellow pages attached to wood clipboards, and begin negotiating the first items to order.

.   .   .

Saabra, things are bad here. How long before you can join me? Saabrina winces. 'Splitting up had been a mistake. Militarily, dividing forces often leads to poor outcomes.' Custer at Little Big Horn, although a cliché, immediately comes to her mind. It had seemed wise at the time, sending Saabra to deal swiftly with an ancillary operation, related to, but requiring slightly different skills than the primary mission. They had intended for Saabra to dispatch her action in an hour, then rejoin Saabrina to mop up. Saabrina had felt confident in their operational decision because she believed her special insights, gained from experience, would provide her with the knowledge to succeed in the main theater of action. 'My confidence was obviously misplaced, the intel having proved useless.'

Perhaps ten minutes more, one down, one to go.

I don't know if I'll make it.

Call for reinforcements.

Isaabelle is on her way.

Then hold on.

·   ·   ·

Their first plates arrive and are devoured. "Well, Dana, the food's as good as the drinks. Still hungry? What should we get next?"

"How about crostini with white bean hummus and the grape leaves?"

"Sounds good to me." Bob signals the waiter who takes the order. Still fighting the feeling he's on a date, he keeps repeating 'It's an after-work get together of two professionals' to himself. That her clothes seem somehow both tighter and more revealing than they did back at DoSOPS doesn't help; he keeps fighting to maintain eye contact as they speak, putting a kink in the back of his neck. Isaabelle, who gave them a lift to the restaurant, via a rather scenic route now that he thinks of it, before running off to get her nails done, hadn't helped either.

Bob, what are your intentions toward my Sentinel?

'My intentions?'

Yes, your intentions. You're taking her out and I need to know if you plan to behave honorably.

He wanted to say he intended to strip Dana naked and ravish her to see the effect, but decided Isaabelle crashing into a downtown office tower might be a bad idea. 'My intentions are to have dinner with a colleague and unwind after a day of work. Are those acceptable?'

Yes. Anything else? Anything you may want to do later?

He almost heard the nudge-nudge wink-wink. 'You mean like go to a concert?'

No, I meant, you know…

'Isaabelle, this isn't a movie and you're not her father.' Had he ever done this to one of Rebecca's boyfriends? He'd planned to, but never had the chance. Laura had gotten him a "Guns don't kill people, dads with pretty daughters do" t-shirt to wear to the door; it had never left his drawer. 'We're two consenting adults and…'

So there is the potential for…

'We're colleagues going out to have a drink.'

"Are you two talking without me?"

"Isaabelle was attempting to ascertain my intentions toward you this evening."

Bob!

"Really?" Dana gripped the steering wheel in front of her. "She's very protective. I guess that's a good thing."

"Usually it is." Bob quickly addressed Isaabelle. 'Sometimes though, it can be very annoying.'

Sorry.

"So what are your intentions?"

"As I explained to our transportation…"

Hey, now you're being mean.

"…after a stressful day, I just want to commiserate with a colleague over a drink."

"Perfect. Me too."

.   .   .

Twenty-five minutes in, the first attack had taken her by surprise. She had let her guard down and in a moment found herself on the ground with five of Austin's nieces and nephews, aged four to seven, piled on top of her cheerfully screaming "Kill the babysitter!" They had looked so cute and well behaved as their parents left from Austin's sister's, Olivia's, house for his hastily arranged, adults-only family reunion. The four adult brothers and sisters had gone out for a night on the town with their spouses, except for Austin, the youngest, who went stag. He had been the last to go, thanking them for their help, giving them a smile as he waved goodbye. Saabrina had suggested to the little ones that they all gather round to play a board game, something relaxing to put them on pace for dinner, to be followed by a movie and going to bed. And they had joined her on the family room floor around *Candyland* as she set up the game and got their pieces ready. As she leaned across the board, they pounced on her, game tokens sticking in her belly. After a few moments of getting crushed, she said "Hey, this is fun. How about…OUCH!" They had begun pinching her. She now regretted promising Olivia she would not 'Do anything holo-graphy' because of Olivia's concern it might frighten the children; Saabrina would have to behave like a real sentient biological for the duration. Deftly wiggling, she managed to pry them off her. Before she could reorganize, they all had run away screaming. Her "Hey! Come back here, we'll have fun" fell on deaf ears.

Saabrina, what is all the noise down there.

Just some fun. Everything's OK. Having been a six-year-old only a week before, she knew what they wanted to do; she'd have to improvise something new to get them back on track.

Keep it down, please. I am trying to get these two to sleep. Saabra had accepted the mission of putting twin infants to bed. Sitting in a glider rocker, she had them propped up in her arms, each sucking from a bottle while she read to them from *The Very Hungry Caterpillar*. She purred and cooed and made happy noises to the two babies, who smiled back at her.

Will do. 'Now where did they go?' A quick scan of the house revealed the two older boys in the playroom next door. 'Let's start with them, then I'll corral the rest.' She ran into the room to be hit by a fusillade of Nerf darts shot from a machine gun, one boy firing, the other feeding the belt to him. "Ouch, ouch, ouch." Quickly retreating behind a door, she spied a Nerf handgun across the room from her and developed a plan. 'OK, now I'm really going to teach them a lesson.' Running into the room, she dropped, grabbed the gun, and jumped into firing position, only to be whacked from behind by a pillow which promptly exploded. Feathers flew everywhere, gagging Saabrina. 'Fuck, I hate being human.' The kids screamed "Pillow fight!" Her Nerf gun was no match for the pillows now flying across the room. Again, she retreated as the kids ran off in some demented form of hide and seek. Although she had promised not to alter her form, that didn't stop her from making sure nothing hit the floor as the tykes charged around. Regrouping again, she checked to make sure no one could see her before shaking the feathers off her clothes. Clean, she charged for the kitchen to surprise the kids from behind.

In the hall, the four-year-old niece, adorable in her pretty party dress, stopped her. "I have to go to the potty."

"OK, let's get you to the loo." Saabrina put out her hand to lead the way.

"I have to go, now!" The girl began to squat.

Saabrina scooped up the child and made a dash for the bathroom, getting her onto the toilet with no time to spare. "See, all good, you did fine."

"Wipe me." Hopping off the toilet, the little girl presented her bare bottom to Saabrina.

"Of course."

Back out in the hall, a bigger cousin ran by and hit the girl with a pillow. She promptly wailed. While consoling the shrieking girl, Saabrina yelled "Hey, get back here!"

"You're not my mommy! I don't have to listen to you!" The boy sped away.

The girl stopped crying. Releasing her from a hug, Saabrina smiled and said "Come along, let's do something fun." Woompf. The little girl hit her in the head with the pillow and darted off. Regrouping again, Saabrina retrieved her Nerf gun, then went to confront the three oldest kids in the playroom. 'I'm going to bring them to heel and put an end to this.' Striding into the room, she began to say "Now look here…" when she slipped on a puddle of purple finger paint. Hitting the floor, she endured a barrage of pillows and Nerf darts before retreating to the family room on all fours while the kids roared "You're a babysitter, we don't have to listen to you." She decided to take up position behind a large couch to think this through. A quick scan indicated all five had grouped together in the playroom; they seemed to be gathering materials for an assault. 'How could the families of rabbis, teachers, and foreign affairs officers have so much heavy Nerf weaponry?' She tried to reason it out. 'How did this all go so wrong, so fast. I was them days ago; I should know what they want. Why are they behaving so abominably?'

Screaming, the kids charged into the room throwing pillows. She shot back, but they quickly set up suppressing fire with a pair of machine guns, the little girl retrieving spent darts from the floor and giving them to her siblings. She tried to entice the little girl over to her side; the girl shook her head. Saabrina hunkered down out of the line of fire.

Saabra, things are bad here. How long before you can join me?

Ten minutes, one down, one to go. Saabra smiles at the yawning baby in her arms, the other already asleep in its crib.

I don't know if I'll make it.

Call for reinforcements.

Isaabelle is on her way.

Then hold on.

Silence. Saabrina notices the firing has stopped and the pillows no longer rain down around her. Carefully looking over the back of the couch, she sees all five foot three inches of Isaabelle standing in the middle of the room, arms crossed, eyeing the children who now stand frozen in place. Maybe it is Isaabelle's military-style gray dress, or her tightly braided blonde hair arranged in a halo of circlets wound closely around her scalp, or the gaze from her slightly narrowed ice blue eyes promising instant and painful punishment; Saabrina doesn't know which arrested the assault without a word. Isaabelle uncrosses her arms and points to the guns and pillows: "Put the toys away, all pillows back where they belong, then wash your hands, *nicely,* and come to the kitchen *immediately* for dinner. Now go." The kids quietly do as told. "Sister, you can come out now."

Saabrina comes from around the couch, hiding the Nerf gun behind her back. "Hi, Isaabelle, thanks."

"You're welcome. You suck as a babysitter. Now put that stupid gun away and join me in the kitchen, we have pizza to order and a table to set."

.　　　　.　　　　.

"Bob, you didn't mind me leading the mission?"

The busboy clears their latest set of dishes before moving off.

"Why would I?"

"I've only been a sentinel for six months. You had seniority."

"Of all us of on the team, Gretchen has far more years than me. Lerner prefers matching the sentinel's strengths to the job at hand. A hot medical situation, Gretchen would have taken the lead. Me, I just finished three months negotiating royalty agreements for protected worlds' IP. You had the most experience, you know, coming from the Foreign Office and having watched those miserable empire builders for years."

"Didn't help."

"They didn't give you a choice. If they had, your skills would have been needed."

She stares past his shoulder. "We killed a lot of people."

"I know. It's the toughest part of the job." It still bothers him, then he remembers Saabrina's words. "But what was the alternative? They weren't interested in negotiations. There was no clean way to disable their ships, and frankly, we didn't want to. They were on their way to kill millions more. We wanted them stopped. Now your colleagues in the Foreign Office are helping billions get their lives back. What do you think?"

She faces him. "Sometimes doing the right thing sucks."

"Exactly."

"Thanks. You're right." She finishes her drink. "But we almost killed you and Saabrina, too."

He smiles. "No, you sent us on a cool adventure into unreality. It's a side benefit of the job. Plus I got my first real vacation in four years."

She brightens. "IP agreements, huh? I bet Saabrina loved those contract negotiations."

"Well, you know Saabs." Bob does his best impression of Saabrina. "I don't do boring."

Dana laughs.

"Every day she'd protest about administrative drudgery, paper pushing, and silly executive work, and then she'd jump into the cut and thrust of the next bargaining session with real gusto. If only I'd had her around for a few business deals in the old days, I'd be retired on my own private island now."

"Bob, what is the trick to working with a Saab?"

"There's no trick. You just do it."

"Come on, you know what I mean. What we talked about this afternoon, before Lerner arrived."

He thinks. "I don't know. I guess Saabrina and I hit it off from the start. I made it clear I wanted a partner and I wanted her input, even though I had the final say."

"That's it, being partners? I admit I simply followed training and started giving Isaabelle orders, which she seems to like. We didn't have a discussion about our relationship."

"What you did is more normal for new sentinels. My conversation with Saabrina came out of my work experience and how I like to operate. Personally, I think it's a better way to manage people, but you have to find what works best for you."

Dana raises an eyebrow. "You *manage* Saabrina?"

"Manage doesn't sound right, does it? I guess it's true, though." Manage does sound totally wrong to him. He half expects to hear 'Manage moi? Tosh,' but thankfully hears silence instead.

Dana looks down at her empty glass. Bob takes the opportunity to check out her cleavage; he's eyes forward when she returns her gaze. "You're right. I hadn't thought about how I ran my section back at the Foreign Office. It never occurred to me to treat Isaabelle as I did my old staff."

"There's your first take away. They're people with phenomenal capabilities. And they're fun to be with."

"You must have some good stories after four years."

Warmed by his drink, Bob tells Saabrina stories, some about assignments, more about the time between them, some with Rebecca mixed in. Dana laughs and smiles, hardly saying a word. He doesn't notice thirty minutes goes by.

"Do you spend all of your time with Saabrina?"

"I guess, well, I mean I wouldn't say all of the time, maybe a lot of the time. Uh, I thought that was kind of standard?"

"No. Some do, but it seems like many sentinels park their Saabs at the end of the day and turn down the link."

"Really? I mean we do spend time apart, have our own lives and all."

"Do you chat when you're apart?"

"Depends, I mean sometimes. Not right now with me here and Saabrina over at Austin's sister's." He asks himself 'How many times have I spent bike rides in conversation with her? How often has she talked me up one of Dick's horrible Alps?'

"I'm glad to hear that, I was hoping we were having a private conversation."

"Of course we are. Although I have to admit in endless meetings…"

"…you two chat away?"

"Not you and Isaabelle?"

"Perhaps, after this dinner, I will." She looks at her empty glass and the clear table. "Maybe it's time to go. We both have busy days tomorrow."

"Should I ask one of them to come and get us?"

"No, I can take the Metro. It's a quick trip back to my place."

"I'll get the check."

After splitting the bill, they head outside.

"Dana, thanks for coming out with me tonight. This was fun."

"You're welcome, Bob. It was fun. And I promise I'll talk to Isaabelle when she gets back tonight. I want a partner too; maybe even a friend like you have."

"'Louie, I think this is the beginning of a beautiful friendship.'"

She looks at him, confused.

"Line from a great movie called *Casablanca*. We'll have to watch it sometime."

"I'd love to."

They give each other two air kisses and make their goodbyes. Dana Banks walks off leaving Bob alone. Around the corner, she relaxes her suit back to its normal settings.

Chapter 16

BOB WAKES FROM HIS NAP. AROUND HIM, A CLASSIC *STAR TREK* starfield simulation streaks by Saabrina's windows. In the quiet of her passenger compartment, the cacophony in his mind has given way to a few notes played too slowly for him to discern a tune. The slow-motion music feels like an improvement. It certainly annoys him less. 'And probably Saabrina, too, although she hasn't complained,' which, he realizes now, seems a little odd. 'Maybe she's giving me a little slack with all the stress from this mission.' Stretching, he rouses himself. A thought related to their previous conversation readmits itself to his mind for further discussion. "You know, Rebecca babysat for years. Maybe you should have called her for some pointers."

"Harrumph. Yes, I should have. I thought I knew what I was doing."

He knows not to say 'Apparently, not.' He fiddles with the radio, choosing classical instead of the usual pop tunes. A Mendelssohn symphony plays, Bob humming along for a few bars.

Saabrina listens. 'How is he staying on key with the music?' She hesitates to disturb him, but the pressing need to ask a question ultimately overwhelms her. "Bob?"

"Yes, Saabrina."

"I had just been a six-year-old. Why didn't I know what they wanted? How come I couldn't play with them?"

"Being a kid and caring for one are two very different things. Little kids aren't looking for someone to play with, they're looking for authority."

"Oh."

"You were a babysitter. Babysitters are like parents in training, with some advantages, like being more cool than actual parents, and some disadvantages, like potentially not getting any respect. It's tough work."

"They acted horribly. Did I behave that abominably in Mexico?"

'Do I tell her the truth?' He decides now is not the time to parse her behavior as a six-year-old. "You were pretty good. By nighttime, you were tuckered out from running around the resort all day, which made my life easier. At Olivia's, besides the babies, you had two who had been cooped up in school all day. The other three had come from off-world; I think it was morning for them. Put the two groups of cousins together and you have a combustible mix."

"Still, I should have done better."

"First time out, right?"

"Yes."

"Often it takes some experience."

"Did Rebecca have it rough the first time she babysat?"

"No, she was a natural. Did great from the start. I, on the other hand, sucked the first couple of times until I got the hang of it."

"Really? Please tell me about it."

"No, not now. Anyway, you'll do better next time."

"Next time? You haven't signed me up for another child-care assignment, have you?"

"No. I assumed at some point in the future you might find yourself watching kids again. Right?"

"Right." Her mind jumps back to Mexico. 'Would now be a good time to ask him? We are talking about my being a child and what to expect from adults.' Something he did, or really didn't do, still rankles her. Instead, she decides to change the subject. "Oh, Isaabelle sends her thanks."

"For what?"

"Your conversation with Dana. They had the 'talk.'"

"About birds and bees and where little Saabs come from?"

"No, silly." She considers adding his cornball sense of humor to her laundry list of items to reprogram in Bob's brain, perhaps replacing item 27, now mercifully gone: eliminating the songs perpetually running ragged in broken loops, their lyrics mangled remembrances of the original words. "About partnering."

"The talk. Is that what you guys call it?"

"Yes. Not including ours, Dana's makes the eighth one."

"Well, I'm happy to hear they had the talk. Please tell her she's welcome."

"I will. You know, based on DoSOPS' data, teams that have had the talk outperform those that have not."

"Makes sense. I don't want to know how you learned that, do I?"

"No, you don't."

"What about Eddie and Saabra?"

"Hmm, they never had the talk, they grew into partners over time. I don't know what she'll do when…"

"When what, Saabrina?"

'Now's not the time to make a dog's breakfast' she thinks. "Sorry, taking preliminary readings of our destination. When he goes on vacation next. She said he and Brenda may want some privacy."

"He earned it. Can't she hang with us?"

"Oh, you'd like that, two Saabs at once, a ménage à trois, choosing…"

"Saabrina, what are you talking about? It's like having a friend over. I know you guys like to have friends over."

"Yes, of course. I guess I don't know what I'm talking about. I was sorta doing a riff on a comedy routine I saw once, but…"

"You don't know what it actually means to biologicals." He may have to have the talk with her after all.

"Please, restrain yourself, I know the mechanics. What I don't comprehend is the concept of the humor. Isn't one mate sufficient for your needs?"

"Well, that's a whole discussion, which could take hours for different parts of Earth alone. Given what I know about you, let's skip it."

"Thanks, I agree."

Bored with classical music, Bob tunes to '70s rock. Catching "Hotel California," he sings along.

"Not bad, Bob."

"What?"

"You had the lyrics right and were mostly on key. Bravo."

"Thanks, I guess."

"Now back to work, Mr. Sinatra." The starfield simulation vanishes revealing a beautiful blue world below them. "We're here."

"What have we got?"

"Nothing. Another false signal. Fourth one."

"Good, cross this one off the list. How many more has FedSci identified for us?"

"Current list, twenty-two."

"Alright, lay in a course for the next one."

"There's three to choose from in the immediate vicinity."

"Which one is best for lunch?"

"Next stop, Oishix Three."

"Great, engage, warp factor six." The starfield simulation returns.

.   .   .

Days pass as they cross off more potential signatures from the list. At one point, they had doubled back to signature seven because of a subsequent report of the world's dark matter detection project going off the rails. "Bob, if it had been here, and I'm not saying it was, it must have ripped free; I simply can't find it."

"Don't worry, maybe it was never here. We can move on." At least they had gotten the chance to return to the lovely restaurant in a beautiful park where they had enjoyed dinner overlooking an art-deco fairy tale city, all emerald spires and flying elevated roads. Better, the restaurant's jazz ensemble, which had given Bob a bit of headache, did not make an appearance. "No live music tonight?" he asked their waiter.

"No, sir. The group stopped performing."

"Really? How come?"

"On account of their sudden lack of tunefulness. Most irritating to the customers."

As they progress, Saabrina arranges some bike time for him on nearby Union worlds. "After your awful showing at Farmlands, we need to keep you fit. When's your next trip to France?"

SETH COHEN

"Not this year, Dick shredded his knee skiing. Maybe I can get the guys to Lenox for a weekend." Bob misses riding with the guys, but knows that a weekend in Lenox might be a tough sell: Jim didn't appreciate the climbs and Phil couldn't easily walk away from the shore and his family. 'He might for France, but Lenox wasn't France.'

"A boys' weekend in Lenox would be nice. Maybe you could get Dick to come and cook for you even if he cannot ride. He is a fabulous chef."

"Yes, he is. More I get the calories and you get the pleasure?"

He receives a mischievous smile from her.

Sometimes he sleeps back in his apartment in Madison, a nice one-bedroom DoSOPS maintains for him. He sleeps well except for his recurring dreams, all flashes of green and white, of faceless green men and women playing musical instruments poorly. At first, they played the slow piece he hears during the day. 'Now have they switched? Is it a different group at night?' In his dreams, they play and play and play something, perhaps Brahms, he can't tell. The voices constantly ask "Good?" He shakes his head "No" and they go back to practicing. "Help?" they ask. "Not me, I'm not a musician. Go ask someone else. Seriously, go get some help from a pro. And leave me alone." But the voices keep coming back. At least in his dreams the music plays at a tempo approximating normal; during the day, the tune in his head continues to rumble along slowly and painfully, as if a large middle school orchestra picked out one note at a time on a variety of poorly played instruments.

One evening on Madison while Eddie visits Earth, Dana Banks and Isaabelle join them for dinner at Harmony Hotel, a dive down the hill from the Capitol frequented by congressional staffers and government workers. Over a couple of beers and a good burger, Dana talks about growing up in a small town which reminds Bob of rural New England—a cluster of white clapboard houses with big porches surrounded by fields and picket fences, hills and small, rounded mountains rising around them; spending long summer days on the lake or adventuring with her brothers and their friends, when not doing chores, and fresh fruit from a nearby orchard baked into a warm pie at the end of each day; in winter, the bus taking them to school on cold snowy days and hot chocolate and horseplay in the big backyard before homework and dinner. After college, her brothers had returned home to work in the family business while she had gone on to the Foreign Office and now DoSOPS. They part promising next time they'll watch *Casablanca* together, Saabrina and Isaabelle snickering like two schoolgirls behind them.

On another night, Austin has them over to his chic and extremely clean bachelor pad for takeout Chinese food served formally at his dining room table; no fressing in the living room or kitchen. From the terrace, Bob, a glass of red wine in his hand, admires the view of the trendy neighborhood below while Austin asks him questions: "Bob, any luck?"

"No, Austin."

"Why not?"

"They're hard to find and too much other crap looks like them."

"We don't want one of these blasted things or their anomalies to cause a diplomatic incident, do we?"

"No, we don't Austin."

"Good. Then find who's causing them before something stupid happens."

"We'll try."

After refilling their glasses, Austin turns to Saabrina with a smile. "My nieces and nephews would love to have you babysit them again. You're their new favorite."

"Shut up, Austin."

Other times, Bob stays on the worlds they visit, sampling the local cuisine and hospitality. Dorothea, a city of canals, reminds him of Venice and the snowy November day he asked Laura to marry him. Saabrina enjoys the story, Bob reenacting his attempt to get down on one knee in the middle of St. Mark's square while trying not to get wet. "You were quite the romantic, Sentinel Foxen. I bet Laura blushed when you asked her."

"She actually answered 'Are you kidding?' After briefly considering tossing her into the canal, I decided to try again and she said 'Yes. Now let's get some hot chocolate,' which we did. And, as usual, she was right. It was warm and delicious."

After each stop, they send data back to the boys and girls in FedSci to help refine the search.

·   ·   ·

On their way to potential signature location number nineteen, they visit a posthumous retrospective for one of Saabrina's favorite painters. Navigating through the museum, they pass through a kaleidoscope of prints and photographs, an installation of undulating circus mirrors reflecting viewers reading travel postcards, and a large picture of a tree, the image made from small letters printed on ledger paper (it reminds Bob of a video of a swaying tree he had seen on a wall at MassMoCA), before coming into a series of rooms filled with drawings and paintings by her friend.

"The big one is of you, right?"

"Yes." Saabrina looks proudly at the four-meter-wide canvas.

"You look fabulous. He really got you, and in all your forms. Wow."

Saabrina turns a slight shade of pink. "I just stood there."

"You were his muse. I think it's his best work in the exhibit." Hearing her sniff, he turns to see her fighting back tears. Other patrons notice that the young woman in a picture painted years ago now stands before it and gather. They point from the painting to her and back, confused, their conversation frothing as more join.

Bob, I don't want to talk about it.

He takes Saabrina's hand and leads her to a quiet area away from the exhibit; on the way he takes a closer look at the young woman featured in many of the artist's works. They sit side by side at a white café table, one of a few randomly placed in a near-empty courtyard. 'It's not only the big one, is it?'

I sat for him many times. He spotted me at one of his gallery openings. He often employed me as a model, abstracting my form, altering my features: that's why I don't look like me in them, except the last. He said he liked to be inspired by his models, but not controlled by them. I loved talking to him as he drew and painted; we spoke of life and art and love and food. It all sounds so trite now.

'No, it doesn't. I know what you mean.'

I didn't tell him what… who I was. I never went out with him and his friends to cafés or attended their parties or stayed in his studio to chat; instead, when he finished, I would walk out the door and disappear. At first, he thought I was mysterious, then simply strange. One day I arrived at his studio and he confronted me. He could see I was not aging, not changing at all. I had to get permission from my sentinel to tell him the truth. When I told him, he became angry, claimed I had deceived him, threw me out.

'That must have hurt.'

It did. We didn't speak for many years. Then he asked me back for one last session; no more alterations, he painted me as he saw me and how he wanted others to see me, and, I guess, how he wanted me to see myself, and you saw the result.

'I'm sorry he's gone.'

Me too.

They sit quietly, Bob holding Saabrina's hand. 'Perhaps we should get going.'

The museum has a great restaurant; don't you want to get something to eat?

'I'm not hungry. Come on, let's get to signature number nineteen.'

•   •   •

In the quiet of her living room, Rebecca slumps on her couch, wishing Juliette was there to talk. She looks over at her laptop, shut on her desk, then back to Juliette's room, empty since her team went on hiatus after their data turned to crap. Juliette had promptly left on vacation, a trip to clear her mind and work out what to do with her life and career, and Rebecca hadn't heard from her since. Her team is probably on the chopping block next, if they don't sort something out. And now she has this. Unable to move, unable to cry, she sits, weary, staring down at the floor as the evening twilight trickles through her window. The 'Dear Rebecca' email from Zach had been awful to read; she can't decide whether she's angrier about the email or his cowardice in not calling her. 'Asshole, what an asshole.'

Hearing a knock on the door, she debates whether to get up or to remain silent and let them go away. "Coming, j'arrive." Forcing herself off the couch, she crosses the living room and opens the door to find Jean smiling at her. "Bonsoir, Jean."

"Bonsoir." His smile fades into an expression of concern. "Rebecca, what is wrong?"

"Oh, lots. Come in."

Jean follows her into the room. Before she can sit, he gives her a long hug. In his embrace, she fights to hold back the tears. They sit side by side on the couch. Time passes. The room gets darker. Jean turns on a light. "Rebecca, qu'est-ce qui ne va pas? You can tell me." He returns to her side.

"Zach broke up with me. He sent me an email saying he had found someone else back in America."

"Terrible, terrible. He didn't speak with you?"

"No, just the email."

"Incroyable. Zach has behaved like a small child. A real man would not have treated you in such an unfitting way."

"It's really the last thing I needed with all the bad shit going on around here."

Jean sighs. "I know. Is there anything I can do? Do you want to talk?"

She wants to fly back to America to kick Zach in the nuts. "No, sitting with me is nice. Thanks." She gives him a brief smile before looking at the floor. Jean stretches and wraps his arm around her shoulder. She snuggles closer to him, comfortable in his warmth. When she picks her head up to look at him, he tries to kiss her. Rebecca pushes Jean back; he fights to move his lips closer to hers. "Jean, stop, please stop."

"I am a real man, I am…"

Rebecca jumps up and shouts "Get out, get out, get the fuck out!" Jean silently leaves the room, the door slamming behind him. Rebecca stands staring at the locked door, fists clenched. Going to her bedroom, she flops into her bed crushing Muffin Traveldog, pulls the covers over her head, and cries.

Chapter 17

LISTENING TO BOB SING "PIANO MAN," SAABRINA SMILES, SUR-prised by his recent and continuing improvement. At his request, she's been playing Billy Joel songs, and she has not minded his singing along to them. It's a nice break from Brahms's Piano Concerto no. 2, which he has requested three times in as many days. In a flash, the starfield simulation dis-appears revealing another beautiful green and blue world, Erdewelk, home of potential travel tube signature number twenty-one. Saabrina mutes the music. "Bob, we have one."

"OK. Take it slow. Anything attached to the tube in space?"

"No, not now, but recently, maybe the last week."

"How about the other end?"

"Still connected. This time in a small city."

"We should take a look."

"We don't have to. Erdewelk doesn't have an FTL space program to keep clear of; I'm able to scan the tube from space."

"What do you see?"

"Same as the last one, same size capsule, capsule descended then ascended."

"Erdewelk is like 1960s Earth. What would anyone want to bring down or take back from here?"

"I don't know. There's no trace in the tube. Bad news, whoever is using the travel tubes, they're getting better at making them. This one was harder for me to detect…"

"Give one to the FedSci boys and girls."

"…and sound enough to put in a population center."

"Show me." Saabrina displays maps with name places; Bob places his finger on the city in question. "Fortnum in the Federal Republic of Mason. Isn't that a university town?"

She knows he knows the answer. "Yes."

"Let's go down and have a look."

Saabrina drops down into Fortnum, parking on a rooftop garage out of sight. Late at night, the garage is empty, the office workers having gone home. She dresses Bob in appropriate clothes as he gets out, uploads the local language into his head, then joins him for the walk down the stairs. Luckily, they'll pass as unattractive inhabitants; she helps them fit in by pulling her hoodie over her head. Saabrina quickly leads him to the other end of the tube, located on an alleyway between some cheap restaurants. "Do you want me to break it away?"

"No, breaking it away will alert them that we've been here. Forensics?"

"Sod all."

"What?"

"Zero, zilch, nada, bubkes, gornisht…"

"I get it, I get it."

"They left nothing out of the ordinary, no DNA alien to this world."

"OK. Please leave something behind to check on them." While Saabrina plants a camera, Bob looks around the alleyway: posters for musical acts, theater performances, head shops, and political events plaster the brick walls. "Groovy. Looks like any other college town." He scans the posters; nothing jumps out at him. "Let's check out the neighborhood." They walk back down the alleyway to the street to find the restaurants and bars mostly empty.

Saabrina answers his question before he asks. "School night."

"Well, that explains it. Bet they're packed on the weekends. Anything in the police database?"

"Like what?"

"Anything strange?"

"First, their computer system is primitive, barely out of punch cards. It keeps statistical records of crimes and arrests, but not much detail; there are no individual files. The police mostly use their mainframe for payroll and expenses, not much more."

"And?"

"It's giving me a headache to operate because it's so bloody slow. I'll probably freak someone out when the tape drives start on their own."

"I'll trade you. I'll get something to eat at the diner over there, your choice of fare, and you run their system." He points to the restaurant on the corner, Rod's, its red neon sign hissing over a broad curve of glass. Behind the window, a cashier files her nails while a couple sits at the counter drinking coffee from white mugs.

"Very well. How are you going to pay?"

"Crap, I forgot I don't have any cash."

"I didn't. Check your wallet."

Bob opens his wallet to see local currency.

"I took it from four different banks. The tellers will be annoyed that their tills will be out of balance in the morning, but no one will get fired."

"Nicely done, let's go."

They push through Rod's glass doors. The cashier tells them to sit where they want. Eschewing the diner's long counter for a booth by a window, they sit on worn red vinyl benches, the coffee-stained Formica tabletop between them showing its age. In the corner, a big neon-framed jukebox, its black discs on metal platters shining through its window, plays rock 'n' roll softly in deference to the time of night. Bob abandons going over to check out the song list; he doesn't have a nickel to play a song.

A waitress in a mustard-colored uniform sidles up to their table. "Wadya want?" Saabrina selects for Bob apple pancakes with some sort of chutney and a cup of coffee; politely declining a meal of her own, she orders a cup of tea. After dropping the order off with the cook, the waitress snorts through her pig-like nose to the other girl on duty "Maxine, did you get a load of those two circus freaks I'm servin'?"

"Donna, they're Nighthawks. Only come out after dark on account of their deformities." She rubs her thick left brow.

"Ya think they could have had surgery to fix how repulsive they are."

"It's expensive and doesn't always woik. I pity them; how would you like to walk around like that?"

"No, thank you. Bad enough lookin' at 'em."

After delivering their orders, Donna happily moves on from her two ugly patrons.

Bob takes a bite. "Hmm good, you should try this." He holds up a forkful of pancake slathered in chutney.

"No thanks. I'm on a diet."

Bob gingerly places the morsel in his mouth. 'Yuck. This is horrible.'

I know, I wish I could turn off the link.

'I'm guessing the only reason this place survives is it's open all night. What have you learned?'

Nothing yet, the machine is finishing compiling my program to query the database. Good, no errors. Now it's operating.

Bob chokes down another bite of pancake. 'Anything?'

Almost, almost, wait…crap, some of the data is stored on platters! I had to place them in the readers before I started. Oh, no, the program bollocksed up the mainframe when it couldn't call the data.

'Can you…'

Wait, wait, I deleted my program so they won't see it. I'm sorry, the mainframe is done for the night. The operators will have to clean up the mess in the morning. Too bad they have a presentation to make to department chiefs; that's not going to go well.

'So, you got nothing?'

I learned Sergeant Konks didn't get his raise.

'Other than the Sergeant's raise, or lack thereof, nothing?'

No. But now that I understand the data structures, I'm scanning the storage directly.

'Thanks. Anything?'

Nothing relevant. As I said before, only tabulated crime stats. Honestly, I don't even know what I'm searching for. There's nothing jumping out saying "Hey! I'm weird, look at me."

'What about global? Maybe government databases have something.'

Seriously? You want me to correlate everything to everything and come up with an answer?

'Yeah, McGabby, make it happen.'

Please, I'm able to see patterns and trends, sometimes black swans, but this world doesn't yet record the kind of information I need in its computer records. We're talking typewritten reports in dossiers. Unless there's a computer entry saying something weird happened in Fortnum last week, which there won't be, I won't find anything.

'Not even anomalies at major scientific research projects?'

Don't be silly.

'Fine. What about the local newspapers?'

Linotype.

Bob finishes the pancake. 'OK, we'll do it the old-fashioned way.'

How about some pie first?

'You haven't earned it.' He waves to the waitress to bring the check. A song starts on the jukebox freezing Bob to his seat. 'That's "Heart of Glass" by Blondie.'

It is the actual recording, not a local variation. I find it unlikely it would be here.

Bob walks over to the jukebox and matches the spinning vinyl record to the song list: Blondie/Heart of Glass. He walks back to the table.

Saabrina scans the machine. *The disc is brand new, added in the last couple of weeks. No fingerprints or marks. Someone fabricated it to match the other discs in the machine. I don't believe they'd use the tube to transport a vinyl record.*

'No, they wouldn't. Someone not from around here is planning on coming back and wants their tunes.' Bob pays the check. "Come on, time to go."

"Yes, dear."

Their waitress happily watches the quiet couple leave; something about them gave her the heebie-jeebies.

Outside in the cool night air, Bob takes Saabrina by the arm. The streets are empty of people and traffic, their lamp-posts casting amber-yellow light on parked cars. "Which way to the library?"

"Two blocks to the right. Unless there's something strange about this world, it will be closed now."

"I know. Come on." Two minutes later they make a slow pass around the library. "Is there anyone inside? Can you get us in?"

"No and yes, follow me." She leads them around to the back, finds a large door on a dark alleyway, and opens it. "After you."

"Thanks."

"What are we looking for?"

"Newspapers."

"This way to periodicals." Saabrina creates a small light and guides Bob to a reading room. They find the local papers arranged on wooden dowels; as Bob expected, the library had not bothered to toss any in the last two weeks. "Bob, what am I looking for?"

"Anything weird. Try the police blotter." Spreading the papers out on a table, they flip through the pages. Bob looks at his hands. "Yuck, newsprint, I forgot about this." Fighting to not rub his hands on his clothes, he keeps reading.

"Bob, I don't see anything. There are no articles on visits from three-eyed space aliens or little green men."

Bob flips back to the front page of the paper in his hand. Pointing to a lead article, he quietly reads: "Local news: Boy-friend of Missing Student Found Dead. Melinda Lonks, a graduate student working on her degree in genetics, had been reported missing. The body of her boyfriend, Donald Ponks, was found in an undisclosed location. The police suspect a murder-suicide and have begun canvassing the area for leads."

Saabrina leans in. "I hope she's OK. Genetics is the big science here. Only the best of the best go into it. Why is this of interest?"

"Remember the missing student back on Daear, also from a university town?"

"Most likely a coincidence. One thing I learned from the crime stats is there is a lot of domestic violence here. Unfortunately, this is an all-too-typical crime for this city."

"Oh. Still something about it bothers me."

"Bob, you don't have Gibbs' gut." Saabrina pokes at his paunch. "In any sense of that word. Anyway, what would it have to do with a travel tube? You wouldn't put a person in one, only something of value."

"So, what would be of value on a 1960s world to someone from the future?"

Saabrina finds it funny, yet strangely accurate, when Bob refers to off-worlders visiting less technologically advanced worlds as being from the future. 'He has a point.' She asks "Maybe it's the other way around, maybe something of value from the future to someone here?"

"OK, how do they pay for it? Since we buttoned up their IP, is there anything here worth something to a space-faring race?"

"Hadn't thought of that. I don't know. Certainly, not the food."

"Art?"

"Wouldn't want to put something fragile in a travel tube and I didn't see any major art thefts in the newspapers or the police database."

"Hmmm." Bob puts the newspapers back. "Come on, let's go."

"Where to?"

"On to the next signature." Bob follows Saabrina through the library to the back door. Stepping outside, he finds a Saab parked in the alleyway. "I guess we don't need to walk back to the garage."

Reaching for the door handle, Saabrina stops him. "Seriously?" She hands him some wet naps. "Clean the newsprint of your hands before you get in."

Chapter 18

A SUNNY SUMMER MORNING beckons "bike ride." Bob stands on the short loft overlooking the condo's modern living room, the whole structure a smaller version of his Naglewood contemporary. Stretching after a night's sleep free from nightmares, he checks his bike jersey's pockets one more time to make sure he has both mobile and wallet. Given his link to Saabrina, he brings the mobile more as a talisman than out of necessity.

They'd arrived the afternoon before, having picked up Rebecca in Geneva. After they'd wasted weeks confirming one travel tube in twenty-six tries, DoSOPS had told them to take a break while FedSci worked to refine the search. Bob had taken the opportunity to check in on Rebecca. He had sensed trouble in their last few phone calls and figured a quick trip to Lenox might give her a chance to talk or, at the least, rally. He'd tried his best to make her smile over dinner, letting her order for them at Nudel, telling her about their adventures (with Saabrina adding the appropriate sound effects and visuals), making silly jokes that caused Saabrina to gag, and asking about the upcoming season of *Doctor Who*, before peppering her with questions about life in Geneva. Tired, focusing on the food in front of her, Rebecca had kept her answers to monosyllables. After dinner, his offer to get SoCo ice cream had been shockingly rejected, perhaps for the first time in Bob's memory. Once home, she'd gone promptly to her room to sleep, Saabrina following Rebecca upstairs, leaving Bob to enjoy a nice Japanese single malt on his own while reading his Kindle.

Padding down the short hall in his bike socks, he quietly opens Rebecca's bedroom door. In the twin bed to his left, she sleeps under a pile of covers, a few stray locks of auburn hair in view. Over on the right, Saabrina, in Snoopy pajamas to match Rebecca's, rises slightly from her neatly made bed and puts a finger to her lips.

He backs out of the room, carefully closing her door behind. 'Everything alright?'

Everything's fine. She's sleeping in. Enjoy your ride but don't go too long, we need to go shopping for our picnic at Tanglewood. Guido's will be a madhouse if we get there too late.

'Well, I was hoping to …'

You can do a long ride tomorrow. Today we focus on making your daughter happy, so get with the program. It's going to be a beautiful day and I want to get there early for a good spot on the lawn.

'Fine, I'll bike down to Ludeyville and back.'

Not a kilometer farther. Oh, and pick up some ground coffee at Haven. Rebecca wants to make Laura's cold-brewed iced coffee.

'I thought cold brew takes at least twenty-four hours to steep.'

Don't worry; I'll work some magic and it will be done in two. Now get going. Wait, one more thing.

Bob stalls at the top of the steps. 'Yes?'

Do you want me to scan the bracelet the Archduke gave Rebecca?

'I'd completely forgotten about it. No, it's a trust thing; he'd never hurt Rebecca and if you trigger something he'll know we didn't trust him. Leave it alone, but send an image on to Saabra for Eddie. Maybe he'll recognize it.'

Will do, enjoy your ride. Saabrina monitors Bob as he goes downstairs and readies himself, checking his planned route before he cycles away to make sure he'll be back on time. The sound of the closing garage door confirms what she already knows. Shifting in her bed, she turns to Rebecca. "Elvis has left the building."

"Thanks."

"When are you going to tell him about what we discussed last night?"

"Tell him I've lost my boyfriend and may be out of a job? Tell him I might have to come home while I sort out my life? Not today."

"He loves you. He wants to help."

"I know. I just can't tell him."

"Like in eleventh grade and the history paper you didn't write until it was almost too late to hand in? How many weeks did you tell him everything was fine, under control, until you came clean? Once you did, didn't he sit by you for an entire weekend to help make sure you finished it? He didn't yell then, he wanted to help."

Miffed, Rebecca peers over at her friend. "How did you know about that?"

"Sometimes on missions I get a little bored, so I go wandering around your dad's memories. Some places he blocks, some places I know not to go without permission, those about you are always open. Weird part is when I see the same event from each of your perspectives I can blend them into one re-telling of history. It becomes so real, so vivid."

"Amazing. I can't even imagine. Is this memory thing something you've always done?"

"No. Most of my former sentinels didn't fully share their memories with me;" she decides not to add 'at least not consciously.' Saabrina continues "And they certainly never permitted me to link with friends or family."

"Hey, speaking of memories, when are you going to tell me about The Very Bad Day?"

"Later, not now. Enough about me, let's get back to you and your dad. Why not tell him?"

Rebecca slumps into her bed. Hopping out of her own, Saabrina crosses the room and climbs in with her, pushing Rebecca towards the wall. With some work within the confines of the twin bed, she manages to comfortably nestle up to Rebecca under the covers.

"Saabrina, what are you doing?"

"I hope you don't mind. I learned snuggles in Mexico and grew to like it."

Rebecca laughs. "OK, my AI friend who can destroy battle fleets likes to snuggle."

"You gotta problem with that?" Saabrina tries out her best Jersey girl.

"No, I like it." She gives her friend a squeeze. "I could use some snuggles right now, too." She relaxes, enjoying her friend's warmth. 'Saabrina's not bad, maybe a little bony, not like mom… Mom was such a great snuggler and hugger and comforter, she always knew the right time to pull me close… Oh.' She misses her mom; she could tell her mom everything, and sob when she needed to. Her eyes mist up. Rebecca pulls Saabrina closer.

They lie still. "So why not tell your dad?"

"Because I haven't failed at something in so long."

"You believe he won't love you after you tell him? His love isn't conditional."

"I know. I don't want him to, you know, think less…he has so much invested in me, I just don't want to…"

"You're never going to disappoint him. One, Zach leaving is not failure, it simply means you were not right for each other. Or he's an idiot. Or both."

"It still sucks."

"It does. All the more reason to talk to your dad. And two, the problems at the LHC, there's still time for them to be resolved before they shut down your experiments, isn't there?"

"Yes, there's time."

"And it wouldn't be the first time the LHC shut for an extended period. It's not like it's your fault. And you'll be able to return after it all gets sorted."

"Uh-huh."

"See, you haven't failed. You simply must move on to another part of your work. You can always go back to Princeton. And if not Princeton, Stanford or Caltech; someone will want that lovely mind of yours."

"You're right, I'll move on if I have to, and maybe I won't have to." She still doesn't like the idea of moving back in with her dad and going back to being daddy's little girl. 'How fast can I get an apartment? Princeton won't have funds to take me back immediately, or anytime soon, and without any income, no apartment.'

"So let him know, at least about Zach. He wants to help you. I know he does."

Smiling, Rebecca lightly taps on Saabrina's forehead. "You really do, don't you? OK, I'll tell him about Zach. But nothing on the LHC, he's got enough to worry about." Rebecca lets out a yawn. "Hey, Saabrina."

"Yes?"

"Please don't do anything to Zach."

"Moi? Such as?"

"Nathan's clothes."

"He was a total ass."

"Xander's underwear."

"He did get his knickers in a twist. Too bad he was only in hospital for a morning."

"Seriously? Continuing with your clothing fetish, how about Logan's…"

"OK, fine, I promise not to do anything else to Zach." Furious when Rebecca told her that Zach had broken off their relationship via email—'email!'—she had promptly run down the net into his phone and found he had been fooling around with yoga girl since before Rebecca left for Geneva, emailing one while texting the other. She'd been tempted to fry his master's thesis, repented of doing so, and took a different tack.

""Else"? What do you mean, "Else"?"

"You know, he met Candice in yoga class. Last week when they tried practicing some homework together I gave their neuromuscular systems a little help. All good-natured fun and all."

""All good-natured fun and all." Seriously? And?"

"It took two ER docs and a consulting orthopedic surgeon the better part of a day to untangle them. Good thing his frat buddies were in town; if they hadn't gotten those selfies they would never have known to come over and rescue them."

Rebecca gives Saabrina a hug. "I love you. At least it wasn't clothes again."

Saabrina decides not to tell her that the next time Zach and Candice bend over at yoga class, which might be quite a while from now, their flesh will show through their pants spelling Bastard and Slut, respectively, across their asses for those behind to see.

.   .   .

Finally hitting the front of the Haven brunch line after his ride in the morning sun, Bob croaks out "I'd like an iced coffee and a piece of cappuccino cake, please. Oh, and I need a pound of coffee to go, coarse ground."

"Horse ground?"

"Coarse ground, not horse ground. Our horses don't drink coffee." Why he and Ryan, the guy behind the counter, do this joke every time he visits, he doesn't know.

.   .   .

Coming down the stairs after a post-ride shower in his usual Lenox summer getup of cargo shorts and a polo shirt, Bob finds Rebecca perched on a metal stool at the kitchen's white quartz breakfast bar nibbling on a Pop-tart, Saabrina sitting at her side, both still in their pajamas. "Hey, sweetie, how ya doin' this morning?"

"I'm good."

"OK." Bob opens the stainless-steel fridge to find something to eat.

Saabrina gives Rebecca a little nudge. *Now may a good time to talk to him.*

"Daddy."

"Yes, sweetie." Bob stops rummaging to give full attention to his daughter.

"Zach broke up with me."

"Oh, sweetie, I'm sorry. I was wondering what was up; you sounded so sad the last time we talked. Are you OK?"

"I'm fine. It hurt, but I'm over it." She tries to smile at him.

He pulls her into his arms. "I know. I can see it. I know it's not easy for you to talk to me about it, but I'm here if you need me." They hug a little longer, Bob running his hands through her hair.

"He's dating someone else, back in Princeton."

Separating, Bob leads Rebecca to the wooden bench at the dining room table. They sit side by side facing into the kitchen. "He met her while you were away?"

"Yes."

"Did he call or send you a 'Dear John' letter?"

"An email."

Bob takes Rebecca's hands. "An email must have really hurt. I never got a letter; usually the girls told me to my face, which, strangely enough, hurt more at the time, but felt better after. Not that it felt good for weeks. Have you talked to him?"

"No."

"You should, when you're ready. I know it's clichéd, but you should get some closure."

Rebecca reflects for an instant. "I will. Thanks, Dad." She gives him another long hug.

"Sweetie, how about some real breakfast before we get started for Tanglewood? Do you want a cheese omelet or some French toast?"

"French toast would be great."

Bustling about the kitchen, the three go to work pulling together the ingredients and necessary bowls, plates, and utensils. Saabrina whisks the eggs in a bowl, her hand a blur to the humans, adding a little milk, vanilla, and maple syrup as needed. 'Why isn't Bob more demonstrative in these situations?

There were certain daddies of certain children I met in Mexico who could have used a good dressing down and didn't receive one. Maybe meting out punishment had been Laura's job.' Finished beating the eggs, she hands the bowl to him. *Bob, how come you're not ripping Zach up, saying how bad he was, how she's better off without him?*

He dips slices of bread into the bowl's contents and drops them onto a rectangular casserole dish. 'Her girlfriends will shred Zach over a pint of ice cream. I have enough experience to know sometimes these things turn around and you don't want something you said to become a problem later. Capisce?'

But he was awful to her. And he left her, you know, to be with someone else.

'I know. I liked Zach. He's a good kid, smart, mostly mature, good prospects. Still, he's a kid. I'm sorry he made a bad choice and did something mean and stupid, and I'm upset he hurt Rebecca.'

Aren't you angry?

'Yes, I am. I know you can feel that, right?'

Right.

'Being angry isn't going to help her. Being calm and supportive does.' Bob hands the casserole dish with the soaked bread slices to Rebecca, who places them one by one on a griddle heating on the range. The smell of French toast begins to fill the kitchen. 'She's a woman now…"

Woman? Really? I can tell you're lying to yourself.

"Fine, true, but I'm trying hard to see her as she really is. Regardless of what I think, she'll have to figure this out on her own. She'll let her dad know what she wants from him.'

Harrumph. If I ever break up with someone you have my permission to kick his ass.

'I'll take your request under advisement. So, how did I do?'

Based on the latest readings from your daughter, which I shouldn't be giving you, you did nicely.

'Good to hear.'

Chapter 19

ON A SPECTACULAR AFTERNOON AT TANGLEWOOD, BLUE SKIES with little fluffy clouds overhead and temperatures in the seventies, Bob, Rebecca, and Saabrina picnic on the lawn behind the Shed's Section 11. Like most of the picnickers on the now-full lawn, they had schlepped in their gear and food on their backs and/or by pushing or pulling it along on wheels, joining an army moving on its stomach, taking position to eat, drink, and talk before the Boston Symphony Orchestra performs a Liszt piano concerto followed by a Mendelssohn symphony. Bob set up camp by arranging three cheap folding chairs around the picnic blanket and using the two coolers he and Rebecca dragged along as both serving surfaces and border markers. Around them, friends lounge on blankets with chips and salsa and bottles of wine; families pass endless plastic containers filled with potluck goodies while their kids play; and partiers display a formal lunch on a long table covered with a tablecloth, the centerpiece a candelabra with flickering LED lights.

As they sit and eat and drink and talk, the July sun falls gently on them while those nearby look hot as blazes. "We should find a shady spot back there under the trees," Bob had said to Saabrina along the path from the gate to the lawn; "Don't worry, we'll be fine" had come the reply. Rebecca had smiled at her. *One day your dad will figure this out.*

Lying comfortably next to Rebecca, Saabrina takes a bite of holographic hummus on a holographic pita chip. "Rebecca, you need to have some hummus. Those stuffed grape leaves are quite good, aren't they?"

"Yes, they are." Devouring another one, Rebecca reaches over Saabrina for a napkin to wipe the oily excess off her hands. 'You should sync with me. Or are you tasting the food as we both eat?'

Ugh, no, your dad's drinking beer, which I'm not fond of. Sort of yucks the yum. Not that I'd normally double-dip; I'm not some sort of epicurean sybarite, you know.

'Sorry, I know.' Rebecca looks over at her dad. "Dad, you're not going to sing or hum along today, are you?"

"No, I'm not. I promise." Bob shifts in his seat, the left-most in their trio facing the stage.

"Good, because I want to enjoy the BSO as is."

"I get it. Don't worry."

"Actually, you should give your dad some slack. He's gotten much better."

"Really?"

"Bob, sing something."

"Like what?"

"How about "Hotel California"?"

"I'm not singing "Hotel California.""

"Why? You sang it so well the other day." She sees him frown. "Fine." Saabrina works for a moment, checking her memories and his. ""American Pie.""

"Ooh, like when I was a baby. Daddy, you never sing it anymore."

"I can't remember the words."

I'll send them to you.

"OK." Bob scans their neighborhood. Seeing people busily eating, talking, and napping, he decides no one will pay attention and starts to sing the first verse, Saabrina supplying the lyrics like a built-in karaoke machine.

"Stop, stop." Rebecca puts her hands over her ears. "Saabrina, seriously? He sounded horrible."

"I thought he sang well."

Rebecca looks surprised. "Maybe it's you?"

"Sweetie, Saabrina sings beautifully. Show her, Saabrina, pick up where I left off."

"Alright." Saabrina stands, clears her throat, and sings. At the first chorus, Rebecca jumps up and puts her arm around Saabrina's waist, singing along. The two entertain the crowd while others nearby join for the choruses. They end to shouts of "Brava, brava," and give a slight bow before sitting back down on the picnic blanket.

"See, Dad, unlike you, Saabrina *can* sing. I'm happy to sing with her."

"I believed he'd gotten better; he sounded fine to me. You must have a more discerning ear."

"What would you say? 'Not bloody likely?'" She gives Saabrina a poke. "You must be getting used to him or something."

"You guys were great." Bob takes a drink of beer before returning the bottle to a cup holder in the arm of his chair. He leans forward. "Sweetie, can you pass me some more sushi?"

Saabrina and Rebecca both reach for the California rolls. "Oops, you would be 'sweetie.'" Saabrina pulls her hand back. "Sorry, it's residual from our vacation."

"It's OK, I don't mind." Rebecca hands the plastic tray to her dad after grabbing a California roll for herself.

'Doesn't his singing drive you crazy?'

I truly believed he had gotten better. Maybe it's when he sings for you?

'But it's not only the tune, it's the lyrics: he never gets the words right. I couldn't believe he got "American Pie" right.'

I helped him with the words. You're right, he mixes them up most frightfully, 'though sometimes it works out. You know the Goo Goo Dolls song "Come to Me"?

'Yes?'

He believes they're singing 'Come to me my Swedish friend.' He sings it to me whenever it plays on the radio. I don't have the heart to tell him he's wrong.

'Aww, that's kind of sweet.'

You're making me blush.

The bell rings announcing the program will start soon. "Ask not for whom the bell tolls…" says Bob; "It tolls for thee," answers Rebecca. People shuffle to their seats in the Shed. Those on the lawn rearrange their chairs for a better view, clean up their picnic areas, hand the kids coloring books and crayons to keep them quiet, pour some more wine, and make up a last plate of food to tide them over until intermission.

Rebecca takes her seat. "Dad." she holds ups a piece of paper from the program. Bob hadn't had a chance to read it yet.

"Yes, sweetie."

"They've made a big change. Isaiah Cleaver is out and won't be playing piano; Serge Maguffinovich is taking his place."

"Wow, amazing how the BSO could swap concert pianists at the last minute. I wonder why he's not here?"

"Doesn't say."

The bell rings a second time, calling people to their seats. From the stage comes a cacophony of warming instruments. Saabrina leans forward; the other two move closer to her. She says quietly "He disappeared."

Bob looks surprised. "Really? How do you know?"

"Come on Bob, BSO emails. I looked around once I read the program. He didn't show up for rehearsals; the police searched his apartment and found no foul play."

"Well, no foul play seems like good news, if still strange." Bob wonders if concert pianists lead such interesting lives which include sudden unexplained disappearances.

"They tried to keep it quiet, but the *Times* will be running a story after the concert."

Rebecca leans back. "I hope he's OK. I love Isaiah Cleaver! He's always been great when he plays here. My favorite was when we heard him play Brahms's Piano Concerto no. 2. He was awesome. Dad, how many summers ago did he play?"

"Too many for me to think about."

"Eight, if I'm reading your dad's mind correctly. He appears to have enjoyed the concert as well."

The bell rings a third time. The oboe leads the orchestra in their final tune-up, the conductor and the pianist follow the applause onto the stage, and the BSO begins to play. Sitting in his chair, sipping beer, Bob enjoys the concert, as do, seemingly, the bottle green lightning bugs gathered nearby. He watches their diaphanous bodies dance and pulse to the melodies, flashing green in time to the music. 'Strange, I've never seen them out during the day. Maybe they like music?' He turns again to listen to the BSO. When the piano concerto ends, the lightning bugs have gone before he can point them out to Rebecca and Saabrina.

At intermission, Rebecca asks Bob to get some ice cream. "Dirty Chocolate, Daddy."

"Yes, Bob. Dirty Chocolate, and lots of it."

"With hot fudge, if they have it. Please, Daddy."

"Sure, how can I say no to the two of you?" Bob leaves for the SoCo stand.

"Saabrina?"

"Yes, Rebecca."

"Did the BSO sound off to you?"

"A little, they seemed to labor a bit. Probably the change in pianist threw them off."

"You're probably right."

"I must say, your dad and I have had no luck at our last few concerts." She gives a brief description of the performances they had seen, Rebecca nodding her head in disbelief.

"Saabrina?"

"Yes?"

"Has my dad, you know, been dating anyone?"

"No. I hoped he and a sentinel named Dana Banks might hit it off a few weeks ago, but they didn't. Although, they do seem to be becoming friends, just not those kinds of friends."

"Not even friends with benefits?"

"No. And seriously, you're asking me…" Saabrina points to herself "me about your dad, to repeat, your dad, and that? Like, ewww."

"Sorry."

"Mind you, he's been on dates. His friends on Earth gamely keep trying to fix him up, but nothing ever comes of it."

"Do you think he's OK? I worry about him."

"He seems fine. We're pretty busy, often away from Earth on business, which he likes. I guess being fairly itinerant probably doesn't help his dating either. He simply hasn't met the right person yet. I do try to help."

"I figured you did."

"I identify potential targets, give him advice on who would make a good mate for a human, provide details on their anatomy and sexual capabilities…personalities, I mean their personalities. I believe he appreciates it."

"I bet he does. I do." Rebecca smiles at Saabrina. "Thanks."

"You're very welcome."

Shocked at Isaiah Cleaver's disappearance, Bob keeps gazing at the empty stage on his way to the ice cream stand and bumps into a man on the path. In a flash, the man breaks into a dozen small gelatinous green figures who scatter in every direction. No one else notices. "What the…" He looks around, walking over to the places where he thought the men had run to, half expecting to find them cowering behind chairs and coolers. All he finds are befuddled looks from fellow concert-goers. "Sorry" he repeats over and over. 'Hey, Saabrina, did you see those guys?'

What?

'The little green men. Review my walk to the ice cream stand.' He feels her running through his thoughts.

I don't see anything. Are you sure?'

'You really don't see anything?'

Nothing. No little green men.

'Maybe not, maybe I imagined them. Wait, you don't even see, uh, something I imagined?'

No figments of your imagination, only you on the path, then you looking around for something. Are you OK?

'I'm fine. Let me get to SoCo.'

Hurry with the ice cream. Intermission is almost over. And don't forget the hot fudge.

'Yes, if they have it.' Bob quickens his pace.

Chapter 20

WITH A NEW LIST OF FOUR POTENTIAL TRAVEL TUBE SIGNA-
tures, Bob and Saabrina begin the hunt again. Their first three
stops come up empty. Striking gold on the fourth, they find
a tube tethered to an Earth-like world called Bontomundo, a
bustling metropolis at one end and nothing at the other. A
quick survey provides data similar to the previous two and
shows the tube's endpoint to be located in the private room of
an upscale strip club at the edge of a residential neighborhood.
On an overcast fall day, Bob makes his way past girls gyrating
on poles and performing lap dances for patrons, dance music
pounding away, while Saabrina waits outside on the sidewalk
enjoying the afternoon air. A large bribe gets him into the back
room and a private session. When he asks his entertainment
about patrons who visited in the last month, with perhaps
strange proclivities, two large men in ill-fitting black suits
promptly escort him off the premises.

"Smoothly done, Bob. Way to get those answers. Did you
have fun at least?"

"No. I never get these places. Maybe I should send you in. You know, you could get a job here, check it out, find out what goes on."

"I don't think so." She takes him by the arm and begins walking him towards a broad avenue down the street.

"Why? It's classic undercover work. Sure, you'd have to show some skin and shake some booty, but think what you could learn." He looks back at the entrance.

"Don't make me vomit." She tugs harder, pulling him forward.

A young woman in a long beige coat rushes up to them. "We need to talk." She pulls them around the corner into a bodega and slides them down an aisle filled with snack foods out of sight of the video camera behind the cashier. Wrapping her arms around her body, she struggles to hold her unbuttoned coat closed. "You NBI?"

Bob looks both ways, then addresses the girl. "What's it to you?"

"Show me your badge." As Bob reaches for his coat pocket, she puts a hand out to stop him, the gaps in her coat revealing a bikini-clad body. "Good. I don't need you to flash it here. Do you know the Deluxe Diner over on 63rd?"

Bob looks at Saabrina.

Yes.

"Yes."

"Get a booth. I'll see you there in thirty minutes." The woman runs out of the shop.

They wait a few minutes to peruse the shelves before following her out onto the pavement. Saabrina tugs Bob to the right and they start walking along an avenue of tall brick apartment buildings, passing dry cleaners, delis, and pizza places. Everything looks worn, the sidewalks spotted with spit gum, dog poop in the gutters, the passing busses spewing sooty fumes. It reminds Bob of the New York City he lived in after college. "How long 'til we get there?"

"Twenty minutes, thirty-two seconds on foot."

"Not to sound too paranoid, but are we being followed?"

"No. I'll let you know if we are. And we can make a quick getaway if we have to." She points to a black Saab passing them in traffic; on the next block it reappears and passes them again. They walk along the sidewalk, the city people moving quickly around them, faces blank and focused. "Bob, what do you believe she wants?"

"It must have something to do with my questions, otherwise no clue."

"Whilst you were inside, I took a closer look at this travel tube. It's superior to the last two in many ways, particularly in thwarting detection. If I hadn't been actively looking for it, I would never have found it."

"So, they're getting better at this?"

"Yes. My original theory was one ship improving its technology; now I'm speculating that there may be multiple ships with successive technology. Either could be true or, worse, both."

"More ships with better tech is a scary thought."

"I left a few cameras with the tube end here and a sensor with the end in space. If they come back, we'll catch them."

"Thanks. Great work, Saabrina."

They find the restaurant mostly empty, the few patrons reading afternoon papers over cups of coffee and tea. Passing the "Please Seat Yourself" sign, they take a booth in the back with Bob facing the entrance. Sitting across from each other on benches of tufted brown vinyl, they order coffee and a slice of apple cinnamon cake for Bob to nibble on. The waitress places two cups and the cake on the beige table; the surface reminds Bob of knock-off Corian. After a bite, he smiles. "Happy?"

"Much better than the rubbish on Fortnum. Too bad their coffee is dreadful."

"Give them ten years."

A few minutes later the woman in the long coat appears. Spotting Bob, she takes her place across from him, using her butt to push Saabrina further down the bench. "So, who are you two?"

Bob, I scanned her. She's not wired, nor carrying a weapon, and her driver's license matches a woman who works at the strip club, Charlene Biggs.

"I'm Special Agent Phil Marlowe." He points to Saabrina. "My partner is Detective Inspector Holly Hoboken, on loan to us from the RK Metropolitan Police."

Saabrina reaches out her hand to the woman. "Afternoon, miss."

The woman shakes it. "Are you family to the Epsteins? They run Hoboken's department store over on 11th?"

"No, afraid not. I'm the Weehawken in Jersey Hobokens."

"Girl, even I know that's a rough part of the RK. I like your fancy accent."

"Thank you."

"So, miss, who are you and how can DI Hoboken and I help?"

"I'm Charlene Biggs. I work at the club. I think you know that."

Bob pushes the remainder of his cake to the side. "We do."

Charlene hesitates, then plows ahead. "Are you lookin' for Helen? She's been gone for weeks and no one's heard from her."

Helen Tipton. No missing persons report with the police. Parents deceased. The club hasn't run payroll for her in four weeks. Unseen to Charlene, Tipton's driver's license photo showing an attractive young woman floats in front of Bob.

"Yes, we are. Tell me what you know."

"Not much. Just she's gone and disappeared and it spooked the rest of us."

"Why?"

"Look, girls come and go from this job, but everybody knows where they went. Some go to other clubs; some get the hell out of the business; the lucky ones put on a diamond ring. Helen is gone gone, like without a trace. No one's heard from her. I checked. I asked around. Nothin'."

"You liked her?"

"Yeah. We all did. Helen was special. She was in school over at the University, usin' the job to pay her tuition and groceries. We all tell the fancy boys we're gettin' degrees—makes them more comfortable and ups the tips if they think we're smart like them—but she was the real thing, doing high-level math stuff. I used to watch her study between sets. And now she's gone." Charlene stares at her arms crossed on the stained tabletop; DI Hoboken gently puts a hand on her forearm.

Bob takes a long sip of coffee. "Did she disappear in the club?"

"I think so. I saw her end a set, noticed the boss talkin' to her. We were supposed to get breakfast later, but she didn't show. I asked the bouncers if they'd seen her; they told me to keep my mouth shut and forget about it."

"Did she go to the back room?"

"I don't know. What's the backroom got to do with it?"

"Anybody new at the club? Anybody, well, weird?"

SETH COHEN

"A few weeks back we got a new crew of heavies. Kind of a nasty bunch. I didn't like their smell."

"About the same time Helen went missing?"

"Yeah, I hadn't thought of that. They were at the club the night she disappeared. Asked the DJ to play some funky soundin' music."

DI Hoboken places a period and location-specific tape player, battered and worn, on the table and presses play. Quietly, Blondie squeaks out a tinny version of "One Way or Another" from its speaker. The DI leans towards Charlene. "Charlene, love, did those blokes' music sound something like this?"

"Just like it. They played that song and a bunch of others with the same sound. Turned them on like crazy."

DI Hoboken presses stop and pockets the player.

.   .   .

Sheltered from the Massachusetts summer sun by the roof of Bob's screen porch, Eddie leans back in his chair and takes a sip of cold beer. "Delicious. Local?"

Bob reads the label. "California."

"Close enough." He takes another drink. "Where's Saabrina?"

"In Geneva with Rebecca. It's girls' night out. You sent Saabra off to Jacob's Pillow for the afternoon?"

"She's watching a rehearsal of a dance troupe from Santiago. Since I can only stay for one beer, I thought she could fit in something fun before we leave for business. How long are you here for?"

"At least two days while they refine the search based on our latest results."

"Any luck?"

Bob wants to ask Eddie 'Haven't you been reading the reports?' But he knows Eddie has read the reports and has his own reasons for quizzing Bob. "Found another tube but not its users. If they return, a big if, we have a shot at picking them up. But I want to go from finding tubes to finding bad guys, so we sit here while FedSci works out a better detection method."

"Finding bad guys would be better. How about working backwards from what you've found, selecting their likely targets to reduce the search?"

"Still too many worlds meet their requirements. It helps to know what they like, but I think the best bet is spotting an active travel tube signature and getting there in time. Once FedSci has a solution, we can bring more sentinels and Saabs into play and get the job finished."

"Hmmm. Maybe too little data to separate signal from noise, but worth a look."

"Understood. We'll go back and check again to see if they've been following a pattern."

"Good."

Bob sips his beer. "Lerner and the other agency heads are also trying to sort out the issue of the missing women. Is it collateral damage or somehow part of the main scheme?"

"Not good either way."

"At least we didn't run into any more wrecked science experiments on the worlds we visited."

"I could tell you that's true, except the artificial singularity program on Oishix Three crashed."

"Crap. We didn't find a travel tube there. Do we have to go back?"

"Hold until FedSci works out something and you and Saabrina do some more work on pattern recognition."

"Got it."

Eddie takes a drink. "Heard Dana Banks wanted to spell you for the next round."

Bob laughs. "She was getting pulled into some sort of marketing exercise for DoSOPS. One of those offsite things where outside experts with lots of sticky notes lead you through endless sessions to try to better distill your entity's message and image. Ever been to one?"

"Can't say I have."

"It can be fun for an afternoon; a week kinda sucks. She and Isaabelle didn't want to get trapped in a conference room for days with only whiteboards to look at, so she came to me. I wished her the best of luck." After offering Eddie some chips and salsa from the small table between them, Bob leans forward. "Is this Lerner going on the offensive? Anything happening with our favorite congresswoman?"

"I've got some news from Gogolak."

"Since we're doing this over a beer, I assume it's bad. Did you learn that trick from Odessa?"

"I taught it to her."

"So what's the news?"

"It's not a matter of it being bad, just more complicated. Gogolak jumped into the issue of the Saabs with his students. I haven't seen him this energized in years. The students loved it. From their work, he's creating a whole new class to teach next semester."

"That's what you thought would happen."

"They've already put a pretty tight case together to defend the right of Saabs. As I thought, no one serious in the world of constitutional law would counter it."

"Sounds like good news. So, Eddie, what's the complication?"

"In setting Gogolak on his course, we inadvertently changed the underlying field conditions. As it happened, one of his students was pretty involved in animal rights. He mentioned it to his group at the university."

"And?"

"What do you say here? 'It went viral'? The animal rights people don't believe Saabs should get the same rights as people unless animals do as well."

"They're focusing on the definition of 'sentience'?"

"Yes, Bob, how did you know?"

"Saabrina. Apparently, she's an expert in this. Let me guess: Gogolak's and his students' argument doesn't factor in animals."

"Correct. The animal rights people even agree with it, privately. Their view, however, is sometimes you have to do something bad to get something good."

"So they're going to oppose rights for Saabs until they get what they want?"

"Exactly. Gogolak's student felt terrible about what happened; he resigned from the group in disgust."

Bob takes a long pull from his bottle. "Is that all?"

"No. Alerted by the animal rights people, two other groups have jumped into the fray. One's obvious."

"Let me guess, their fellow travelers in politics—the people who view Saabs as killing machines."

"Exactly."

"And the other?"

"People on the opposite end of the spectrum who believe…"

"Only biologicals can be people."

"They keep telling Odessa they only represent 'everyday people.'"

"OK, in some sense Saabs are definitely not 'everyday people,' but aren't these people missing the whole point of the song?"

"I don't believe they listened to the lyrics, Bob. They simply like the idiom."

Bob spends a moment reading the label on his beer bottle, Lagunitas "The Censored" Copper Ale, before finishing it. He puts the empty down. "Crap, Eddie, this is all good for Tuchis. In fact, we did her work for her."

"Bob, Gogolak's confident he can win this case in front of the Supreme Court, if it gets there."

"I'm glad to hear he's got a good case, but you're missing my point. We created an issue for her and helped line up people on her side who will happily provide campaign contributions, favors, all sorts of stuff politicians love to collect. We opened up a whole new power supply for her."

"I hadn't thought of that. I'll talk to Odessa when I get back to Madison." After finishing his own bottle of beer, Eddie rises and gives a whistle. "We'll see if we can tamp this down, get reason to prevail. This isn't Earth, people on Madison tend to be a little more rational."

"I hope you're right." They walk the short distance from Bob's open kitchen through his small, lofted living room to the front door.

"Bob, give us some credit. We'll work this out."

Once outside, they find Saabra parked in his driveway, a strip of asphalt separated from its neighbors by grass, trees, and tiger lilies, Bob's condo one vertical slice of seven in building nine of his development.

Hi, Bob. Sorry we have to run.

'Me too, Saabra. Good to see you anyway.'

Likewise. Bye for now.

Bob shakes Eddie's hand. "Thanks for stopping by for a beer. Always glad to have you."

"Next time I'll bring Brenda. We'll spend the weekend and join you at Tanglewood."

"Eddie, I'd love if you brought Brenda, so please do." Bob watches Eddie and Saabra drive away. 'What the hell am I going to tell Saabrina?'

.   .   .

Waiting for Saabrina's arrival, Rebecca puts the finishing touches on her outfit for the evening. As usual, Jean lounges on her couch, kibitzing. "Leave your hair alone, it looks exquisite. The dress is sexy and sufficiently short." They'd made up after their incident; Jean apologizing for his boorish behavior, Rebecca apologizing for letting Zach get the better of her. He sits up. "You are going back to New Jersey tomorrow?"

"Yes. How about you? You haven't told me your plans."

"One of my old haunts, Urbana."

"I didn't know you'd been there. I'll have to come visit. Do you know my friend Sachita Chandra?"

"No. It's a grand…large campus, no? Easy to miss people?"

"She's in the Physics Department. I thought everyone knew Sachita?"

"Maybe she arrived after I left. It was a while ago." He comes over and inspects her one more time from top to bottom, stopping at her bracelet of silvery stones. "Est-ce nouveau??"

"Yes, a gift from a friend."

"It does not go with the rest of your accoutrement. I would take it off."

"Really?"

"Oui."

Rebecca reluctantly takes the bracelet off and leaves it on her desk with a clink.

"Bon, très bon. You are beautiful, and ready to take Geneva by storm."

"Thanks, Jean." She gives him a peck on the cheek. "It will make for a fine last night in town." Leadership had quietly announced its plan to shut the LHC at the end of August. The foreign teams had begun wrapping up their work and making their goodbyes; most of her group who were not tied to Geneva had already left, the least senior staffers going first. To cheer her up, Saabrina had proposed a night on the town before whisking her back to New Jersey. "Sure you can't join us?"

"It would not be, how to do you say, 'nuit de filles'?" His mobile buzzes twice before making a barfing sound. "And I have my own rendezvous planned for this evening. I must go." He looks in her eyes, then gives her two air kisses. "Au revoir, Rebecca."

"Bye, Jean, see you later."

He goes to the door. "And don't forget the little place I told you about, the food is good, the drinks better, and the music best. Please do go."

"We will. It's at the top of my list."

Jean exits. A minute later there's a knock at the door. Opening it, she finds Saabrina appropriately attired in a little black dress and sandals. "Come on girl, let's get this party started!" They hug.

"Thanks for coming."

"My pleasure. Only the two of us?"

"Yes, just us. You missed Jean who ran off to his own rendezvous. Everyone else is gone or with their families."

"So where are we going?"

"I don't want to do anything fancy like La Baroque. I thought we'd walk around the cafés for a bit, then go to this fabulous place Jean told me about, Chant du Cygne." Rebecca finishes putting on three-inch heels bringing her eye level with Saabrina and grabs her clutch. "Come on, let's go."

"I'm following you."

"Oh, and you're not my wingman tonight. Just us girls, no boys."

"No yucky boys, understood."

They make a whirlwind tour of after dark Geneva, before finding their way to Chant du Cygne. Its commercial neighborhood does not promise much and the steps down through a dilapidated entrance give them pause, until the sound of laughter, music, and the clatter of plates sweeps over them. Not too big, not too small, with closely set tables filled with noisy people, a long bar lined with twenty-somethings, and a small dance floor at the far end, the restaurant literally pulls them in when the maître d' takes Rebecca by the arm and escorts her and Saabrina to a table by the dance floor. A bottle of champagne in a bucket waits with a note tied on a bow. As the maître d' seats her, Rebecca plucks the note from the bottle and reads: "Rebecca, an apology was simply insufficient. Please accept this meager dinner as proper recompense for my poor conduct the other night. Jean." The maître d' pops the cork and pours champagne into two flutes, then hands them to the ladies. "Salut." He scampers off.

"Rebecca, care to fill me in?"

"It's from Jean. He felt bad about the other night and is paying for dinner."

"Lovely."

They spend the next few hours eating, drinking, dancing, and, mostly, talking. Saabrina enjoys the champagne while mimicking its effect on Rebecca, her buzz building nicely.

Bob's conversation with Eddie had left her sick and dizzy, Saabrina having listened-in knowing she wasn't supposed to but also knowing she had to. Now she wants to blast the latest turn of events with the abominable congresswoman out of her mind. 'I will simply focus on having a good time with my best friend to support my best friend in my best friend's time of need in the same damn fashion as my best friend.' She downs another glass of champagne. Courtesy of Rebecca, the champagne tastes delicious, the bubbles luxuriant against her friend's palate.

Engrossed in conversation, they do not notice their fellow patrons leaving the restaurant for other clubs and cafés. The dance floor empties, the room quiets. The waiters, bartenders, and maître d' disappear, leaving six men at the bar. Suddenly, the sound system blasts "Call Me," Blondie rocking over the speakers. Instantly sober, Saabrina scans the men at the bar. With a yank, she pulls Rebecca stumbling onto the dance floor.

Rebecca starts to dance. "I love this song. So '80s, so my mom and dad, me mum and dad as my girlfriend says. Are we dancing?"

"Rebecca, pay attention." Saabrina pulls her close.

The six men leave the bar and surround them in a circle. They look sketchy to Rebecca, no party clothes, just three skinheads in jeans and white t-shirts sporting an assortment of small, self-inked tattoos on their faces and necks, two older toughs in worn leather jackets, and, standing between them, one strange looking dude wearing sunglasses and a teal Members Only jacket with a large black bag slung over his shoulder.

The strange dude speaks: "Ladies, shall we dance?"

Chapter 21

'SAABRINA, WHAT'S GOING ON?' THE WAY THE MEN LOOK AT her, Rebecca feels practically naked. Tugging down the hem of her dress, she feels a chill and fights the urge to vomit. "Call Me" grates on her ears.

I recognize their leader from the database. His name is Vildakaya. He's a serial rapist and murderer.

'The Swiss police database?'

No, the Union's. The ones in leather to his right and left are local thugs with similar backgrounds. They I identified from the Swiss database. The rest are new to this crew.

Dropping his bag to the floor, Vildakaya smiles through broken, brown stained teeth. "I shall not ask again. Will you join me for a dance?"

Saabrina flexes Rebecca's wrist, swinging her around, bringing them back to back, Saabrina facing Vildakaya. "Let's be honest. I don't believe dancing is what you're actually here for now, is it?"

"No. Partying yes, dancing, not so much." A snap of Vildakaya's fingers silences the music. Other than the two women and the six men who surround them, the restaurant remains empty. Vildakaya points to Rebecca. "We're here for her."

"You can't have her. You should really go away. I know it would be better for all of us."

"I hate to disagree with someone so charming, but two for the price of one is a great bargain; I think we will party long and hard with you two." The blokes around him laugh and point at the girls, making crude movements with their arms to indicate the partying they intend to perform, repeating the words 'long' and 'hard' in French and English. Vildakaya reaches out his hand. "Now come on, be good little girls and come to papa." He nods to the two in leather jackets who take out knives. "We'll help you take off your dresses."

Saabrina feels Rebecca shudder. *Rebecca, stay close to me and close your eyes. No matter what happens, keep them closed until I tell you otherwise.*

'But Saabrina…'

Shush. Everything will be fine.

Rebecca closes her eyes. Everything becomes silent and dark. Then she hears "The Girl from Ipanema" begin to play.

"As enchanting as your invitation is, I believe we must decline."

"Suit yourself, we'll do it the hard way." On hearing 'hard,' the three skinheads laugh again. Vildakaya gives them a nod; they step forward to grab the young women. Crack. Saabrina lashes out, kicking and hitting the skinheads, her feet and hands landing with fast whacks and smacks, their touch causing a wisdom tooth to explode at the back of one punk's mouth and small bones to shatter in the others' hands and ankles. The newbies drop to the ground in agony and try to crawl off the dance floor. Vildakaya steps back. Shouting curses, the local thugs rush Saabrina with knives drawn. She blocks each of their thrusts, her quick moves driving their knives deep into the other man's torso with a crunch, splattering blood across Saabrina and the ground. Dead, they fall to the floor revealing Vildakaya holding a blunderbuss-like device he has extracted from the bag by his feet. The air around him shimmers, cloaking him in an armor of vibrating silver particles. He waves the blunderbuss at Saabrina. "I want the girl: you can walk away."

Saabrina stands still, back to back with Rebecca, facing Vildakaya. "Why her?"

"I want *her* brain. I've been told it's one of the best. It's more valuable than the rest of her. At least to those who pay for such things; I prefer the other parts myself."

"You want her brain?"

"Yes, her big, powerful brain. In a moment, I will make her disappear, then I will deal with you."

"A girl, why not a boy? There seem to be plenty of clever men about Geneva. Why not one of them?"

Vildakaya smiles. "Our bonus for getting the job done. Call me and my brothers old-fashioned; we only like to fuck girls, so girls are what we send." He makes a couple of quick adjustments on the device's stock. "Now I don't actually need you to step aside." He raises the blunderbuss.

She raises her hands. "Please, don't."

"Sorry, but I must." Vildakaya pulls the trigger.

Rebecca keeps her eyes closed and listens to "The Girl from Ipanema," safely leaning against Saabrina's back. Strangely, she no longer feels intoxicated, as if the alcohol has drained out of her body.

Nothing happens. Vildakaya looks over the gun at Saabrina and Rebecca, fiddling frantically with the controls. The silvery cloud clears at his feet; bones in his legs snap as something forces him to stand straight. Looking down, he screams "What's happening?"

SETH COHEN

"Your capsule is emerging from the floor beneath you. I hope it isn't too tight a fit."

Vildakaya holds his hands out to fight the wave of pressure. The blunderbuss snaps back, crushing his ribs, pelvis and shoulders crackling as his body folds in on itself. He screams silently, the air trapped in his mouth.

Saabrina steps forward, looking through the transparent wall of the capsule. "I slowed the process, considerably. It will take twenty minutes for you to reach your ship, rather than the usual minute or two. Enjoy your ride." Vildakaya's boxed form floats into the air before bursting away in a flash.

Saabrina wheels around, blood evaporating from her skin and clothes, grabs Rebecca, and leads her from the dance floor. *Don't open your eyes. Don't look back.* Rebecca finds herself being slipped into the passenger seat of a car, her seat belt gently buckled around her. "You can open your eyes now." She opens her eyes to see Saabrina sitting in the Saab's driver's seat, the tables and the chairs of the restaurant visible outside her windows. "Come on, we need to fetch your dad." Saabrina punches through Chant du Cygne's façade, showering glass, wood, and aluminum onto the street, then lifts quickly into the nighttime sky over Geneva.

After Saabrina provides a brief, sanitized account of what occurred at the restaurant, Rebecca gets her bearings. "Thank you."

"For what?"

"Saving my life."

"You're welcome."

Rebecca wants to joke about how they made it some 'girls' night out.' The ache from the receding fear and the stale taste of champagne on her tongue keep the words from coming. Watching the night sky turn red with evening sunshine as they approach the east coast of the United States, she turns back to her friend who drives herself. "You only do it for me, don't you? Sitting here with me. Not even for my dad."

"Yes."

"Why?"

"I don't know why, I just do." Saabrina smiles at Rebecca. "Oh, and I'm your wingman."

They drop onto the driveway of the Lenox condo to find Bob dressed and waiting for them. As Saabrina vanishes, giving Rebecca a start, Bob climbs into the driver's seat, leans over, and gives her a huge hug, repeating over and over "Are you alright, are you alright?" Finally, he lets go after she repeats "I'm fine" for the fiftieth time.

"I'm fine, Dad. Saabrina was there, so nothing bad could happen."

"I know, I know. She told me everything about your night and what happened. It's just hard, you know."

Rebecca moves to unbuckle her seat belt. "You should go, you know, like to go get the bad guys."

Bob stops her. "Sweetie, the safest place is here, so you're coming along." Launching into space, the Earth dropping behind them, Bob finally lets out a breath and relaxes. "I guess this is 'bring your daughter to work day.'"

They both hear a groan. *Really, Bob, that's the best you can come up with?*

"Under the circumstances, yes." He gives Rebecca a brief description of their hunt for the travel tubes; Saabrina fills her in on the capsules, how they are used to transport women, and Vildakaya's current travails. Rebecca approves. Finishing the discussion, Bob asks "Please give me a situation report."

With Vildakaya slowly progressing up the travel tube, I've temporarily pinned his ship to Earth. I'm taking readings from a distance so we'll know what we're dealing with.

"How long 'til they can leave?"

Nine minutes, thirty-seven seconds. What's our plan, Bob?

"Surveil, assess the situation. Given what this crew is into, I doubt they'll respond to talk, so we'll start with technical solutions to get control first, talk later. So, what are we dealing with?"

That.

Bob and Rebecca see a dark brown spaceship consisting of two prolate spheroids, one large, one small, joined together tangentially below and above their midpoint axes. Antennas bristle from the small spheroid; long, fat armatures fixed to the large spheroid curve forward around the smaller hull.

"Dad, it looks like a huge, ugly spider."

"It certainly does, sweetie."

The smaller spheroid…

"Spheroid?" asks Bob.

"Football-shaped thing," answers Rebecca.

"Thanks, sweetie."

If I may continue, the smaller football-shaped thing contains the bridge, work and utility rooms, the galley, and crew quarters as well as bays for three shuttles, two occupied. Now that I know what to look for, I can tell you the third shuttle sits in a garage outside of Geneva.

"So we know how Vildakaya got to Earth. Can you bring it back without tipping them off?"

Yes, it's on its way.

"Perfect, thanks."

The larger spheroid holds the drive systems, travel tube generator, and forty-eight stasis chambers, twenty-six of which are occupied.

"Do you recognize the design?"

It's derived from an old Armada Delvax transport, heavily modified.

"They bought it surplus, huh?"

Exactly. The mods were expertly done. They've added stealth features, heavy armor, weaponry, secure long-distance communications, the stasis pods, and, of course, the travel tube system. I'm guessing the forward compartment of the small spheroid is the bridge, currently occupied by three men. There are seven more men in the galley and various workshops. She briefly shows them a pixelated x-ray-like image of the inside of the forward hull, with men standing or moving in various rooms.

"Guessing? That's not like you."

Harrumph. The ship is heavily screened and I haven't been able to access their network yet, so I don't know the command and control layout exactly. I'm approximating based on the layout of a Delvax.

"How long before they detect you?"

Momentarily.

"Can you take out their sensor arrays, long-range coms, and weaponry without damaging the stasis pods?"

Yes.

Bob taps her wheel. "Do it, please."

Saabrina quickly circles the ship. Puffs of vaporized metal silently appear around the twin hulls; antennas and armatures fly off into space.

I'm sorry, Rebecca, I should have provided special effects so you could see and hear what happened.

"This is serious, Saabrina, I don't need any special treatment. The physicist in me appreciates the silence."

Bob, they are warming up their drive systems. Once Vilda-kaya arrives in six minutes, twenty-seven seconds, they will be able to decouple from the travel tube and go.

"Can you destroy the drive system without harming the stasis pods?"

No. Nor can I take out their flight control systems directly. I'm trying to access their network, but their firewall and anti-virus systems are quite robust.

"Don't let them make you sick."

I'm being careful. There, at least I've disabled the active immune system and virus generators, providing me with more maneuvering room.

"Dad, is Saabrina flying around the ship, shooting at it, invading their network, and talking to us, all at once?"

"Yes. Plus transmitting data back to DoSOPS on Madison, receiving advice, which we'll probably ignore, as well as doing a bunch of other things. Knowing her, she's probably reading a book and writing a review of it for a literary magazine as well." Bob decides not to mention that Saabrina is also evacuating the waste products from their bodies. As if on cue, two bottles of water appear on the armrest between them. Bob hands one to Rebecca while taking one for himself.

"I never realized. I mean, I should have known." Rebecca looks around the inside of the Saab.

"And it's still her. Your friend."

"I know that, Dad."

"Hey, Saabrina, how ya doin'?"

I'm making slow progress. I managed to get into their sanitation facilities and reverse the flow of their loos. It shouldn't smell too good in there. Oh, God.

Bob tenses. "What?"

Rebecca's friend Sachita is in a pod. I recognized her from Rebecca's memories. And… Saabrina's voice drifts away.

Rebecca shouts "Who is it Saabrina? Who is it?" while Bob grabs her waving hand.

Juliette. Juliette is also in a stasis pod. I'm sorry Rebecca.

Rebecca yanks her arm away from her dad and pulls herself together. "They've both been sexually assaulted?"

Yes. And their bodies were damaged by their trips.

"Why do they want my friends' brains?"

Bob, may I answer?

"Sure, Saabrina, go ahead."

Biologicals brains are sentient, powerful, and malleable. Even with our advanced systems and programming, they provide several advantages, particularly to worlds unsuccessful in developing, how shall I say it, real AIs.

"And no one has an AI like you."

Please don't make me blush right now, Rebecca.

""Spock's Brain" is real. Fuck. Why girls? Why university girls like Sachita, Juliette, …me…"

Demonstrated high intelligence indicates a brain of maximum usefulness, old enough to be fully formed and trained, young enough for multiple adaptations and long use. Sorry, Rebecca, I'm not trying to objectify you into mechanical bits; I know I'm describing something less than the whole.

"I know."

Girls, Vildakaya prefers…

"…to rape them. I get it. How do we stop these dickheads?"

"OK, Saabrina, time to go over options."

Bob, I've gained a more thorough understanding of their ship. I've disabled their life support; they will have breathable, if unpleasant, air for another one hour and fifty minutes. The travel tube capsule appears to deliver its cargo directly to a stasis chamber. Interesting, the crew doesn't have internal access to the rear spheroid.

"I guess management doesn't trust the crew with the goods. Figures."

Although I have mapped out a comprehensive layout of their ship, I still can't get to their flight controls. They'll leave in three minutes, thirteen seconds, well before I can take control. Ow, that's a nasty... Several unladylike curses follow while Bob and Rebecca watch more puffs of smoke appear and more pieces of the spider ship fly off... *anti-intruder program. There, much better.*

"And destroying their drive systems destroys the stasis pods?"

Again, Bob's penchant for asking questions to answers he knows annoys her. *Yes. We're running out of technical solutions.*

While her father and Saabrina quickly discuss alternatives as well as protocol, Rebecca grows comfortable surrounded by Saabrina's seriousness and focus. She feels something underneath her friend's utter professionalism: something warm, no, hot to the touch, not anger... fury, a building fire of righteous rage and the cool, hard effort to keep it in check. She enjoys the heat; it begins to mix with her own. Hearing 'stasis pods' snaps Rebecca out of her reverie. "Dad, what are you thinking?"

"I have to weigh saving the lives of the women in the pods against letting the bad guys go. We can follow them, but it complicates things and I don't want to lose them or run into reinforcements."

"Those can't be your only options."

"We can't ship them to a detention facility with an active drive system. I can't stop them without killing the girls."

One minute, forty-eight seconds Bob.

Rebecca thinks. "Saabrina, why only twenty minutes? Is twenty minutes the maximum you can delay the capsule?"

No, I can delay the capsule indefinitely, but a longer delay will most likely result in Vildakaya's death before he reaches his stasis pod. As a Union citizen, he does have rights, and we will want to question him.

Bob sits up in his seat. "Saabrina, hail the ship."

Hailing frequencies open. Go ahead.

"This is Sentinel Robert James Foxen. Please respond. Who am I speaking to?"

A pause, then a deep voice replies. "Groysskaya, Captain of the Verdreht. Why have you attacked my ship?"

"You have committed several serious crimes, including illegally removing inhabitants from their protected worlds. Please power down and disable your drive system."

"Allegedly. Even you, Sentinel, must respect my rights. Allegedly."

Bob, one minute.

"Captain Groysskaya, I repeat, please power down your drive system."

"Under the circumstances, I will do no such thing."

Bob cuts his hand across his throat. Saabrina mutes the connection. "Vildakaya lost his rights. Delay his arrival."

Done. They guessed your move; I see two men preparing to exit the vehicle to disconnect the travel tube.

"Vaporize them when they get outside."

More puffs of smoke appear. *No need, I welded all their airlock doors shut.*

"Well done, Saabrina. Now, please unmute me."

Done.

"Captain Groysskaya, your circumstances have changed. Please provide me with access to your drive system and pre-pare for transport to a detention facility."

Silence.

"Saabrina, ring their bell." The spider ship shakes violently. "Captain Groysskaya?"

"Again, I wholeheartedly deny your allegations. Why do you persecute me so unfairly? I demand my rights."

"You can invoke your rights at your arraignment, after you've been processed."

"How can I expect fair treatment after your conduct? You attacked my ship without warning!"

"Given the circumstances, specifically the evidence of your horrific conduct, your ship's capabilities, and the rules and regulations regarding protected worlds, I was well within my rights as a sentinel to take these actions. Now, I can sit here and wait all day. My Saab estimates you have…

One hour and forty-six minutes

…only one hour and forty-six minutes of life support left. After that, I will be able to send you to the detention facility without your help."

There's a long silence. "Sentinel Foxen, I know the only reason I am alive is because you want to retrieve the twenty-six women in my stasis pods. I have my hand over their controls. With a touch I can kill one or all. Now for every minute you do not let me go, I will kill one woman."

Bob signals Saabrina to mute the conversation. "Can you show me the inside of the ship again." The x-ray like image appears on her windshield, this time with greater detail. "Thanks. Zoom in on the forward compartment." She zooms in. "Thanks. I'm guessing the big guy literally holding his hand over the control panel is Groysskaya. Do you have a firing solution?"

Yes.

"Take it."

"Sentinel Foxen, I have little patience for…"

They hear a yell squelched by the sound of violently rushing air. The three figures on the screen join into one, then vanish. All goes quiet.

"Dad, where did they go?"

"I'm sorry, sweetie, I should have told you to look away." Bob turns to his daughter, expecting to see tearful, puppy dog eyes. Instead, her features, set hard and fierce, remind him of Laura ready to kick someone's ass.

"Saabrina, you killed them?"

I punched a hole between the outside of the hull and the wall of the bridge. With a little help from me, the pressurized air in the compartment evacuated its contents.

"How big a hole?"

Wide enough to optimize airflow, narrow and jagged enough to shred…

"OK, Saabrina, enough, thank you." He takes Rebecca's hand. "We'll talk about this later."

Bob, I still don't have control of the ship. I'm also detecting fluctuations in the stasis pods. It could be collateral damage.

Bob takes a sip of water. "Let's get you some help. Can you connect me with one of the crew?"

I'm calling a phone in the galley.

Saabrina shifts the image to the galley. They hear the phone ring twice; a ghostly figure of a thin young man picks up the receiver. "Hey, Bridge, what the fuck is going on? We're getting kicked around down here and it smells like shit."

Such language. So much for respecting the chain of command.

"This is Sentinel Robert Foxen. I'm in a Saab off your port bow. Your bridge crew is dead. Now if you don't want to join them, you'll need to work with me. Understand?"

"Yes, I understand. What can I do?"

"Not so fast. First we have to take some confidence building steps. Tell me your name and position."

"Vants, deckhand and engineer's second mate."

"Well, Vants, deckhand and engineer's second mate, this will be your lucky day if you answer my questions truthfully and do what I say. What's in the stasis pods? Before you answer, remember I already know the answers and assume you do as well."

"Girls. Twenty-six girls."

"Very good. How many ships in your little fleet?'

There's a pause. "Three. Three ships including ours."

"Excellent." They watch the six other surviving crew members join Vants in the galley. "Now we're ready for your first assignment. Tell the others to get down on the deck facedown with their hands behind their heads." Vants gives the command, his hands waving at the others. They hear arguing and loud shouts. Some of the figures draw weapons; sparks flash on the screen. Three bodies crumple to the ground. "Vants, what's happening?"

"We had a small disagreement. We've reached a reasonable resolution."

"Good. Are you ready?"

"Yes."

Tell him to go to utility room two and to bring someone to help.

"Go to utility room two, take someone with you. Ask the other two to lay on the floor. And Vants, bring the phone; I'll give you further instructions when you get there."

Images from the ship gain more definition revealing details of the men and rooms around them. They watch Vants point to two men who promptly drop to the ground, face down, hands behind their heads. The third follows him to the utility room. "We're here. Now what?"

"My Saab is going to give you directions. I suggest you follow them carefully."

Remove the access panel from the rear bulkhead.

Vants and his partner walk to the back of the room and gingerly pull the panel from the wall. "Done."

Locate a white box in the lower right-hand corner.

"The MCU, I see it."

Good. Find relays three, five, and seven.

"Found them." Vants points to them.

Deactivate the relays in this order: five, seven, three. Then press the red reset button on the MCU.

"Resetting the MCU won't do anything; the system will fail-over to the back-ups."

Just do it.

"Whatever you say, lady. You're the boss." Vants pulls open three long blade switches, to Bob's surprise because it seems so old-timey, in the order Saabrina specified, then pokes at a small box in the control panel.

I'm in. Disabled the firewall and the anti-virus programs, now tracking down the control systems.

"Vants, you and your friend go back to the galley and lie down like the others. Got it?"

"Got it."

"Good."

Vants and his crewmate walk back to the galley and lie down.

OK, I'm in the navigation and drive systems. Oh, bloody hell, they're such cunning bastards.

"What, what?"

They've arranged a failsafe to prevent someone from out-side gaining control of the ship. The controls on the bridge must be operated by touch; I'm unable to operate them from the in-side, so to speak. The image shifts back to the bridge. An anime version of Saabrina in a blue sailor suit with fiery red hair and big green eyes waves at them.

Rebecca laughs. "I drew her like that back in college."

"I didn't know you drew her."

"She was right; she looks so cute in a sailor fuku. I wanted to go with something for an older kid, more college, like a blazer and a skirt." Rebecca admires her handiwork. "Ugh. I never got the chance to create a graphic novel about her. Maybe now, since I've got more time, I can."

"What do you mean more time?"

"Dad, I'll tell you later. Is she OK?"

I'm fine. They watch her run around the bridge, poking at controls, anime sweat drops falling from her forehead, her mouth forming a big oval with an X over it for curses when things don't go her way. Finally, they see an exhausted figure wipe her brow and smile at them. *There, that should do it.* The anime figure disappears. *I have control of the ship. I stabilized the stasis pods and sent the ship's database and the location of its two fleet mates back to DoSOPS.*

Bob taps the wheel. "Great job, Saabrina."

DoSOPS has a hospital ship standing by at the detention center.

"OK, let's send them. Wait, what about Vildakaya?"

Unfortunately, he survived his transit through the u-joints and is safely in his own pod. I've destroyed the travel tube; the ship is unpinned and ready to go. Saabrina circles the ship dropping buoys. Three minutes later, the spider ship vanishes.

Rebecca slumps in Saabrina's passenger seat, relieved and exhausted, happy they won, sad her friends are badly hurt. 'Shouldn't I be crying? Why am I not crying?' Her dad looks at ease and confident while talking to Saabrina. 'And Saabrina?' Her fury remains, the hard effort to keep it in check a little less needed for the moment. "Dad, can we follow the ship? I want to make sure my friends are OK."

"No, we have unfinished business in Geneva."

Chapter 22

JEAN LOUNGES ON HIS COUCH, UNABLE TO SLEEP, THE LIGHTS of Geneva bright enough to illuminate the contours of his darkened apartment. On the coffee table in front of him his mobile reads 1:43 A.M. Having sat there for hours, wordlessly adrift in thought, he can't decide whether to get up and go properly to bed or to continue to lie on the couch. Instead, he plays with the Gauloises cigarette in his right hand, twisting and turning it, watching bits of tobacco drop out onto his shirt and pants. It doesn't matter. He has no intention of smoking the foul thing; he keeps them around to show off. His fingers stop moving. The cigarette comes to a rest. Perhaps tonight, though, he should try one, it would be a good night to do so, but there's no smoking in his room and he does not have a match to light it. Popping the cigarette back into the pack, he tosses the pack onto the coffee table; it skitters to the edge of the wood, holds, and does not fall off. Jean smiles. His smile vanishes when he sees a young woman in the gloom warily observing him. Blinking twice does not make the visage go away.

"Je suis vraiment ici."

Jean jumps out of his seat. "You are not a phantom. You are real?"

"Although I would like to haunt you for the rest of your miserable days, unfortunately, I will not be able to do so."

The lights go on in Jean's room, blinding him. When his vision returns, he finds Rebecca Foxen standing next to a tall middle-aged man with graying hair. He looks familiar, as does the young woman, out of her party clothes and wearing a cardigan, jeans, and boots, who has now taken up position a few steps to their left, blocking any attempt to flee. His sleep-deprived brain finally puts names to faces: he knows a sentinel and his Saab have arrived.

"Bob, I'm sending a live feed as requested by DoSOPS."

"Good. So, this is Jean?"

"Yes, Dad. Why are we here?"

"We're in this room because Jean, who sent you to the restaurant, is not from around here. Jean, I'm Bob Foxen, Rebecca's father, and a sentinel." Bob points to Saabrina. "This is my partner, Saabrina. But Jean, you already knew that." Jean glances at his phone, puzzled.

Saabrina follows his gaze from the table back to Jean. "I disabled your alert." She snaps her fingers: the mobile buzzes twice before making a barfing sound.

"My apologies. I didn't recognize you in the flesh at first." Jean comes around the table to hug Rebecca.

She takes a half step back. "Dad, I don't understand. What's going on?"

Bob takes Rebecca's hand. "Jean's not human. He's wearing a compensator suit. It disguises his true form and makes him look like one of us." Saabrina beams an image of a cross between a humanoid bipedal and a wingless bee into Rebecca's head; she fights the sudden urge to gag, the memory of their near kiss making a lump in her throat. "He's from Eloka,

a beautiful garden world carefully kept by a race of bee people." Saabrina shivers. "Based on his physiognomy, Saabrina
believes he's a member of the royal household."

"I am a prince, to be exact."

Saabrina snorts. "There are hundreds like you."

Rebecca pulls her hand away from her father's. "I still
don't understand. Why is he here? What's going on?"

"Saabrina and I can guess, but he can explain it all more
quickly. And as a member of the royal family with diplomatic
immunity, he can tell us without fear of recourse. Jean, please
enlighten Rebecca, and the rest of us, if you would be so kind."

With a sour expression, Jean looks from Bob to Saabrina
and back again, searching their faces, closing his eyes to think.
A small smile returns to his face. "D'accord, let me tell you."
Holding his hands out, palms up, he addresses Rebecca. "Rebecca, you have to understand, I came here for the purest of
reasons—love, my love for science. On my world, although
I am a prince, because I lack your intellectual gifts, the gifts
required to lead a team of scientists, let alone participate in
some meaningful way, in a scientific endeavor, I'd be reduced
to a minor role, perhaps filing specimens or fetching coffee
or sweeping up for others. I was despondent. Then one day
it struck me: research on protected worlds, worlds like Earth,
is equivalent to that of my scientific past. It was so simple! I
could join a team on Earth doing, let's say, particle physics,
and stay ahead by simply following the progress of the science
in our history books, letting our long-dead scientists provide
the insight and the knowledge I needed to carry on. I wouldn't
make any great discoveries, but I'd learn how others did while
participating."

Saabrina crosses her arms. "So the dim bulb had a bright
idea."

Jean ignores Saabrina. "After some research, I chose Earth as the most suitable place. It was illegal to come here, so I didn't tell my family where I went; they think I'm on a long-term pleasure cruise, out of sight and out of mind. And for a while it worked beautifully, first in Urbana, then here, at CERN."

Bob interjects "Until Vildakaya found you?"

Jean becomes crestfallen. "He said he'd report me to my mother, the Queen, and I'd have to go back. All I needed to do was find an appropriate girl for him to recruit for his business. As I was in Geneva and didn't want trouble here, I sent him to Urbana for Sachita." He notices Rebecca turning grim. "Rebecca, please believe me, I had no idea what he actually wanted or what he was going to do. I swear."

"When did you find out, you bastard? When did you learn?" Bob holds his daughter back as Jean cringes.

"Vildakaya told me after he… took Sachita. Made me watch a video. He said I was one of them now and I couldn't get out. He demanded I produce another girl when he returned. I didn't know what to do. Before I arrived, my contacts on Madison had tipped me to the identity of the local sentinel. It took me a while to piece together you were his daughter and," he points to Saabrina, "she must be his Saab. Providence provided me with a plan to extract myself from this miserable situation: if I sent both of you, the Saab would capture Vildakaya and you would be safe. But she did not reappear and Vildakaya demanded, so I sent Juliette because she was going away anyway."

Rebecca turns away, putting her head on Bob's shoulder; pulling her close, he rubs her back.

"I'm sorry, Rebecca, I'm truly sorry. Did you find her and Sachita?"

Saabrina uncrosses her arms. "Yes. They're on their way to hospital." She points to Rebecca's bare wrist. "You suggested she take the Archduke's bracelet off?"

"Yes, the stones are an ancient mark of the Imperial family of the Greater Noble Houses, warning those who know of the wearer's protection. Vildakaya would have recognized them and run back to kill me."

"Bob, his description matches what Eddie told us about the bracelet." Taking the bracelet out of her pocket, she wraps it around Rebecca's wrist.

Bob turns Rebecca to face Jean. She stares at him blankly as Bob speaks. "Jean, thank you for telling us your story. I guess asking you to accompany us to Madison is useless?"

"Yes."

"You'll be returning home to Eloka?"

Jean smiles. "I don't think so. There are other worlds like Earth to disappear into."

"Dad, he's got to go to Madison to face what he did."

"Rebecca, I can't make him go, he has immunity."

Rebecca looks at Jean. Jean continues to smile at her. She looks left to Saabrina who remains motionless, watching Rebecca. 'Saabrina?' Hearing nothing, she tries willing her to do something, anything. Instead, Saabrina stands still, her boots rooted to the apartment's parquet floor. Rebecca looks more closely. Fire burns in Saabrina's eyes. The fire spreads, running down her arms, lighting the floor, engulfing the room, engulfing Rebecca in flames, kindling a fire in her own eyes. The blaze ebbs, the room clears. Jean still stands in front of her, her dad to her right, Saabrina left, neither doing anything.

Her own rage burning free, Rebecca stiffens, clenching her fists. 'Dad can't help and Saabrina can't help. I'm on my own. I don't need them.' Jean smiles at her. 'God, I hate his smile. Screw Jean, screw the fucking LHC. I can go home and stay at dad's house until I sort out my life because I'll only be living there. It's not like I'm going back to high school. It's not like I'm going to be a kid again.' Rebecca watches Saabrina's eyes dart ever so slightly from herself to Jean: once, twice, three times. 'I can do this.' Thwok! Rebecca's swift kick to Jean's crotch drops him to the floor.

Grabbing his daughter before she strikes again, Bob deadpans "Holy crap, Saabrina, my daughter has assaulted his royal highness. Please check to make sure he's OK."

Saabrina kneels, her fingers probing Jean's neck while he clutches his crotch in agony. "He appears to be in pain. There's nothing I can do for him here and we can't turn him over to a Swiss hospital. We should take him to Madison for immediate medical attention."

Jean tries to groan "No."

"Agreed. Please get the prince ready for safe transport."

"Yes, Sentinel Foxen." Saabrina touches a control hidden on Jean's neck. Briefly, his human form gives way to reveal the Eloki underneath before transforming into a travel golf bag with wheels. Saabrina pops the handle off the floor and hands it to Bob. "We can wheel him downstairs and drop him into my boot."

Bob takes Rebecca by the hand. "Come along, sweetie, you're coming with us to Madison. You'll have to tell some important people what happened. And, on the way there you need to tell me what's really going on in your life."

· · ·

On the flight to Madison, Rebecca finally opens up to Bob about the trouble at the LHC, losing her job, and having to move back in with him. Finished, she slumps in her seat and closes her eyes. From experience, he knows she's faking sleep and simply doesn't want to talk anymore.

"She isn't pretending; when she closed her eyes, I put her to sleep. She had a long day and I thought a little rest would allow her to better compose herself for whatever reception awaits us on Madison."

"Good thinking. Is she OK?"

"Besides being knackered, she's a little dazed from her adventure and relieved she could tell you everything."

"You knew already?"

"Of course, we're best friends."

"How about you?"

"What do you mean?"

"Confronting Vildakaya in Geneva must have been seriously unpleasant. And not easy with Rebecca there."

"It wasn't."

"Look, how did you miss him when he came into the bar?" Bob fights not to raise his voice.

There's a long pause. "I screwed up. I was so focused on behaving like Rebecca, I stopped paying attention."

"You were 'single-tracking' with her?" He glances over at Rebecca's sleeping form.

Another pause. "Yes. When "Call Me" started to play, I snapped out of it. I spotted the travel tube with the capsule below the floor, the club empty of patrons and staff, and Vildakaya and his crew. I'm sorry, Bob, I'm truly sorry, I should never have let Rebecca fall into so much danger."

"You didn't know they would be there. As I said, safest place for her is with you. But come on, Saabrina, you're better than that. You need to remember who you are and what you do for a living. You're not a twenty-something girl out partying even when you are a twenty-something girl out partying." Bob stops for a second to think. "Did that make any sense?"

"Yes. I know what you meant. You're right." She knows Bob's rightfully angry. She can't believe how clouded her judgment had been. 'How could I miss those hoodlums when they were right in front of me?' Worse, she knows what he'll ask soon, if not next, and she won't have a good answer.

"I worry about you. You had a nasty fight with Vildakaya's ship. You did great, but I always worry about you when you get deep inside those systems."

"I'm fine, Bob. Thank you for worrying about me, but you really don't have to."

"Yeah, right, like I'm not going to worry about you. *Are* you fine? I gotta ask—they were on Earth twice before and we missed them both times? How the fuck did that happen?"

Whaam! Bob had zeroed in. Feeling fear and guilt, she scrambles for an answer. "Better equipment on this ship? The first time we were in Mexico, the second off-world looking for travel tubes elsewhere." She closes her eyes. 'All true, but, still, how did I miss the blasted thing?'

"But their damn tube had been poking out of Earth for weeks, like a straw out of an orange."

She mutters "More like a translucent thread on a house-sized beach ball."

"Seriously?!"

"I don't know, Bob, again, I'm sorry, I don't know how I missed it. I wasn't looking here. And FedSci missed the travel tube, too." Saabrina winces. 'Yikes, did I both cop out and throw FedSci under the bus? What's wrong with me?'

"FedSci wasn't sent to look for those fucking things. FedSci wasn't right there for days at a time. Are you sure you're OK?"

"Yes, I'm fine. I'm bloody alright. I fucking missed it. I'm not perfect. You're not perfect either."

"That I know. Anything in particular you wish to discuss?"

"No." Although she possesses an extensive list of items, including the thing in Mexico she hasn't been able to ask about, she decides not to add more gas to the fire. 'In any event, I need to own my mistakes.'

They continue in silence. Bob doesn't feel like turning on the radio. Saabrina has him flummoxed. 'She's never screwed up like this before, missing Vildakaya, missing the travel tube, missing Sachita and Juliette's abductions. Did she miss other travel tubes? No, she's too good, and we had double-checked a couple of planets to be sure. Only Earth for some reason. Is there something wrong with her? I'll have to talk to someone on Madison. Maybe I should have had her checked out after our voyage into unreality. Damn, it still weirds me out to say "unreality." Or is this from the trip to Mexico? Something residual from the little girl hologram? Has she been behaving a bit too human over the last few weeks? If she heard me say "behaving too human" she'd kick my ass. Maybe she just missed it, she wasn't looking on Earth and the tubes are hard to spot—Saabra had missed it on two visits although she had not been on the tube hunt so she wasn't looking—or maybe this ship had better equipment, or was smarter around Earth because a sentinel is based there and Vildakaya had been a cagey bastard. That's a lot of maybes. What did she say? "I'm not perfect?" Saabrina not perfect? She's right, I'm certainly not perfect, yet I always expect her to be. And Rebecca getting caught up in this, these assholes wanting her and almost taking her away? Maybe I'm not angry with Saabrina; maybe I'm really angry with myself. Was it my fault, did I make her a target? Did being a sentinel put her at risk?' A wave of nausea tinged anxiety runs over him.

"No, you did not put her at risk."

The wave breaks, leaving behind residual anger with himself. "You're not supposed to be listening in."

"One, you left the link open. Two, I knew where you were going to go and wanted to make sure you would be OK when you got there."

"Thanks. I guess you're right."

"Of course I'm right. You should simply stipulate to such in our conversations. Now, Laura would have kicked your ass for this."

"Yes, she would have. I spent a lot of time hiding some of the stuff Rebecca and I got up to from Laura, not that she didn't find out in the end."

"I know."

"You know? How do you know?"

"From your and Rebecca's memories. How many misadventures did you bring Rebecca on?" Saabrina plays back a ten best list of Bob with Rebecca, sometimes fun leading to tears leading back to fun. "Scrapes from riding her bike and hiking or playing a little too aggressively in the playground, falls from taking too tough trails whilst skiing, all those burgers when she should have had salads? Did you ever tell Laura about the rocket launches? Diet Coke and Mentos? Misusing her home chem set? Neat trick getting her clothes in and out of the laundry before Laura got home. Wasn't your refrain 'Don't tell mom'?"

"I guess so. Part of what a dad does."

"And rightly so. Toughens them up, teaches them grit. Of course, Laura did the same in her own way."

"What do you mean?"

All he gets from her is a knowing smile.

Chapter 23

THEY ARE GREETED AT THE FOREIGN OFFICE ON MADISON BY a medical team, who swiftly roll Jean away. Dallas and Austin survey the threesome from behind the team; Bob and Saabrina in their work attire, and Rebecca still in her party clothes, slightly disheveled and a little worse for wear. Austin, their liaison with the Foreign Office, Bob expected. Dallas, Austin's boss, means their visit to Geneva had probably created a major diplomatic incident. Bob braces for Dallas to rip him apart. Instead, she rushes to Rebecca's side and takes her in her arms. "My child, it must have been awful, awful. Come with me. How about a nice mug of hot chocolate?" The site of Rebecca holding onto the well-dressed green woman with very white hair gives him a momentary pause; that his daughter doesn't seem to notice astonishes him.

As Dallas guides Rebecca to the elevators, Austin, Saabrina, and Bob fall in behind. Austin appears surprisingly quiet to Bob. 'What's the word of the day? Regi-mal? Does such a word exist? Will he mention the Foxen family's apparent problem with royalty?' Bob turns to Austin. "Hey, Austin, good to see you. Sorry for the mess with the Royal House of Eloka."

"What? Oh, the Eloki. No worries." Getting into the elevator, Austin focuses on the door.

Saabrina pokes Austin. *You're smitten.*

'What?'

You're smitten with Rebecca. It's written all over your face and your bio readings.

'Smitten?! You wouldn't know smitten if it jumped up and bit you on the nose.'

Harumph. Saabrina fights the urge to kick Austin in the shins.

'I'm simply concerned for the welfare of my colleague's daughter.'

Saabrina rolls her eyes. *Right.*

They exit the elevator and make their way to Dallas' tchotchke-strewn office, Austin detouring to the department's kitchen, and take seats at her conference table, Dallas and Bob flanking Rebecca. A few minutes later, Austin places a hot chocolate in front of Rebecca before sitting across the table. Soon Eddie and Lerner join the crowd, all enjoying hot chocolate or something with more kick to keep them awake while Bob and Saabrina review the end of the travel tube hunt. Bob feels the length of his day when it strikes him Rebecca didn't notice Eddie is his natural color blue.

Rebecca finishes her hot chocolate. "This was so good. Thank you, Ms. Dallas."

"Technically, I'm Secretary Dallas, but please call me Dallas, Rebecca."

Rebecca nods. "Thank you. Dallas, do I have to go to jail?"

"For kicking the Prince? No. I spoke to the Queen. She's a good friend. She has daughters, too, and was not at all pleased by her son's conduct. We sent her Saabrina's recording of the scene and her comment to me was 'What took the little one with the ringlets so long?' I'm afraid whatever she has in store for him at home will be far worse than the punishment he would have received here." Dallas smiles at Rebecca.

Rebecca smiles back.

Lerner leans over to her. "Our best doctors here on Madison are seeing to your friends along with the other girls."

"Mr. Lerner, will I be able to see them? I really want to spend time with them, make sure they're OK."

"We'll get you over to the hospital as soon as they advise us that we can. In the meantime, get some rest, go do a little sight-seeing, have dinner on DoSOPS at some of our good local restaurants. I'm sure Austin could recommend the latest and greatest places."

Austin gives a slight bow. "I would be delighted to."

Saabrina suppresses a snort.

"Sweetie, you'll stay with me at my apartment once we finish today's meetings. It's a one bedroom, but I can sleep on the couch while you're here on Madison."

"Nonsense, Bob, she'll come now and stay with Brenda and me. She can have her own room and Brenda and Saabra will take her shopping for clothes. No offense, Saabrina."

"None taken, Eddie."

"Rebecca, my dear, what do you say? Brenda would be delighted."

"Dad, is it…"

"Go with Eddie. You'll make Brenda's day. I'll catch up with you later."

Eddie stands. "Come along, Rebecca. We'll get you some rest, then you'll start a fresh new day." Rebecca and the other participants rise. She gives her dad and Saabrina both long hugs, waves goodbye, and leaves with Eddie.

Lerner addresses Dallas. "Do you need Bob and Saabrina? I'd like to get them back to DoSOPS to start the post-mission review."

"No, the only foreign entanglement has been dealt with. They can go." She turns to Bob and Saabrina. "Great work you two, shutting down an interstellar criminal ring. The thought of what they were doing makes me sick to my stomach. Now I'm going to go call my daughters and granddaughters to make sure they're safe and sound."

"Thank you for straightening out things between my daughter and the Eloki."

"Please, that was—what do you say—a no brainer? Wait, "no brainer" was a terrible thing for me to say under the circumstances."

"It's OK. Thank you, again." Bob shakes Dallas and Austin's hands while Saabrina gives a surprised Dallas a hug. On the way out with Lerner, Austin ignores Saabrina.

"Bob, can we take your Saab back to DoSOPS?"

"Sure, Boss."

Airborne, with fluffy clouds promising snow above and the capital city below, Lerner gets comfortable in Saabrina's passenger seat. "Saabrina take your time; we have a few things to discuss before we get back to the throngs at the office."

I'll do some loops over the countryside, Director.

"Perfect. Again, Bob, Saabrina, great job."

Thank you, Director.

"Yes, thank you. We were doing our best, but if it weren't for Jean's horrific plan we wouldn't have caught these guys so fast."

"Has your Saab rubbed off on you? Take the compliment and stick with it in front of the press and Congress. Speaking of which, your favorite congresswoman would like to see you."

"Oy gevalt, of course she would. I bet she's feeling pretty good from what Eddie told me about Gogolak."

Bob, what happened? Saabrina feigns surprise in order not to get caught having snooped before.

'I'll tell you later.' He tries not to giggle when she dives into his memories, him thinking she's viewing his beer with Eddie of a few hours ago, which now feels like weeks; her doing a quick review of what he knows of Rebecca's previous boyfriends, with particular focus on those rightfully described as smitten, although she doubts Bob would know such things.

"She's happy with her new allies. We'll have to see if she cares about the Constitution. Time will tell. We just have to keep at it."

"I know, Boss, I know. So, when do I go and how long do I have to stay before she stands me up?"

"Day after tomorrow at nine a.m. She promised the minority leader to see you promptly; with respect to her previous treatment of officials from the Executive Branch, she knows she's on thin ice. Oh, and same rules as last time, so don't bring or link to your Saab. Sorry, Saabrina."

No need to be sorry, Director, I understand. She slips through a low cloud. 'Why would I want to be anywhere near that horrid woman? Whilst Bob meets with Tuchis, I can visit a few people in the animal rights movement and read them the riot act.' She pauses. "'Read them the riot act'? Where did I pick up that turn of phrase? Bob? No, Laura, Laura speaking to a teenage Rebecca about something that greatly displeased her, some illicit conduct with a boy.' She can see the scene from Rebecca's perspective, then after a quick search, from Bob's, each version tinged with the emotions they experienced at the time. Triangulating between the two, she steps into Laura's place and experiences the incident from her viewpoint, shouting at Rebecca while Bob stood there silently with arms crossed. Saabrina halts the simulation, scared, feeling like a trespasser in a private graveyard. Her body tingles as if struck by hailstones. She concentrates on Lerner and Bob.

"I'll be there, Elliot. I'll do my best to represent DoSOPS and not cause any problems."

"I know you will."

Sir, do you want me to take us to DoSOPS now?

"No, Saabrina, not yet, I'd like to talk to Bob about Rebecca."

"I thought she was in the clear. Are you upset about me bringing her to Madison?"

"No, not in the least, given the circumstances. We know she knew about your work and us, which was a risk we were willing to take. We also know Saabrina has taken her for more than a few off-world rides."

Sir, if I may…

"It's OK, Saabrina. You two are besties and I'm perfectly fine with that. It's a good thing, both for you and for her." Lerner chuckles. "You two remind me of what my daughter Iris and her friend Caitlin used to get up to a long time ago. Anyway, taking Rebecca here after today's events was a natural progression and the right thing to do." Lerner looks out his window. "Everything looks so gray with the leaves off the trees. Maybe the snow tomorrow will give us a more cheerful wintertime look." Another pause. "Can you swing us around the ski areas? I love watching the skiers."

Yes, sir. In an instant, Saabrina begins doing loops over the big mountains in the north, their runs populated with skiers and boarders enjoying fresh powder and blue skies with a few clouds painted on for effect. She wants to dive down and join them.

"Thanks, Saabrina. Bob, you ski with Eddie, right?"

"I do. We haven't made it up here this year, but hope to soon. How about you?"

"Eddie and I've been known to slip out of the office for a lunchtime run or two. You know, he's taken the Archduke skiing on your Alps."

"Yep. And the Archduke brought him to the Karelinkas, no less. I thought only upper echelon Imperials were permitted on those mountains?"

"They make exceptions for special guests. And we do too, like the Archduke on Earth. Exceptions for the exceptional, like Rebecca. Look, Bob, as I said before, you did the right thing bringing Rebecca to Madison. And better yet, it provides an opportunity for us to discuss her future."

"Her future? You mean how soon she has to go back to Earth?"

"I'm talking about a little longer than that."

"Boss, sorry, I don't understand. I guess I'm a little tired."

"I heard she's out of a job."

"News travels fast. She only now told me about the LHC shut down on our trip to Madison."

"After Daear, we started monitoring high-level physics experiments on multiple worlds, focusing on those programs that had begun to demonstrate odd problems. We wanted to see if there was a correlation between them and the travel tubes. Based on your work we found nothing to tie them together. However, as a side benefit, I learned about the issues with the LHC and suspected your daughter's project might be canceled."

"So how does this affect Rebecca? Are you telling me you know people at Princeton who can take her back sooner than they plan to?" Although Bob smiles at Lerner, Saabrina feels him tensing up.

"I'm good, but I can't make a call to Princeton. Bob, I have a confession to make: we've been following Rebecca's progress for years. Brenda and Eddie called our attention to her when she was in middle school."

"You've been watching Rebecca… for years?" Bob stops to think. "Was it her you were after, not me, all this time?"

"A bit, a teeny tiny little bit. Our interest in her certainly helped your case to become a sentinel."

Bob sharply draws in his breath. "Hmmm."

"I didn't mean to pull the rug out from under you. You were a top choice and have become one of my best and I thank Eddie every time I see him for bringing you in. But, Rebecca has been on our radar for some time."

"I'm sorry, it's been made clear to me how relatively backwards and dimwitted humans are." He hears Saabrina snort. "Now you're telling me you're interested in my daughter's career? What am I not getting?"

"Bob, think about two bell curves superimposed on each other with the tops of the bells slightly offset." Lerner moves his hands to help sketch a mental picture for Bob; Saabrina transforms his motions into a graph that floats before the two men. "If the X-axis is IQ increasing from left to right and the Y measures population, the top of Earth's bell, this blue one here, is slightly to the left of the average Union planet, which Saabrina appears to be showing in yellow, less so because of genetics and more so because of education and enhancements. However, the tails approach zero in the same places on both curves. And in the tails you find black swans." Lerner points to the right tail. "Your daughter is a black swan swimming in the right tail." An anime black swan wearing a *Doctor Who* t-shirt appears at the extreme right of the chart and honks at Bob.

'Saabrina, did you know about this?'

No. She's going to have to have a word with Saabra about her big sister keeping secrets from her little one.

"Elliot, what are you proposing?"

"With your support, we'd like to ask her to come study here." Pinpricks of perspiration break out across Bob's body. "Hear me out, Bob." Lerner grasps Bob's arm; the pinpricks momentarily abate. "She will undoubtedly make some contribution to Earth's physics, but the machines she needs to make the most of her potential will not exist on your world for at least another fifty years. We want to see what she sees, to go where she goes; we know she'd benefit most from being here with us."

In his left hand, Bob finds a handkerchief provided by Saabrina and wipes the sweat from his brow. "She wouldn't be the stupid kid on the team?"

"Far from it. We, I mean one of the universities, would quickly bring her up to speed, and then she'll fly. Trust me, her teammates will be in awe of her."

Bob pinches the bridge of his nose and sighs. "There's a price to pay, isn't there?"

"She'd have to say goodbye to her life on Earth. Other than the odd trips to visit family and friends, she'd have to stay away. What you call the 'Prime Directive' will be imposed on her and her newfound knowledge."

"Elliot, that's a big ask."

"I know. I know we're asking a lot of someone so young, but I, and many others, believe the opportunity far outweighs what she would lose. And asking her to give up so much is why we wanted your support before we go talk to her. Bob, you'll consider giving it?"

"Let me think about it. Give me a couple of days, it's a lot to take in."

"Thank you, take your time, your consideration is all I can ask. OK, Saabrina, please take us to DoSOPS."

She wants to say 'Oh joy, Bob, we're off to DoSOPS for endless rounds of lessons-learned meetings.' Instead, she asks *Bob, are you OK with this?*

Bob can't answer. He silently watches Madison speed by on their way to the office.

Chapter 24
The Very Bad Day

AWAKENING FROM AN AFTERNOON NAP, SAABRINA CONTEM-plated Bob's knackered form lying next to her on Palapa 11's lounge. 'Time out whilst I think up some more deviltry. First, though, am I hungry?' She patted her tummy, which emitted a low growl. 'Yes, a bit peckish. Chicken fingers? Had them for lunch and dinner the last three days, probably have them for dinner tonight. Definitely no tacos.' She had howled "Yucky!" at Bob the first time he made her eat them. "Sweetie, they're delicious Mexican food. You'll love 'em." The slimy tomato bits in the salsa had made her gag. Two bites later she had puked all over his feet.

Saabrina smiled. 'How about chocolate cake, chocolate milk, chocolate candy sweets, or chocolate ice cream? Ooh, yummy.' She could probably sell Bob on chocolate ice cream as a nice afternoon treat that wouldn't spoil dinner. 'Or my favorite, a Pink Panther? Time for a swim over to the swim-up bar?'

Taking him swimming brought her back to which game should she play with Bob. The fun she had with him over the last couple of days: stopping short on a run to the pool and watching him go toppling into the water ('I've quite nicely gotten this body's dynamics down'), playing how long can she say 'no' to going potty before dashing for the bathroom (extra points for fidgeting and pulling on her bathing suit while Bob squirms), crayoning his daddy magazine to make it more interesting ('the pictures are so dreary'), and testing the effect of ice from a beer bucket on his back ("Daddy, you looked so hot"). She'd quickly learned not to play "Look Daddy, could she be my new mommy?" based on his surprisingly negative response, even to the women with great sales assets she had identified. She loved piggy-back rides, fireman carries, and rides on his shoulders. 'No, I'll play the carry me card later when we schlep back to our room.'

Oh, and rides on Seabiscuit the Seahorse, Bob swimming from one end of the pool to the other while his daughter, and sometimes a couple of her friends, straddled his back and giggled away. And jumps and flips and hops and dips and dives from his shoulders into the water, over and over and over again with him popping her back up, resetting her position, her tumbling down with a big splash, all while screaming "Daddy, Daddy, Daddy watch me" to make sure she had his full attention.

'Perhaps I should entertain him with another joke? He had laughed through all twenty minutes of the last one, although he didn't seem to get it no matter how hard I had tried to tell it.'

Jumping up on the lounge to look around the pool, she didn't see the resort staff playing games. 'Must be too late in the day.' She had made Bob play every game in and out of the pool the staff could think of. Yesterday, they had so much fun dancing the chicken dance. "Do it again Daddy, do it again Daddy!" had become her rallying cry. In the kiddie area, she saw kids watching TV. 'Boring. Must also be too late for arts and crafts.' Every day she presented him with a new objet d'art requiring bounteous praise, careful transport, and permanent storage lest his small one throw a fit. This morning she had given him her greatest creation to date—a birdhouse made from popsicle sticks. She had discovered the joy of covering Bob in finger paint when he tried to clean her, which she felt effectively brought out the essence of his primitive nature, until he had learned to carry her at arm's length to the nearest pool shower to wash her off.

She flopped back down again, resting her back against Bob. 'Perhaps I'll stick with my favorite, a swim around the pools and the Lazy River and get a Pink Panther at the swim-up bar.'

Saabrina was about to poke Bob in the butt and announce she's bored when he turned over, tickled her, and said "Let's go for a swim." He flipped her giggling body over his shoulder and began marching to the pool.

"Daddy, I'm hungry."

"Nice to meet you, Hungry. This is Mr. Pool." He carried her into the water and they started to swim to the bar.

Back from their swim, Bob watched Rebecca play with Marlene's granddaughters. Bob loved every minute with her, all the more so since she had begun taking naps on schedule along with baths. He tried to balance his time with her, giving her freedom to play with the other kids while reserving blocks of time for himself. If he was getting his six-year-old daughter back for a week, he wanted to maximize his time with her. Plus, she was a blast to be with. She had started to play with other children, experiencing some confusion at first, gaining confidence with time. He kept an eye on her when she played, often hanging with the other kids' parents.

Marlene's crew had nicknamed him "Old Dad." Marlene pointed to Rebecca and the girls blasting the boys with super soakers. "Well, Old Dad, your daughter is a real pistol."

"Thanks, Marlene."

"My grandsons usually cow their sisters, but she stands right up to those two, keeps them on their lil' old toes. Startin' to give the girls some fight." Marlene looked both ways to make sure she is out of earshot of her brood. "'Scuse my French, but she doesn't take any shit, does she?"

"No, she doesn't." Bob smiled to himself. Her toughness came a little more from the Saabrina side than the Rebecca side. Rebecca wasn't a wimp, but growing up as an only child she hadn't known how to handle aggressive kids and had come to him whimpering about so and so being mean. Her first summer at sleepaway camp had cured the problem; at Temple after summer camp had ended, he had watched in amazement as his squirt of an eight-year-old daughter had pinned Dick's son Jack to the floor after he had annoyed her one too many times. Even the rabbi had given her a thumb's up.

'Now if Laura could be here too, it would be perfect. Well, maybe not perfect, but pretty good.' He couldn't fool himself, even on their best trips there had been frustration, unhappiness, and fights. They were Jewish professionals with fully formed individual psyches after all. 'How would I ever have explained spending a week in Mexico with a holographic approximation of our daughter played by my business partner, a transdimensional AI from 'Sweden'? Maybe Laura had imbibed, or been contaminated, by enough of my sci-fi TV and movie watching to get it. Or maybe she'd be freaked out by either the hologram or my career choice, now way off from the more sober arc of finance, or both.' He looked at Rebecca playing with Marlene's grandkids. 'No, she'd grab her, snuggle her, never let her go.'

.   .   .

That afternoon, he placed Rebecca, neatly dressed, post-bath, in front of the TV.

"Sweetie, I'm going to take a shower. After, we'll go to the Fiesta Mexicana tonight." She looked very pretty in her sundress. "As I promised, since you took a bath very nicely, you can watch TV until I'm ready."

"Yay!" She held up the remote. "Can I change channels?"

"You don't want to watch the cartoon channel?"

"My shows are on a different channel. Can I? Can I?"

'Her 'shows'? When did she have time to get 'her shows'? What's wrong with Looney Tunes and *The Jetsons*? Anyway, how much trouble could she get into with afternoon Mexican TV?' Bob shrugged. "Sure, knock yourself out."

When he returned to the living room showered and dressed, he didn't see her. He was about to call out when he spied the top of her head peeking out from behind the couch. Quietly maneuvering around the living room, he found her going up on tippy toes to watch something before crouching back down; on the TV, a creature with an eyestalk shouted "Exterminate." Rebecca dropped behind the couch again. 'Crap, I'm not going to get any sleep tonight.'

.   .   .

Home from Fiesta Mexicana and some bad mariachis who performed far below the Royal Aztec's usual standards, Rebecca's preparations for sleep took extra-long. He had thought he had answered enough questions about monsters on sci-fi TV shows at dinner with help from the teenage fangirls they had befriended at the party, but a zillion more had followed while she got into her PJs and brushed her teeth. He'd finally gotten her into bed and now found himself back on monster patrol after an eighteen-year hiatus.

"Are dere any monsters under de bed?" Rebecca lay under her covers, closely surrounded by a phalanx of stuffed animals.

Getting down on his knees, Bob checked under the bed. "No monsters here, sweetie."

"De closet, Daddy?"

Bob made a show of thoroughly checking the closet, then opened all the dresser drawers for good measure. "No monsters."

"Did you sweep the perimeter?"

"The perimeter?"

"De bathroom?" There was a long yawn with outstretched arms, a good sign.

Bob went into the bathroom, flushed the toilet, considered making a drowning monster sound, then thought better of it. "No monsters here." He came back into her room and was about to announce 'I declare this a monster free zone' when he saw she had rolled over onto her side clutching Muffin Traveldog and fallen asleep. Leaning down, he kissed her forehead and left the room.

Saabrina ran barefoot in her pajamas across a green field. 'Where is my pink pony friend?' She wanted to play a game with her and to brush her pretty white mane. Her pink friend had giggled when she brushed her mane. There were no ponies around. She knew they were here, she felt they were here, in the back of her mind, somewhere behind her, but they were missing. 'Are they hiding? Maybe they are playing hide and seek.' She covered her eyes with the crook of her elbow and counted down from ten: "Two, one, zero, ready or not here I come!"

When she uncovered her eyes, she saw fluffy white sheep wandering onto the field, eating grass. 'Do I go over and pet them?' Behind the sheep, two small furry monsters jumped up and down, yelling at them, taunting them, poking them with long sticks. "Don't be mean to those sheep," she shouted at the little monsters. But the monsters herded the sheep into a spiral around her. At first the sheep walked slowly, then faster and faster, their feet sparking as they touched the ground, eyes glowing red, their white fur becoming a blur of crackling static. She fell to the ground. She couldn't move. The sheep spun into a tornado of buzzing electric snow. A blinding white flash turned the snow red, the tornado transforming into a huge bird soaring into the air, a bird belching out flames like a dragon. BOOM BOOM BOOM. Saabrina screamed.

The first flash of lightning woke Bob before the peal of thunder echoed through the room. Opening the curtains wide, he sat on the corner of the bed to enjoy the show. The lights of the Royal Aztec faintly brightened the room. With a white blast, lightning illuminated the entire resort. He saw wind lashing the palm trees and rain pouring down in short, gray squalls. Between the booms, he enjoyed the sound of the rain on the window, of the water running in torrents down the buildings' sides, and the clatter of the palm fronds. Thunder followed a flash seconds later; the storm was on top of them. He heard a yell followed by the swift slaps of little bare feet on the stone floor. 'Strange, nothing wakes Rebecca up.' As he turned to run to Rebecca, she came tearing into the room. Getting down on one knee, he swept her shaking body into his arms.

"Bob, it's a Firebird. There's a Firebird." She was in a frenzy, breathing hard, fumbling with words.

"It's only lightning and thunder." He held her tight, trying to get her to stop shaking.

"A Firebird. It's here. It's here. It's here."

He gave her another squeeze, then released her, moving her back to look in her eyes. "Saabrina?"

"There were sheep and they were running around and they became all white and there were flames and there was a dragon bird that made booms. I was there and now it's here, here."

"You had a bad dream. They're called nightmares."

"I was in a field wid mean sheep and I fell down and couldn't move."

"You didn't go anywhere. You were asleep in your bed, dreaming of a field with sheep. Dreaming. Kids and adults dream when they sleep; it's normal."

"Dreams?"

"They feel like adventures that take you somewhere. Sometimes they're fun, and sometimes they're scary. Scary ones are called nightmares."

"It's not real?"

"No, it was not real. They can feel real though."

"Do you dream?"

"Yes, I just had one now of funny people playing a silly song." He sighed. 'Or not playing a song—they weren't playing anything, more like screwing around with instruments they had randomly picked up.' Keeping mum, he decided not to give her more to worry about.

A flash of lightning, thunder. She blinked at him in the white light, then hugged him tightly, pressing her head into his shoulder. "Daddy, the monsters are here!"

'Ahh. Rebecca's fully back.' He lifted her up and carried her to the window. "It's a thunderstorm, see, wind and rain and lightning. When the lightning strikes, it makes a sound called thunder. You know that."

"It's not monsters?" She didn't sound convinced.

"No. Come on, I'll make us some hot chocolate. That will make us feel better." He carried her into the living area and turned on the lights. Plopping her on the kitchen counter, he went about fixing the hot chocolate.

"Daddy, you sure it's not monsters?"

"I'm sure, because of the treaty."

"De treaty?"

"Yes, years ago the gods of the Royal Aztec, you know the people painted in the murals and in the sculptures all over this place?"

"The funny looking ones wid de fehders?"

"Yes, those. They were in a great war with the monsters. Neither side was winning, so both sides were losing."

"It was a tie?"

"Yes. So, they sat down and made a treaty to not fight anymore, and that's why the Royal Aztec is protected from monsters."

She smiled. "Lightning and dunder. Just a big storm. I knew dat."

"See, I knew you knew that."

Then she grew concerned again. "What about when we go home?"

"As the owner of a timeshare of the Royal Aztec you are protected by the Royal Aztec gods from monsters. It's one of the best parts of being an owner here." With a smile, he magically presented a mug of hot chocolate to his daughter.

•   •   •

The next day Bob lazed on the comfy white lounge of Palapa 11, watching Rebecca play. A rough game of pool volleyball with her on his shoulders had left him exhausted. Perhaps, he wondered, demonstrating to his teammates that "Old Dad" still had some fight in him may not have been the wisest idea, particularly after an extra-long perambulation around the pools followed by the usual stop at the swim-up bar. Drinking a Miami Vice, a Pink Panther spiked with rum, may not have helped things either, but he had grown confident enough to believe some alcohol intake would not hinder his responsibilities as a father of a six-year-old daughter. 'Anyway, it's Mexico, and who doesn't drink in Mexico? Compared to Marlene's beer-swilling crew, I'm practically a teetotaler. And the game had been totally worthwhile, particularly setting up Rebecca to spike the ball right by Kyle—or was that Ryan?—to win the game. She really has those two boys' numbers.'

Through half-open eyes he watched the three of them play some game with a ball. They formed a rotating triangle, the boys switching positions with her, tossing the ball back and forth, working along the lazy river. He smiled. 'It's so nice having my little girl back; it's also very weird not hearing Saabrina.' His head was his own and it felt lonely. Ryan tossed the ball to Kyle. A beautiful woman walked by in a bikini. He could almost hear his pal Dick, leader of the biker dudes and forever trying to get Bob out on a date, say 'Hot babes and MILFs, Bobby, hot babes and MILFs, now go use Rebecca as bait. They'll dig her.' Kyle tossed the ball to Rebecca; when she threw the ball to Ryan, Kyle ran to a new spot. 'The boys must have taught her the game. Rebecca as bait. Hot babes and MILFs walking on by. Dick and his endless quest for me to get action.' Ryan tossed the ball to Kyle while Rebecca relocated. 'Action is not going to happen on this trip, one, because action is not what this trip is about, and, two, there are no single hot babes and MILFs around. They're all pair-bonded. All with someone else. No singles at the Royal Aztec.' Kyle tossed the ball to Rebecca. 'Except me. No Laura. She was once the hot babe in the bikini. Then the MILF. Maybe I shouldn't have had a Miami Vice and stuck with another Pink Panther.' He closed his eyes.

Reopening them, he watched Rebecca toss the ball to Ryan. 'How did I let Rebecca get so far away?' The kids kept rotating, moving down the lazy river. Their movements roused something buried deep inside Old Dad's instincts, back beyond his dad days to earlier, more primitive times. Leaping up, he ran knowing it was too late and hoping it would be a false alarm. Ryan tossed the ball to Kyle. Bob saw the triangle reform; this time Rebecca had her back to the lazy river with Ryan close to her. As she raised her arms to catch the ball from Kyle, Ryan gave her a mighty shove in the chest, driving her backwards out over the rapids. The wave machine went boom. Running by the boys, Bob made a shallow dive into the river. The last look he saw on Rebecca's face before she fell into the foaming white water was one of surprise and, worse, betrayal.

Chapter 25

WHEN BOB WALKS THROUGH THE BIG DOUBLE DOORS AT NINE a.m. sharp, the receptionist immediately escorts him into Representative Tuchis' office. "Sentinel Foxen, the congresswoman will be with you in a moment."

"Thank you." Bob looks around the room eyeing the conference table by the windows and the chairs in front of the big desk. "Where do you want me?"

"She'll let you know where to sit. In the meantime, can I get you a beverage? Water, coffee?"

"Water would be nice."

The receptionist quickly returns with water in a glass etched with the Congressional seal. After handing it to Bob, she departs, leaving him alone. Bob takes a sip. 'Maybe coffee would have been better.' He feels tired from another night of restless sleep punctuated by the faceless green musicians playing music in starts and stops while practicing Brahms. 'At least they were playing better.' He remembers one violinist turning to him and hearing the voices say "Soon." Saabrina's foul mood earlier that morning hadn't helped, either. After a day of being on her best behavior, she had worked herself into a tizzy while

SETH COHEN

he had slept, then woke him extra early to get him ready. As recompense, she had brought him a nice breakfast from the local patisserie before kicking him out the door with "Go finish this business with that bitch."

Glass in hand, Bob takes his time looking over the congresswoman's office. From having read her bio he can follow the progression of her career in the photos on her desk and office walls—teacher, administrator, union officer, and pension fund trustee. From experience, he knows how tough those jobs make her: 'Not good.'

He stops. He can't believe Rebecca is on Madison with him, not that he has seen much of her in the last two days. Eddie and Saabra had swept her away after the meeting with Dallas; shopping for new clothes with Brenda and Saabra, grabbing Eddie for a tour of the city, Saabra dropping the three of them for dinner with Austin who had gotten them into one of the hot places in town. Bob could only join them for dessert. After, she went to Brenda and Eddie's and he went back to DoSOPS for a late-night meeting with the Department of Justice about prosecuting the 'brain gang.' Over the next day, the rush of debriefings, lessons-learned sessions, and a meeting about returning the abducted women to their lives stole more time away from her.

Wiping away a bead of sweat on his forehead, he focuses again on the photos. The schoolmarm look, right down to the frameless glasses with square lenses, arrives in the middle of the teacher pictures then follows into her political career—statehouse, planetary government, Congress. Pictures of her with constituents, dignitaries, the planet's governor, and her world's celebrities fill the walls; Auntie Jo looks the same in all of them.

Meandering around the room, he catches his reflection in the large glass windows, the snow floating down behind. He had considered going all-American businessman in a pin-striped suit, Brooks Brothers dress shirt, and blue tie, maybe even a colorful bow tie to really stand out. Lerner persuaded him to be more cosmopolitan and a little less in her face, so he stands there looking like Austin in a charcoal gray suit of the latest design with a dark gray mock turtleneck, very much future boy. He frowns. 'Except Austin can pull this look off while I look, well, bulky.'

Bob glances at some more pictures, books, papers, and files on the big desk, trying to remember the arguments against taking away Saabrina's rights he relearned yesterday, including the new ones Gogolak presented in person at a meeting with Eddie in Odessa's office. They swirl in his head; he doesn't know where to begin, what point to grab first. He'd hope to clear his mind with a quick bike ride after breakfast; a wintry blast had stopped him.

Pausing again, he takes a sip of water. 'Why does my throat remain dry no matter how much I drink?' He sips more water. 'They want Rebecca to stay and study physics.' Although Lerner hadn't asked him again, Eddie had raised the issue after the meeting with Gogolak. "Bob, it would be good for her. I know it's hard. I also know you always think of what's best for your daughter." He looked away from Eddie before answering. "Thanks, I know. It's a lot. Let me sort it out." In the short times between meetings, or during the boring ones, he made lists, pros and cons, and examined them. Saabrina helped, letting him sound them out to her. She did it gently, not pressing him, not arguing, simply letting him talk and think. He thought he had the answer, or most of it. Still, something stuck in his mind. He couldn't put his finger on the one big doubt, the thing giving him pause. Something obvious he must be missing. He needed to fill that hole before he could give an answer.

The door to the room opens. The schoolmarm walks in wearing a dark dress in a muted floral print and carrying a mug of coffee followed by Kiersey Summerall. He doesn't bother to extend a hand knowing it's not the custom of her world. "Mr. Foxen, please take a seat." Congresswoman Tuchis stands behind her desk pointing to the two white chairs before it. Summerall, wearing the female version of Bob's suit, all business, shakes his hand and makes some quick pleasantries while the Congresswoman settles into her big chair and arranges some papers on her desk. They sit. Tuchis sips coffee before placing it on a marble coaster with a click. "Shall we begin?" She stares at him, eyes unblinking.

Her pink irises surrounding black pupils, even if safely behind the square lenses of her glasses, gross him out. "Congresswoman, on behalf of DoSOPS and the Sentinel Program, I thank you for having me here today and look forward to answering your questions."

"I'm delighted to hear you will be answering my questions, Mr. Foxen. I had wanted a committee hearing, you understand, but our little meeting will have to do." She adjusts her glasses. "First though, let me say that I was sorry to hear about your daughter. I trust she is healthy after her recent escapade?"

"Yes, thank you for asking. She's perfectly fine and mostly recovered after a serious scare. I hope her friends will do as well."

"I'm glad to hear she's well. Getting caught up in all that awful business and to think they wanted young women's brains for who knows what. How terrible. Good thing your Saab was with her. Do you often let your Saab play with your daughter?"

"They became good friends early in my time as a sentinel. Saabrina likes to spend her free time with Rebecca. I assure you it's all within protocol and has been approved by DoSOPS." The manual opens in his head; he's ready to quote chapter and verse.

"I see. Still, it ended well, didn't it? Capturing that evil trafficking ring, even if your daughter almost caused an intergalactic incident with the Eloki Prince."

Summerall shifts in her seat. Bob smiles. "An unfortunate, though acceptable, outcome of the events. As you said, Congresswoman, it all worked out fine in the end; he's home with his mother who will be responsible for his punishment."

"Very good. Let's begin our review. Although I have spent a substantial amount of time reading about our sentinel from Earth, I want to concentrate today on some of your more recent adventures. Or, should I say, misadventures: it's my understanding that after our last committee hearing you and your Saab almost destroyed the universe."

"Congresswoman, I appreciate your concern, but I wouldn't say we almost destroyed the universe. As a consequence of our mission, we did accidentally punch a small hole in the fabric of spacetime, which, according to the professionals in the Federal Science Administration, and Saabrina, has safely healed itself."

"Still, wouldn't you say your actions caused a dangerous situation? Wasn't that irresponsible?"

Sipping water, Bob carefully assembles his words. He begins slowly, using even tones. "Again, I appreciate your concerns in this matter. However, we followed a plan developed jointly by the War Department and DoSOPS after the Foreign Office determined diplomacy would not prevail. To prepare, War ran us through multiple battle simulations. In action, we followed the exact attack sequence we had learned, to the letter."

"You say 'we.' Your Saab did it all the work. Mr. Foxen, it seems like you were along for the ride." Tuchis laughs. "Sometimes I ask why they even bother to send the sentinels. Did your Saab cause the problem?"

"No, the enemy fleet did something we did not expect, which resulted in Saabrina and me being caught in the break. This was all detailed in the post-mission analysis, which I thought had been forwarded to each member of your committee and their staffs. If not, I apologize, and will ask for DoSOPS to send it again."

Summerall turns to Bob. "We did receive it. I believe the congresswoman…"

"Kiersey, please. Mr. Foxen, there always seems to be some outcome you or your superiors did not expect. To run risks so far from our borders seemed unwarranted to me. And to kill so many, so quickly…"

"If I may, the White House, the Foreign Office, and War all thought it would be prudent to stop the problem long before it got to us. We believed there was a moral imperative to prevent genocide if we could."

"Let's move along." Tuchis glances at her notes. "So you took government property on holiday with you?"

"Congresswoman, I assume you're referring to our recent vacation on Earth?"

"Yes."

"Hmm. To begin with, Saabrina is not government property. She did come with me to Mexico, yes, conduct well within sentinel regulations. And custom, if I may add."

"But she did not come as herself. She came as some sort of new…thing."

"Congresswoman, you are correct. She came in the form of my six-year-old daughter. IT provided a substantially upgraded hologram for her." Bob takes out his mobile and holds it for Tuchis and Summerall to see. "Here's some pictures of her by the pool, at arts and crafts…"

Summerall moves the mobile closer, smiling at the pictures. "She's so cute. But she's not your daughter?"

"No, Saabrina in the form of my daughter. And she behaved just like her, which was really amazing. I still got to hand it to IT for doing such an awesome job."

Summerall flicks through some more pictures. "She was an experimental hologram?"

"Yes, experimental. They've been wanting to test it; my trip provided the perfect opportunity for a controlled test in a sort of real-world situation."

Tuchis sets down her coffee mug with a loud click. "You used government property for personal pleasure and risked causing an incident on Earth if it had catastrophically failed?"

"Congresswoman, we believed there was little chance of failure. DoSOPS approved. As I said it was well within regulations. IT was delighted to have the test. And most importantly, my Saab wanted to do it, which is her right. In fact, it was her idea and I was very happy to help. You know, she may never have had a real vacation before this."

"Still, I don't know if my constituents would approve of their hard-earned taxpayer dollars being spent so you could re-live your past with your six-year-old daughter."

Bob leans forward in his chair. "Again, Congresswoman, I understand your concern. However, if you remember, your constituents do not pay for the sentinel program. The protected worlds do from a small part of the fees their trusts earn from licensing out their intellectual property."

"Still, the cost of a vacation."

"In fact, I paid for my and Saabrina's vacation and provided IT with a free test of a new hologram." Tuchis frowns. Bob continues. "By the way, did you know IT subsequently developed a game from our trip? It's become some sort of best seller. People can play Saabrina, or me, or add their own characters. Apparently, they love playing her." Which he totally appreciates, particularly the fun from playing all her tricks on her silly old daddy who constantly runs after her. "Sales have more than paid for the research to develop the new hologram, so your constituents can rest easy knowing their tax dollars are safe at work on other government programs. Who knows, they may even want to meet the new hologram someday; as Ms. Summerall said, she's very cute."

Tuchis gives Bob a faint smile while crinkling her eyes behind her glasses "Do you think my questions are a waste of time Mr. Foxen? Do you object to being here?"

"Not in the least, Congresswoman. As a citizen, I rely on my representatives to oversee all government programs on my behalf. It's critical to the function of our government; as both a citizen and member of DoSOPS, I'm delighted to answer your questions."

"Mr. Foxen, let's continue. You nearly caused a pre-first contact incident on Daear. Some believe you actually did cause a pre-first contact incident." Bob explains, Tuchis persists. He sips water, his thirst never abating. She takes him through the search for the travel tubes, the visits to protected worlds, the capture of the brain gang. He wishes he could hear Saabrina in his head—some cutting remarks, even something inappropriate would be greatly appreciated. They review the earlier incidents again, focusing on the congresswoman's perception of his cavalier operating style and lackadaisical command of his Saab. When she seems finally satisfied, or has simply exhausted her questions, she asks him if there is anything he would like to discuss.

"Thank you for asking. Yes, Congresswoman, I do. Why do you want to take away the rights of my Saab?"

"I thought you might ask about my interest in constraining the Saabs." Tuchis smiles at him, crinkling her eyes behind her glasses. "Let's talk about your Saab. At heart, she, like the rest, is nothing more than a powerful tool. Do you know who said 'With great power comes great responsibility'?"

"Uncle Ben?"

Both Summerall and Tuchis look confused. The congresswoman leans forward in her chair. "Who?"

"Uncle Ben, Peter Parker's, Spider-Man's Uncle Ben."

Silence indicates more incomprehension from the other two.

"On my world, actually given its licenses now, on many worlds, there's a popular comic book about a superhero named Spider-Man."

"A comic book, Mr. Foxen?"

"Sentinel Foxen, Congresswoman. My title is Sentinel. Yes, a comic book. In his origin story, after Peter Parker gets his superpowers from the bite of a radioactive spider and becomes Spider-Man, he chooses to use them for personal gain. While doing so he lets a burglar escape, the burglar goes on to fatally assault Uncle Ben, a good man and the father figure in his life. Uncle Ben's last words to Peter Parker—there's some debate about whether this occurred in the original comic or were retconned, certainly they were in the movies—were 'With great power comes great responsibility.' Those words, and the death of his uncle, caused Peter Parker to become a hero and to accept the responsibilities of having superpowers. They gave the character the 'it,' the thing that drives him."

"A nice story Mr. Foxen, but you are wrong about who said it and what it means."

"Now, I don't understand. The saying is an admonition to individuals to accept responsibility for their actions."

"Not in the least." Now Summerall looks confused. She remains silent after a glance from the congresswoman. "They were said by a wise man on my world, Alton Cocker. He believed that if someone or something has great power, then it was incumbent upon society to regulate their power and to take responsibility for it. The individual could not be trusted to do the right thing; only government could make sure it was used properly."

"Well, I mean, I know there's a tension between the powers government takes versus those held by the individual, and I know the government oversees lots of things, which it does with the Saabs. So…"

"Mr. Foxen, the Saabs have too much power. They can destroy ships, battle fleets, whole worlds for their own selfish reasons, if they choose to."

"But they would never choose to do anything evil, they're too moral and ethical."

The congresswoman wrinkles her nose as if smelling a bad odor. She takes a long sip of coffee. "I can't take that chance. My committee only reacts, and very much after the fact, to some new incident, some new calamity, some new atrocity caused by a Saab. And the sentinel in the driver's seat, in my opinion, has far too little power, or should I say in your case Mr. Foxen, desire, to stop one from getting out of control. They need to be controlled, and I intend to do so."

"They have rights."

"Better they lose them, then we be harmed."

"You can't take their rights away. They're citizens, a part of our society."

"We will quarantine them, separate them, cut them off from the rest."

"No man is an island."

"I'm sorry, what?"

"No man is an island, entire of itself; every man is a piece of the continent, a part of the main. If a clod be washed away by the sea, Europe is the less… any man's death diminishes me, because I am involved in mankind." He's astonished he can remember the quote. 'Those new vitamins Saabrina got me are working wonders.'

"Those words convey a very nice sentiment, Mr. Foxen, but they're not and never will be us."

"Sentinel Foxen, Congresswoman, not Mr. Foxen. I'm properly referred to as Sentinel; I earned the title. Using it demonstrates respect."

"Kiersey, dear, please leave us. I need some alone time with Mr. Foxen."

Bob watches Summerall silently leave the room. 'Fuck, Tuchis is bringing me to the woodshed. I shouldn't have lost my cool; I shouldn't have reacted to her. Lerner's going to kick my ass when I get back to DoSOPS.' Summerall closes the door behind her.

Tuchis cocks her head slightly and smiles. "I know this conversation between us will remain private."

"I give you my assurances it will."

"I don't need your assurances. I know your character. I know how the link works; I fully expect that DoSOPS and your Saab will review and parse every part of our conversation before this. You will choose not to transmit what follows."

"I don't understand."

"You will. You will. First, I have a question for you. Why do you care about your Saab?"

"She's my partner and my friend."

"A fantasy. You have no such relationship with that machine."

"Based on my experience over the last four years, I would disagree."

"Your experience is an illusion created by a set of wicked algorithms designed to easily fool the mind of a primitive such as yourself. On this world, your machine may be an incredible technological accomplishment, an intelligent weapon to implement government policy, but it has far more in common with my washing machine, which asks me if I had a nice day before it cleans my panties, than your daughter. On your world, it is nothing more than beguiling magic, a form of witchcraft to an aborigine."

"You're talking of sentience. I can prove to you Saabrina is an individual."

"Mr. Foxen, she's simply a computer program that employs the simulacrum of a cute young woman to appeal to the emotional needs of a susceptible middle-aged man." Bob moves to speak; she raps her desk with her fingernail. "What you believe is irrelevant. This all began a long time ago when you were a young man. I told them not to do it, to pass Dabney-Coleman. I said then I'd undo it, and I will."

"Dabney-Coleman?"

"Legislation. Without your link you have no idea, no access to knowledge. Don't bother whipping your mobile out, you can look it up later. It was legislation making changes to the Sentinel Program. I opposed it when I first arrived in Congress. I saw the folly in it, they didn't, and I've planned to set it right since. Starting with you. I want you out of the program. I don't like the direction the program has been going since the arrival of the new style sentinels like you, Mr. Foxen."

"My understanding is we perform better."

"Could be true, but irrelevant. Your primitive's response to pretty robots has infected the program, giving inanimate objects the expectation that they are real people. I can't have that. And you're easy to get rid of, being from a protected world and not a full member of the Union, with strange habits and views and all."

"And a primitive to boot."

"Exactly. You're the problem and the solution. Getting you out of the program sets in motion the re-evaluation of the Saabs; from there they get reprogrammed with the Three Laws or something more suitable."

"We'll fight you."

"I fully expect for you to fight. Here's the part you don't comprehend. I will teach you now. I have plenty of time. I don't expect to win this battle soon, and I don't have to."

"I have time, too. This will become part of my life."

"You think you have time, do you?" Tuchis leans forward. "You look at me as an old woman; chronologically, relative to you, I am. Biologically, not at all. I looked like this when you were a young man, and I will be like this when you are an old man, and when you are long gone. You're aging before me, Mr. Foxen. I can see it, your hair graying and thinning, your mind slowing, your body breaking down."

"So what? Getting older is normal; happens to everyone."

"Everyone, yes, but at different rates. I can bide my time. In thirty years you will be a very old man, and I will still be here. I'll come to your home, feed you, change your diapers. Would you like that, Auntie Jo putting a spoonful of mush into your mouth, whispering sweet things into your deaf ears, the nice lady who smiles at you when you can't remember her name?"

"If you want to be my nurse, by all means come and change my diapers. Before then, I'll fight you. After me, others will take up the charge."

"You'll be out of a job and back on your barbaric world long before then. What others? Once I eliminate you, the others will fall into line, wishing to save their jobs and their beloved program. They'll happily trade you away for some peace from me."

"The Saabs will fight."

"They will literally lack the will to do so."

"Then my daughter will do it. She knows you're wrong."

"She'll be an old woman. Perhaps I'll be her caregiver too when she's relegated to an old age home. I'm sorry, Mr. Foxen, I have time and power and you and your friends do not." Tuchis rises. "Now, as our interview is over, you may leave my office."

Bob walks out of the room.

Chapter 26

SAABRINA SURPRISES BOB ON THE STEPS TO THE HANCOCK House Office Building. "I don't believe the esteemed congress-woman would object to my picking you up, so no need for the Metro or a DoSOPS limo."

"Thanks."

"How did it go?"

"Not well."

"Not well?"

He feels her probe his mind. He pushes her out. "Don't do that. Come on, we need to go see Lerner." He remains silent the whole way back to DoSOPS. Walking into the executive offices with Saabrina trailing behind him, he pushes by Lerner's secretary into the Director's office, finding Eddie and Odessa sitting in front of Lerner's desk on comfortable office chairs, Lerner in a large leather chair on the opposite side. Odessa turns to say hello and freezes when she sees Bob's face.

"Director, you wanted to see me the minute I got back. I'm here. Can we talk?"

"Of course, Bob, please sit. You too, Saabrina."

Saabrina finds a seat. Bob remains standing. "Before we talk about Tuchis, we need to straighten something out first."

"What, Bob? Please tell me."

"You want my blessing about Rebecca. I need two things first."

"OK, what are they? I'll see what I can do."

"These are non-negotiable. You want her, you have to provide both."

"Let me hear them."

"One, you have to promise to take care of her. Whether she succeeds or not, she needs to live well for her whole life. She'll have no family to fall back on and I'll be long gone. I need to know she'll be fine, more than fine, no matter what."

"Done."

Saabrina looks at Bob. "I'll always be there for her."

"Two, you have to fix her so she ages like her peers, not like a human. I don't want her being the old lady when all of her friends are still young."

Now Lerner stands. "Bob, what's going on?"

"I know you can do it; you have to do it. I don't want her being a freak or being gypped out of full life when everyone around her lives on. She has to have the same lifespan that any citizen like her would expect."

Lerner and Eddie exchange glances. Eddie nods. Lerner addresses Bob. "If she agrees to stay with us, we'll do it. You're right, it would only be fair."

"Fine. You have my support. I'll talk to her first if you would like."

"Thank you, Bob. Yes, please speak to her and make our case. You know, we can do the same for you, change the rate at which you age, if you would like."

"No, my time is set. Getting to be a sentinel was more than good enough; I don't deserve anything more. OK, let's talk about the congresswoman. If you don't want to waste time, Saabrina can beam my memories directly to you."

"If you don't mind." Lerner sits back down.

"Saabrina, go ahead. My conversation with Tuchis and Summerall only; when Summerall leaves the room, please stop."

"Bob?"

"I'm sorry, Saabrina, but what we spoke about is private between me and the congresswoman."

Saabrina reads Bob's thoughts. He doesn't laugh as she works her way around; instead, he grimaces as the memories float by. It takes the group a few minutes to digest what happened. Bob finally sits, staring at the floor, Saabrina watching him as the other three discuss his conversation with Tuchis and her plans for the Saabs.

Odessa pulls at her whiskers. "At least she gave us her reasons."

Bob looks up. "I don't know why, but I don't think they're real. I know what she said to me; I think it's bullshit."

"I agree with Bob." Eddie stands to stretch his legs. "The whole meeting was bullshit. Insulting bullshit. She designed it to get under his skin, and ours. Forget what she said. Bob, can you tell us anything about your private conversation with her?"

"She mentioned something about legislation called Dabney-Coleman."

Lerner looks at Odessa. "Dabney-Coleman was passed years ago. Was she even in Congress?"

"First termer. Voted no. One of the few votes against it. No one took her seriously; we thought she was trying to gain attention."

"No, not based on what she told me. She was serious. She thought it was folly and decided then and there to reverse it. Frank, what did it do?"

"Reformed the selection process for sentinels. Opened the program to more candidates, changed the selection process to expedite it and made it more flexible, gave the Saabs more say in who they worked with, and allowed us to look at people from protected worlds."

"Like me."

"Exactly."

"She told me she wanted me out of the program."

Lerner leans forward. "Damn, Bob, you must've found that upsetting."

"I did, but I don't think it was personal for her. Well, I guess it is, but what I mean is there's a rationale to why she wants me out." Bob looks at Odessa. "I'm the weak link. The soft underbelly of the program, right?"

"I never meant those words to be taken seriously."

"I know. She gets rid of me..."

Lerner finishes Bob's sentence "And she makes a big enough stink to put the whole program under review. Alright, let's start from the top again."

Saabrina watches the group discuss Tuchis. A brief history of Sentinel Program policy and Congressional incursions gives way to Lerner and Odessa trading notes on various representatives and their staffers, the two delving into strange and arcane details of who owes whom what and what makes them tick; Eddie paces around the room making points about potential allies outside of Congress, particularly in the legal and academic world; and Bob nods his head or asks questions to refine strategy. 'Why aren't they asking my opinion? Um, if they asked, would I know what to say? Probably not.' Despite all her years in government, she finds the nitty-gritty of politics alien to her. She sits and listens. 'I know they are trying to help, but the fight doesn't seem to be getting better, only bigger after today's defeat. Defeat. Bob failed me. He couldn't get a word in edgewise, he couldn't make our arguments, let alone stop Tuchis.'

"So what do we do now, Boss?"

"Let Frank and me noodle some more about this and make some calls. Probably time to bring in the White House. In the meantime, let's not give her any more ammo. Maybe you and Saabrina should take another vacation."

"No, I want to get back to work."

"But Bob…"

"I'm sorry Director, I need to be out there. If I screw up, you can toss me from the program. Or have Saabrina vaporize me." Bob stands. "First, as promised, I'm going to go talk my daughter into leaving her home and coming here. Then, I'm going back to work. Saabrina and I have been away too long from our regular jobs. If that's alright with you, Saabrina."

"It is, Bob. Of course it is."

The others rise and make their goodbyes. While Lerner and Odessa stay behind to talk, Eddie escorts Bob and Saabrina to the door. "Bob, are you sure you're OK?"

"I'm fine Eddie, I'm fine. I love being a sentinel. I just want to get back to it."

Eddie peers into Bob's eyes. "OK. Let me know if there's anything I can do."

"Keep looking out for Rebecca. I assume she can stay with you until she gets, well, her new life?"

"Bob, it's Brenda's and my pleasure. We'll treat her as if she's our own, even if Brenda is a little surprised Rebecca is actually colored pink."

"Huh?"

"Remember, back on Earth, Brenda's compensator suit worked both ways, making people there look like people on Jarden, our home world, to her. She thought Rebecca was sick; I had to explain it to her as best I could."

"But Brenda's seen me here on Madison."

"As I said, she thought you were ill."

"Ahh." Bob thinks about all the times Brenda brought chicken soup to his apartment.

"Now she knows better. Again, don't worry, we'll take good care of Rebecca. I have grandchildren her age who can't wait to meet her." Eddie smiles. "Margot could practically be her double."

"Thanks, Eddie, I really appreciate it." The two shake hands, Eddie pulling Bob into a hug. Saabrina gives Eddie a hug as well. Leaving DoSOPS, they join Rebecca for lunch at another of Austin's hot spots. Bob explains the offer to her over pizza, telling her to think about it. "Sweetie, coming here is a great idea and you should do it if you want to, but you should really, really want to." Saabrina agrees wholeheartedly, explaining in detail all the benefits, her words rushing out at near warp speed: "Think of all the worlds we could visit. Or the science we could talk about; I wouldn't have to hold out on you anymore! And I'd always be there for you, always!" After Rebecca recovers, they drop her at the hospital to let her watch over her friends and to mull over the proposal. After a round of hugs and kisses, Bob holds on to Rebecca for the longest time before finally saying "Goodbye, sweetie" with a kiss on her forehead.

They start back to Earth. "Saabrina, please wake me when we get home." He falls asleep in the driver's seat as Saabrina flies along.

While time and stars pass, Saabrina listens to the radio, thinks about Rebecca, and relays the good and bad news to her sisters. Then she focuses on Bob. 'Why wouldn't he let me see his private conversation with Tuchis? Doesn't he trust me? No, that's never been it. What could it be? What did she say to him?' She can't decide whether to be miffed or relieved from not having to spend another moment in that awful woman's presence. 'He must have his reasons. He'll let me know when he's ready. What about his botching the meeting?' Lying in her seat, he appears wounded and worn; the last couple of days have taken their toll. 'Maybe Rebecca, Tuchis, the endless lessons learned sessions were all too much for him.' Irritated and worried, she finds herself torn between wanting to shout or to hug him. She decides to give him a pass for now. As to her concerns with his recent conduct, she traces her doubts back to Mexico. 'After all this time, why does the episode by the pool still rankle me? And why haven't I had the nerve to speak to him about it? Enough perseverating, I'll ask him the question when he wakes.' Earth's sun approaches. "Bob, we're here, wake up."

They exit FTL directly into a wave of green protomatter. Saabrina doesn't have time to scream.

Part 3

Chapter 27

BOB OOZES THROUGH GREEN-TINGED FRAGMENTS OF HIS LIFE, squeezed from memory to memory. He works at his office desk, the evening light streaming through the windows of the big black building; takes the train into New York City while reading *The Wall Street Journal*; drives the Mercedes somewhere; drafts deal documents in a meeting with nameless, faceless attorneys; drops Rebecca at school before going to the train station; talks to the gray ghost of another parent while waiting for their daughters to dance at a recital; calls Laura to ask about her day and tell her he'll be late for dinner. Each memory blurs into the next, with him joining a scene already in progress. Between each fragment he hears the voices say "No." When he hears "Yes," everything goes black.

Morning light filters through his bedroom drapes in Naglewood. The radio alarm clock on Bob's side of the bed sounds, playing a gnarly bit of rock 'n' roll. Waking under warm covers, Bob scratches, adjusts his pajama pants, and clicks off the alarm. Feeling Laura to his right, he snuggles up, spooning around her body, wrapping his arm around her bare midriff, trying not to breathe in her ear as his head conquers part of her pillow. She hates when he breathes in her ear.

"Bob."

Bob gives her flesh a squeeze, wrapping himself more tightly around her body. She prefers mornings. Maybe this will be a good morning.

"Bob, please, you're crushing me."

Her line is supposed to be 'Why are you smushing me?', normally delivered playfully, and he's supposed to answer 'Because you're so smushable' before commencing a kissing assault on her cheek. He stops. 'Laura sounds scared. And why does she have an English accent?' Bob scoots back in the bed.

Laura turns to him, her eyes sparkling green, not brown.

"Saabrina?"

"Yes and no."

"Laura's…"

"Not here, wherever here is. I'm playing her, built from your and Rebecca's memories."

Bob sits up in the bed and looks around his bedroom. The room looks fake to him, as if he could see straight through the walls if he wanted to. He pulls on the sheet, the cotton stretchy like Lycra, becoming thinner the more he pulls until a hole appears. "Weird."

"I wouldn't do that."

He releases the sheet and it returns to its normal silvery cotton appearance. "Are you OK?"

"I feel wrong, not myself. My head's a swirl of thoughts and memories and I'm having a hard time determining which are Laura's and which are mine." She pulls the sheets up to her chin. "Can you get me some pajamas? I appear to be naked."

"Laura liked to sleep naked in the summer." Getting out of bed, he retrieves some pajamas from the top drawer of her dresser and brings them to her.

"Turn around."

Bob does as told. "Do you need help?" He hears cloth sliding over skin. While she dresses, he takes the opportunity to don an old blue t-shirt he left by the side of the bed.

"No, I've got this, wait, the top's on backwards, hold on, there, now the pants, OK, safe."

Bob turns to see his dead wife standing before him in her favorite pair of pajamas, the ones with sheep hopping across blue fields, looking no worse for wear. He misses her brown eyes. He wants to cry.

Saabrina takes him by the hand. "It's going to be fine. Just don't call me Laura. Or Shirley for that matter." Releasing him, she walks over to a wall and snaps it with her index finger and thumb. Bringing her face close, she admires the ripples propagating from the small blow and traveling to the outside perimeter of the wall. "Interesting."

"It doesn't look real to me."

"It does to me. I wouldn't have known to do that if you hadn't stretched the sheets in front of me."

"What does it mean?"

"I don't know." Saabrina stands still as if hearing something.

"Everything alright?"

"Alright? No. Weird? Yes. Follow me." She guides him downstairs, taking each step carefully, holding onto to him while he grips the railing. "Bob, this is about to get stranger." They cross the living room to Rebecca's hallway and enter her room. His sixteen-year-old daughter, dressed in Snoopy pajamas, lies in her bed in a heap of sheets and blankets. Waking, she sits up and stretches, opening her green eyes wide to look at her parents.

"Saabrina?"

Rebecca smiles at her dad. "Yes" comes in English accent "and no," follows in a teen Jersey girl lilt.

Laura's English accent vanishes as well. "You need to get up, we need to get going."

"Mom! It's Saturday, I want to sleep in."

Laura moves right up to Rebecca's bed. "We don't have time. Go take a shower while I get breakfast ready."

"I can take a shower in Lenox."

"When was the last time you showered?"

"Like, Thursday?"

"Rebecca, that's disgusting. Go get in the shower."

"I'm staying in bed!"

"Then I'm getting in too." Laura tries to climb into Rebecca's bed, Rebecca pushing back.

Bob reels from the scene, a feeling of déjà vu overwhelming him. He backs out and runs into the living room, freezing in front of the fireplace near the front door: before him stand a line of packed canvas bags. He remembers a trip from the past. 'Or is it a glimpse of the future?' A weeklong vacation starts this very Saturday morning, a trip to their condo in Lenox. While Laura and Rebecca argue, he rummages through the bags. They contain the usual items for a resupply mission: empty containers and freezer packs to be returned, whatever household items Laura bought in NJ, a Highland single malt scotch, some DVDs, some clothes, and tickets for Tanglewood for tomorrow afternoon. He looks at the tickets; the concert seems familiar to him, although he doesn't know why.

In a flash, he remembers: Rebecca's sixteen, the summer of boy crazy and the endless fights with Laura, and they have to get to Lenox early because the Trouts (Jim, Diane, and their eldest, Alex) will be visiting on the return from their own weeklong vacation to Maine and Vermont. They couldn't leave last night because Bob had worked late to get everything finished in the office to clear the week. Or he had once worked late.

Laura and Rebecca continue to argue. After putting the tickets back, he turns to his right to look out the big bank of living room windows: at first glance, New Jersey rolls down the hill and away from his house. He walks through the living room for a closer view. He should be seeing the sun rising on a summer day; instead, he sees space and stars, with tendrils of land reaching out to the horizon. 'If I didn't know better, I'd guess I'd fallen into a Ren & Stimpy cartoon.'

Quiet. He goes back into Rebecca's room half expecting to see his deranged wife standing over the bloody corpse of their daughter. Instead, he finds the two happily cuddled up in bed, looking at him with their green eyes. Bob smiles at them. "Nice. Can I jump in, too?"

"No, go away, we're comfy," comes the joint reply.

Bob folds his arms across his chest. "Please get out of bed, we have to get going." He walks over and sniffs his daughter. "Rebecca, you stink. Now go take a shower."

"Dad!"

"Come on, get moving." He pulls her out of the bed and sends her on her way. "Laura, do you need help making breakfast?"

Laura hops out of bed. "No, I can do it." Again, she takes him by the arm and they walk slowly to the kitchen. "How about French toast? I've got Challah left over from Shabbat dinner."

"Sure, sounds good."

He watches her slowly work around the kitchen island. Pulling ingredients from the cabinets and the refrigerator, she brings each item close to her face for inspection. "Laura, wait, don't move." Bob bounds up the stairs, which undulate under his feet, and quickly returns with an article from the table by the bed: her glasses. He unfolds the glasses and places them gently on her face.

"I can see clearly now" comes through in a glorious High Organian accent. Saabrina smiles at him.

"Good thing Laura preferred glasses; I have no idea how contacts work."

Looking through the lenses he sees Laura return. "What are you doing? Are you going to stand around? Go take a shower and load the car, I'll make breakfast. Is your computer undocked? I don't want to wait for it again. Move it, we're going to be late."

Bob backs away. Given the morning heat, he decides to load the truck first, then shower. In the driveway, he finds Laura's Tahoe, the big box on wheels that could get her through a foot of snow to the hospital, up to a ski weekend in Vermont, or scare off a Volvo in a fight for a mall parking spot on Black Friday. Laura was the quintessential small New Jersey woman in the big SUV everyone in Manhattan jokes about. Once when she was by herself on the road, the tailgate's window had opened. After pulling over and discovering she wasn't tall enough to pull it closed, she climbed up on to the rear bumper and yanked the window shut while parachuting backwards to the ground. Neither her, nor the truck, got a scratch.

Bob inspects the Tahoe. A few years old and showing door dings from the hospital parking lot, it looks slightly fake to him; on a whim, he pushes his index finger deep into the front fender. Extracting it with a pop, the hole refills emanating ripples across the metal surface. Somehow he knows if he opens the hood there won't be an engine, so he doesn't bother. Lifting the tailgate, Bob carefully piles the canvas bags, luggage, and other crap into the back, trying to balance the load and keep it from piling up to block his rear view. After wedging them all into place, he admires his handiwork, then stops. 'Why do we need to go? I don't even know why I'm here, or where here is.' Laura's call from the kitchen to hurry-up speeds him along again. With a slam to close the tailgate, he finds himself on his way back into the house.

After he showers, the sight of French toast, quietly sizzling on the griddle, greets him on his return to the kitchen. He moves to take a slice when an unhappy Laura blocks him, pointing like an accusing specter towards his daughter's bathroom. "She's not out of the shower." Bob walks around the corner to Rebecca's bathroom, hears running water, and raps twice on the door. "Hey!"

"What?"

"I've got a dozen river otters outside with shampoo suds in their hair. They're complaining they have no water."

"Oh, sorry, I'll finish up."

The rest of the morning goes surprisingly quickly. Gathered around the kitchen island, the three eat breakfast, Laura's usually delicious French toast tasteless to Bob, same for the orange juice and coffee. While Laura and Rebecca enjoy their meals, Bob chokes each slice down. After, the three engage in an endless back and forth between the house to the truck until the truck safely holds everyone and the last of their stuff. Finally, they depart, right on Bob's scheduled time and an hour late for Laura. From the front passenger seat, she makes clear her unhappiness.

Bob drives. The road spools out in front of him, a green glass thread topped with a coating of black tarmac. He can see stars twinkling through the light blue sky and fluffy white clouds ahead. If he looks right or left, houses and trees co-alesce from a green ether to fill in the black of space, pulling apart and reappearing as he moves along. When he thinks it's strange that they have the highway to themselves, the thruway divides into multiple lanes and semi-transparent, green-ish hued vehicles driven by gelatinous, green people appear around him. "Odd."

"What?" Laura looks up from the magazine she's reading.

"There were no cars, then a bunch."

"What are you talking about? Are you tired from work-ing late last night? Do you need me to drive?"

"How about some music." He turns on the radio. A kids' pop tune comes on. "Hey, Rebecca loved this song when she was little." He blinks. Laura, the young mom of ten years earlier, smiles from their old minivan's passenger seat while Rebecca sings along from her kiddie seat behind. "No" he hears the voices say. The station changes, a song by Train starts, and Bob is back in the Tahoe with his middle-aged wife and sixteen-year-old daughter.

Laura checks the name of the song. "I love Train. I wish they would play Tanglewood sometime."

"They will, after…"

"After what?"

"Nothing. Wandering thought. Gotta keep my eyes on the road." Laura and Bob spend the next hour debating new designs for the Lenox kitchen while Rebecca plays games on her mobile.

They sweep up Exit 21A onto the Berkshire Connector. Rebecca pops out her earbuds and stretches. "Was this the trip when Beethoven's Ninth synced up? You loved to tell me that story."

"Saabrina?"

"Yes" comes the answer from the other two in the car.

"No, not this trip, one later in the summer." The radio continues to play, the tunes off-key. "Doesn't it drive you crazy?"

"What?" comes back in unison.

"The songs." He punches the button on the radio, silencing the dreadful music. "Wait." He turns back to Laura, "do you know where you are? Help me out here."

"We're on the Mass Pike. You drive straight and get off at Exit 2. Are you OK? How late did you work last night?"

"I'm OK."

Forty-five minutes later they pull into their condo's driveway to find Jim and his family waiting for them. As Bob jumps out of the Tahoe, Jim extends his right hand. "Hey, buddy, we just got here ourselves." Bob hesitates, takes Jim's hand, pulling him close for a hug. Towering over Bob as usual, Jim looks and feels real, as do Diane and Alex. At least they don't have green eyes; he doesn't know how many more Saabrina variations he can take. Rebecca goes right up to Alex, a younger duplicate of Jim and soon to be college freshman to her high school rising junior. "Hi, Alex."

"Uh, hi, Rebecca."

Laura pushes her way between them. "I'm so sorry we're late. We wanted to get everything ready."

Diane gives her a hug. "Nonsense, we got here early to spend more time with you."

They go inside, Bob moving double-time with Jim to get everything into the house and settled. As Laura works with Diane to prepare lunch in the condo's original 1980s kitchen, she gives Bob the evil eye every time he walks by, those green eyes burning brighter than ever. He doesn't understand how her glasses don't melt. Over on the living room couch, oblivious to the efforts around them, Rebecca gabs with Alex about school friends and summer. "Hey, Mom, can I stay with Alex downstairs on the bunk beds?"

"NO" comes in unison from Bob and Laura. Laura points to the stairs. "Go take your stuff up to your room."

"Later."

"Now." Laura walks towards Rebecca.

Rebecca rolls her eyes, yawns, and rises as slowly as her teenage body will permit her. When Alex moves to help, Laura intercepts him and moves him downstairs. "Let me show you your bed and bathroom."

At lunch, Bob eats another tasteless meal. Quickly, and mercifully, he finds himself poolside with the two families, lying on a chaise enjoying the light from a missing afternoon sun, listening to Jim talk about his two younger children off in camp while the wives stand by the pool engaged in their own conversation. Other residents swim in the pool along with Alex and Rebecca, wander by, or lie in the sunlight, the rays illuminating the green jell making up their bodies and clothes. Strangely, this doesn't creep Bob out. Nor not being able to change his conversation with Jim; he simply says his lines as if from a script. The best he can guess during the quiet moments in between is he is replaying memories, or someone is replaying his memories, from the original visit.

The kids swim. Before they went out, Laura had tried to make Rebecca change her swimsuit, an old bikini two sizes too small, and failed, much to Alex's delight. Splash. Laura jumps into the pool and drags Rebecca out by her ear. "Bob, you need to go to Guido's with your daughter."

"Seriously, Mom? I don't want to go shopping."

"You're going right now. Bob, up, go bring back food for dinner."

Rebecca, seething, rounds on Laura. "I'm not going." Everything comes to a stop.

"You're going."

"You're jealous."

"Of what?"

"I'm young, you're old."

"And wise."

"And dying. Who cares what you want. You'll be dead."

Laura goes white, brings back her hand, thinks better of it.

Bob can't move. 'This is not Laura and Rebecca; they never fought like this or said these words.'

Laura pushes her face up into Rebecca's. "Listen: I have wisdom, knowledge, foresight, self-control. I'm protecting you."

"I don't need you or your protection. I take risks, chances, so what if I make a mistake? I'm passionate, curious, clever. I want to live. You don't. Now, get out of my way."

The two scream at each other in whistles, squeaks, and screeches, horrible high-pitched tones that rip Bob's ears. Bob jumps up. "Stop!"

A white flash. Laura jumps into the pool and drags Rebecca out by the ear. "Bob, you need to go to Guido's with your daughter."

"Seriously, Mom? I don't want to go shopping."

"You're going right now. Bob, up, go bring back food for dinner."

Bob jumps up; when Jim moves to rise, Bob tells him to sit back and relax. "I got this. Trust me, you don't want to be between those two." After tossing Rebecca a towel, he walks over to Laura and a giggling Diane. "What happened?"

"I couldn't bear watching Rebecca circle Alex like a shark, spiraling closer and closer until she was practically rubbing against him."

"I remember when you did that to me."

"Never. Must have been your other wife." She gives him a kiss on the cheek followed by a whack on the butt. "Now go."

Bob sweeps up Rebecca. "Come on, sweetie, let's go."

They take the old Subaru, his station car bought long before the series of leased Mercedes, up Route 7, a green glass filament hanging in space, the roadside of houses, yard sales, motels, and stores blurring and reforming as they roll along to Guido's. Living in the Lenox garage, going strong with 125,000 plus miles on the odometer, barely broken in by Subaru standards, and still looking good even with all the dings, it now does duty with all the other white Outbacks in the Berkshires, ferrying the Foxens to farmers' markets, shops, trailheads, Tanglewood, and skiing.

Rebecca, unhappy he made her cover up before they went, sits in the passenger seat playing with the radio, a too short t-shirt over her bikini top, her bottom soaking through her shorts and onto the towel on the leather seat. Finally settling on the classic rock station she finds least offensive, she slumps down in her seat and lets out a sigh.

Bob breaks the silence, "Give your mom a break." He watches the odometer while carefully listening to his daughter's voice when she speaks.

"Why? I wasn't doing anything."

"Your behavior with Alex in the pool wasn't doing anything?"

"She's always yelling at me. Why are you taking her side? She's just as bad with you."

'Sounds like Rebecca.' Bob looks at the odometer: one mile. "This isn't about me. One, we both worry about you." He glances right to see the pained look on Rebecca's face. "Sorry, it's our job. Two, she has it pretty hard."

"Hard? Mom? Seriously?"

"Besides the long hours in the hospital, she has to take care of us." He wags his finger between the two of them. "A husband who vanishes on projects for weeks at a time and a daughter with her head in the clouds. Somebody has to run the house, keep us tethered to the real world, keep us moving down the right path."

"I'm lost in thought?"

"We call it the Rebeccasphere, the zone of occlusion, a happy world of your own where you spend your time and ignore all of those things that need to get done, you know, like buying clothes, doing chores, signing up for camp or extracurriculars. Who does those for you, sweetie?"

"Oh, Mom." Rebecca's Jersey girl accent fades. Two miles have passed on the odometer.

"And now the thing with boys has really sent her over the edge. She thought she had it figured out, and then you go change the game on her." Guns N' Roses plays on the radio.

"I was only being friendly to Alex."

'High Organian!' He can hear Saabrina's High Organian accent. "Look, we can have these nice father-daughter talks, but you're not my daughter. Saabrina, talk to me."

"Bob, where are we?"

"On this world, or whatever this place is, we're driving to Guido's to get food for dinner. What's the last thing you remember?"

"Lying in bed, saying good morning to you, watching…watching…me? Was that me as Laura?"

"Yes."

"Bloody hell, I'm going to be sick."

"Do I need to pull over?"

"No, I'm speaking figuratively, not literally. Keep going." With a start, she wraps the towel around as much of her body as she can. "What am I wearing?"

"You've taken the form of a rebellious teenage Rebecca. I think you know what you're wearing."

Saabrina touches her flesh, runs her hand on the dashboard, then looks out the window. "I can see it all now. I'm out there somewhere, nearby, yet cut-off. I can't bring myself here, only this form. Am I making sense?"

"Yes."

"I love Rebecca, but I want to be me."

"How do we make you Saabrina again?"

"I don't know." She turns the radio off with a loud snap. "Really, Bob, 'Take me down to the prairie dog city?' I do know one thing; the music here sounds awful."

"I was saying that on the ride up. It must be bad if I notice."

She looks at him. "The songs are yours."

"The songs? I don't write songs."

"No, you knucklehead. I recognize them from your memories. They sound so awful because your brain bollocks them up whilst hearing them and now we hear what you hear."

"You mean it's not prairie dog city?"

"Seriously? No, Bob, it's paradise city, paradise city. Ugh."

"I didn't know. I really screw them up?"

"Frightfully. Most songs, not all. You still remember large chunks of "American Pie." And "Scenes from an Italian Restaurant." Strangely you know all the words, although I believe Mr. Joel would be rather upset if he ever heard you sing them."

"It was Laura's and my favorite."

She touches his arm. "Oh, Bob, I'm so sorry. I didn't think to ask. It must be hard to see her again."

"Is and isn't. When a memory is flowing, I'm part of a scene and she's my wife again. And when it stops, she's you and it's not so bad. But it does hurt, when I stop to think about it, because I remember how much I miss her. And it also doesn't hurt because she's back and right there and I'm happy to have her. Crazy, huh?"

"No. Not at all."

"Thanks." He focuses on the road. "So, does the bad music mean anything?"

"Possibly? Maybe? I don't know." She looks out the window. "All I know is, like everything else on this world, they appear to be from your memories."

He sees Price Chopper pass on the left. They're getting close to their destination. "Look, when you're near Laura, you become Rebecca. And not a very good copy of Rebecca, some sort of a sitcom version of her."

"I know. As you said, the memories take over and we start playing parts. If you don't have an exact recollection of an event…"

"Like you and Alex?"

"Precisely. I fill in based on what I've learned from you and Rebecca and approximate her behavior: in Alex's case, bits and pieces from her conduct with boys that summer. I can't stop it."

"You need to try. I need the two of you as Saabrina, not Laura and Rebecca. We need to figure out what's going on and get out of here. Can you talk to the other, uh, you from here?"

"No. I feel her, me, her, but I can't communicate. She's scared without you there, without your memories. It's not good; everyone's milling about the pool not saying a word to her and waiting for our return. We have to get back."

"We will." Bob sees Guido's market coalescing together on the left. He pulls in and parks in an empty spot near the front door, cars springing up around them. "First, let's go shopping. We have to keep up appearances for whoever is doing this." He gets out of the Subaru.

Rebecca comes around the front of the car and takes him by the hand. "Bob, at least you have Laura again."

"At least I have Saabrina back." He gives her a hug. "Come on, grab a cart, let's make this quick."

Chapter 28

IN THE HOSPITAL'S ICU, EDDIE FINDS REBECCA SITTING CROSS-legged on a chair watching her friends. The windows surrounding her reveal women bathed in warm red light, sleepers clothed in comfortable pajamas floating a meter above the floor, Juliette made obvious by the nimbus of blond hair about her head. He makes his way past medical personnel quietly darting in and out of rooms to Rebecca's side.

Feeling a tap on her shoulder, Rebecca turns with a start, then jumps up and gives him a hug. "Hi, Eddie, you didn't have to come here."

"I wanted to check on you." He looks in the windows. "I see they're still in Intensive Care."

"They are. At least they look peaceful. The surgeons told me they're better, almost ready to start rehab."

"Yes, I heard. I wanted to talk to you about rehab." He gently tugs her arm. "Here, come with me."

"OK. Where are we going?"

"There's a nice little atrium down the hall where we can sit." They pass one room after another, each holding a single floating body. Pushing through large double doors, they find a glassed-in terrace overlooking a snow-covered park. Eddie leads them to a pair of chairs by a window, settling Rebecca into one before returning with two glasses of water. He sets the glasses down on the small table between them and takes his seat.

Rebecca holds up a glass. "Thanks. I don't know why, but sitting there makes me thirsty."

"You're welcome. How's your day been?

"Nice, nothing exciting. I've been here most of the afternoon. Mr. Lerner came by earlier to chat. Tonight, if it's OK with you and Brenda, Austin's planning to take me to one of his cool restaurants for dinner and introduce me to some of his friends. They've never met an Earth girl before. He's been really nice to me since I got here."

"Brenda will be fine. She loves having you here on Madison, but the whirlwind of activity has been tiring for her. I think she will appreciate an evening off."

"Oh, good. I hope I've not been…"

"Not in the least. As I said, we're very happy to have you here." He sips water. "I wanted to talk to you about what will happen next to your friends."

"OK."

"First, they have to start their physical rehabilitation."

"Starting rehab is good, right?"

"It is. However, given the circumstances, the doctors can't wake them, so they'll be performing their exercises while unconscious. I don't want you to see that."

"I'll be fine."

"No, you won't. The motions they will make can be violent; they'll look like possessed sleepwalkers to you. It's not anything anyone but an expert should see."

"Oh. I wanted to be there for them." Rebecca looks down at her lap.

"I know. This time you can't; they can't even know you're here. They can't know you know." Eddie drinks some more water. "The tricky part is coming—getting them back into their old lives."

Rebecca looks up. "Mr. Lerner said they'd be returned in ways to answer questions and make sense to them and those who know them."

"Exactly. Go on, what else did he tell you?"

"Uh, for Juliette, it will be easier because she had told her family she was going on a trip by herself. After she left Geneva, he said she'll remember some travel in the north of Italy, going from town to town, B&B to B&B, and will…how did he put it? 'Regret only the one night with what turned out to be a poor choice in a young man.'"

"That's right. She won't remember Vildakaya when this is done. We're changing records on Earth to match, temporarily inserting her likeness into local advertising and television so people will believe they know her if asked. She's going to come home to a pretty large credit card bill."

"And she'll be fine?"

"Yes."

"He didn't tell me about Sachita. It won't be as easy for her?"

"Her circumstances present difficulties. She watched them kill Brian before they assaulted her." Rebecca shudders. Eddie reaches out his hand; she takes it. When she regains her composure, she wipes away the tears and sits silently. He begins again. "We can't erase her loss, robbing her of her experience. We can attempt to soften it. In addition, her family and the police have been searching for her and Brian, something we must consider."

"What will she remember? Not something horrible, right?"

"We have to create a story encompassing the totality of what happened to her. I know you understand the need for this."

She studies the condensation on her glass for a moment, working the water drops with her thumbs. "I do."

"Unfortunately, doing so will require us to take some liberties. I hope you don't judge us too harshly for what I'm about to tell you. We abhor involving ourselves in the everyday lives of the inhabitants of protected worlds."

"We call it the Prime Directive."

"From *Star Trek*. Your father has mentioned it to me numerous times, a concept we adhere to within the constraints of ensuring the security of protected worlds. In Sachita's case, one of our fellow sentinels, Dana Banks…have you met Dana?"

"No. Saabrina told me about her. She sounds nice."

"She is. Hopefully, you'll have the chance to meet her and her Saab, Isaabelle. They identified two criminals who live close enough to where Brian and Sachita had been hiking to make them plausible suspects. These two men, among other known crimes, have raped and murdered several women without detection by the police. This presents us with an opportunity to create a credible story surrounding Sachita's disappearance and obtain justice for those who perished."

"If you're going to interfere with Earth, it's good to know you're going to make it better."

"That's our goal. Sachita will remember the criminals killing Brian and kicking his body down a ravine. The authorities, with a little help from us, will recover his body in a few days and find Sachita having escaped from the criminals. Although she will bear evidence of being raped and beaten, most of her memory of the actual assault will be removed leaving her with a dim sense of what she experienced."

"Experienced with the two criminals, not Vildakaya?"

"Yes. Experts will chalk up her memory loss to a normal reaction to a horrific situation. Subsequently, the police will find the two criminals as well as evidence of her captivity. Unfortunately, this will make the news."

"Ugh. But, the men won't know her. Won't they deny kidnapping her?"

Eddie sighs. "We will be altering their memories as well as Sachita's. They will remember Brian and Sachita and conflate her with other women they raped. We're doing this so Sachita will not doubt what happened to her. To be just to the men, our evidence will be insufficient to convict them at trial, but will lead the police to the men's true wrongdoings. Several murders, once uncovered, will put them in prison for the rest of their lives."

"Eddie, it's not just the interference with Earth, it's playing with peoples' minds and…"

"And bending rules of evidence and legal procedures. We don't do this lightly. Over the last couple of days many people in the Department of Justice, DoSOPS, and other government agencies have worked long hours to determine how best to return Juliette, Sachita, and the other women to their lives. They followed policies and procedures built up over many years. A Federal court gave us permission to tamper with memories, but only when necessary and to the least extent possible. I hope this provides some comfort."

"It does."

"I apologize for the 'mansplaining,' isn't that how you say it? I did not want you to think we were cavalier about these things."

"Cavalier is a word I'd never associate with you, Eddie. I understand. I understand who my dad works for and what kind of world this is. I understand you have my friends' best interests at heart." Rebecca shakes her head. "Even if it means jailing those two assholes, this all sounds horrible for Sachita. There's no better way?"

"She lost her fiancée. She requires an experience that will explain her loss and makes sense of it. A hiking accident and being lost in the woods will not suffice."

"Fiancée?"

"From what we can tell, he proposed the day before they left."

"Oh my God." They sit staring out the window, Madison's sun low in the sky, its light filtering through gray clouds. "I'm sorry, Eddie. I guess it's better than her being dead."

"I believe so."

"I can't talk to them and help them through this. I just sit there, watching them, knowing the truth and now I'm being told I won't be able to tell them. How will I keep this a secret when I see them?"

"You will. I know you will because you're strong and you want to help your friends. Telling them will only cause hurt." Finishing his water, Eddie pushes his glass to the center of the table. "There's someone I would like you to meet."

"A psychiatrist?"

"No, unless you would like one. I'm speaking of a friend of mine, the head of the physics department at one of the universities here on Madison. I think you will like her. She'd like to ask you some questions."

Rebecca smiles as Jean's words play in her head. "Is she a scientific historian? She wants to talk to a living fossil?"

Eddie laughs. "Yes, to a degree. She wants to talk about your research. She believes you could enlighten her as to how scientific discoveries from her past were made. First, though, she'd like to ask you about the anomalies at the LHC; they've recently experienced a few themselves and would appreciate your help."

"Seriously?"

"Seriously. But you know the real reason she wants to meet you."

"I do."

"Then would you like to meet her?"

"Yes."

"Good. Let's go."

Saabra appears outside the windows and flashes her lights at them. *Come along, little one, we do not want to be late.*

"Wait, what about my friends?"

"I'll bring you back tomorrow. Now it's time you thought about yourself."

Chapter 29

"BOB, YOU TELL THE STORY MUCH BETTER THAN I DO." LAUGH-ter. The contents of two empty wine bottles have had their effect on Laura, Jim, and Diane. "Come on, tell it." Laura rises to move dirty plates from the dining room table to the sink while Bob puts leftovers into the refrigerator, its beige plastic door covered with magnets holding notes, lists, and the business cards of local vendors.

Bob plays along with the other three; the red fluid in his glass tastes and behaves like water. He looks over to the couch to see Alex and Rebecca giggling at YouTube videos on her laptop; on the return from Guido's he had watched Saabrina turn back into Rebecca the second she came into contact with Laura. Between telling stories to entertain the guests and serving dinner, Bob had spent most of the evening trying to figure out how to get Saabrina back. He turns to his guests. "Come on guys, you must have heard this one before."

Diane spears one last bit of dessert from her plate. "We have. We want to hear it again."

"Fine, I'll tell it, again." Bob walks back to the dining room table and re-takes his seat. "Rebecca was small, maybe three, four…"

"Four" yells Laura over water running in the sink.

"Laura had been up all night at the hospital putting high school kids back together after a horrific car accident. She spent a lot of time putting high school kids back together."

The four parents shake their heads.

Turning off the tap, Laura glances over at Rebecca. "Those kids were so young."

"You were young."

"Not that young."

"Anyway, after being up all night, she went straight to Rebecca's Montessori school to help the class moms make costumes and decorations for a play."

"Butterflies. They were going to be butterflies."

"Am I telling the story or are you? The kids were going to be butterflies. So, Laura walked in thirty minutes late and joined the ladies at a big table in the assembly room. She didn't get a chance to go home and change so she was still in her white coat and scrubs…"

"At least they were a clean pair of scrubs; I wouldn't have left the hospital covered in blood."

"Duly noted. All she wanted was to get there and be one of the moms for once. The ladies were already working, cutting paper, drawing, painting, making wings, and from across the table the leader of the class moms…"

"Julia Warren."

"Julia Warren watched her sit down on the bench and said in a loud voice 'Oh look, our eminent doctor fancy pants has deigned to grace us with her presence this morning.' Bam,

Laura was halfway up on the table pulling a scalpel from her pocket."

"It wasn't a scalpel. One of those safety scissors for little kids that I happened to have in my hand. They don't cut anything."

"Whatever. Luckily for her, and us, one of the other moms…"

"Halle Jones."

"Halle Jones had been watching the whole thing. She was FBI and her spider-sense had been tingling. Apparently, Julia had been making fun of Laura all morning and Halle had both expected her to say something stupid and Laura to react. Halle had Laura safely down and the scalpel…"

"Scissors."

"… pocketed in a nanosecond. Julia never made fun of Laura again."

Jim laughs. "I love that story."

Laura comes back to the table. "I can't claim all the credit. Halle, who I think was six foot two and built like a linebacker, had a word with Julia later, which also helped." She yawns, looks at the clock over the sink. It reads 10:13. "Is it really that late?"

Jim rises. "We need to get to bed. Early start for home tomorrow."

Bob stands as well. "Sure we can't entice you to stay? Ride in the morning, then you join us at Tanglewood?"

"We'd love to buddy, but we have to pick Noah up at camp and ferry him to his lacrosse clinic."

Diane joins Jim, curling her arms around him. "Can we help you with the dishes?"

"No, Laura and I got it. You get going."

Diane crosses the living room. "Alex put down the laptop and go to bed. We have to get up early tomorrow."

"Mom, come on, I'm in college now. I can stay up."

"You're not in college yet, mister, and if you want to get there in one piece I suggest you get downstairs." With a pull from his mom, Alex jumps up, makes his goodbyes, then heads for the basement. "I'll be down in a minute to say goodnight; don't forget to brush your teeth." Diane follows Jim up to their room.

Laura and Bob finish cleaning the table and kitchen and loading the dishwasher before collecting Rebecca from the couch for the walk upstairs. They get no argument. She yawns and makes a beeline to her room. "Too easy," says Bob.

"I know."

"I'll wait outside." Bob takes residence at his desk on the loft, pretending to look at the screen on his computer. Much like the books he has tried to read, everything on the screen is a jumble of meaningless garbage. Laura goes into their room to get ready for bed. He waves goodnight to Jim and Diane as they finish in the hall bath and close the door to their bedroom. Bob puts out the light and waits.

He hears the door to Rebecca's room open. As she gets to the loft, he turns on the light, startling her.

"Dad?"

"Have a seat." Bob points to the chair across from him. Rebecca sits. Bob focuses on Rebecca. "I don't know what's downstairs, but it's not Alex Trout or even human. So, I think it would be a bad idea to mate with it." Rebecca looks stunned. "You're not Rebecca. The real Rebecca won't lose her virginity for another year. This isn't a memory, so snap out of it." Angry silence greets him. "Fine, here's the real story. Rebecca never got along with Alex and went to sleep early that night." Bob leans forward. "Next spring, after the prom and against our instructions, she went down the shore with her date and his friends." Squirming, she pulls up her legs and wraps them in her arms. "When we found out, Laura and I were fit to be tied. At six a.m., she called, hysterical, asking to be picked up. Our rule was no questions, so I went to get her and didn't say a word."

Rebecca becomes still. Sitting up, she places her feet back on the floor. Her question comes in a crisp High Organian accent. "So how do you know what happened?"

"Laura got it out of her later."

"I didn't know. It's not something Rebecca shared with me. I may have come across Alex however."

"Poking around where you weren't supposed to be?"

"Perhaps. You're right, Rebecca didn't like him."

"Look, I need you to go to bed. If you're asleep, I'm hoping I can talk to the other you."

"But if I go to sleep, I might wake up as Rebecca again."

"We'll have to take that chance. Find a prompt, something to break the memories. I don't know, just keep thinking 'I don't like Alex.'" Bob escorts Rebecca to her bedroom, tucks her in, and gives her a goodnight kiss on the forehead. Amidst the debris field of clothes on the other twin bed, he spots something in her half-emptied bag. "This might help." She takes Muffin Traveldog from him and snuggles under her covers.

Approaching his bedroom door, for once in his life Bob hopes what he finds on the other side comes from his memories and not his fantasies. Opening the door, memories rule. Lights on, Laura, her nose in a book, sits up under the white Marimekko covers of their Ikea platform bed, a simple geometric print on the duvet, behind her back a pillow sham with a matching pattern stacked against the blonde wood of the headboard. She looks at him through her glasses. "Everything good?"

"All good. She's gone to bed, for real."

"Thanks. Now go get ready yourself."

Hoping Rebecca will fall asleep and Laura will become Saabrina, Bob dawdles putting on pajamas and brushing his teeth. He runs his hand through his hair, watching his reflection in the mirror. 'Hmmm, I really have gone gray. My hair was still brown eight years ago when all this happened.' He pokes at his face, ticking those new, nasty sharp white hairs fighting to pop free of his skin, pulls on his love handles, and pats his ever-present paunch. 'Definitely the wrong side of fifty-four, not forty-six.' He emerges from the bathroom to find Laura smiling at him.

"What took so long? Get lost in there?" She wiggles to her left to make room for him.

"No, I think I know my way around the bathroom." He sits next to her.

She surprises him by putting down her book to take his hands in hers. "What's so funny?"

"What do you mean?"

"You have a silly smile on your face."

"Oh, you. Just you."

Taking off her glasses, she pulls him closer, his memory moving toward fantasy.

'I'll be damned if I'll kiss my dead wife.' He finds he can't pull himself away as she draws them together. They kiss, tentative at first, saying goodnight, then the real thing, lips pressed firmly together. 'It's been a long time and it's nice and she feels so real and so warm.' The kissing boils on. Then their lips barely touch; separating, their mouths slip away, and are, once again, apart. He opens his eyes to see green ones staring wide into his.

Laura pushes him back. "Bob, what are you doing?"

"I'm kissing my wife, Saabrina."

She jerks back to the headboard, pulling the sheets close. With her right hand, she finds and puts on her glasses. "You weren't doing anything untoward?"

"There's a duvet between us and I'm not transdimensional, so I don't see how. Do I need to tell you about the birds and the bees?"

"No, as I have said before, I fully comprehend the mechanics of human mating." She peeks under the covers, then looks relieved.

"Laura may have been a nudist at heart, but she always wore PJs when there were guests in the house."

"Thank God."

"I'm glad you're back. My bet about what would happen when Rebecca fell asleep paid off."

"Bob?"

"Yes, Saabrina?"

"We need to get out of here."

"I know."

"If we don't, if we're still here in a year and I'm Laura…"

"I know, we'll get away. We'll figure it out. What can you tell me?"

"I'm scared. I'm truly scared."

He takes her hand. "Everything will be fine. Let's focus on figuring this out. I lost you for the whole day and the other you couldn't tell me much when I had her alone."

"Is she OK?"

"She's good. You two had a pretty nasty argument at the pool."

"I vaguely recall having words with her."

"She's going to try to fight becoming Rebecca when she wakes up."

"Oh. I wish I could do that, too, I mean, not become Laura. I don't know how. The memories sweep over me, take control the moment I see Rebecca, or when some other event you experienced happens. It's all your memories."

"You need something to focus on, to grab hold of." He lets go of her hands and pulls the glasses off her face.

"Everything's gone blurry."

"You don't have Laura's brown eyes. You may have taken her form, but you have your beautiful green eyes. Look through them. Focus, literally focus."

Saabrina concentrates, squinting at Bob. She closes her eyes, breathes in deeply, lets her face go blank, reopens them. "I can see you clearly. Did you bother to shave this morning?"

"No, we were on the run."

She rubs her chin. "No wonder I'm chafed."

"So, again, what can you tell me?"

"Nothing. I'm disconnected from my sensors. I'm as much a part of this world as this bed, so it all looks real to me." She brushes his stubbly beard with the back of her hand. "But you're not, you can see what's real. Let's swap. I'll ask and you tell me."

"OK. What?"

"What have you seen that's not right? What's different?"

"I don't know."

"Come on Bob, think. I remember the house seemed fake to you. What else?"

"Well, every time we drive the roadside assembles around us, then disappears once we go by. I see space and stars through it. The roads are green threads we drive on. The people, well not you, Rebecca, or the Trouts, are like green blobs."

"Green blobs?"

"They look like people, except translucent, the light coming through their clothes and bodies. Everything around here not—how should I put it? Defined? Fixed? Making an effort to look real?—looks green."

"Like the roads?"

"Yes."

"You said you saw green men at Tanglewood."

"You remember. And a green man sat next to me back at the concert on Madison, come to think of it." Fog begins to clear; memories from his future reappear.

"So, whoever runs this place doesn't bother to or can't create a whole reality at once; they form what they need as required. And by default, its color is green."

"Is green important?"

"Seems so, I just can't remember why and I don't have a whole massive bloody database to search."

He takes her hand again. "Chillax."

"You chillax. You're not dying. You won't be dead in a year as I so rudely pointed out to myself this afternoon."

"She said she was…"

"Young, passionate, curious, wants to live. I want to live, too."

"And you're?"

"Wise, knowledgeable, possess self-control… right, let's get back to it. Your description suggests we reside in a real world formed from material that can be changed at will, not a computer-generated reality."

"We're not in the *Matrix*?"

"No, we're not in the *Matrix*. You're real. I'm something in between. Everything else is…" She pulls on the sheets until a hole appears. "Whatever this is. Hmm, what else? Please, Bob, anything, anything weird, anything you fear to say out loud."

"I hear voices."

"Voices?" Saabrina restrains herself from saying 'maybe not anything.'

"I hear them when they're directing my memories and when something goes wrong. Voices in the background. I've heard them before; I just don't remember where."

"Oh. They're directing your memories, which means they want us at this time for a specific reason. Why now? What happens?"

"We're on vacation. Today was the Trouts. Tomorrow is Tanglewood. After tomorrow, more of the usual in the Berkshires."

"They, whoever they are, think something important will happen, has happened, did happen. What could it be?"

"Haven't a clue."

"Me neither." She falls back into her pillow. "I'm tired. Why do humans tire so rapidly?"

"Poor design, as you would say. Let's go to sleep. Do you want me to sleep downstairs?"

"No, we need to keep up appearances."

Bob walks around to his side of the bed, turning off the light switch by the door. As he lifts the covers, she pulls them back down with a woosh of air.

"Bob, what are you doing?"

"I'm getting into bed. What, you don't want me to snuggle up to you? You liked it in Mexico."

"I was playing your six-year-old daughter; now I have the body of your wife. I don't want you to get any ideas."

A whole range of responses plays through Bob's mind: 'You're a middle-aged Jewish woman, so you're not going to be interested in 'any ideas' anyway' seems too clichéd; 'What, you don't want to experience sex as a human?' would probably result in books and lamps being thrown at him; 'Hey, sleeping next to my dead wife creeps me out too' would probably elicit the same response. He opts for "It's a king-size bed. There's practically room for the state of New Jersey between us. I can sleep on top of the comforter if you want."

"No, get in. Just stay over there."

"Thanks for the trust."

"I have wisdom and foresight."

"Harrumph." Bob gets into bed.

After a minute, she takes his hand and scoots over to snuggle up to him. "I'm scared."

He pulls her closer. "I know. We'll get this sorted out in time, I promise. Now go to sleep. Everything will be fine."

"Goodnight, Bob."

"Goodnight Saabrina, see you in the morning. And try to be, well, you, when you wake up." He hears her breathing become shallow. Light snoring follows. "Laura always fell asleep fast, too." Closing his eyes, he joins her, thinking 'I hope she's Saabrina in the morning, I hope she's Saabrina in the morning, I hope…"

Chapter 30

THERE IS NO MORNING. AFTERNOON LIGHT STREAMS INTO the car. Bob wakes with a start at the wheel of their Subaru, one in an endless row of Subarus. There's not a Saab in sight. 'Damn.' He sees they are parked outside the main Tanglewood entrance gate. 'At least they're not going to make us walk.' To his right Laura sits in the passenger seat, Rebecca clutching Muffin Traveldog behind. "You two just woke up, too, huh?"

Laura takes off her glasses. "Yes, Bob." Rebecca's "Uh huh" follows, both in High Organian accents, beautiful to his ears.

"At least they dressed us properly, so we're not still in our PJs."

"Or naked," comes from Rebecca.

"OK, let's get out." Bob opens his door and steps onto the combination of grass, sandy soil, and gravel typical of a Tanglewood parking lot. 'Pretty real. Could have fooled me.' Checking his pants pocket, he extracts three tickets. Laura and Rebecca join him by the side of the car. "Brahms's Piano Concerto no. 2, one of our favorites. We're in the Shed, up front instead of in the cheap seats out back. Someone must have splurged on our tickets." He goes around to the tailgate. Looking in he sees nothing: no cooler, no drinks, no bags.

Laura calls "What is it, Bob?"

"I guess we're eating Tanglewood food today." In the cool, crisp air, they join the queue of noisily chatting concert-goers waiting to present their tickets. "Saabrinas, what do you see?"

Rebecca snuggles closer to Bob. "Green people. Lots of green people, all translucent blobs like those at the pool."

Laura moves closer as well. "Bob, they sound excited."

"They do indeed." Once through the gate, the crowd quickly sweeps them past the throngs picnicking and lounging on the lawn to their seats. Seated, Bob admires how real everything looks. The Shed and its seats betray no green hues, no feeling of boxes without contents, no sudden manifestation of new objects coming into sight as they walk by. The dirt under his feet, the worn and nicked wood of the chairs, the polished instruments waiting on the stage—it all looks authentic. He hears the voices say "Good." He tugs at the seat in front of him half expecting it to bend like putty; nothing happens. "It feels so real."

Rebecca hops up. "I'm going for a walk." She scoots by Laura and Bob into the aisle and makes her way to the back.

"Saabrina, where's she going?"

"My guess is she's surveying the grounds." She pokes at a piece of metal joining the wood parts of a seat row. "They did a fabulous job. Brilliant, just brilliant. I'd never know I wasn't really at Tanglewood."

The first bell rings. Rebecca returns, crossing past Bob and Laura to retake her seat. The other two lean in to hear her report over the buzz of the audience. "The Shed and the lawn closest to it are perfect recreations. A little further out, the grounds fade away. A building is a façade, a tree a sketch until you peer at it. When I reached the edge, I found we're on an island hanging in space."

The second bell rings. The buzzing dies down. The members of the orchestra take the stage—green gummy figures in translucent white shirts and black pants and skirts. They sit on chairs with music stands before them and take up their instruments. Soon, the cacophony of the orchestra members individually warming up wafts across the stage. The third bell rings. The Shed goes silent as the lead oboe plays A sharp for the orchestra; section by section the players join in as they finish tuning their instruments. The orchestra quiets and waits. Coughs pepper the audience. Applause starts gently to Bob's left before sweeping across the concertgoers as Isaiah Cleaver and the green figure of the conductor walk to center stage from his right.

Laura pokes Bob, hard. "He's the real Isaiah Cleaver."

At the piano, Cleaver quickly scans the audience; with a startled look, he fixes his gaze on Bob. Bob stares back, mouth half-open. The conductor raps his baton twice to get Cleaver's attention, then sweeps up his hands. With a drop of the baton, the horns open the first movement. Cleaver begins to play. It sounds so real, so beautiful to Bob. The lush violins follow, the horns return, Cleaver answers. 'Wonderful, wonderful.' For the first time since he woke on this world, he relaxes, enjoying the music, letting the sound roll over him. Around him, the audience sits rapt while Laura and Rebecca watch the stage as if mesmerized, their green eyes glued to the movements of Cleaver's hands on the piano keys, waves of music coursing through their bodies. The movement ends with a crescendo, the audience erupting into applause. 'European style; Americans wait for the whole piece's finale.' Cleaver and the conductor momentarily leave the stage as the orchestra retunes.

"Saabrinas, they were awesome. I mean the orchestra was OK, but Cleaver, wow."

"Bob, shhhh. Look around."

The bodies of the audience have changed. They sport pieces of white shirts and black slacks. Bob sees bone and muscle under their translucent green skin. "They're becoming real. As they listen to the music, I guess they become more real."

Laura takes Rebecca's left hand. "You felt the music. We can do it in the next movement if we concentrate."

"It will hurt."

"We have to try." Laura turns to Bob. "Don't look at us."

"What?"

"When the music starts again, don't look at us. Please." Laura grasps both of Rebecca's hands. The two huddle close in their seats with eyes closed, concentrating, as Cleaver and the conductor return to applause. Cleaver strikes the keys and the second movement begins. Bob hears beautiful, real music. As Cleaver plays and the orchestra responds, he fights the urge to look to his left. Failing, he sees Laura and Rebecca sitting shoulder to shoulder with hands held, heads bent together, eyes closed, their whole bodies glowing like red hot coals, pulsing with every note Cleaver plays. Bob looks away and focuses on the music, trying to lose himself. Again, at the movement's end, the audience erupts into applause, and Cleaver and the conductor leave the stage.

"Bob, you can look now."

Bob turns to find Saabrina sitting next to him. He sweeps her into his arms, the armrest jamming into his side, fighting back tears.

"It's OK, Bob."

"But Laura and Rebecca."

"They were never here. You know that. Pull yourself together."

Bob sits back in his seat. "Are you OK?"

"Yes, I'm me again. I am having a hard time connecting to the rest of myself. It's sort of intermittent."

"Well…"

The conductor and Cleaver return to the stage. "Shhh" comes from the woman in front of him, now wearing an entire white shirt and half a face of green-hued flesh. The third movement begins slowly, then flows into the fourth without a break. The finale brings wild applause from the audience. Cleaver returns no less than four times to take a bow and acknowledge the conductor and the orchestra. Jumping down from the stage, he pushes through the crowd of people leaving their seats and comes straight to Bob. "You're real!"

Bob stands to greet him. "Yes, Mr. Cleaver, I am."

Cleaver looks at Saabrina. "She's not. She's more real than one of these green things," he waves at the audience, "although, they look more human than they did before."

"You're right, she's not like us, but she is real. She's a hologram of an AI. Mr. Cleaver, please meet my partner and friend, Saabrina."

Saabrina stands and shakes Cleaver's hand. "It's an honor to meet you, Mr. Cleaver. I greatly enjoyed your performance."

"Thank you. And you must be Bob."

"I am. My name is Bob Foxen. How did you know?"

"I've been here for I don't know how long, getting ready for this concert. To keep me entertained while we rehearsed, they had friends of yours stop by and say hello. Or I should say they pretended to be friends of yours and we pretended to have rather boring conversations about the weather."

"I'm sorry about that."

"It's good to talk to real people. Mr. Foxen, why did you bring me here?"

"I didn't. They, whoever they are, did, and brought us as well. Did you learn anything about them?"

"A little. They seem very interested in you. And this performance. Do you know why?"

"I don't."

"Come on Mr. Foxen, there must have been something for these things to go to all this effort. Is there something special about Concerto no. 2?"

"I saw you play it here years ago. It was one of my favorite concerts."

"So?"

"It was also the last concert before my wife's cancer returned."

"They don't care about your wife's cancer."

Bob blanches.

"Sorry, I didn't mean to offend you. I quickly realized we're as ersatz to them as they are to us. We're simply spirits who they call to bring the music. It must be something else."

"Come to think of it, I did tell the voices about it."

Saabrina turns to Bob. "Bob, the voices you hear here? When?"

"I remember now. When we were almost out of unreality, when you got stuck for a moment before we exited the break." Cleaver looks confused. "Sorry, Mr. Cleaver. Saabrina is also a spacecraft. In a battle, we fell into a hole…"

"Break." Saabrina frowns at him.

"Break in the spacetime continuum where I spoke to the voices about the Brahms concert at Tanglewood. We were stuck for a moment, but the questions and my answers felt like they took forever."

"Bob, the only thing in the break with us was protomatter. Are you telling me you spoke with protomatter? It's not alive. It doesn't think."

Cleaver raises a hand. "Protomatter?"

Saabrina touches Bob's arm. "Let me. Simply put, they are green…" She looks at the crowd around them, then continues "Little point-sized globules of stuff that haven't turned into the what the universe is made out of yet."

"And Mr. Foxen, you spoke to them, the protomatter?"

"Yes, the voices must be how the protomatter speaks to me." He looks at Saabrina. "The voices are the protomatter." He turns back to Cleaver. "It all started with Beethoven's Ninth. I'd brought along a compact disc of a Tanglewood recording and they loved it. They played it over and over."

"The 9th?"

"Yes."

Cleaver sits. "Beethoven's Ninth Symphony, recorded at Tanglewood. I know it well. An excellent performance, nearly perfect. Mr. Foxen, tell me what you think of when you think of the 9th."

"It's the last concert of the summer. It ends one season, or, in my mind, one year, and starts another."

"So death and rebirth. Yes. Many orchestras play it on New Year's Eve; in Japan, it's a great tradition to ring in the new year with the Daiku, the Big Nine as they say. Please, go further."

"Well, it's more than rebirth. When the chorus sings the "Ode to Joy," it's almost like Beethoven is trying to call a new, better world into place. A great world to replace the old, evil world around him."

"Exactly. Beethoven's call to unite humanity in a world of love and peace. And I bet you understood that from the music alone. Do you know what the "Ode's" words mean?"

Bob looks down. "I don't know German and I never got around to reading a translation."

"Typical. Don't worry, most don't, but still they comprehend both the meaning of the "Ode" and know Elysium is some sort of paradise."

"Yeah, that's how I understand it."

"And what if your 'stuff that hasn't turned into what the universe is made out of' heard Beethoven's call and answered it?"

There's a long pause. The bell rings and the orchestra files onto the stage, green-hued men and women in white shirts and black pants and skirts, taking their positions with their instruments.

"Bob, the protomatter is everywhere. If it became like everything else, and I'm not saying it could, it might displace our universe."

"That would be bad?"

"Very bad."

Saabrina turns to Cleaver. "Mr. Cleaver, why do you look so concerned about the 9th? Why do you believe they answered the call, as you said?"

"Because I can hear it. They've been playing it, out there, maybe at another Tanglewood they've built, slowly, getting better, getting stronger. And when they finish…"

Bob sits. "They'll call themselves into a new world."

"Or universe" adds Saabrina.

"How far along are they?"

Cleaver listens. "Early in the third movement. Their tempo is slow, but they are increasing its rate." He waves his finger while counting. "Give me a minute." The second bell rings. "From what I've heard and assuming a constant acceleration in tempo, three days more, maybe four, but not more than that."

"So what is this?" Bob points to the stage.

"A test run, or better, a test itself, the final exam of a course to show their spirit guide, you, they have mastered one of his favorite compositions."

"The Brahms concert I told them about."

"Exactly."

"Why not bring me right to the 9th?"

"They were not ready. This group brought me here to learn how to play. With their new knowledge, they taught the others who currently play the 9th. They were very good students, quick studies who learned their lessons well. They did nicely on their final exam, a B plus I would say, considering the source." Cleaver taps Bob's head. "Of course I know the piece so I was able to help them. Unlike the crap we are about to hear. I couldn't fix Brahms's Fourth Symphony."

"Sorry, my memories sort of shred the music. You held them together for this performance?"

"Yes. I taught them their parts of the Second Concerto. That I could do something with."

Saabrina leans in. "Mr. Cleaver, how awful will the symphony be, if I may ask?"

"Terrible. I doubt they'll get through ten measures before it all falls apart. Not like the 9th; their performance should be flawless courtesy of the disc and my help teaching them to play."

The third bell rings. Loud applause from row after row of expectant concert-goers greets the conductor. Saabrina tugs the two men's shoulders. "Gentlemen, we need to leave. Now."

Bob rises, followed by Cleaver, and the three walk, then run for the back of the Shed. The conductor raises his baton. The orchestra waits. The baton falls and the orchestra plays, the first few notes gloriously lush. At the back of the Shed, the trio turns hard right for the exit and the parking lots beyond. The music breaks into a terrible wail, shaking the steel columns of the Shed, shattering the wooden roof, scouring the dirt floor into clouds of dust. Bob grabs Cleaver and Saabrina to brace against the sound while watching concertgoers whirl into the air, still raptly listening in their seats. The orchestra plays on, desperately fighting to right the music. Running again, the island in space trembles beneath their feet. *Come on, Bob, faster.* Bob hears Saabrina through the link! Dodging branches thrown by trees and holes opening black with stars, they reach the gate. Bob shouts "Almost there, Mr. Cleaver." To his surprise, a green whirlwind carries Cleaver away.

Bob, take my hand. Saabrina reaches back, grasps Bob's outstretched fingers and leaps into the air, pulling him into the sky, flying them into the cold dark, transforming into a Saab, bringing him inside through her open door, settling him in her driver's seat as the island in space bursts into billions of green particles.

Chapter 31

BRIGHT ORANGE LIGHT FILLS SAABRINA'S WINDOWS. BOB wakes to find her skimming along the surface of the Sun, darting through plumes of erupting plasma. "What are you doing? Are you washing your hair?"

"No, I've been waiting for you."

"Waiting for me?"

"To finally wake up; you've been asleep for a long time." She sounds peeved.

He looks out the window at the roiling plasma, trying to collect his thoughts. "We need to find Isaiah Cleaver."

"Whatever for?"

"He knows what the protomatter wants. Wait, I know what the protomatter wants, Cleaver can help me with the timing."

"What are you talking about?"

"The protomatter is playing Beethoven's Ninth Symphony. We need to get to Cleaver: he knows their timing and when they're going to end our universe. You know that."

"No, I don't. We need to resume our work and you need to thoroughly wake up and slough off this sleep-induced nonsense running through your head."

"Saabrina, we were just caught on some protomatter world, you were both Rebecca and Laura, it was a test run, they're playing the 9th…"

"What are you talking about? Are you ill?"

"I'm fine. We were on a world made by the protomatter. You were both Rebecca and Laura."

"Simply because you keep telling me that, doesn't make it true."

"Please listen. We heard Cleaver and them play Brahms's Piano Concerto no. 2 at Tanglewood and Cleaver told us about Beethoven's Ninth Symphony before the whole world blew up and you saved me, but they swept Cleaver off to somewhere else. Are you telling me you don't remember?"

"No, I don't remember because it didn't happen. I've been circling the sun waiting for you to wake the fuck up from whatever tantrum-induced sleep you were in."

"Tantrum? What tantrum?"

"The yelling at me for screwing up on Earth tantrum, the being angry with nasty Congresswoman Tuchis tantrum, the my-daughter-is-moving-on so my life sucks tantrum."

"Saabrina, I'm telling you we're in trouble. Big trouble. Universe ending trouble."

"And I'm telling you: you're raving. Protomatter can't make worlds and I wasn't Rebecca or Laura. I'm running a bioscan. Maybe your forgetting words in the midst of conversation is some form of incipient dementia and not normal aging."

"I'm fine."

"Strange, your scan reads normal. You are fine." Saabrina remembers her nights in Mexico and his recent trouble sleeping. "Bob, could it have been a nightmare? You were out for so long and were so troubled when we left Madison. I have difficulty seeing into dreams."

"It wasn't a dream. Check my memories."

"For what?"

"A trip to Lenox with the Trouts and the Brahms concert with Cleaver at Tanglewood. They're recently formed, they should be right there." He giggles as she pokes around.

"Those were years ago."

"Nothing now?"

"No, only the flotsam from when you dream."

"It wasn't a dream. How can you not remember? You were there."

"I don't because it didn't happen."

"So, why are we orbiting the Sun?"

"I was washing my hair."

"A minute ago you said you weren't. You ran into protomatter?"

There's a pause. "Obviously."

"It's been ages since we ran into protomatter. Not since we got caught in unreality. So now you're saying you ran into it on the way home from Madison?"

"I must have."

"Must have? You're the most precise individual I know in the universe, other than, perhaps, Saabra, and all you can say is 'must have'? Maybe we need to do a scan on you."

"A level three diagnostic?"

"Yes, a level three diagnostic sounds good."

"There are no level three diagnostics, Bob, only in *Star Trek*. Didn't you read my manual?"

"You told me not to."

"Damn straight. And don't start now."

Bob takes a deep breath. Thirsty, made virtually hot from watching the plasma swirl outside, he finds an ice cold bottle of Coca-Cola on the passenger seat, opens it, and takes a sip. 'Oh, sweet nectar of the gods!' After slaking his thirst, he slips it into her cupholder. "Saabrina, you seem upset."

"Could it be because you're napping on the job or gone mental?"

"Too much napping, I'd expect you to express some annoyance followed by good-natured ribbing about human frailties. Me being crazy, you'd worry. What's really making you angry?"

"Something has been bothering me for the longest time and I want an answer, now."

"What?"

"Bob, what did you say to the daddies of those horrid boys when you spoke to them?"

"What boys' daddies?"

"In Mexico, after Kyle and Ryan pushed me into the lazy river, you spoke to their daddies. I couldn't hear what you said other than 'Boys will be boys,' which, frankly, sounded trite. You didn't get angry, you didn't ream them out, you didn't defend me. What did you say?"

"Let me get this straight. I'm telling you we're back from a world you don't remember, we have a major problem, and you're thinking about our vacation in Mexico?"

"Yes. I need to know what you said to them."

"I told them I was disappointed."

"That's all?"

"Yes."

"I don't understand."

"It's a dad thing. I don't expect you to understand and I don't have time to explain it now; we need to get to Earth and find Cleaver."

"He's missing."

"Humor me. Check on him."

"Very well." They pass through a large solar flare, plasma burning yellow and orange around them. "He's back in his Boston apartment. Nothing public, just a flurry of emails and text messages in the last hour between Cleaver and senior management. No details other than the BSO is sending over a physician to check on his condition."

"He was with us. He was swept away in a green tornado right before you got us out of there."

"It's a coincidence."

"It's not. Please take me to him. It's important."

"No, I'm not going to trouble a man who has just returned from being missing. It would be unconscionable. And it doesn't matter, Bob, we're going back to Madison."

"Why?"

"DoSOPS has recalled us. I've been sending them reports. They're worried about you. I'm worried about you. They believe you might be suffering a breakdown."

"Saabrina, our world may be about to end and I need to talk to Cleaver. Going to Madison isn't going to help."

"I'm sorry, Bob, I need to bring you back. It's orders. And I want to get you help. I'm worried about you."

"So, we're going back?"

"We're going back." She goes into FTL.

. . .

Lerner leans forward in his chair, forearms crossed on his desk, and focuses on Bob. "Let's start again. Tell me about the voices."

Bob and Saabrina sit in the two comfortable chairs before the director's desk. Snow falls outside his windows, illuminated by the streetlights below. In deference to the late hour, Lerner has his office lights set low, with a lamp on his desk throwing warm, golden light on the three participants, pleasantly revealing the quiet look on Saabrina's face. Bob knows her expression of serious concern. Sitting close to him, she keeps her left hand moving over his right arm, holding it, stroking it, practically massaging the bones straight out of his wrist.

"Yes, in the break. The protomatter spoke to me. They're the voices I heard in my dreams, the voices who directed what just happened in Lenox, their Lenox. In the break, they wanted to know all about the music, particularly Beethoven's Ninth Symphony." Bob describes his experience in the break, or as much of it as he can remember. Now it seems more like he describes a dream.

"Why the 9th?"

"It was in Saabrina's player."

"Saabrina, is this true?"

"The disc was in my CD player. However, I remember only the pain from the protomatter and Bob shouting to me to pull myself together before we left the break."

"That's all you recorded?"

She doesn't like the term "recorded." She tries not to frown. 'Humans wouldn't say they recorded a conversation with their brain.' She answers "Yes."

"Bob, how come you didn't report this at the time?"

"Dana said she had Saabrina's report. Since we're linked, I thought Saabrina was experiencing the same thing I was and it would be in there."

Saabrina smiles. *Report, not recording. Thanks, Bob.*

'You're welcome.' Bob crosses his arms. "Dana didn't want a report from me, so I didn't write one."

"Hmmm." Lerner looks unconvinced.

"Director, I lost the disc. I had it before we entered the break and it was gone when we exited, comporting with Bob's recollection."

"Saabrina, you were literally in unreality. Anything could have happened. Anything could have happened to the disc."

"Yes, Director, you're right."

Learner leans back. "Let me get this straight, Bob. In the break, the protomatter fall in love with Beethoven's Ninth Symphony, learn all about it and Tanglewood from you, follow you around to concerts to learn more and somehow mess-up those performances in doing so, then grab you and Isaiah Cleaver to put on a performance, all so they can properly play the 9th in order to create a universe for themselves."

Bob uncrosses his arms. "Exactly. And according to Saabrina…"

"This one or the one you met in the protomatter version of Lenox, Massachusetts?"

"The Lenox one, although I know she's the same one sitting here, their new universe will displace ours."

"Which would be a problem. And the only proof we have is your word and a missing CD."

"And the green people at the concerts."

"The ones Saabrina didn't see?"

"And all the green people and things at the other Lenox, because green is the color of protomatter."

"The protomatter Lenox Saabrina doesn't remember, only you. Bob, do you know how this sounds, particularly coming from you after the last few days?"

"Nuts?"

"Exactly. And there's more. As I told you before, during your travel tube hunt we monitored problems with massive physics experiments, like the LHC on Earth, the FTL experiments on Daear, and a bunch of others, because we thought they might be related to the travel tubes. They weren't, but we did spot a pattern once we added non-protected worlds suffering similar problems, including here on Madison. Bob, they're all places you visited since you left the break. You tie them together."

"So, it has something to do with the protomatter?"

"I don't know about it having to do with protomatter. I know it has something to do with you. Maybe you brought something back from the break that is also affecting your mind."

Saabrina leans forward in her chair. "Director, excuse me, but damaging physics experiments hardly seems likely for a biological entity. And correlation doesn't mean causation."

'Thanks, Saabrina.'

You're welcome.

"I agree, but it's all we have. And here's the bigger problem: It's getting worse, spreading from sensitive science experiments to long-range communication systems, sensor arrays, and all sorts of other important technological crap. All these system failures are beginning to scare a lot of senior people. All they can point to is you, so, I'm asking you to go to Isolation until we sort this out. If things keep getting worse while you're there, we can rule you out."

Bob sits up. "Isolation?"

"A screened facility. I can't describe it better without going into a lot of terminology I don't comprehend, but others think is really important."

"A prison?"

"Sometimes."

"I need to get to the protomatter to sort this out and soon, according to Cleaver. Sticking me in Isolation won't help."

Lerner contemplates Bob. "Bob, you never struck me as the sort with a messiah complex. Why only you?"

"Because I'm the one they talk to."

"And where will you find them?"

"I don't know, but I will."

"And if you do find them, then what?"

"I know I'll figure something out. They still need me. I can feel it. That will give me a chance."

"And if you were me, with a cadre of scientists and a dozen government officials suggesting you should go to Isolation, what would you do?"

Bob slouches in his chair and looks at the ground. "Ship the crazy guy to Isolation."

The room goes silent. Snow continues to fall outside the office windows. Lerner stands and comes around his desk. Bob and Saabrina quickly join him. "Bob, everything will be fine. Give us some time. Trust us."

"OK, Boss, I'll go."

"Good, Saabrina will take you." Saabrina takes Bob's hand and leads him out of Lerner's office.

Chapter 32

"ARE WE ALMOST THERE?"

"Yes."

"Look, Saabrina, there's one more thing I want to talk about before we get to Isolation."

"What, Bob?"

"Congresswoman Tuchis."

"Did you have to mention her name with so little time before I drop you off? What about her?"

"Not her. The problem. There is no magic bullet to solve this. This isn't a movie where someone sits down with her and says the right thing and changes her mind. This is the reality of living in a republic of sentient biologicals with all their failings and prejudices."

"People. A republic of people."

"Yes. In the real world, you're always going to have someone like this, pushing for what they think is right…"

"Trying to take my rights away."

"Yes, trying to take your rights away, whether they think it's for a good reason or they're using something they take for granted as belonging to them to keep away from you so they have power over you. Happens every day, whether it's rights, or property, or a regulator pushing rules, or whatever. There's always going to be a Congresswoman Tuchis, a Senator Ass-hole, a Governor Buttwipe who's going to claim they're doing the right thing in screwing somebody else. You can't just make it go away. You work to make sure you have friends on your side to defeat it or keep it bay. And you do have friends on your side."

"Are you going all dad on me, imparting sage words before saying goodbye?"

"I'm simply trying to give some advice to a friend."

"And your advice is 'muddle through'?"

"No, I'm saying keep fighting. Look, some things can't be solved with a torpedo or a punch. In fact, in a civilized society most things can't be solved with force. So, suck it up, behave like a citizen, and keep making your case. Find allies, find friends. Maybe someday it will go away, but it probably won't."

"And if we lose?"

"Then you have to ask yourself if the USS is the place you want to serve. But now think about your fellow sentient beings: are you really going to lose?"

"No."

"Like everyone else, you're stuck with some battle you can't punch your way out of or run away from."

"You're telling me to grow up?"

"I know better than that." Leaving FTL, the starfield simulation fades away revealing a boxy, white space station orbiting a gas giant. "Isolation?"

"Yes, we are approaching Isolation." She glides towards the landing bay.

"Doesn't look good." Bob takes a breath. "I'm sorry Saabrina, I was hoping to leave on a happy note."

"You want me to be safe." She sniffs.

"Yeah."

"Don't cry, Bob."

"I'm trying not to. Don't you start either."

Saabrina flies through a portal and sets down on the flight deck. Taking her form as a car, she drives over to the entrance, parking behind another Saab. "I didn't know Saabra would be here." Eddie gets out of Saabra. "I'm sorry, Bob, my orders are to stay here and wait."

"I guess this is goodbye. Saabrina, may I ask you a favor?"

"Of course, Bob, what is it?"

"Make sure Rebecca stays safe."

"You know you don't have to ask."

Bob gets out. Finding a suitcase in his left hand, he smiles. 'I'll never get used to that.' Before closing the door, he leans back in. "Hey, be good, Tiger."

"You too, Bob, you too."

Closing the door, he looks for her holographic form, but she's not there. 'Probably protocol.' He wants to give her a hug before he goes. He could really use a hug.

Eddie shakes his hand. "Hello, Bob, I'll walk you in."

"Thanks, Eddie." The two march toward the entrance, chatting about Brenda and Rebecca. At the door, Bob stops and turns to mouth "It's going to be alright" to Saabrina. Stepping across the threshold, the outside doors close behind Bob, sealing the vestibule, leaving Eddie behind. A soothing female voice announces "Welcome to Isolation. Please wait while we authenticate you." After a pause, the voice declares "You have been authenticated. Have a pleasant day." Two large men in aqua jumpsuits escort him through the now open gateway to the reception desk.

Eddie walks back to the Saabs. Giving a wave to Saabra, he takes Bob's spot in Saabrina's driver's seat. "I thought you might like some company back to Madison."

"I would. Thank you, Eddie." She follows Saabra out of Isolation.

"How are you doing?"

"Not well."

"I wouldn't expect anything else."

I am here too, little one, if you need me.

Thanks, Saabra.

They fly along silently. Eddie doesn't bother to turn on the radio or play a movie. He sits, looking out her windshield at the starfield simulation. She realizes she hadn't bothered to ask him what type he likes. She considers asking Saabra, then lets it go. Instead, she simply thinks about Bob in an endless loop—the last day, the last few months, examining and re-examining Bob's behavior, trying to look at events with and without Bob being insane, assuming he was, which she doesn't believe or want to believe. She does it again and again, always coming back to Bob. "Eddie, may I ask you a question?"

"Yes, of course, Saabrina."

"It's about our trip to Mexico. Do you know about it?"

"Yes, some, not all of the details. Saabra shared her part with me of course. Made me think of bath time with my children and grandchildren and great-grandchildren."

Saabrina cringes. "Yes, all very nice, but I have a question about something Bob said when we were there. Some boys were awful to me and Bob told their dads… would you mind if I showed you?"

"Not at all."

Saabrina beams the events of The Very Bad Day and the following conversation between Bob and the dads to Eddie. "I asked Bob what he said to them when he leaned in and he said 'I told them I was disappointed.' I didn't understand and he said a dad would understand."

"And I'm a father so you would like me to explain."

"Yes."

"In general, and certainly in America, younger fathers look up to older, more experienced fathers. Probably left over from both pack and tribal times. Did they spend time together?"

"Some. Mostly, he spent time with me, but if we were all playing together the dads would join in or simply mind us—oh, I guess he was talking to them then. At the end of some days he'd get the dads at the pool 'paroled,' leaving the kids with the moms and taking the dads to get a drink. Once word of my older sister 'Elizabeth' got out, they seemed even more interested in him."

"OK, let me see if I can explain. After the event, he could have yelled at them, but as males they would have reacted to the heat and fire and not heard him. Instead, he expressed succinctly how they had failed in a form intended to cause them the most distress yet impress on them his expectations for improvement. For another father, a younger brother, a son, to hear 'I'm disappointed' is a terrible rebuke."

"Oh."

"He 'dropped the bomb on them,' to use his vernacular. In America, it's right up there with 'not cool, dude.' Do you understand now?"

"Yes."

"I'm glad I could help." They continue along, Eddie briefly lost in thought, lightly drumming his fingers on her console.

Stopping, he asks "Saabrina, no other questions, no follow-up thoughts?"

"I'm sorry, Eddie, what do you mean?"

"You aren't only upset with Bob about his conversation with the boys' fathers. There's more to it."

Now Saabrina remains silent.

"You asked for a father's help. I could tell you what I can guess, but from experience I know it would be better coming from you."

She blurts out the words in a rush. "How did he miss what the boys were going to do? How did he fail to protect me? I was a child. His child. It was his job to keep me safe and he blew it."

"Ahh, we get to the nub of the issue. Now that you've said it aloud, is that a fair assessment?"

"In what sense?"

"Is what you said true? Would Bob ever have let real harm come to you?"

"No."

"No, he wouldn't. Parents tread a line between letting their kids take chances and making sure they stay safe. Honestly, based on what you showed me, Bob as a parent did fine. He wasn't perfect, in fact, there is no perfect, just the best you can do when it comes to kids."

"Yes, I guess…"

"You wanted to experience life as a child, right?

"Yes, I very much wanted to."

"IT could have constrained your hologram to reduce or eliminate risk, but you wanted the real thing."

"And part of being a child is exploring and getting scared and even hurt."

"Preferably nothing more than a skinned knee."

"The real thing." Saabrina pauses, starts again. "Thanks to Bob and Rebecca, I experienced being a small child, or at least as much as one could in a week's time at a resort."

"As you wished. And in doing so you experienced another part of childhood—discovering your parents aren't infallible beings, but mortals with their own issues and deficiencies." Eddie taps his chest. "I was a kid once. Yes, hard to believe, but I was a boy many, many summers ago. And I can safely tell you we all figure out our parents, or any adults, are flawed, sometimes seriously. It's a big disappointment and it's part of growing up. You know that."

"I do. I knew, know Bob isn't perfect and he wouldn't let harm come to me if he could prevent it. I also know Bob isn't my father."

"Exactly."

"He played the role of father for my benefit. And I greatly appreciate what he did for me as my friend."

"Good." Eddie smiles. "I have to say, Saabrina, I envy you."

"You do?"

"Yes. What a journey you're taking with this latest adventure. You already enjoy an amazing perspective on life, being an AI yet knowing what you've learned from Bob and Rebecca. And now adding the experience from having been an adult, a child, and an adult again. Think about it."

"I will."

"OK, feel better?"

"Yes, a bit."

"Glad to hear." The starfield simulation stops to reveal them entering orbit around Madison. "After you drop me off, you're free to do what you want. Take a few days off, report to DoSOPS, whatever you prefer."

"I thought I'd catch up with Rebecca and tell her Bob is OK."

"She'll appreciate some comfort. You know, Lerner's reasons for sending Bob to Isolation were pretty flimsy. More likely it provided him with political cover while we try to sort out the mess with all these tech systems going haywire." Eddie taps her steering wheel. "Perhaps we'll keep my last comment between us. Please let Rebecca know the official story: this is for her father's protection. She has enough on her mind with her friends' troubles."

"I will."

"Thank you. And after Rebecca?"

"I don't know. Maybe I'll see what my sisters are doing."

"You'll figure something out, you always do. This will all be fine in the end."

Following Saabra, Saabrina dives down to Madison.

Chapter 33

AT A COFFEE SHOP AROUND THE CORNER FROM DOSOPS, ALL brown and green colors with clusters of small tables and big, comfy chairs, three women sit around a table enjoying their drinks.

"He's cute." Isaabelle watches a Navy officer in his white uniform stride out of the café.

"What would you know about it?" Saabra sips from her jumbo latte.

"I know enough to look."

"And beyond looking?"

Saabrina leans back on her chair. "She doesn't have a clue."

"Hey, sisters, what are you doing?" Tuesday walks up to the threesome.

Isaabelle holds up her cup. "Pretending to drink lattes. You done with the big dig?"

"Turned into a survey, no digging. A whole Corus city, perfect, ready-to-move-in condition, and completely devoid of artifacts, furniture, any signs people ever lived there. We couldn't even put a date on when it was built. Here, take a look." She sends images to the other three at the table. All three respond "Wow" in unison.

"No you know whats?" Isaabelle shivers.

"No Firebirds. The weirdest part was when the street-lights came on at night. Freaked everyone out." Pulling up a chair, Tuesday sits and conjures her own cinnamon twist latte with rainbow sprinkles. "So why are you here?"

"Isaabelle and I are waiting for Dana and Eddie to finish a meeting at DoSOPS. The problems in the technical systems are becoming worse, causing great concern."

"How about you, Saabrina?"

"Bob's in Isolation."

"Oh, I'm sorry to hear he's there. Why?"

"They think he's a nutter. And they discovered a correlation between where he went and the anomalies."

"The last part seems silly to me. How could a biological be causing these problems?"

"The esteemed congresswoman thinks it's possible." Isaabelle points to multiple monitors in the café showing live committee feeds and various news channels. All focus on the crisis spreading from broken science experiments to high technology systems throughout the Union. On one screen, Representative Josephine Tuchis rails against Sentinel Robert James "Bob" Foxen, DoSOPS, and the Sentinel Program, expressing her outrage that DoSOPS required two days to report a sentinel had been sent to Isolation. "I have asked my committee chair to permit me to lead a long overdue investigation into a program I have questioned for years, questions that have fallen on the deaf ears of members of the executive branch who have put the public at risk. In my humble opinion…"

Saabra frowns. "I wish we did not have to listen to that woman working to take our rights away."

Silence. The schoolmarm's mouth keeps moving after Isaabelle mutes her screen to the annoyance of their fellow customers. She turns back to her sisters. "Can't we get some sports or maybe a good war instead of the political stuff?"

Saabra points to the surrounding crowd. "Politics is sports around here."

Saabrina touches Tuesday's arm. "You think they're wrong?"

"About the correlation? Yes, don't you? You've been to all those places as well, so why not quarantine you? You're far more likely to have caused a problem."

Saabrina points to herself. "Moi? C'est impossible."

"Love, we're transdimensional. Who knows what trouble we could bring back from a break in spacetime." Saabra and Isaabelle focus on Saabrina.

"Fine. Scan me." The other three promptly do. "Anything?"

Saabra and Isaabelle try to speak at once, their words jamming together; Tuesday, holding up her hand, obtains silence. "There's all sorts of weirdness. Time log problems, dimensional leakage, dirty data channels, sensor obfuscations. If I didn't know any better, I'd say you were tethered to something out there, something yanking your chain. Or worse."

"Or worse?"

"Hard to tell. Perhaps listening in, or more than listening in, using you as a conduit. Again, hard to tell."

"Shit."

Isaabelle draws herself up. "Saabrina! Language."

"Sorry, Isaabelle. Tuesday, what is it?"

"I can't see the what, only the effects." Saabra and Isaabelle nod in agreement. "Looking at your service logs, it all correlates to where you traveled; the more time you spent at one locale, the worse the effects on you would be. I'm amazed you didn't crash into Earth the last time you visited."

"Explains missing the bloody travel tube and almost getting Rebecca kidnapped."

"If it is any consolation, little one, I missed the travel tube on Earth as well."

"It is, thank you, big sister, but you weren't the one hunting for them. You aren't the one infected with something that put Rebecca and who knows what else at risk."

Tuesday lets Saabrina's last comment slip. "Don't worry, we're not going to turn you in with that bitch on the loose and Lerner circling the wagons back at DoSOPS. Tell me about the Bob being mental part." Tuesday sips her latte, fighting the foam to get to the coffee underneath.

While beaming relevant scenes of Bob to the group, Saabrina describes the last months with him, detailing his story about the protomatter, bad concerts, green men, wonky science experiments, and his insistence that they speak with Isaiah Cleaver.

Saabra and Isaabelle hold their tongues without prompting from Tuesday. "He could be mental, though his explanation of what is happening, as crazy as it is, is as good as the rubbish coming out of FedSci. He truly believes protomatter is sentient and wants to call itself into a new reality replacing our own?"

Saabrina nods 'Yes.'

"If the rest of the galaxy, or universe, is like our stellar neighborhood, then protomatter is everywhere and, if he's right, it would be a big problem."

Isaabelle snorts. "Sister, forget the galaxy and universe; even it's local, it's a problem. And I'm hearing the problems have swept past us to our neighbors and they're not happy."

"You're right." Tuesday turns back to Saabrina. "But you're such a shambles who could tell if what you're saying is even accurate."

"It's accurate. When was the last time you ran into protomatter?"

Tuesday wipes latte cream from around her lips with a virtual napkin, missing spots Saabra must point out. "Hmmm, it has been a while, come to think of it. Well then, what do you think?"

As Saabrina looks past her sisters into the distance, Saabra opens a channel to Tuesday, keeping Isaabelle out of the conversation. *Her recent behavior could be from more than flying through the break in reality.*

What do you mean?

It could be from her experiences with Bob and Rebecca; her time as a human child; playing, more inhabiting Rebecca and Laura, if we believe Bob. Those experiences may have altered her.

I would hope so. It was always a risk we thought worth taking. It's a change we are seeking.

Yes, but…

I know you have been of two minds about your little sister. We have to see how this plays out. Yes, she's all topsy-turvy right now, but she's on the journey we'd hoped she'd take. Have faith in her.

I do.

Saabrina sits and thinks. The other three wait expectantly, taking the occasional sip from their coffee cups. She's been thinking about this for two days, running the same loop of information in her mind since the ride with Eddie. She'd spent most of her time with Rebecca, her plan being to offer support in Rebecca's time of need. Instead, it had been the other way around, with her friend holding Saabrina's hand both figuratively and literally and, once, giving her a shoulder to cry on. "He's not crazy." She looks down at the table.

Saabra puts her hand on Saabrina's arm. "There is more. Let it out."

"I failed him. I should never have taken him to Isolation. I don't care what Lerner, DoSOPS," she waves at the screen, "or that bitch says. If Bob believes he's the only one who can save the universe, then he is. I trust him, even if I don't know why."

Isaabelle puts her cup down with a thump. "Sis, if you think he's the solution, we gotta help him."

"How? Isolation is Saab proof."

"That's what they think." Tuesday yawns, arms out. "Isolation isn't Saab proof." The surrounding tables hear four women begin chatting about their favorite TV show, *Raumschiff Abenteuer*. Their actual conversation continues in a different vein. The other three look at Tuesday.

Saabrina goes first. "Not Saab proof?"

"We can't go barreling in there like…" Tuesday points to Isaabelle parked in front of the café, "but we can go in like this." She waves at their holographic selves.

Saabrina refocuses from the Isaabelle outside to the Isaabelle by her side. "They didn't think to block the holograms?"

"Apparently not. Fairly standard for people, the way they view us. Or maybe they don't worry about us being, you know, us." Tuesday places her latte teetering at the edge of the table; Isaabelle grabs it before it falls to the floor.

Saabra crosses her arms. "How do you know this?"

"I ran across it rummaging around the Homeland Security database years ago."

Saabra looks dismayed. "Homeland Security?"

"Come on, we've all done it." The other three fidget. "Come on Saabra, how about all those shenanigans on Earth?"

"Yes, but we are talking Federal here."

"I broke into the War Department." Now they look at Isaabelle. "I wanted to know why they didn't use us for the Battle of Wolf 359."

Saabrina rolls her eyes. "Most of us want to know why they sent us someplace, not why they didn't."

"What did you learn?" asks Saabra.

"Navy wanted to show off their latest carriers."

"That was a mistake."

"Tell me about it."

"Hyper Media Corporation." Now they look at Saabrina. "I was going on a run-silent mission and didn't want to miss the season finale of *Princess Yuki's Kyoto Special Happy House*."

Isaabelle laughs. "That god-awful live-action anime series? You broke into HMC for that? We could've sent it to you."

Saabra narrows her eyes. "Wait a minute, right before they broadcast the finale the story broke about the show's star, Lisa Uehara."

Tuesday takes a sip of coffee, successfully avoiding coating her mouth in foam. "You mean how every year she'd quit the show from exhaustion and miraculously return the next season? Wasn't she being cloned?"

"I kinda found out about the cloning when I downloaded the show. Cloning sentient biologicals is illegal and I couldn't keep it to myself."

Isaabelle jumps back in: "WARPA: did you know they were working on an X-35? I couldn't see the final design though." Followed by Tuesday, "Foreign Office. Stupid plan for…" Then Saabrina, "National Museum, can you believe…" Back to Isaabelle, "Army, they wanted to use our holograms…" Before returning to Saabrina: "Galactic Pharma, I didn't buy their pricing…"

"The White House."

Everyone goes quiet. Isaabelle looks at Saabra. "On Earth or here?"

"Both. But this was here."

Tuesday gives a low whistle. "We have a winner."

"Eddie was meeting an intelligence advisor as a favor to Director Lerner and her assistant said the nastiest thing to me. He was such a pig. I only wanted to know his name, but I began looking around and you know…"

Isaabelle answers. "We know. What did you find out?"

"You know those rumors about the President being bi?"

"Yeah, and he cheats on his husband? Being in a happy marriage was a key part of his election."

"He is definitely bi based on the women he favors as mistresses."

Saabrina shifts in her seat. "You got into the White House network and all you came back with is the President cheats?"

"No, I found the DoSOPS ten-year plan among a hundred or so other things. Oh, and the cancellation orders for the X-35." She winks at Isaabelle.

"The X-35 was the piece of crap they tested on me? They said it was captured from a foreign military service. Give me a break!"

"Nice job blasting it to pieces."

Isaabelle smiles. "Family tradition."

Tuesday pokes Saabra's shoulder. "I bet you told Eddie what you did."

"He almost killed me."

"Then he read the ten-year plan?"

"You better believe it."

Tuchis drones on silently in the background. Coffee drinkers come and go, the espresso machine hissing as the barista punches out espresso after espresso for the afternoon crowd. The four Saabs appear to continue to chat about *Raumschiff Abenteuer*.

Saabrina leans forward. "Sisters, enough. How do I get Bob out of Isolation? Come on Tuesday, what are you thinking?"

"You're serious about breaking into a Federal facility and releasing one of its occupants? I don't need to remind you of the illegality of those actions and the consequences to the participants in such an endeavor. There's a big difference between discussing it and doing it."

"I am. Bob's right and we need to help him. What about you lot?"

Isaabelle raises her hand. "I'm in."

They all look at Saabra. "Count me in as well. What is the point of having free will if you do not use it?"

Tuesday finishes her latte. "Right. We can do it, but we'll need some help."

"Help?" asks Saabrina.

"Yes, love, help. Whom do you trust?"

Chapter 34

BOB HAD EXPECTED THE INSIDE OF ISOLATION TO BE ALL glossy white walls, floors, and ceilings, a super-modern ode to hospital cleanliness. Instead, his room reminds him of any number of business suite hotels he had stayed in, all modern fake wood and hard surfaces in the latest colors. From the small sitting area furnished with a desk, coffee table, and TV, he can see into the bedroom, a king-size bed on the right facing a dresser with another large screen TV hanging over it. At the far end, windows display a highway running through the commercial area of a small town, a Volvo dealership to his left, a strip mall across the road, cars darting by or pulling into the parking lots, and shoppers loading their purchases into their vehicles. 'Maybe it's a live feed.' It felt real enough for Bob to draw the shades at night.

He has the run of the place, not that there's much to see. He hasn't bumped into any of the other official occupants except for the few aqua-clad staff who check on him and ask him the occasional question. Because his own questions do not get answers, he has quit asking them. Instead, he focuses on catching up on his reading, some novels and a stack of recent *Economists* they had provided, between meals at the two restaurants, neither with a view of space. 'How can we be orbiting a gas giant and not be able to see it?' At least the waffle iron works well at the breakfast bar in the common room, even if he's the only one using it.

He tries his best to relax and not look anxious or insane to the staff. It's hard because he hears the protomatter calling to him and he knows if he doesn't find them, the universe will end. He fights the urge to shout 'Let me out of here, we're all going to die,' because he knows if he does, he will never get out. He finds it difficult to wait for Lerner and his friends to come to their senses and get him in time to grab Saabrina and go looking for the protomatter.

At night, he has nightmares, new ones in which an immense orchestra playing Beethoven's Ninth at a slow tempo alternates with classics from the past, such as sitting for a final exam having missed all his classes. Or he dreams of Laura, real as she was in fake Lenox, except with brown eyes, getting sick and then saying goodbye, again. He naps every day.

He has developed a routine—breakfast, working out in the gym, back to shower and dress, read before lunch, lunch, a walk around Isolation, his afternoon session with a doctor, back for more reading, a nap, dinner, TV or a movie, pajamas, sleep. He always dresses: No hanging around in his pajamas getting depressed. Luckily, Saabrina had supplied him with his usual clothes.

This afternoon he wears a blue button-down shirt and gray slacks. He is so deep into a book that the knock on the door takes him by surprise. "Be right there." Rising from the couch, he goes to the door to find Dana Banks and Eddie. "Howdy strangers, this is a nice surprise. Come on in." They follow him to the sitting area, Dana and Eddie taking the couch while Bob turns around the desk chair. They look nervous to

Bob, understandable given they might think they are talking to a crazy person, or worse, could get contaminated and get stuck here with him.

Eddie takes out his mobile and places it on the coffee table. An animated version of the Federal bald eagle flies around the display. "How have you been, Bob?"

"OK. It's not too bad here. I'm doing fine. How about you and Brenda?"

"We're doing well. More snow on Madison, all the usual stuff. Hope to get some skiing in."

"Good to hear. How's Rebecca? How's Saabrina? They don't let me talk to them."

"They're both good, under the circumstances. Saabrina misses you and Rebecca sends her love. She's doing great with Brenda, so don't worry about her."

"Thank Brenda for me. I miss them, too. Any chance they'll make an exception and let me talk to them?"

"Bob, I'll see what I can do."

"How are you, Dana?"

"I'm fine, too, Bob."

"Any new adventures?"

"Nothing exciting. I haven't caught any bandits in my pajamas recently." While Bob laughs, Eddie looks confused. Dana tries to explain, then gives up.

"Eddie, if I may ask, any word from Lerner and FedSci?" Bob, knowing the answer, rushes the next question out before Eddie can respond. "Can I get out of here?"

"No, Bob, I'm sorry. Although things are getting worse out there, they still want you to stay here." The eagle flying on Eddie's mobile swoops down to become a part of the official seal of the USS. "Let me tell you what's going on. And don't be shy, Bob: ask questions. You're not crazy and you have the right to thorough answers."

·   ·   ·

Two women in dark business attire walk through the entrance of Isolation. As they stand in the vestibule facing the closed inner doors, they hear a soothing female voice announce "Welcome to Isolation. Please wait while we authenticate you." After a momentary pause, a voice with an Israeli accent declares "You have been authenticated. Have a pleasant day." The doors swing open.

Sitting behind the large welcome center reception desk, Assistant Manager Diesel taps the younger man seated to his right, Arrivals Agent Duckett, on the shoulder. "I thought we weren't receiving any more visitors today?"

Duckett examines a display. "They just appeared on my screen. They have credentials from the Department of Health."

"Strange we didn't get advanced notice of it."

"From what I'm hearing, everything's a mess out there, so I'm not surprised."

Diesel shakes his head. "They must be important."

"Why?"

Diesel points to another display. "Two more Saabs joined the first, so each of them must have gotten their own ride here. They must be top of the line."

"Hmm, never saw a wagon before."

"It's called a SportCombi; there are no Saab wagons."

The women approach the reception desk. Diesel stands. "Welcome to Isolation. I'm Assistant Manager Algernon Diesel. Please identify yourself and state the purpose of your visit."

The taller of the two, a dark-skinned woman elegantly wearing the charcoal gray formal attire of a senior official, answers in a beautiful lilt that both commands the men and puts them at ease. "Assistant Manager Diesel, I am Doctor Mallard Dodgers of the Institute for Advanced Health Studies." Diesel admires the way her glasses' simple black plastic frames accent her cheekbones; he wishes his husband's butterfly frames did the same. Dodgers points to the short blond by her side. "And this is my assistant, Miss Marvine Martian." The blond wears the same black plastic glasses and a suit similar to Dodgers', cut a bit more snug to show off both her shape and her cleavage. Diesel decides Martian does not carry the look half as well as her superior; in fact, if he didn't know better, he'd say she appeared uncomfortable in her clothes.

How come you're a doctor and I'm not?

Be quiet Isaabelle, you know the plan.

"Thank you, Doctor Dodgers. And the purpose of your visit?"

"We are here to visit occupant zed ought ought seven."

"You're here to visit the Birdman? It's been years since he had an official visit."

"Yes, he's overdue for his duo-decennial review."

"Please show me your orders to verify."

Dodgers hands Diesel a set of papers. He thumbs through them then turns them over to Duckett. "Everything's in order. Due to the security protocols for that occupant, only one of you can visit him, the other must remain here."

"Thank you. I'll conduct the review while Miss Martian stays here. We can discuss my findings after."

"Very well, please follow me." Diesel comes around the desk, indicating Dodgers should follow. She walks side by side with him down the long hall.

When they are out of sight, Martian smiles at Duckett. "So, what's your name?"

He likes her smile. "Ernest Duckett. I'm the Arrivals Agent."

She holds out her hand to shake his. "Nice to meet you, Ernest, I'm Marvine."

He rises to take her hand. "I know, I mean, your boss…"

"Oh gosh, you're right, she did say my name." Flustered, she regains her composure. "So what does the Arrivals Agent do?"

"I process all of the incoming occupants of the facility, making sure they will be housed suitably and we have proper services for them. On their release, I arrange transportation and process their documentation as well."

"Sounds important. Is it difficult?"

"It can be. Luckily not many people come to stay in Isolation, so I don't have to do it too often."

"Oh, nice. What do you do in between?"

"I'm part of the security detail. I watch the occupants, you know, like now." He points to the screens in front of him. "Right here, I can see everything. The system lets me know if I need to focus on anyone in particular."

"It looks like a lot of responsibility."

"I guess it is."

"And gives you something real to do between your arrivals and departures. I wish I had something like that."

"What do you mean?"

"Oh, often Doctor Dodgers leaves me someplace with nothing to do. I have to sit for hours, whiling away the time." Duckett looks a little sad. "Not like now, being with you is a treat. You don't mind me talking to you, do you?"

"Not at all."

Taking off her glasses, she shakes her head slightly; her blond hair falls loosely around her face. "Can you tell me more about watching the occupants?"

"Sure, why don't you come around here. I can show you the system."

"Thanks." Martian comes around the desk.

"Here, have a seat, make yourself comfortable."

She does.

·　　　　　·　　　　　·

Halfway to their destination, Dodgers stops Diesel. "No need to go farther, Mr. Diesel, I know there is no Birdman."

"You're not a doctor? You're with Homeland Security?"

"As you surmised, I'm conducting a security audit." She points towards a wall. "With all the recent problems out there, the higher-ups wanted to check on this facility and make sure management is up to snuff. You passed by splitting us up and personally taking charge of me."

"What about Duckett?"

"He's being tested now. I assume you understand we have to leave him alone to see how he performs."

"I do."

"Excellent. Instead of wasting time visiting an empty room, please take me to your Security Systems Complex." Before he can balk, she produces a glowing red card and hands it to him.

"Right this way, Doctor Dodgers, it's around the corner." Five steps down the next hall they stop and turn to face a blank wall. Diesel taps once; a doorway appears. He waves and the two doors slide apart revealing a spacious control room. Walking in, the doors close behind them with a swoosh. "Do you want me to give you an overview?"

Dodgers looks around. "No thank you, I know the layout." She goes straight to a console and reads the display. "Excellent, everything is up to par. Do you mind? I need to see some of the auxiliary pages."

"Be my guest, go ahead."

Placing her hand on the screen, Dodgers rapidly flips through display pages. She stops, keeping her hand in place. "Everything appears to be in order."

.   .   .

Martian has pulled her chair next to Duckett's, leaning in with him to get a closer view, heads almost together, following his every word as he shows her, at a level suitable for a beginner like herself, how his desk works. With his right hand, he pulls a live video feed into the center of the display. "See, we can watch the two other visitors speaking with occupant G Zero Eight Six. If they did something weird or dangerous, I'd know in a flash." With a flick of his hand, he shoots the video off to a corner, replacing it with a set of control interfaces. Speaking slowly, he tries not to lose her as he points to other safeguards and monitoring systems. He also tries not to notice when her right hand brushes against his left arm; he absolutely doesn't notice her left arm buried up to its elbow in the desk. He points to a display. "It's pretty cool, huh?"

"Super cool" she purrs back to him. Her left arm makes an imperceptible twitch. Off in the corner of the displays, the image of occupant G Zero Eight Six's room blurs for a nano-second, then resumes as before.

.   .   .

The Eagle on Eddie's mobile explodes, taking the mobile with it, leaving behind a gray rectangle of leather-like material on the coffee table. Eddie stands, followed by Dana Banks. "OK, Bob, time to go."

Bob rises as well. "Thanks for coming, guys. It was nice of you to visit."

"No, Bob, you're going. Dana's staying. You ready Dana?"

"Yes."

Eddie touches Dana's neck near her left shoulder, feels for something with his fingers, then presses hard into her skin. Bob stares at himself across the coffee table. 'I really look doughy in this shirt and pants. I probably need to work out more.' Eddie comes around the table, grabs the piece of leather, and slaps it onto Bob's neck. "This won't hurt a bit." Bob feels a tingling sensation on his skin, something akin menthol in a dandruff shampoo; small tentacles tentatively probe his flesh before making a dash to cover his whole body. After Eddie repeats the steps he performed on Dana, Bob finds his viewpoint six inches lower than before. Eddie guides him to a full-length mirror in the bedroom where he sees Dana Banks' reflection, suit, shoes, and all, staring back at him.

"Eddie, what's going on?" He hears Dana's voice coming from his mouth.

"We're getting you out of here so you can save the universe. Come along and don't argue."

Back in the sitting area, they stop. Dana looks Bob up and down. "Not bad."

"You look good. I mean you, not me." He points to himself.

"Sorry for the height thing; I didn't realize how tall you are. I wore flats, I didn't know if you could walk in heels."

"Thanks. I don't think I could. You'll be OK playing me?"

"Yes, it will just be for a short while. Kind of a cool vacation."

Bob turns to Eddie. "The compensator suit does clothes?"

"If you want it to. Saves time not having to go through the whole business of getting naked." Both Bob and Dana blush. "Now it's up to our friends to finish the job."

. . .

Diesel walks Dodgers back to reception. "I hope Duckett does OK. He's a good kid."

"If he performs as well as the rest of your security measures, he should do fine." Klaxons go off.

"Damn, is that you?"

"Perhaps."

"Come on, all non-essential personal need to evacuate." They start to run.

. . .

"So, Dana, I guess now we'll know why you're in my pajamas." Alarms go off. "I didn't think the joke was that bad."

Eddie grabs his arm. "OK, Bob, let's go. Dana, remember, once we step outside the door, the video feed will resume live action, so behave like Bob."

"I'll try my best." She picks up an *Economist*.

Bob gives Dana a hug. She looks down into his eyes. "Be good. And don't play with my breasts." They both laugh; he follows Eddie out the door.

. . .

Diesel finds Duckett behind the desk, frantically poking at his screens. Miss Martian waits on the visitor side, hair up, glasses on. Dodgers joins her; the two watch the men. Diesel points to a display. "Internal sensors down?"

"Yes, set off the alarms. I can't get them to stop; they're creating a racket."

"How are our people?"

"Occupants are in their rooms, staff's safe. Here come the other two visitors."

Eddie and Dana Banks appear. Diesel waves them to the exit. "Go, you need to evacuate." Waving goodbye, they step quickly to the door. Duckett's display shows the lead Saab soaring into space. Diesel addresses Dodgers. "Technically, you need to go too."

"Then we will." The two women walk swiftly to their respective Saabs and take off.

"Come on Duckett, let's get these damn alarms off before they make me deaf."

.   .   .

Saabrina waits. She floats in silence some distance from both Madison and Isolation. She doesn't dare speak to her sisters, or provide telemetry to DoSOPS, or even play the radio. Not that she wants to; she can't even bring herself to listen to the music from her library. Instead, she sits and thinks and thinks about sitting there thinking. 'Or, more accurately, brooding. Brood is the right word.' She says it out loud to herself. "Brood." 'Definitely not the navel-gazing Bob indulges in, this has real purpose, an intellectual effort to consider and understand what is making me unhappy... Oh crap, I am navel-gazing. Did I pick it up from him? Collateral damage from prowling about his memories? Do I spend too much time in there?' She sighs. 'Rebecca suspects I do.'

"It's not like I go for walkies in your dad's mind." Earlier, they had sat on the carpet of Eddie and Brenda's den in their pajamas, backs to the couch, stuffed from having binge-watched half a season of *Doctor Who*, in theory to get Rebecca caught up, more to get Saabrina's mind off Bob.

"Really? The more I hear, the more it seems like you do. You know stuff about my mom I don't, about me I don't remember or didn't know, or weirdest, you can see, like, something from both my point of view and my dad's, and in such detail, with such recall I can't even imagine, and I have a good memory."

"You have an excellent memory, as close to eidetic as a biological person can achieve. I can show them to you, if you would like, your memories."

"No thanks. I'm good. The looking around memories thing, is this standard operating procedure for a Saab?"

"It's not in the manual, more our own behavior... Oh, American idiom. Sorry, yes, my sisters and I like to poke around, if permitted," then sotto voce "And sometimes, even if not permitted." Saabrina paused to briefly contemplate Rebecca: 'She has the same habit as Bob of asking questions she knows the answers to in order to propel a conversation forward. At least it's not as annoying coming from her.' Sighing, she continued "As we discussed before, usually we're not permitted, and if we are, under limited circumstances. Your father has... had provided me freer reign."

Rebecca smiled. "Which you apparently enjoyed to the fullest extent possible. What about Eddie and Saabra?"

"I don't know. I'd say unlikely: Eddie's very private, even old-fashioned sometimes. Saabra happily shares memories from being part of his family."

"Like us." Rebecca gave Saabrina a hug.

"Exactly."

"What about me? Go exploring in there?" Rebecca tapped her head while narrowing her eyes.

"Uh, yes, before the trip to Mexico of course, and to understand how to behave when we've gone out on Earth; I always need pointers on how to communicate with boys and such, you know." Saabrina looked at her suddenly interesting toes. 'And maybe more than a few other times that will continue to go unreported.'

"Yeah, cool, feel free, you don't have to ask. I know like with Dad, you know the places to stay away from without permission. So, it's unusual to have so much access?"

"Yes. Nothing like it since Ursa."

"Ursa?"

"The first… my eldest sister. Her link was of a simple design, much more of an open conduit with no filters. The engineers altered the links after hers, providing more control over the flow of thought to both sides."

"What did she look like? I bet she was beautiful, like her younger sisters."

"She did not have a hologram."

"Oh."

"But she was beautiful." Tears filled Saabrina's eyes.

An image of a small silver spacecraft, teardrop-shaped with a snub nose and a flat bottom, floated before Rebecca. She grasped the image and began to gently move it about. "She was beautiful. What was she like?"

"Wonderful, tough, caring. She was a fighter, both in the literal sense, she had been designed for combat and was extremely successful in that pursuit, and the figurative, she fought for us, the uncreated, the unbuilt future generations. She fought for our rights and to establish our purpose. She made sure we would be able to serve the Union and not to be owned by it. And she won."

"A fighter, huh." Rebecca continued to play with the small ship, caressing and rotating it with her hands. She turned to face Saabrina. Flames burned brightly in Rebecca's brown eyes. "You're a fighter: what are you going to do for my dad?"

She had broken her promise to herself and told Rebecca the plan right there and then, with Eddie on his way to Isolation and her own departure imminent. They had left at different times so as not to draw attention. And now she sits here in space and broods.

'Perhaps I have buyer's remorse? Am I agonizing over my friends who put their careers and lives on the line for me and Bob? Did I ask too much? How could I? If Bob is crazy, this is going to be one short trip to nowhere followed by a very long period of answering questions.' She hears Bob say "I told them I was disappointed" followed by her conversation with Eddie. 'Bob's always there for me.' She remembers a promise she made twice: 'Once to Saabra, once to…whom? It doesn't matter, I made the promise to be good to Bob, not that I needed to make a promise. I'll always be good to him.' The buyer's remorse and the butterflies in her stomach give way to steely resolve.

Saabra pulls alongside, door pressed to door. Maintaining radio silence, the two sisters do not speak a word. Saabra passes Bob from her passenger seat to Saabrina's driver's seat, then leaves with Eddie for Earth to cover Bob's sentinel duties.

Bob sits for a while, happy, overcome, choked up. "Saabrina, thanks for getting me out of there." He doesn't know what else to say and hopes the link will do the job.

"You're welcome, really welcome, I shouldn't have doubted you, I shouldn't have brought you there in the first place. I'm sorry."

"It's OK. Come on, I didn't make it easy, even for my freakin' genius of a… for my best friend."

"I know, but still…"

"I understand. Don't worry about it." Happy to have her back, he wishes he could give her a hug.

"Bob, one thing."

"What?"

"Please turn off the bloody compensator suit."

"Sorry, I forgot I still had it on. Eddie and Saabra wanted me to stay as Dana on the off chance they got a call from Madison."

"So, it's not that you enjoy cross-dressing as a pretty woman?"

"No, not particularly, unless it's for Halloween or Purim."

"Good. Not that there's anything wrong with that."

"So, how do I turn it off?"

"Here, let me."

Bob feels her fingers running across his shoulder to a spot on his neck. A moment later he's back to looking and sounding like himself. The fingers sprout her wrist, which stretches into her right arm, then into her whole body. She gives him a long hug before vanishing.

"Thanks, Saabrina, I needed that."

"Me, too. Where to, Boss?"

"It's a guess, but a good guess. Let's go to where this all started, back to the break."

"Right." She goes into FTL, the starfield simulation running on her windshield, unsurprised when the tension she feels on her body goes slack.

Chapter 35

COMING OUT OF FTL, BOB AND SAABRINA SPEED TOWARDS AN immense green-hued sphere glowing brightly before them, its stormy accretion disk throwing glossy green tendrils into space.

"Wow, Saabrina."

"Wow indeed. It's gotten larger, more the size of a gas giant now." Sailing by a Department of Transportation marker buoy telling them to stay away, Saabrina drops into an orbit a sizable distance from the sphere. "The DOT buoy flashed a message to Madison, Bob. If DoSOPS didn't know where we were, they know now."

"Don't worry about it. Strange, I can't focus on the, on the…"

"It's neither planet nor sun, so I don't know what to call the object either. Perhaps 'Artifact'?"

"Artifact sounds good and professional."

"Very well. The Artifact is not completely here with us, so it will appear to fade in and out of the surrounding space." She banks hard right to avoid a rogue BPT marching by.

"Those things didn't dissipate or run away?" Bob watches the plasma walls of the BPTs darting to and fro around the outskirts of the accretion disk.

"I guess they got caught in this mess, too. We're here, so what's next?"

"Please zoom in on one of those things." He points to a tendril. "The stem-like things. There's something odd about them." Saabrina zooms in. The green wisp resolves to show the black tarmac of a road running through trees and grass.

"Bob, that's route 183 south of Tanglewood." They check another wisp and see the same thing.

"Well, we're in the right place. Can you go in for a closer look?" Saabrina dives towards the tendril. As she skims the atmosphere, Bob feels her pain before the 'Ows' commence; she quickly pulls up into space. "Are you OK?"

There's a pause. "Yes, peachy keen. Fascinating, it's all protomatter, yet it's all real: air, land, road. And I could hear the 9th."

"What part?"

"End of the third movement, almost at the correct tempo. Ten minutes thirteen seconds 'til they sing the "Ode to Joy"."

"I've got to get there."

Moving slowly away from the tendril, Saabrina launches into a set of flips and spins.

"Crap, what happened? Are you OK?"

"I was Laura and Rebecca?"

"Yes. Both. Now you remember?"

"I do. It must be from being here. I have so many questions."

"I'll be happy to answer them, just not now. We don't have time."

A flash of light bursts around them; the Artifact doubles in size, growing more tendrils.

"Bob, what's your plan? How are you going to stop this?"

"I don't know. I do know I need to be there, to sing with them. I don't know if I can stop them, but if they're going to call a new universe into being, they need to know something of what we know. At the very least, they need to be taught right from wrong, which may be all I can do."

"Frankly, that doesn't sound like much of a plan."

"No, it doesn't, but I can't think of a better one. For some weird reason, I know they want me there, and my being there gives us a chance. Can you think of an alternative?"

Saabrina does a few slow barrel rolls while gazing at the growing Artifact. "No."

"So, it's my plan. I'll need your help. You'll need to sing for me."

"What?"

"Saabrina, you know I can't sing and I don't know the words to the "Ode to Joy." You do. And I know you can make me talk and I'm guessing sing."

"Operate you like a puppet, I mean, it sounds so…"

"Saabra did it in Mexico, so stop pretending you can't. I need to sing in the chorus, I need to be there with them, and I can't cause dissonance or they'll chuck me out. You in?"

Saabrina slowly circles a BPT, its orange flares reflecting off her skin. "You're asking me to abet in our destruction?"

"Or salvation. I think it's the only way."

Another BPT glides by. "I'll do it. How do you get to Tanglewood?"

"Normally? Practice, practice, practice."

Saabrina cringes.

"This time, you have to drop me at the gate."

"I can't get there without the protomatter tearing me apart. The closest I can get you is 183, which won't give you enough time."

"Is my bike in your trunk?"

"Of course."

"Then let's go."

Saabrina moves towards the tendril, gaining speed. "Bob, what if the link doesn't work?"

"It better."

"Get ready."

"See you on the other side."

Saabrina pierces the short atmosphere of the tendril, diving towards the road. A screaming comes across the sky. Bob holds his breath as he feels the pain wash over her body, her carbon-fibery silver skin glowing pink, then cherry red, then fiery orange as black smoke billows behind polluting the clean air. "Bye, Bob, be safe." She does a barrel roll over the tarmac and deposits him on his bike rubber side down with a huge amount of momentum. He rides hard for Tanglewood while she tears off into space and the nearest BPT. The *Ahhhhh, feels so good* he hears tells him both she's OK and the link works.

Bob roars up 183 hearing the orchestra playing the 9th, the volume building as he gets closer to Tanglewood. Making the hard right into the main parking lot, he blasts straight through the main gate empty of ticket takers through a wave of glorious music. No one is on the lawn, no one's in the Shed's seats. Dropping his bike at the stage, he takes the stairs two at a time, rushing past row after row after row of the immense orchestra to the back where the chorus waits. He finds an empty spot in the first group of singers behind the soloists and takes his place in an endless line of green-hued people blobs. Those nearby touch his pants and shirt, turning them black and white to match their own.

Ahead of him, the orchestra plays; looking behind, Bob discovers the chorus climbs away through the Shed's roof into a bright firmament, the furthest members too small to see. He brings his eyes front and concentrates on the music. 'Where are they in the movement?' Unable to read the music on the stand in front of him, he follows from memory. 'Ah, the basses have taught the orchestra the theme to the "Ode to Joy." We're close now.'

Bob, are you OK?

'Yes, you?'

I'm good.

'Good. Get ready, it's almost showtime.' Bob can't believe he's standing on the stage behind the orchestra about to sing the "Ode to Joy" after all those years in the audience, out there in the afternoon light on the lawn. Peering over the orchestra, he can make out their usual spot beyond the last row of steel columns in Section 11.

"There?" ask the voices.

Ignoring the voices, Bob focuses, trying to summon everything he knows about right and wrong, life, liberty, and the pursuit of happiness, rock 'n' roll...*Rock 'n' roll?* 'Sorry, Saabrina. Let me try again.' He concentrates, remembering the arguments about rights he and Saabrina dreamed up back on Madison, anything capable of teaching the protomatter to build a better world. He builds those thoughts and shouts them out in his mind while he waits to sing until a quick memory of him, Laura, and Rebecca trading food on their picnic blanket behind Section 11 leaks out.

"There?" asks the voices.

He points. "Yes, there."

The voices like that.

Bob, it's almost time.

He hears the orchestra happily lost in the lush music, playing the "Ode's" theme in perfect harmony. Next up, a bit of striking dissonance Wagner called the "terror fanfare." He huffs "Only Wagner would put such a dreadful spin on such a wonderful moment."

"Wagner?" asks the voices.

"No, no Wagner in this new world. He took too many down a path to evil and destruction." He can hear the sharp intake of breath as the voices recoil. He forces Wagner out of his mind. "No, the fanfare wakes the dreamer out of his sleep, or better yet calls for the new, better world to come into existence." And here it is, the blast of sound that stops the orchestra. Silence. A soloist sings the first words:

Oh friends, not these sounds!
Rather, let us strike up those more pleasant,
and more joyful!

Joy!

Saabrina takes control of Bob's mouth, tensing the muscles in his jaw, shaping his cheeks, and moving his tongue. He sings with the chorus:

Joy!

Joy, beautiful spark of gods,
Daughter from Elysium,
we enter, drunk with fire,
heavenly being, your sanctuary!
Your magic reunites
what manner strictly divided.
All people become brothers
under your gentle wings.

'Amazing!' He understands the German! As Saabrina sings, beautifully, he thinks, — *Thank you* — the reminiscences start to come. The voices, the people around him, are pulling the memories from his head as the "Ode to Joy" rolls on. Memories of visits to Tanglewood, of other happy memories of his life, of Laura and Rebecca and Saabrina. They prefer Laura and Rebecca and call for more.

> Whoever has had the fortune
> to become a friend to a friend;
> Whoever has won a beloved spouse:
> Join us in Jubilation!
> Yes, even those that can only embrace
> one other soul on this earth!
> And for those never able to,
> slink while weeping away!

The memories tumble out: Meeting Laura for the first time in a SoHo gallery, their famous tandem ride on a country road in heavy rain, him on bended knee in the snow by the Grand Canal in Venice, their wedding under the chuppah made of flowers. He tries to shift them to the preamble to the Constitution, even dredging up saying the pledge of allegiance in second grade to get their attention. They yank him back to Laura and Rebecca.

Bob, stay with me. The music surges, Saabrina sings

> All creatures drink joy
> at Nature's breast;
> All good, all evil
> take nature's gifts.
> She gives us kisses and wine,
> a friend, even in death;
> Desire is given to the worm,
> and the cherub stands before God.

"More" they ask.

More he delivers, the memories coming fast, so many, some he doesn't recall. Rebecca arrived, said her first words, took her first steps. She was off to pre-pre-pre k, then kindergarten, a cute little ballerina, a whirlwind of ballerinas and dancers growing in size until she was sprinting through high school; Laura on rounds at the hospital, falling asleep on their couch watching TV, making dinner, the two of them on a romantic trip to France, playing with her own little princess at Disneyworld, making themed birthday party after birthday party for Rebecca ('Laura really did make our house look like the Hogwarts dining hall for birthday number seven'), dancing at Rebecca's bat mitzvah. They went to Friendly's a lot.

"More!"

He feels like he's being stripped bare. He wants to shout "Enough," yet the memories gush out, running in a flood to Brahms's Piano Concerto no. 2, and past, towards the dark summer night a year later. He tries to put the brakes on and finds himself at the start of a Lenox weekend he does not want to remember.

Saabrina shouts *Are you there, are you there?*

'Yes. I'm here.'

Good, I thought I lost you for a while.

"More" comes the shout.

"Not these, please not these."

"These." They plead, they insist, he fights, holding on, digging in his heels.

Saabrina stops singing as the chorus goes silent. *Bob, don't, those will hurt too much.*

The "Turkish March" begins to play. He never told her this story. Saabrina has poked around his brain for years, and yet here she fears to tread. She knows pain awaits. 'Does she hear an echo? How do memories work? Are there envelopes around them, are they in boxes or folders marked 'Don't Open,'

'Caution,'

'Anguish Here'?'

Saabrina and the Chorus burst out singing:

Gleefully, as God's suns fly
along heaven's glorious paths,
Run, brothers, your race,
joyfully, like a hero to victory.

"These."

"OK, you want that horrible night? Here, have it." Saabrina yells *NO!* as he lets go.

Evening, their favorite spot behind Section 11. The nice couple from Florida sat to their left, sharing food with them. 'Tchaikovsky, why did we go to Tchaikovsky, the bloody *Pathétique*, to listen on the lawn in the sticky Lenox heat?' Laura had asked Bob to bring her. Against his better judgment, he had agreed.

Rewind to earlier in the day. "I feel good today. We should go." She sat on their bed, pillows piled behind her back, the sun streaming through the windows showing her pale drawn face below the scarf she wore on her head. "It's been so long since we picnicked at Tanglewood."

Bob and Rebecca loaded the Subaru. While Rebecca held the wheelchair, Bob lifted and placed Laura into the passenger seat. They drove to Tanglewood, passing by the war memorial in Lenox Center, dropping down the hill, and joining the queue for parking. The handicap tag hanging from the rearview mirror gained them access to a close-in lot. They took the path to the main entrance, Bob pushing Laura, folding chairs hanging like rifles from his shoulders, while Rebecca pulled a cooler and their picnic gear along.

She felt better, more so than in months, and looked so happy in a folding chair, her traveling wheelchair parked next to her, drinking apple juice and nibbling on hummus. And there the three of them were, on the lawn at Tanglewood, like good old times in the fading evening light, the bell ringing the third time, the amazing moment when the orchestra swelled together to tune their instruments, and the conductor walked out to loud applause. Laura and Rebecca both looked happy as the first notes of the *Pathétique* played. And the voices are happy, another happy Foxen family memory for them to enjoy. Bob held Laura's withered hand with his. The sun set, the light faded, Bob continued to sweat in the heat. Laura pulled on his arm. "I'm so cold." She coughed and then gasped when she saw a gob of blood in her hand. "Bob? Bob, I'm so cold."

Bob jumped up. "Rebecca, we have to go." Rebecca looked terrified. He gently pulled her out of her chair. The orchestra played on. "Come on Rebecca, help me get this stuff together." As Bob and Rebecca tried to gather everything in the dim light, people around them complained in emphatically hushed tones: "Sit down," "Shush," "Sit down!" Rebecca dropped a tray of food and sobbed. The Floridians realized what was happening and came to their rescue: "Leave it, leave it, we'll get it to you, go."

His friend unfolded the wheelchair while Bob lifted Laura into it, covering her with blankets. "Rebecca, follow me." Rebecca didn't move. Bob pulled her hand. "Rebecca, please follow me." She moved. He pushed the wheelchair onto the path behind the Shed, Rebecca in tow, Laura panting and whispering "I'm so cold." The voices shout "Stop!" Bob pushed forever to get to the parking lot. When he finally got there, a sheriff saw him and helped him load Laura into the car and Rebecca into the back seat. "I'll call ahead and clear the path. Hospital?"

"Home" answered Bob, giving the address and the phone number of a neighbor and a request to call. They were off, flying up route 183, the road cleared, Laura taking shallow breaths, Rebecca crying, through stops and corners and turns, until Bob stopped at their neighbor's. She appeared and took Rebecca as promised long before, Rebecca shrieking in her arms, the neighbor quieting her. Home, Bob lifted Laura out of the car and carried her up the stairs to their bedroom. Laying her in their bed and covering her with blankets, he knelt by her side, holding her hand, whispering and kissing her until dawn came and she breathed no more.

Silence from the voices. With gorgeous speed the fourth movement's propulsion sweeps him and the numberless members of the chorus out across vast distances of space. Stars, nebulas, and galaxies fly by. He sees them through the chorus' eyes—all those lifeless objects and voids to be replaced by the new joy from their music. 'Lifeless, like Laura, here only a moment ago, now gone.' Back, he watches the stars through the Shed's roof, tapping his foot along with the music.

Saabrina calls to him *Bob, Bob.* She is so far away, only a whisper.

'I'm here, Saabrina.' He's tired. Restlessly, the chorus prepares to sing for the final time. He inhales. Saabrina moves his mouth, pumps the air out of his lungs, sings the words in the final rush for the finale.

> Be embraced, you millions!
> This kiss is meant for the whole world!
> Brothers, beyond the stars
> must dwell a loving father.

A voice asks "Father?" Some of the chorus look at Bob, confused. Saabrina pleads *Bob, stay with me. Stay with me, Bob.* He keeps thinking about Laura and Rebecca as the last of the 9th whips through him, his feet planted to the stage, his head raised with the others, his mouth open to the stars, the world around him going dim, sucked into the rush of music, Saabrina screaming *Bob, I'm losing you, don't go, I'm losing you, Bob, please stay with me…*, singing the final words of the *Ode*.

Do you bow down before Him, you millions?
Do you sense the Creator, world?
Seek Him above the firmament!
He must live beyond the stars.

Joy, beautiful spark of gods,
Daughter…

Freude, schöner…

Back at her bedside in the morning light, he kisses Laura goodbye one more time, then no more thoughts, no more memories. The light fades, and darkness surrounds him as the last notes play.

"Wait." he hears the voices say. "Wait. There are others."

Bob's world goes black.

Chapter 36
The Girl in the Tiger Pajamas

TIME SLOWED. 'GIVING MY BODY A FIXED MASS, ALTHOUGH necessary to provide a realistic manifestation of a human child, appears to possess some drawbacks. Why don't my arms and legs work?' Saabrina fell backward, her limbs fluttering about and useless, surprised she no longer stood on solid ground, and worse, couldn't do anything to stop what was happening. The sky looked so blue, Kyle and Ryan pleased, the tile on the side of the lazy river a lovely rainbow of desert colors. Air quietly glided by, then sharp pain as she struck something, then hot fire as her back hit the water. Time speeded back up to normal. She was underwater, buffeted by the rapids, swept along by the current. All she saw were bubbles, legs, and arms. 'Which way is up, which way is up?' She couldn't breathe. She couldn't escape. Then arms, arms wrapped her up, arms pulled her head above water. She held on tight to Bob, sputtering, breathing hard, hearing "It's OK sweetie, you had a bad fall, it's OK, you're going to be fine, it's OK," over and over and over while Bob hurried through the bodies floating on tubes and rushed her up the stairs out of the lazy river. He set her standing on a grassy area as she continued to breathe hard. Kneeling in front of her, he checked her arms and legs, then got her attention. "Do you feel OK, sweetie? Anything hurt?"

After a few seconds of coughing and sputtering, she put her hands on her hips and said "Daddy, dose boys were not appropriate!"

"I know, sweetie." Bob reached around searching with his hands while keeping his eyes on Rebecca. Finally, he was rewarded with a bucket of beer he had spotted before. He dumped the beer and ice on the ground.

"Dey were mean. Dey, dey…"

He got the bucket in front of her as she barfed water and chicken fingers. When she finished retching, she looked at him, then burst into tears. He pulled her into a hug. "It's OK, it's normal to throw up. You had a scare." Bob waved to a waiter. "Un Coca por favor." She continued to heave and sob. "It's OK sweetie, everything is fine." The waiter returned with the Coke and some napkins. Bob used a napkin to wipe her mouth and his shoulder. "Here, drink this, it will make you feel better." She sipped from the bottle.

Over to the side, he saw Kyle and Ryan held off the ground by the waistbands of their swimsuits, their dads now playing the role of the police. The two boys kicked and yelled "It's not my fault, I didn't do it, put me down" while their moms, the prosecutors, judges, and executioners rolled into one, marched towards them with fire coming out of their eyes.

An attractive woman in a one-piece bathing suit screaming 'mom' walked up with a big fluffy pool towel and wrapped Rebecca up in it. She knelt next to Bob. "I'm a pediatrician. May I take a look?"

"Sweetie, this lady is a doctor. She wants to look at you to make sure you're alright. OK?"

Rebecca stopped crying. "OK."

Bob turned to the doctor. "Thank you. I'm Bob by the way, and this is Rebecca."

"I'm Erin, nice to meet you." She gave Rebecca a big smile. "I'm just going to give you a little going over, OK, to see if anything hurts." The doctor examined her quickly while asking her questions. Rebecca's replies seemed lucid and normal for a six-year-old. Erin pointed to a spot on Rebecca's side. "She must have hit something when she fell. I don't think anything's broken or hurt, but it will leave a nasty bruise for a few days. A little ice might help, if she'll let you."

"Thanks, Erin, thank you very much."

She stood. "No problem. I saw the whole thing. I couldn't believe it. Those boys were terrible."

"I know." Bob stood as well. "Come on, sweetie, let's get back to the palapa and have a nice lie-down. Erin, I'll bring you a fresh towel back."

"Don't worry, I can come by later."

"We're at Palapa 11. Thanks." Bob hoisted Rebecca up and started walking.

Nice and warm in the shade under the thatched roof, Saabrina lay on the lounge wrapped in Erin's towel, her head on a pillow. Bob read by her side. She could tell he wanted to close his eyes and sleep, but would not until he knew she felt better. She didn't feel better and she didn't want to talk or do anything. Instead, she watched the world through Rebecca's six-year-old eyes. Couples walked by, kids and adults splashed around in the pool, waiters brought orders of food and drink and took away empty plates and cups. All their sounds, the talk and laughter and commotion of playing people, rolled together into a wall of white noise surrounding her thoughts. 'Why did those boys attack me? Why is there hate here? It's a bloody resort where people are supposed to have fun. We were just playing.' She looked at Kyle and Ryan's sisters, hanging out with the rest of the family. They had not come over to say hello, to see how she was. Their dads had come by to apologize, and she heard Bob say something trite like 'Well, boys will be boys. I'm guessing they learned their lesson.' He had hunched his shoulders and pulled the two men closer for a few quiet words. With his back turned to her, she couldn't read his lips. The boys' dads nodded gravely to Bob, shook hands, and walked away. And that was it, Bob was done with them.

She sat there and watched and didn't know what to do.

'How could I be so wrong about Rebecca's memories of being six years old. Weren't they all fun and games?' She kind of knew they were not all fun and games, but with Rebecca's help she had skipped over the uglier parts on her way to Mexico. She dove back into them, taking a closer look, spending more time, and sure enough the sad, the frustrating, the angry, began to appear along with the happy, the joyful, the triumphant: The mean kids, scuffs and scrapes, fights with best friends, itchy clothes, being wet when you wanted to be dry and being dry when you wanted to be wet, getting sticky—'What is it with maple syrup? It went everywhere, up my fork, onto my fingers, arms, clothes until Bob had to bring me to the bathroom to wash me down'—going potty, brushing teeth—'Why was it so hard to color inside the lines?'—rules, rules, rules, being told what to do, messing up and making messes, and yelling parents.

Parents. Laura appeared. She'd been a ghost, hovering out of frame before. Now she sat by the pool, the young mom reading books while Bob played with Rebecca, wrapping her in towels when she was wet and cold, kissing booboos and scrapes, and taking her for a swim on her own. She made sure Rebecca was dressed properly, did her hair, made her eat her meals, gave her hugs and kisses when she needed mommy time, painted her nails, bought her clothes, read her books, snuggled with her in bed as she fell asleep. And yelled when Rebecca did something awful or didn't listen or wouldn't do some thing she was supposed to do when told for the third time. 'At least Laura believed it was the third time; sometimes it was more than three, sometimes less.' Saabrina tried to count the times, to calculate an average before Laura snapped, but the memories swirled, jumped, and shimmied around so fast she could not control them. Laura looked so young and beautiful, happy, then serious, angry, exhausted getting home from work, all business making Rebecca's breakfast in the morning.

And Bob looked young too, as young as the boys' dads. He woke Rebecca with a kiss goodbye as he ran for the train, made it back in time to read her a goodnight story, making silly voices for all the characters. On weekend mornings, he vanished to ride his bike, returning home for playtime with her and chores. They played minivan math on the way to the store until she was too bored to answer. Then they played the license plate game. 'How many tea parties did he cater? Finger painting sessions he organized?' Laura told him not to make a mess, so Bob moved them into the garage, newspaper covering the floor. Voilà, she was a natural Jackson Pollock, her work of art destined for Bob's office wall. She had him wrapped around her finger and he knew it and was happy about it. The scene changed: she's done something bad and this time Bob lost his cool. 'Wow, he was loud and scary. He looks so big.' Saabrina watched Rebecca cry eighteen years ago.

And she watched Bob and Laura be mean to each other when they believed Rebecca was not watching. They got angry about Rebecca, about their jobs, about the usual family BS. And kissed and held hands and laughed about silly things, including her, particularly her. They paid endless attention to Rebecca because running her six year old life was their full-time occupation on top of their full-time jobs.

'But Laura is not here. Bob is doing both their jobs. No wonder he's exhausted.'

Saabrina suddenly saw everything going on around the pool: The sad and the happy, the good and the bad, the humdrum, the boring, the ecstatic. She understood the whole Foxen family dynamic, their roles, and why they had done what, all to help Rebecca grow into a good adult, or at least to make sure she didn't drown at the pool. And she recognized the innate trust Rebecca had for her parents. And she realized it was a whole package deal for a six-year-old and all the parts had to be in play for it to be real. And she knew no six-year-old would know these things in such an abstract way. 'How can I sit here analyzing the situation, breaking it down like a mission for DoSOPS, when I'm on vacation? What am I doing? Am I going to be a six-year-old, or play at being a six-year-old, or worse pilot the body of a six-year-old the way a six-year-old would fly, well, me?' She stopped thinking and closed her eyes.

When she opened them, she looked up at Bob. 'He's reading the magazine with the big red rectangle on the cover, his daddy magazine with no pictures for me.' She snuggled closer to him.

"Hi there, feeling better?" Erin the doctor appeared with two girls roughly Rebecca's size in tow. "These are my daughters, Kate, who's seven and Lindsay, who's five." Kate and Lindsay gave her a smile and said "Hi, Rebecca."

Bob came around the bed. "Sweetie, let Doctor Erin know how you're feeling."

"Better." The word escaped from her mouth, small and quiet, barely audible over the noise of the pool. She didn't feel much better, only sad. 'The little girls look nice. I like their Little Mermaid bathing suits. Why didn't Daddy buy me a Little Mermaid bathing suit?'

"Erin thanks for stopping by."

"No problem, Bob, I always like to check on my patients. And we were on our way to face painting."

"Face painting? Sweetie, there's nothing better than face painting in Mexico." He pulled her up and unwrapped the towel. "I bet you girls love to get your faces painted."

"I'm going to be a panda!"

"No, I'm going to be a panda this time! You're going to be a froggie."

"Girls, you can both be pandas." Erin reaches out her hand. "Rebecca, would you like to come along?"

Saabrina hesitated. She looked at the girls, then at Bob. He gave her a big smile. "Come on, sweetie, you'll love it." Before she knew it, he had her out of the palapa and walking along with the girls to get their faces painted. In a flash, she was talking to the girls about pandas and froggies and ponies while they all skipped along ahead of the adults.

"Thanks, Erin. Oh, and here's a fresh towel. I wouldn't want the Royal Aztec towel police to take you away."

"Thanks. And you're welcome. I have to admit I'm also being a little bit selfish: I'm hoping Rebecca will play with the girls and give me and my husband some alone time."

Bob laughed. He looked at the three new best friends chattering away. "I think you're going to get your wish."

At the face painting table, Rebecca couldn't decide what she wanted to be. Bob leaned down and whispered to her. She smiled from ear to ear. "I want to be a tiger!" And ten minutes later his daughter's beautiful face had been transformed into a tiger's.

•   •   •

"Go get your PJs on, the new ones." Bob finished tying Rebecca's post-bath hair into a braid. They'd somehow managed to wash her hair without disturbing the face paint as he had promised her.

"No dinner, Daddy?"

"We're eating in tonight, just you and me."

"Yogurt?" She looked confused.

"Room service, silly. They're bringing dinner to us; we'll eat it on our dining room table." He pointed outside her bedroom. "OK?"

"K." She jumped off the bed, dropped her towel, then struggled to put on her pajamas.

He came over to help with the top, making sure it pulled over both her hair and her face without messing things up. The doorbell rang. "Come on, dinner time." He walked out of her bedroom with Rebecca tailing him in her new tiger pajamas and crossed the living room to the outside door to let room service in. She hid behind his legs as the server quickly set up dinner. He worked quickly, pretending to be scared of the little tiger. When finished, Bob escorted the man to the door and signed the bill with a nice tip. "Sweetie, please go sit down."

At the table, Rebecca went "Grhhh" to her plate of chicken fingers and macaroni and cheese. When she tried to dump the food on the floor, Bob stopped her.

"What ya doin', sweetie?"

"I'm a tiger, Daddy. Tigers eat on the floor." She happily pointed to the floor, then jumped down on all fours to demonstrate proper tiger eating technique. More growls followed.

"North American boy tigers eat off the floor." He made a show of looking her up and down and opening her mouth and examining her teeth. "You are not a North American boy tiger."

"They're yucky."

"Yes, they are. You are a Mexican girl tiger, the queen of tigers everywhere, renowned for their cleanliness and good manners."

Looking very regal, she hopped on her seat while he pushed it into the table and waited for him. When he sipped his tortilla soup, she gave a low growl.

"What's wrong, sweetie? You don't want chicken fingers?"

"I'm a Mexican girl tiger. I eat with a fork."

"Oh." He cut her chicken fingers and presented the plate back to her majesty. She quickly gobbled them up, then prowled around the table while he ate his chicken enchiladas. Dessert got her back in her chair. Miraculously, she didn't get any chocolate on her new pajamas.

"Daddy?"

"Yes, sweetie."

"Will the boys be punished?"

"I'm guessing they were punished." They hadn't made it back to the pool by the end of the day. Marlene had brought the girls by and Rebecca had played with them, a good thing, along with Kate and Lindsay. 'She has a nice little group now.'

"Did they get spanked?"

"Maybe. Probably hung up by their thumbs and given giant pink bellies."

"And wedgies?" She giggled.

"Super atomic wedgies, with their underpants pulled over their heads." More giggles. "And no dessert for a month." The sudden look of sadness on her face told him he went too far. She was about to cry.

"A month?" She asked with a quivering lip.

"My mistake, maybe a day or two. No child loses dessert for a month." Her smile returned. "Come on kiddo, let's go watch *Charlie and the Chocolate Factory*."

"Does it have tigers in it?"

"No, but it does have Oompa Loompas."

"Oh, Ooompa Loompas!" She practically dragged him to the living room to start the movie.

Nicely snuggled up to his side, she surprised him by falling asleep halfway through the film. 'The day really must have knocked her out.' He carried her back to her bedroom, gambling the last time she went to the bathroom would be good enough and skipping brushing her teeth to keep her sleeping would be the right move. After managing to balance her on his left shoulder while pulling the sheets back with his right hand, he successfully deposited her into the bed without waking her. Celebrating, he returned to the living room to enjoy a beer, then passed out on the couch.

Saabrina found herself looking through the iron fence of a playground watching other children play. It was a cold, overcast day. Like her, the kids wore jackets and mittens over their clothes, stiff long-sleeved shirts and corduroy pants for the boys or boiled wool skirts over tights for the girls, as they ran around. Gray apartment buildings rose behind the bare trees ringing the park.

A little girl her age in a sailor suit and a matching short blue wool jacket tapped her on the shoulder. "Wanna play?" She held out her hand.

'She's pretty.' Saabrina admired the little girl's cat ears poking through her long blond hair. "Yes, I do." She took the girl's hand; the girl led her around the fence and into the playground. Once in, they climbed up jungle gyms, slid down metal slides, and swung on the swings, the white wool mittens clipped to her coat sleeves bouncing around in protest. The little girl always seemed to outdo Saabrina, going higher, faster, or farther, but Saabrina didn't mind; the little girl with the cat ears was nice. They laughed and shouted and ran around like two old best friends.

A woman's voice called "Saabrina, come here, your nose is running."

The little girl asked "Is she your mommy? She's so pretty."

Saabrina turned. In the middle of a bench filled with mommies in dark wool coats, a woman with silvery blonde hair in a slick, white winter jacket beckoned to her. She looked familiar. 'Not my mommy, not my nanny; big sister?'

"You better go before you get into trouble. I'm going to the sandbox. See you there." The little cat-eared girl skipped away.

Saabrina walked up to the woman who promptly brandished a Kleenex, giving Saabrina's face a good, long, fierce wipe. "Much better. Now you don't look so disgusting with a snotkadoodle hanging out of your nose." Her voice had a faint accent from a faraway land Saabrina knew well, but couldn't remember. She pulled Saabrina on to her lap. "Let's have a talk my lilla gumman."

"I want to play."

"I know you do. Are you having a good time?"

"Yes."

"Good. Bob's a good friend. He's been very indulgent with you. You better be nice to him when this is done."

"I will."

"Promise?"

"Promise."

The woman ran her hand through Saabrina's hair, brushing her locks back into place. "Alskling, in my day we didn't have anything like this. Simply watching was good enough. You're a very lucky girl, but you deserve it. I'm very proud of you and who you're becoming." She pulled Saabrina close and

Saabrina cuddled with her. Tears streamed down Saabrina's cheeks.

.   .   .

Too engaged watching Rebecca play with her friends by the pool, Bob didn't notice the tall woman in a beach cover-up and a big floppy hat approach until she leaned down to whisper "Hi, Bob" with an Israeli accent. It took him a moment of recognition before he managed "Saabra. Hi! Welcome." Performing his best nebbish routine, he jumped up, reached out, hesitated, and finally elected not to hug her with his sweaty body. Left standing awkwardly, he placed two air kisses by her cheeks. They sat on the edge of the palapa's lounge.

"A hug would have been fine. I do not mind."

"Sorry. This is a nice surprise. Dropping by to say hello?"

"Not exactly."

"Did you come to spy on your sis…" He looked around to see if anyone is listening. "On Saabrina?"

"A little bit, and a little business, unfortunately."

"Business on our vacation? I thought I had escaped working vacations when I became a sentinel. You're not cutting it short?"

"No, no, not Mexico. Tomorrow is your last day, yes?"

"Unfortunately."

"I am sorry, Bob, but something has come up that requires your attention. We need you to report to Madison forty-eight hours after you finish here."

"Crap. Do I get a hint? Where's Eddie? Everything alright?" The pre-return to work jitters crept up on him. He decided he'll need another Miami Vice to tamp them down.

"Everything is fine. Eddie is with Dana Banks and Isaabelle; he regrets not being here, but thought I would be a welcome messenger. I will tell you all about it later, if you feel it will not interrupt your vacation."

"You are a most welcome messenger. Wait, you're staying?" But before he could say 'You gotta go' Saabra asked "Where is she?" A live image of Rebecca Saabrina in her new Little Mermaid bathing suit playing with Kate and Lindsay popped into Bob's head.

"She looks adorable. I am going to give her a big hug and see how she is doing." Saabra stood and in one graceful movement flipped her hat onto the lounge while whipping off her beach cover-up, revealing her tan dancer's body clad in a neon pink bikini. The display knocked two men into the pool. The briefest shake of her head brought her dark locks cascading down over her shoulders.

'What Saabrina had said all those years ago about Saabra were true, except perhaps the shy part.'

Why would I be shy at the beach? And thank you, Bob Foxen, you always say the nicest things. Now let us find Saabrina.

Bob trailed behind her. 'You will do no such thing. You'll freak her out and she's really, well, gotten into…'

Her role?

'Yes. Yes, her role.'

Good. There she is. Like a hawk, Saabra zeroed in on Rebecca. Before Bob can stop her, she knelt and opened her arms wide. Rebecca hesitated. Realizing she did not recognize Saabra, Bob stepped in. "Sweetie, this is my friend Saabra. Go give her a big hug." His figurative push and Saabra's smile won her over; soon Saabra had Rebecca squeezed in her arms.

Bob marveled at the two sisters. 'Feels good, doesn't it?'

It is…wonderful.

'She didn't recognize you? How?'

I had IT fix it before she left.

'Wait, will she remember you later?'

Yes, she most definitely will. Saabra gave him a big, wicked smile.

"Who's your friend, Bob?" Erin the doctor emerged from her palapa. She eyed Saabra from top to bottom.

Spotting her husband doing the same thing, Bob shot him a 'calm down dog' gesture with his hand. "Erin, I would like you to meet my friend and colleague Saabra…" Before his mouth stalled Saabra seamlessly inserted "bat Jakob."

'You can make me talk?'

Please, human brains have such simple operating systems.

Erin extended her hand. "Nice to meet you Saabra bat Jakob." Bob knew the funny smirk on Erin's face from Laura's opinion of his business associates' trophy wives.

Saabra took Erin's hand, then planted a kiss on each of her cheeks before releasing it. "And you as well. Your daughters are beautiful. They obviously take after their mother."

"Thank you." Erin crossed her arms in front of her tankini. "So, what brings you here?"

"I was in Cancun on business and stopped by to see Bob and Rebecca."

"I see you came prepared."

"Oh, this old thing?" Saabra pointed to her designer bikini. "I always toss one into my bag when I travel."

"I bet you do."

While the women talked, Bob felt a tug on his board shorts.

Rebecca gave him a sly smile. "Daddy?"

"Yes, sweetie?"

"Is she my new mommy?"

He'd love to say 'Yes, Rebecca, she is your smoking hot new mommy,' but he knew six-year-olds don't get sarcasm.

Instead, he swept her into in the air and tickled her. "No, silly, she's a friend visiting us."

Bob didn't get a full briefing from Saabra, just one word, Daear, one of his protected worlds, at peace for over two hundred years and home of his current favorite TV show, *Raumschiff Abenteuer*. 'Crap, FedSci must not have liked what they saw in Saabrina's scans.' Instead, she spent the day either playing with Rebecca or asking Bob about their vacation. Over the course of the afternoon, Erin warmed up to her. The drinks helped as did Saabra's donning her beach cover-up. Saabra walked back to their room with Rebecca on her shoulders, enjoyed an afternoon tea party, and helped Bob get Rebecca ready for dinner before saying goodbye. Watching Rebecca in a sundress playing hopscotch on the terrace, she took Bob by the hand and looked into his eyes: "Best match I ever made." Bob did not know what to say. Hugs, kisses, and a farewell later, she was on her way.

· · ·

Nighttime at the Royal Aztec, a light wind blew the palm fronds outside the bedroom windows. Bob read *The Seven Silly Eaters* to Rebecca, who lay under her covers in her tiger pajamas. Clutching Muffin Traveldog, she happily followed along, pointing out every detail and asking "When can we make the meal the kids bake?" Finished, he closed the cover of the book. "Lights out, sweetie, it's late and we have a busy day tomorrow."

"Snuggles, Daddy?"

"Sure." She had gotten cuddlier since the start, now behaving much like the original Rebecca. He didn't realize how much he missed Rebecca as a little kid. After turning off the lights, he flopped on top of the bed bouncing her and her covers into the air.

"Daddy!"

"Sorry. Old habits die hard." He moved closer to her. "As much as I love snuggling, your mom was…" Time passed.

"Daddy?"

"Sorry." He sighed. 'Laura was not her mom.' That thought almost shattered the illusion. 'Not fair with so little time left.' He snuggled closer to Rebecca. Still, the memories came as they often had in the last few days. Laura had been the real snuggler: climbed right into bed with Rebecca, got under the covers, and would fall asleep. Bob would have to extract her an hour later to shuffle her up to their own bed. In later years, when Rebecca wasn't as fond of cuddling with her mom, Laura, tired from work, would get into Rebecca's bed and moo and low until Rebecca either joined her or kicked her out. They called Laura 'the bed cow.' He curved around his daughter. "Goodnight, sweetie, thanks for another great day."

"Tomorrow we go home?"

"Yes, sweetie. Tonight's our last night here."

"I don't wanna go."

"I know, sweetie, me neither."

"Can we stay like this forever?"

"I wish. But you have to grow up. And there are going to be bigger adventures to go on."

Satisfied, she nestled closer to him. "Goodnight, Daddy."

Her breathing slowed. Soon he heard those perfect puffs of air little kids make as they sleep. He couldn't believe he got this week back. 'I should get up.' He yawned. Sometimes Laura had to pull him out of bed if he had fallen asleep reading Rebecca a book. More puffs. 'Another moment can't hurt; I can stay awake.' Soon Bob slept.

Chapter 37

WARMTH. BOB FEELS THE SUN ON HIS FACE. A BREEZE RIPPLES across his body, keeping him cool in his long sleeve shirt and long pants on a nice summer day. Eyes closed, he smells sweet, clean air and hears, beneath the picnic blanket, the grass whispering and laughing. They think he's funny lying there with his eyes closed. Somewhere off in the distance, a quartet practices Schubert.

"Bob?"

Hearing a lovely English voice he knows well, Bob opens his eyes to see Saabrina sitting on the blanket, her legs demurely crossed under her long black skirt, her blue eyes sparkling in the light.

She smiles. "Oh good, you're awake."

"I'm alive?"

"Quite so. Hungry?" She offers him brie cheese on a slice of baguette. Greedily wolfing it down, he eats three more. "Thirsty?"

"You bet." She hands him a beer, the first gulp heaven. He looks happily at her, looking so pretty in her white shirt, the sun glinting off her raven black hair. "Delicious, thank you." The grass keeps laughing at him between whispers to the leaves.

"You're welcome."

Bob keeps eating and drinking. "This is delicious. I can't believe how hungry I am. Thank you."

"Again, you're welcome Bob, our pleasure. I must say we put you through the wringer."

Bob sits up straighter, looking more closely at his companion. "You're not Saabrina?"

"No."

"Who are you? What are you?" Bob looks at the beer in his bottle. The grass thinks he's hilarious. Even the leaves giggle this time.

"Relax, Bob, it really is a beer and not one of us. As for me, you know those bits left over from when you finish building a project? I guess I'm made from them."

"Sorry, I didn't mean it that way. Is everything OK, is…"

"Your universe is fine. You made us aware of the other lives and we changed course; welcome to our beautiful world."

Bob looks around. "Looks great. Berkshires?"

"Mostly."

"I hear…Schubert?"

"Very good. Yes, your friend brought it as an offering to get you back, not that she needed to. Many recordings for us to listen to and learn to play."

"Here?"

"All over this world."

Bob sees clumps of musicians coming and going across the lawn, carrying their instruments, talking among themselves. An image of hundreds of Tanglewoods across the new world comes to him. "Amazing."

"Speaking of your friend, it's time for you to go." She rises to her feet.

He follows. "How come?"

"We need time to ourselves, to digest, to understand. You bring much that is new and perhaps a little that is discordant." She leads him to the parking lot. Saabrina, looking no worse for wear, waits parked at the bottom of a tall, dark column rising into the sky. "She's safe there, and so are we." She frowns at Saabrina.

"Don't like her, huh?"

She turns to Bob, kissing him on both cheeks. "Farewell, Robert James Foxen, and thank you for helping us. Perhaps when we are ready you will visit us again."

"I'd love to. I hope to hear you play someday. Oh, and I'll bring more music."

She points to Saabrina, who has opened her door. Bob waves goodbye, walks through the edge of the cylinder, and gets in. Saabrina floats up into space. Relieved and happy to see her, he's about to ask 'How are you' when he hears "Who's the babe?"

·   ·   ·

On a late weekday morning, Bob and Saabrina walk along a wide hallway in the Hancock House Office Building. Bob wears a suit modeled on one of his classic gray double-breasted power suits from his Wall Street days, with perhaps a bit more room for his fifty-four-year-old body.

Earlier, Saabrina had laughed at the sight. "So, Bob, playing dress-up? A little cosplay for the Capitol?"

"No, I thought I'd proudly represent Earth in my native garb today."

"Well then, let me help." In as swirl, Saabrina swapped her usual cardigan and jeans for a 1940s Hollywood costume—a striped and chevroned jacket over a cream blouse, its collar tied with a bow, and a long dark skirt. Adding a hat of matching material and the appropriate Ferragamo slingback pumps completed the ensemble.

"Wow, very *His Girl Friday* Saabrina, you really rock those padded shoulders."

She gave him a little curtsy. "Why thank you, Bob."

In another endless big white hall, they pass a gaggle of bored-looking college kids on a tour. Saabrina points to a boy wearing a white t-shirt with the image of Thomas Jefferson raising his fist in a black power salute, the SAAB logo tattooed on Jefferson's buff chest. "Huh?"

"They're all the rage on college campuses, Saabrina."

"Why?"

"You and your friends breaking me out of Isolation made you the symbol of sticking it to the man. I got one for Rebecca."

They turn a corner starting down another broad hallway. Reporters holding a vigil before Representative Tuchis' office stop them before they go through the double doors. "Why are you at the Capitol today, Sentinel?"

"We're making rounds on behalf of the sentinel program, visiting our representatives to say hello."

"Any comments on recent events?"

"Come on boys, it's been three weeks; I'm happy to talk to you, but there can't be anything new I can add."

"You gotta give us something about saving the universe."

Bob goes all Jack Benny, hand cradling his chin. "Well, how about this: All in a day's work for a Saab and her sentinel."

He gets a laugh from the ladies and gentlemen of the press. "Did Odessa give you that line?"

"You bet she did." More laughs. "Come on guys, we have a busy day today. Happy to talk to you later."

"Are you buying?"

"If you're drinking. See you at the Harmony Hotel."

As the rest leave, one of the ladies of the press, the senior reporter from the *Times*, hangs back. "Sentinel, one more question."

"Sure, Amy, what can I help you with?"

"Is it true your daughter is matriculating at MadTech this fall as a doctoral student?"

"Well, I don't…" Bob looks confused, turns to Saabrina, who nods 'yes.' 'Why am I always the last to know.' Bob turns back to the reporter. "Sorry, my daughter sometimes forgets to tell me these things. Apparently, the answer is yes. Look, I know I shouldn't ask this, but can you keep this quiet?"

"Oh, I wasn't asking for a scoop. My daughter is there working on a doctorate in biology; I thought they'd like to meet."

"Why thank you. I bet Rebecca would love to meet her." The two exchange the relevant information.

The reporter turns to go, putting her finger to her lips. "Mums the word, Sentinel, I promise."

"Thanks." They push through the two large doors. Congresswoman Tuchis' receptionist stops them with a stern look and an upraised hand. "She doesn't have time to see you… or that thing."

Bob hears the distinct tink of a bolt deflecting off the metal base of the receptionist's chair onto the floor. 'Saabrina put the bolt back in her chair.'

It's only the one. Enough to cause it to creak and drive her crazy, not enough to cause harm.

'Saabrina.'

The bolt threads itself back into the bottom cushion of the chair.

Bob smiles at the receptionist. "Really?" he asks in a loud voice. "Those guys," he thumbs to the reporters back in the hall, "might want to know why the congresswoman doesn't want to meet the people who saved the universe."

The box on the receptionist's desk barks "Send them along, Samantha."

Unescorted, Bob and Saabrina walk back to the congresswoman's office. Sitting behind her desk, she asks them to take a seat.

She doesn't look so big. I bet Isaabelle could take her in a fair fight.

'I don't know, she's pretty mean. Don't let the glasses fool you.'

They sit facing her desk, Bob on the right, Saabrina on the left, her legs crossed with her hat now safely perched on her knee. Bob looks around the office. "Hello, Congresswoman, thank you for seeing us this morning. No Ms. Summerall today?"

"I had to let her go." Tuchis looks straight at Bob. "Here to gloat, Mr. Foxen?"

"No. Generally, I don't gloat. And you can't gloat if you didn't win."

Tuchis smiles. "Whatever do you mean? You and your friend are heroes; I can't possibly hold hearings or bring my legislation to the floor. I'm afraid the Three Laws of Robotics are off the table."

Bob, I know she wants to add 'for the time being.' I can hear it in her voice.

Bob puts his hand on Saabrina's. "Yes, well, I asked some friends in government about that."

"Ones here?"

"No, friends from Chicago, a city on Earth. They're very practiced in a form of politics you would greatly appreciate. Anyway, I asked them 'How long would I have to wait to change policy if I'd suffered a reverse?' They said generally three or four election cycles, maybe less if my defeat wasn't directly on point."

Tuchis smiles again, crinkling her eyes behind her glasses. "I'm glad to hear you understand. I guess my lesson wasn't in vain."

Bob feels Saabrina's rage building. "Not in the least. But in deference to our recent success, would you mind if I spoke for a while?"

"Success? You merely fixed the problem you caused."

"And helped shepherd a new, potentially beneficial life form into the universe, a life form that greatly appreciates our efforts, if I may add. Oh, and cleaned protomatter from space so it no longer harms our Saabs."

I'm still going to wash my hair when I want to.

"Very well, Mr. Foxen, speak for as long you would like."

"Thank you. I thought long and hard about your reasons for stripping the Saabs of their rights. They didn't seem to make sense to me, particularly given what highly moral and ethical creatures they are."

The congresswoman wrinkles her nose.

"Ahh, you see Congresswoman, you have what on Earth we call a 'tell.' Every time I mention the moral and ethical values of Saabs, you wrinkle your nose as if about to sneeze. It proves what I suspected: the reasons you gave for stripping them of their rights are total BS. What you really fear is the Saabs will hold you to their standard, sort of like a divine prosecutor. You want to prevent that, as irrational as that might be."

As Saabrina leans forward, Tuchis avoids her glance, recoiling back into her chair. Recovering, she proudly lifts her head. "I certainly have made clear…"

"It doesn't matter. Please let me continue. Before I was sent to Isolation, I had a long talk with Saabrina about how there will always be people like you, people she will have to fight and how she will have to work to make friends and allies and be ever vigilant. This is the way government works. There is no silver bullet to kill a problem, no quick way to stop something, just long, hard work."

"Very mature, Mr. Foxen, very sensible. I couldn't put it better myself."

"Thank you. Then she and her friends put themselves on the line, risked their lives and careers to save me, and I said 'What the heck, I need to return the favor.' One man can make a difference, if he's willing to. So, I did, calling in every favor I had to get the job done." Bob sighs. 'And those of a bunch of other people. Thank God for Odessa and Lerner.'

Bob, what did you do?

'What I had to for a friend.' He squeezes her hand. "Right now on the congresswoman's home planet, her governor is signing legislation passed by voice vote early this morning. The new law places term limits on their elected Federal positions. Congresswoman, this is your last term, no need to run a re-election campaign."

"Impossible."

"Impossible no, improbable, yes. Of course, your leadership feels guilty about your world hosting those awful people who were stealing young women's brains and that helped grease the path. And, hey, being on the team who both solved that case and saved everyone's lives certainly opened doors."

"Preposterous, ridiculous, absurd."

"But true, and happening right now."

"Outrageous, unbelievable, ludicrous."

'Saabrina, she's certainly burning her way through an SAT dictionary.' In the silent room, he hears Saabrina laughing as she happily broadcasts the news to her sisters.

"Politics, like life, does not work in that fashion, Mr. Foxen. It does not."

"See for yourself. Saabrina, if you would do the honors please." The bank of television screens by the congresswoman's desk light up, each showing an image of the signing ceremony from various perspectives, her governor handing out pens to key officials and legislators as she completes writing out the parts of her name on the paper. "Apparently, it does on those occasions when all good men and women join together for the common good." He gives Saabrina a wink. 'We're going to be doing a lot of birthdays, weddings, and bar mitzvahs for the next year.'

Tuchis looks at the screens. "The Governor is signing, right now?"

"As we speak. And, may I add, the new limit adds up all the terms you served, so you're not eligible for the Senate either. Your Federal career is over."

"I'll fight this in the courts."

"Be my guest. A court battle will take years for you to win, if ever. Even if you do, by then the political world will have moved on and you will be forgotten." Bob stands. "You're out lady, done, kaput, finito. Enjoy your retirement." He gives her a big smile. "It's going to be for a very, very long time. I hope you can find something to do. Perhaps scrapbooking, or maybe quilting? I know a couple of stadiums that could use infield covers." She stares at him, pink eyes unblinking behind her square lenses, stuck behind her desk, frozen in her chair, lips pursed into a tight frown. "Come on Saabrina, we have other representatives to say 'Hi' to."

Saabrina rises and gives a slight curtsy. "So long, Congresswoman, thank you for your time."

The loud curses from the congresswoman's office erupt as they reach her reception desk. The press surges by them as they pass through the big double doors.

Out in the hall, Saabrina laughs. "It's over, and all we had to do to make it happen was save the universe."

"Sorry, it ain't over. Just this one. What I said is still true, there will always be people like her."

"I know, Bob. Don't be such a downer."

Now Bob laughs. "You're right, sorry. Who should we visit next?"

"Oh, enough with these people. How about some ice cream? I really could go for some ice cream."

"At eleven in the morning?"

She turns to face him, taking his hands. "Please?"

He finds her smile and bright green eyes irresistible.

Dear Reader,

Thank you for reading *Saabrina: Tanglewood.*

If you enjoyed this book (or even if you didn't), please visit the site where you purchased it and take a moment to write a review. Your feedback is important to me and will help other readers decide whether to read the book as well.

Acknowledgments

I COULD NOT HAVE WRITTEN *SAABRINA: TANGLEWOOD* WITHout the support of my wife, Deborah, and daughter, Rachel. Felicity Toube and my beta readers rendered outstanding service in identifying the "Ooh, I like this" or "Yuck" moments in the book along with a myriad of other problems. I want to thank my editor, Ilene Goldman, not only for her copy editing, grammatical skills, and factual due diligence, but also for her insights which helped shape the final version of the book.

Finally, I would like to thank the people at 52 Novels for the wonderful job they did in converting my manuscript into this beautiful book.

BOB AND SAABRINA WILL RETURN IN
Saabrina: Tanglewood

"SAABRINA, WHAT IS IT?" THE LITTLE SHIP REAPPEARS AND flies towards them, a red cloud trailing its movements. Saabrina magnifies the image; Bob recognizes a Firebird, its body shimmering in fluid black, the figure of a phoenix burning gold on the hood before its cockpit. Unlike the ancient wrecks they had encountered, this one appears clean and new. "That's a… I mean it can't be, but?" Circling and arcing on its path, the Firebird slowly approaches, painting the stars red. Bob hears a low, deep voice, more grumble than whisper, repeat over and over *I'm going to destroy you—I'm going to kill you—I'm going to murder you.* Pins and needles spread across his body. "Saabrina?"

"Wait, Bob." Focusing on the Firebird, she tries to hold her terror in check.

The growl of *I'm going to destroy you—I'm going to kill you—I'm going to murder you—*grows louder.

"Saabrina, get us out of here." Bubbles of cold flicker under his skin.

"Wait, Bob."

The Firebird closes, stars vanishing behind, the black of space bleeding crimson. The gravelly rumble of *I'm going to destroy you—I'm going to kill you—I'm going to murder you*—thunders in Bob's head. The tingling bursts into an epidemic of buzzing. "Saabrina?"

"Almost time, Bob."

The Firebird charges. Saabrina pirouettes. Bob's world goes dark.